"Sherman certainly knows how to make a Western gallop, but his real skill is in his gifted creation of gritty characters who must pay the price of greed and ambition."

—*Publishers Weekly*

"An outstanding storyteller. Sherman portrayed the characters, their problems, and scenes so well it brought back memories of people I've known and ranches I've visited."

—*Tulsa World*

"Sherman paints pictures with remarkable skill. His characters come to life against a rich historical background."

—Janet Dailey

"Sherman's descriptions of daily life and the landscape ring true."

—*San Antonio Express News*

"*The Barons of Texas* grabs the reader by the throat. . . . A rousing good story with larger-than-life characters and a sense of place so strong the reader can smell the mesquite if he closes his eyes."

—*Roundup* magazine

By Jory Sherman from Tom Doherty Associates

THE BARON BRAND

JORY SHERMAN

FORGE®

A TOM DOHERTY ASSOCIATES BOOK
NEW YORK

THE BARON BRAND

Copyright © 2000 by Jory Sherman

A Forge Book
Published by Tom Doherty Associates, LLC
175 Fifth Avenue
New York, NY 10010

www.tor.com

Forge® is a registered trademark of Tom Doherty Associates, LLC.

ISBN: 0-812-53924-9
Library of Congress Catalog Card Number: 99-051787

First edition: January 2000
First mass market edition: January 2001

Printed in the United States of America

0 9 8 7 6 5 4 3 2 1

For my father Keith Sherman's First Family,
my beloved brothers and sisters,
Gordon Sherman, Inka Stroud,
William T. Sherman, and Nancy Grant.

I can speak but little longer, but let my last words be remembered by you. . . . In the far distant future the generations that spring from our loins are to venture in the paths of glory and honor. If untrammeled, who can tell the mighty progress they will make? If cast adrift—if the calamitous curse of disunion is inflicted upon them, who can picture their misfortunes and their shame?

—SAM HOUSTON
September 22, 1860

Cast of Characters

The Box B Ranch

Martin Baron—patriarch of the Baron family
Caroline Baron—Martin's wife
Anson Baron—son of Martin and Caroline
Lazaro Aguilar—blind boy raised by Caroline
Esperanza Cuevas—Lazaro's nanny
Lucinda Madera—works for Caroline
Ken Richman—Martin's friend
Ed Wales—publisher of Baronsville newspaper
Peebo Elves—works for Anson
Jorge Camacho—cowhand

The Lazy K Ranch

Ursula Killian—widow of Jack Killian
Roy Killian—son of Jack and Ursula
David Wilhoit—Ursula's friend
Wanda Fancher—Roy's friend
Hattie Fancher—Wanda's mother

The Rocking A Ranch

Matteo Miguelito Aguilar—Jaime's son by Pilar
Luz Aguilar—Matteo's wife

Others

Mickey Bone—a Lipan Apache
Dawn Bone—Mickey's wife, a Yaqui Indian
Jules Reynaud—a Frenchman from New Orleans

Will Harrison—a friend of Roy Killian's
Tom Harris—nighthawk
Seth "Cullie" Culbertson—nighthawk
Culebra—chief of the Mescaleros
Nancy Grant—new schoolmarm
Doc Purvis—town doctor
Al Oltmen—Texas ranger

1

ANSON BARON HEARD the ominous swish of a horn behind him and the tiny hair bristles on the back of his neck stiffened into needles that made his skin tingle as if pierced by miniature icicles. Then, he heard the angry rake of cloven hooves gouging the earth.

Anson turned just in time to see the huge longhorn steer lower his boss and leap forward in a lusty charge, snorting steam from mushroomed nostrils, hooves pounding the ground to a muffled thunder. Anson saw the spread of the six-foot horns, knew he would be smashed to a blood-soaked pulp if he didn't suddenly sprout wings and fly out of danger. He felt as if his feet were made of lead and his boots mired in quicksand.

The young man started to run to the side, but he knew he was moving too slow to escape the powerful swipe of the steer's left horn. His stomach swirled with a thousand fluttering wings as if five hundred moths had emerged from their dusty cocoons. Time seemed to freeze and unfreeze as if every bone in his body had turned rigid with fear.

A gelid lump rose in Anson's throat and stuck there as he realized that he could not escape that terrible horn, that it would smash his chest flat and crush his ribs and lungs into a pulpy mash.

Anson, as he scrambled to the side to try and avoid the swinging horn, heard a loud shout and the steer swung its head to the right, skidded to a stop. Anson let out his breath and the burning in his lungs sweetened with the fresh air he inhaled.

"Hoo, hoo," shouted the unknown man in a strange loud voice and the steer charged toward the sound.

Anson edged along the corral fence to put distance between him and the crazed longhorn steer and looked off to his left. There, atop a claybank mare, sat the man who had shouted, causing the steer to check its killing charge.

"Better climb that fence, Anson," the man said, "afore this here steer changes his mind."

"What the hell," Anson said, as he turned and grabbed a split rail above his head. "That you, Peebo?"

"Naw, Anson, it's Honest Abe Lincoln."

Anson climbed the fence and straddled the top rail. He looked down into the arena and saw his lariat strung out like a dead snake in the center. The steer had caught him by surprise. He had been trying to rope it and snub it to a post to find out what was making it mean as a copperhead with a bellyache.

"I'm goin' to shoot that mean sonofabitch," Anson said.

Peebo laughed. "Why?"

" 'Cause he tried to kill me."

"Warn't his fault. That steer was more scared than you was."

"He sure as hell didn't act scared."

Peebo dismounted and stepped up to the corral fence and looked at the steer as Anson marveled at his bravery. He was no more than a few inches from those long, sweeping horns.

"You better watch out," Anson said.

"Did you look at his eyes?" Peebo asked. He was a towheaded young man on the burly side, all muscle, tough sinew, face burned umber by the sun and wind, a pudgy set of lips, curious blue eyes, hands cracked by exposure, scabbed like a pair of sea creatures.

"No, I didn't look at his eyes," Anson said. "He come at me for no reason. All I saw was horn and meanness."

"Well, that steer's blind as a bat," Peebo said.

"Blind?"

"Ain't you never seen the 'pink eye' before?"

"No, I reckon I ain't," Anson said.

"Well, by the gods, that there steer's plumb got it, Anson. What in hell you doin' way out here, anyways?"

"What are you doing way out here, Peebo?"

"I come lookin' for your pa. 'Member, he offered me a job did I ever want one?"

"Yeah, I remember. You lookin' for work?"

"Ranch I was workin' on up on the Brazos done went under. Comanch'."

"Comanche?"

"That's right. Wiped old man Bate clean out, pert near."

"You was raisin' horses, wasn't you?"

"Still am. I had me a string over t'nother place what wasn't hit. I brung me some steeds."

"Steeds?"

Peebo laughed. "Horses, son, a passel of 'em. I got 'em over in a draw just this side of the Nueces. Heard all the ruckus here and come over."

"You didn't happen to run across a Mexican out in the brush, did you?" Anson asked.

"Nope. Why?"

"That damned Jorge was supposed to be helpin' me and I ain't seen him since breakfast."

"You bunked out somewheres?" Peebo asked.

"We got a line shack up on a creek that runs into the Nueces."

"Didn't see that, neither. Where's your pa?"

"He's at the main ranch or maybe in town."

"Okay. I want to talk to him about comin' to work for the Box B."

"Well, now, Peebo, you want a job, you got one."

"You runnin' the spread now?"

"Pretty much."

"Don't that beat all, though?"

"What do you mean?"

"Why, you're barely dry behind the ears and already the head honcho."

"Pa, he goes away a lot. Somebody's got to run things around here. 'Sides, I had a bunch of Mexican hands run off this mornin'. There's just me and another hand to finish up the branding."

"What happened? They get the pink eye?"

"No, they said there was some big white bull raisin' a ruckus and it gored one of their horses."

"Sounds like a shuck."

"No. That horse was bad gored, for sure, guts all over. Had to shoot it."

"Then your boys run off."

"They said it was a white devil. I couldn't talk 'em out of it."

"I'd like to see this white bull," Peebo said.

"Say, you working here or not?"

"I guess. Whatcha want me to do, Anson?"

"Tell me what to do with this steer. Shoot him, run him off, drown him?"

"You can doctor him if you got a mind to and give him medicine."

"What medicine?" Anson asked.

"Hell, I don't know. Creosote, maybe."

"You mean boil a creosote bush and pour the juice in its eye?"

"Yeah. Or you can just let that steer loose and let him run. It'll wear off, finally."

"Open that gate," Anson said.

Peebo slipped the thin manila rope off a post and swung the gate wide. The steer turned at the creaking sound and stared blindly at the opening.

"Kick him in the ass," Peebo said.

"You kick him in the ass."

"Hoo haw," Peebo called and the steer charged at him with rheumy pink eyes that did not blink. The animal ran out into the open and stopped, then started staggering around, lost, but free.

"A pitiful sight, ain't it?" Peebo said.

"Nobody told me about the pink eye," Anson replied.

"Anybody tell you there's talk about the South seceding from the Union?"

"What's that?"

"What's what?" Peebo asked.

"See seeding."

"Oh, that means breaking off from the North, becoming a separate country."

"That don't make no sense," Anson said.

"Well, maybe not, but it's got to do with folks holding slaves. North says it's wrong, and the South says it's right."

"Well, I don't hold with slavery."

"No, well, maybe it's all talk, but there's a lot of people talkin' about war and secession. Some towns is gettin' up militias to fight Yankees if they come down and try and take the slaves away."

"Well, we don't hold slaves," Anson said.

"You may be gettin' some visitors right soon who'll ask you and your pa to take sides," Peebo said.

"Likely we'll take no sides."

"Yep, likely," Peebo said, a pixie look in his crackling blue eyes. "Well, what's the work today?"

"First, we put up your horses, then we wrassle the brush for more strays."

"What were you aimin' to do with that blind steer?" Peebo asked.

"Put a brand on him."

"Where's the fire? The irons?"

"I ain't got that far yet. He was the first one of the mornin' and I wanted to snub him up first. He was ornery and it was heck gettin' him out of the brush."

"You're lucky he didn't gore you into next week," Peebo said.

"I wonder how he caught the pink eye."

Peebo shrugged. "They get it from flies or skeeters, hell, I don't know."

Anson grinned. He was glad to have company. He had sent but one of the hands back to the main ranch. He figured there couldn't be more than a half-dozen cattle in the brush left to brand. After letting the other hands go, he and Jorge Camacho had ridden out to this section of the Box B the day before and he had seen little of Jorge since. Jorge was a sullen worker, but always full of fun when the sun went down. He'd bring out his guitar and sing sad Mexican songs, *son huastecos* he called them, and he'd drink aguardiente he made from peaches or persimmons or something and would laugh so hard he'd cry. But, during the day, his face clouded up dark as a thunderhead and he scowled without cracking a smile all day.

"You going to look for Jorge?" Peebo asked as the two men rode together toward the Nueces.

"Naw, he'll show up, I reckon. He knows where the corral is. He and I built it last spring."

"I heard about the Apaches," Peebo said.

"We beat 'em good."

"They run off?"

"Yeah."

"Likely they'll be back."

"We don't expect them," Anson said, but his forehead creased in worry lines. He was just a shade over nineteen, but he had taken on responsibility for keeping the ranch up and taking care of his mother while his father had abandoned them for a time. Now Martin Baron was back, but he spent most of his time in Baronsville mak-

ing deals or talking deals and seldom did any real work
on the ranch.

Anson had grown tall, but he was lean from hard work
and forking a saddle. His dark unruly hair was full of
dust now and one curl hung over his forehead. His hazel
eyes bore the look of an older man because he had seen
much in his young years and he had killed a white man
and some Apaches.

Peebo's horses were hobbled and strung out along a
small creek. They were all grazing. One or two lifted
their heads as the two men rode up. Their coats glistened
sleek in the sun and one of them gave a friendly whicker.

"I count sixteen horses," Anson said.

"And not an ugly one in the bunch."

"Prime stock, then."

"Sound as a sackful of dollars."

"Let's get 'em unhobbled and over to the line shack.
There's a stock tank there with water in it and grain
aplenty."

Peebo grinned. The two quickly unhobbled the horses
and Peebo strung them all on a lead rope. He followed
Anson through brush to a trail that led to a mesquite
fence with a gate. Anson dismounted and swung open
the gate. They rode another half mile and made a turn
onto a small creek. There in a clearing stood a small,
crude shack and a large corral that appeared sturdy despite its primitive construction.

"That your shack?" Peebo asked.

"It's where we bunk."

"Hell, it ain't nothin' but a damned jacal."

Anson laughed. He opened the gate to the corral and
Peebo led the horses in, removed the lead rope from their
halters. He and Anson took the halters off. Peebo
checked the water tank, which was almost full and, together, they walked to a small shed that was closed up
against the weather. Inside, there were sacks of cracked
corn, one opened. Anson took a wooden bucket off a
peg stuck into the wall and filled it with grain. Another

bucket was on the floor and Peebo picked it up and filled it.

When they had finished graining the horses, Peebo went to the shack and opened the door. It had a dirt floor, three bunks, a small iron stove. Utensils stood on a small sideboard nailed against the wall and hung from wooden pegs. A small cupboard revealed staples, sugar, flour, coffee, jerky, chili peppers, salt, pepper and a clay jar of molasses. On a board laid on the floor were sacks of potatoes, onions, sugar beets and beans.

There was a small rickety table and three barrel chairs covered in cowhide. There were bedrolls on two of the bunks.

"Looks just right for three hands," Peebo said.

"Lay your bedroll on that bunk yonder," Anson told him. "We got three more shacks like this one scattered hereabouts. We use 'em all during the gather. I figured we had pretty much worked out this section, so I sent the other hands on back to the main ranch."

"How long do you expect to be out here?"

"Another day or two, maybe."

"When's roundup?"

"A month from now, I reckon. Whenever we finish branding on this section. I got one section to go, closer to home."

"How far's home?" Peebo asked.

Anson laughed. "A good day's ride."

Peebo let out a long whistle. "How much land you got, Anson?"

"I don't rightly know. Maybe near a million acres."

Peebo whistled again. The two men stepped out of the shack and into the sun. Peebo went to his horse and untied his bedroll from behind the cantle. He was walking back toward the shack when both men heard a loud scream and then silence.

"What in hell was that?" Peebo asked, stopping dead in his tracks.

"It sounded like a man in pain," Anson said. He had

been just about to step up into his saddle. Both men listened for a long time, and then they both heard another scream, louder this time and from a man unmistakably in pain.

Peebo tossed his bedroll on the ground and ran to his horse as Anson pulled himself into the saddle. He pointed in the direction of the screaming and was already putting spurs to his horse.

Then, they both heard the sound of galloping hoof-beats followed by a cavernous silence as if a deep moss-black tomb, filled with unspeakably defiled ancient corpses, had suddenly been opened after thousands of undisturbed centuries.

2

Ursula Killian stared at the house a long time before she set the brake on the buckboard. A sadness swept over her like a melancholy fan of molting summer feathers. It was not like the house she had lived in for so many years in Fort Worth. It was not like any house she had ever seen before.

"It—it looks like an orphan," she said, bewildered by her own words.

Her son, Roy, astride his gelding strawberry roan, looked down at her, his face stricken with bewilderment and hurt.

"Ma, it—it's just a start," he said. "I'll make it better. Bigger."

Ursula, still in a musing state, did not seem to hear her son. She continued to stare at the house as memories stirred within her, unbidden thoughts from a faraway time like the vagrant petals of a rose torn by a steady autumn wind.

She was once again a small girl, coming to a new

place with her widowed mother, a small forlorn cabin on a Nebraska prairie with not a tree in sight, their milk cow tethered to a rickety wagon loaded with all of their meager possessions, a washtub, washboard, bed, bedding, cooking utensils, tools, shabby clothing and little else.

Ursula had learned her only skills on that small patch of land, had helped with the washing and ironing, learned to cook and rake and hoe and dig and plant and had seen the skin on her hands dry out and crack open like rivers boiled to dust and her face had turned brown under the hot Nebraska sun until she looked like an Indian. There, with her mother taking in washing for soldiers and settlers and sodbusters, she had learned the ways of men, as well, and when John Fitzroy Killian, her beloved Jack, had come along, she had run away with him, leaving her mother to die in that sod-roofed cabin on the prairie, all alone at the end, her skin turned to umber parchment, her bones under shrunken skin so that her face was all skull, her body mummified like an Egyptian slave's.

She and Jack had gone back to Nebraska to see her mother, Ingrid Grunig, but she had already withered to a skeleton and her brain had become addled from aging. They had wanted to take her back to Texas to live out her years, but that was not to be. Her mother died before the week was out and Ursula and Jack buried her in Omaha, sold her house and land for pennies on the dollar.

Ursula touched a finger to her right cheekbone, traced the outlines of the extrusion. She had lost weight since Jack had died and it showed in her face, as it had in her mother's. Her fingertip lingered on the oval swell of flesh as if that were the place where death first touched, as if to remind herself that she, too, would grow old and die someday.

"Ma, what's the matter? Don't you like your new home?" Roy peered at his mother, trying to see her face under the bonnet she wore. All he could see was her slight frown and a set jaw.

"Why, sure, Roy, it's mighty fine," Ursula drawled. "It's just that it's so bare here. No flowers, no trees."

Relieved, Roy let out a soft sigh. "Why, I aim to plant you some trees and we'll get flowers and everything. I already talked to Ken Richman. He's over to Baronsville, and he said he thought he could get me some box elders and some rosebushes, and pecan trees and figs and persimmons."

"We didn't see any town," his mother said, looking at her son's face just so she would not have to look at the small shack that was to be her new home.

"Well, it wasn't on our way," he said lamely. But his mother knew better. Roy had talked to her long into the nights to convince her to leave Fort Worth and the soldiers she washed and ironed for and sometimes took to her bed. She knew he was jealous of her lovers and resented the attention she gave to men she liked.

"Well, is Baronsville far?" she asked. "I'd like to see it, maybe buy some things for the . . . the house."

"Oh, it ain't far, Ma. It's over yonder some." Roy pointed to land that stretched to the horizon, grassy, rolling land that had few distinguishing features beyond clumps of mesquite and grass peppering the soil that was not yet high enough to measure.

"Why it's back the way we came out," she said.

"Yeah, I reckon."

Ursula sighed deeply. "Well, let's take a look inside," she said. "You built this all by yourself?"

"No'm, I had help. Horky, he's a Mexican, he helped me and some others. Martin Baron give me this land and said I could buy more when I got some money."

Ursula stepped down from the buckboard as Roy dismounted. "I got to put up a hitchrail," he said sheepishly as he tied his reins to the wagon.

"Seems like you've got a lot of work to do, Roy," his mother said, as she dusted off her frock. Gingerly, she walked toward the house, avoiding the cow pies and tumbleweeds that lay in her path. The house smelled of new wood shavings, but the whipsawed boards appeared to be dry, not green. She noticed such things with a critical eye as her mother had before her. Together they had chinked the Nebraska cabin before the snow blew that first winter and they used straw and cloth to insulate the inside walls, pasting them on with glue made from boiled horses' hooves.

Ursula lifted the latchkey and the door, on leather hinges, swung open without squeaking. "Mmm," she said, in approval.

Roy followed her eagerly as she stepped inside the small, two-room dwelling. His mother could almost hear his heart pounding in his chest.

"What do you think, Ma?" he asked.

"Well, it might do," she said. "We'll see when the furniture arrives. When did you say it would be here?"

"Oh, tomorrow at the latest. Them boys I got to haul it are real fast."

"Umm, well, we'll see," she said. There was a bed built into one corner. It was made up, if not fancy, then comfortable enough, with a spread and blanket, sheets, and a single pillow, which was covered fancy in pink satin. Ursula walked to the bed and tested it with a light punch of her fist. She pressed a hand on the pillow, felt its give. Then, she walked around, went in the other room, which was a kitchen with a small woodstove, plenty of kindling and wood, some few utensils on the top shelf and pots and pans, ladles and spoons hanging on wooden dowels nailed into the wall. There was a small homely bunk, with a pair of blankets and a feather ticking pillow in one corner.

"That where you sleep?"

"Yes'm," Roy said.

"It's somewhat Spartan."

"Yes'm."

"Well, I suppose we can make do until my things get

here," she said, opening a crude cupboard to see boxes of staples.

"There's a springhouse I dug out back," Roy said, "and I got meat hanging in it. Prime young beef."

"Longhorn, no doubt."

"Well, yes'm, I reckon."

Ursula smiled at Roy. "You're a good son."

"Thank you, Ma."

"You remind me of your father. He was always a comfort when he was home. Thoughtful."

Roy didn't say anything, but his face was beaming with pride. It had been hard for him to tell his mother about his father's death. She had taken it hard, sobbing for days, crying all night when she thought he was asleep.

Ursula removed her bonnet and tossed it on the bed. She walked to a nearby window and pulled back the burlap sack that covered it. A small cloud of flies that had clung to the outer surface of the drape took flight, their green-blue bodies iridescent in the sun.

"I see you have a well out back," she said, "and a corral. Do you have cattle?"

"A few. Martin gave me three leagues of land to get started and me and Horky are buildin' fence. Next year I'll plant new grass on one section."

"Who are those men out there walking around?" she asked.

"Men?"

"They have horses, but they're carrying sticks and some kind of looking glass."

Roy strode to the window and looked out. In the distance he saw four men, four horses. One man was waving to another who was walking backwards carrying a pole. Another was kneeling down, digging a hand into the earth, while another stood nearby, a rifle cradled in his arms.

"Well, do you know them?" Roy's mother asked.

"No'm, but I'm sure as hell going to find out. You wait here."

"Nonsense," she said, "I'll go with you."

"There might be trouble," he said.

"Trouble?" Ursula's eyebrows rose to twin arches.

"Those are Mexicans out there and I don't recognize nary a one of 'em."

"That one man doesn't look like a Mexican," she said.

"Which one?"

"The one with the telescope. You know what they're doing, don't you?"

"No'm, I don't."

"They're surveyors."

"Surveyors?"

"They're measuring your land. If that's your land out there."

"It sure is." Roy tipped his hat back from his forehead and rubbed his scalp with his fingers just past the hairline. "I wonder if Martin sent them out."

"Let's go ask," Ursula said.

When they reached the door, Roy stopped. "Do you want to get your bonnet, Ma?"

"No, I need some sun," she said, casting a sidelong glance at the cramped room once again. "Until I get a hoe in my hands, it looks as if I'll be a shut-in."

"Ma, please," Roy said, and ushered his mother out the door. Outside, they circled the house and started walking toward the team of surveyors.

"Oh, you have a creek," Ursula exclaimed when she glanced to her left.

"Bandera Creek," Roy said. "That's why I picked this spot for the house."

"And an outhouse," she said. "I hadn't noticed." Off to the right, out of view of the back windows of the house, a small board building stood in a copse of mesquite trees. "It's big, isn't it?"

"I keep my tack in there," Roy said. "There's a wall inside to separate the two cubicles."

"How clever," Ursula said, not without pride.

"I'll build a barn, Ma, and move the tack, giving us a little storeroom."

"There's no end to it," she said. "The building, I mean. You've gotten a good start."

"Thanks, Ma."

As mother and son approached the surveyors, the man at the tripod holding the theodolite stepped away, shaded his eyes as he peered at them. The Mexicans all straightened up and stared, too. All of the men wore holsters and pistols. The man with the rifle did not shift the weapon, but stood motionless.

"What are you boys doing?" Roy asked as he and his mother drew near.

"Working," said the man standing by the theodolite. "I'm Dave Wilhoit."

"I'm Roy Killian and this is my land."

"Yes sir," said Wilhoit.

"You're a surveyor, aren't you?" Ursula asked.

"Yes'm."

"So, do you work for Martin Baron?" Roy asked.

"No sir, we don't."

"You don't?"

"No sir."

"Then how come you're out here measurin' my land?"

Wilhoit removed his hat, looked directly into Ursula's eyes. Her face flushed slightly and she brushed away a vagrant curl that grazed her cheek.

"Ma'am," Wilhoit said. "I don't believe I caught your name."

"Ursula Killian. I'm Roy's mother."

"Why you look more like his sister, ma'am."

Roy swallowed saliva, blinked. He did not look at his mother.

"Why, thank you, Mr. Wilhoit. I'm flattered."

"You didn't answer my question, sir," Roy said.

"We work for Mr. Aguilar."

"Aguilar?"

"Matteo Miguelito Aguilar. He owns the Rocking A Ranch over yonder."

"I know who he is," Roy said. "And he ain't got no business sendin' you boys on out here."

"We have permission," Wilhoit said.

"Permission?"

"Yes sir. Mr. Baron, he told us we could survey."

"Martin Baron?" Roy asked.

"No, it was the younger Baron. Anson."

"Anson? What the hell . . . ?"

Ursula looked closely at Wilhoit. He was nobody's fool, she decided. He was a stocky, handsome man, not very tall, about five foot eight or nine, perhaps, with light hair the color of dusky wheat, and light brown eyes, clean shaven, muscular. He appeared to be in his mid or late twenties, but he seemed sure of himself. There was an air of confidence in him that she liked.

"My," she said to the surveyor, "you must be hot out here in the sun and all. Perhaps you'd like to come over to the house and I could fix you some tea. Roy, we do have tea, don't we?"

"No'm," Roy said, "we ain't got none."

"Coffee, then. We have that, don't we?"

"Yes'm, we got coffee. But not very much."

"That's all right, ma'am," Dave said. "We got to keep working. I want to finish this section before the sun sets."

"What do you expect to find?" Ursula asked. "That my son and I are trespassers?" There was a challenge in her voice now that her offer of hospitality had been rebuffed.

"Why, I don't rightly know, Mrs. Killian," Dave said. "I'm just hired as a surveyor. Mr. Aguilar didn't tell me why he wanted this section surveyed."

"Well, he ought to have," Roy said. "I got papers on this land. Signed by Mr. Martin Baron himself."

"I'm sure you do, Mr. Killian," Dave said, a tone of forced respect in his voice. "I'm sure my surveys will bear that out."

"I could have told you that," Roy said. "No need for

you to look through that glass there and measure my land."

"There's an old saying," Dave said, "good fences build good neighbors. I think Mr. Aguilar just wants to know where your land ends and his begins."

"Mighty dumb of him, you ask me," Roy said. "Man don't know where his own land is."

"Roy, that's enough," Ursula said. "Mr. Wilhoit, David, if I may, we're sure you're doing what you were hired to do. If you get through work early or need to ask any questions, just stop by the house yonder, will you?" Her voice was laden with sugar and Roy grimaced slightly.

"Why, I'd like that, Mrs. Killian," Dave said. "We shouldn't be more'n another day or so. We're camped beyond Bandera Creek. If you've got a chair to sit on, it would be mighty welcome."

"You drop on by," Ursula said, holding up her arm for her son to take it. Roy stared at her a moment before he realized she wanted to go back. He took his mother's arm and started to turn to walk back to the new house.

"You get your business done quick, Wilhoit," Roy said sharply.

"I'll do my best," Dave said, with an engaging lopsided grin. Then, as if to irritate Roy, he spoke directly to Ursula. "Ma'am, I'll surely stop by if I have time," he said.

Ursula waved and smiled at Wilhoit.

She could sense her son's irritation as he began to match her stride.

"How come you're butterin' up that man, Ma?" he said when they were out of earshot of the survey team.

"I wasn't buttering him up," she said. "I was just being polite."

Roy snorted. He looked back once before he and his mother reached the house, but Dave Wilhoit was looking through the theodolite and motioning for one of the Mexicans to move back with the measuring stick.

That sonofabitch better not be looking at my mother, Roy thought. I'll survey his puny ass.

3

THE HORSE GALLOPED past Peebo and Anson, reins dragging, stirrups swaying and flapping like bell clappers. Its ears were laid back and its eyes wide as saucers as it shied away from the two riders and sped off, riderless, back toward the line shack.

"That was Jorge's horse," Anson said as he reined to a halt.

"Like somethin' was sure as hell chasin' it," Peebo said, "or it got spooked somethin' fearful."

"I'll say. Come on."

Anson followed the horse's tracks which led into the brush and then out again. Beyond, they saw movement and both men drew their cap and ball pistols. A man's arms stuck out of a thicket of prickly pear and brambles. Streaks of blood streamed down both arms.

"Jorge?" Anson asked as he rode up.

He heard a stream of Spanish curses coming from the man lying in a clump of cactus.

"That must be Jorge," Peebo said.

"Jorge, what in hell are you doing?" Anson asked.

"*Me muero de dolor,*" Jorge whined.

"Get your ass out of there."

"*Ayudame.*"

Anson started to dismount when Peebo stuck out an arm and blocked him.

"What?" Anson asked.

"Listen," Peebo said.

Anson listened. "I don't hear anything."

Jorge was silent. He lay there, unmoving, on a bed of prickly cactus. Anson looked at him for a long moment. "Horse throw you, Jorge?"

"No," Jorge replied. "Apache."

"Looky there," Peebo said, pointing to the ground beyond the cactus patch. "This here Jorge was dragged to that clump of prickly pear."

"Dragged?" A sinking feeling stirred in Anson's stomach. He saw the drag marks and then he saw the rope lumped up behind Jorge's head. He rode closer and looked down. A loop of rope was around Jorge's neck.

Anson swore.

"We ain't alone," Peebo said softly.

Anson looked up.

"Apache," Jorge said. "Culebra."

"Snake?" Peebo asked.

Anson's stomach seemed to sink deeper and swirl with winged insects. He looked around, his eyes following the contours of the land. There was a low ridge just beyond where they stood and he could not see any farther than that. A quail piped in the distance.

"What do you mean 'we ain't alone'?" Anson asked, a quaver in his voice.

"It sure as hell warn't no snake," Peebo said.

"Jorge wasn't talking about a snake."

"Sounded like he was."

Anson's stomach turned into a pit of fear. "That's the name of an Apache, son of Cuchillo, one that my pa and I killed."

"Uh-oh," Peebo said, reaching for the rifle in his boot, a .40 caliber flintlock, converted to percussion, with a cherrywood stock, made by a German in Tennessee, the thirty-two-inch barrel made from rolled Damascus steel, tempered on a blacksmith's forge. The rifle slipped easily from its sheath.

Anson drew his pistol, the one his father had bought him, a cap and ball Navy, .44 caliber. "Jorge, can you get out of there?" he whispered.

"Much pain," Jorge said. "Rope caught."

Anson swore again. He looked at the loop around Jorge's neck. It was tight against his throat. Below, a section was coiled around three or four paddles of cactus. If Jorge tried to get up, he would strangle.

"Where did Culebra go, Jorge?" Anson asked.

"I do not know." Jorge gagged and seemed to be choking.

"You get him loose, Anson," Peebo said. "I'll cover you."

Anson stepped out of the saddle, holding his pistol out of the way. He tiptoed to where Jorge lay and knelt down.

"*Ten cuidado*," Jorge said. "Be careful."

Anson reached down with his left hand and grasped the rope. Slowly, he began to unwind it from the roots of the prickly pear. He winced, but did not cry out when a slender sharp spine pricked the back of his hand. It was then that he noticed his hand was shaking.

The rope was further pinned by a forked mesquite branch driven into the earth. Anson felt the wooden shaft with his hand. When he pulled on it, the shaft broke off. He saw that it had been cut after it had been pounded into the ground, deliberately cut so that it would break when someone tried to pull the forked section loose.

"Damn," Anson said.

Jorge made a gurgling sound in his throat as the rope tightened.

"Hold on, Jorge," Anson said. "I've got to dig under

this damned mesquite branch. That damned Injun pinned you down good."

"He's turnin' purple," Peebo said.

"Shit," Anson said, and dug his fingers down in between the forked limb.

The forks were long and Anson tugged and twisted until the wooden clasp began to loosen. He jerked the Y upward and when it came loose, he almost tumbled over backwards. He grunted and pulled the rope until there was slack in it. The rope kept getting caught in the spines of the cactus and he cursed as he gained inches at a time. Then, he unwrapped it from Jorge's throat. Finally, he heard Jorge take in a deep breath and then the Mexican was free.

"Can you get up, Jorge?" Anson asked.

"You help me, Anson."

Anson scooted backwards and got into a squat. He grabbed Jorge's left hand and pulled. Jorge managed to get his legs under him and popped out of the prickly pear bed. He winced and tears streamed down his face as he stepped away, Anson helping him gain his footing on bare ground.

"Jesus," Peebo said. "Lookit his back."

Anson stepped around and saw the spines jutting from Jorge's back and arms like little straw-colored and darker brown needles. Jorge stood there as if he were in a state of shock, unmoving, his flesh quivering with the pain.

"It'll take hours to pull all those spines, Jorge," Anson said.

"I am going to die," Jorge said.

"You ain't gonna die," Anson told him. "You're just going to have a lot of bruises and sore spots."

"I no can walk."

"Well, we can't stay here and do it," Anson said. "You have to walk, or ride."

Jorge swore a sacrilegious oath in Spanish.

"That ain't goin' to help none, Jorge."

"I hurtin'."

"Well, hell, how come that bastard jump you?"

"I don' see him," Jorge said. "I feel the rope around my damn back and I am on the ground and the horse she is gone."

Peebo cleared his throat. Anson looked over at him with a querulous look.

"I think that Culebra's still somewheres around," Peebo said. "If you two want to just stand there jawin', I reckon I'll hightail it somewheres else."

Anson turned back to Jorge. "You're just goin' to have to bite the bullet, Jorge," Anson told him. "You want to ride behind me or walk to the line shack?"

Jorge said nothing for several seconds. "I will ride wit' you, Anson. *Jesus,* it hurts."

Anson turned away angrily and caught up his horse. He pulled himself into the saddle and rode over to where the immobile Jorge stood. "Give me your hand and stick your boot in that damned stirrup, Jorge."

Jorge's face contorted in pain as he raised his arm. Anson took his hand as Jorge lifted a leg and poked the toe of his boot into the stirrup. With a heave, Anson lifted Jorge up. Jorge swung his leg over the back of the horse and sat gingerly behind the cantle. Tears flowed from his eyes and streaked his face. He started to blubber.

"Shut up, Jorge," Anson said curtly. "It's gonna hurt like hell and not a damned thing I can do about it. It's your own damned fool fault anyways."

"Please do not ride fast, Anson."

Perversely, Anson kicked his spurs into his horse's flanks. The horse bucked and leaped ahead as if shot through with an electric current. Jorge screamed and squeezed Anson around the waist as he held on fast. The horse broke into a fast gallop until Anson reined him up. The sudden stop caused Jorge to scream out again.

"Sorry about that, Jorge," Anson said, but there was a bitterness to his tone that was not lost on Jorge.

Jorge moaned, which only served to make Anson angrier than he was before.

"Stupid," Anson said in Spanish.

"Yes," Jorge replied.

Peebo caught up to Anson. He was still holding his rifle. "Look back there," he said softly.

Anson turned around. There, on the slight ridge, sat an Apache. He was grinning and he held up his bow and shook it.

"Shoot him," Anson said to Peebo.

Peebo turned in the saddle and brought his rifle to his shoulder. Before he could take aim, the Apache wheeled his pony and dropped from the ridge, out of sight.

"That there would have been Culebra, I reckon," Peebo said drily.

Jorge nodded numbly, tears welling up in his eyes, tracking down his face in streams that left watery scars.

4

CAROLINE BARON TREMBLED every time she entered the barn and she didn't know why. She dreaded going in there after feed for the livestock, or to curry her horse, the bay mare, Rose, whom she loved dearly. Lately, she knew, it had gotten worse, this feeling of despair, of something akin to terror. She had gotten so fearful of entering the barn alone that she had begun to open the front and rear doors wide before she would venture inside.

But now, even the creaking of the doors bothered her so much that she could hardly bear to open them. And each time she did so, she was afraid of what might be in there, in the darkness, what might come out once she had swung the first door wide to let in the sunlight.

She waited this day a long time before even touching the back door and, to her surprise, found that she was listening intently for any sound issuing from the depths of the cavernous barn. She stood there, her legs quivering with a nameless fear, unable to bring herself to lift the latch.

As she stood there, unable to move, she heard a horse inside one of the stalls whicker softly.

"Rose," she said so soft only she could hear the word, and then, with no explanation she could give then or later, she began to weep. She collapsed against the barn door, sobbing out of control, unable to stem the tide of sadness that welled up in her all of a sudden, a sadness she could not define nor name.

Each day seemed worse than the last. Each time she had to come out to the barn, she approached it with a ball of fear in her stomach, a ball that writhed and grew tentacles and these strangled her thoughts and electrified every nerve in her body.

She could not bring her hand up to lift the latch and swing the door open. Not today, she thought. I can't bear to see the darkness, to think about what might be inside, waiting for me, waiting to pounce on me. She felt herself strangling on her fear, felt a shadow hover in her mind like some large dark bird and there was a weakness in her legs, a jelliness in her knees. She felt as if she might swoon at any moment, might fall to the ground and into that pit of black in her mind that seemed to be opening like some chasm of night.

She tried to lift her hand to the latch, but it would not move. She collapsed against the wooden door. Again, she heard her horse nicker and the sound, for some unknown reason, terrified her.

"Oh, Rose," she sobbed and the words so soft and faraway, she thought someone else must have uttered them. Again, she tried to raise her hand to open the door, but her arm was stiff and frozen. It was as if she had no will of her own anymore. The pressure against her forehead was beginning to hurt, but she could not pull herself away, could not stand on her own feet without support.

"No," Caroline shrieked, "I can't."

Several yards away, Lucinda Madera stopped hoeing in the garden to gaze at her mistress. Quickly, she threw the hoe down on the ground and started trotting toward the barn, hiking her skirts up out of the way of her sandals.

"*Señora*," Lucinda called, "*qué pasa?*"

Caroline seemed not to hear her. Lucinda rushed up and put an arm around the weeping woman's shoulder. "Why do you cry?" she asked.

"I don't know," Caroline said. "I—I'm afraid."

"What are you afraid of?" Lucinda asked.

"The—the barn. Something in it. Something not there. Something there. Lucinda, I—I just don't know."

Lucinda pulled Caroline away from the door and turned her around to face the fields and the garden.

"I will open the door," Lucinda said.

"N-no, not yet. I mean, I'll open it. Just give me a minute."

"*Por seguro, señora.*"

Caroline opened her eyes wider and stared out at the countryside. The tears blurred her vision and made the land swim and sway. She gulped in a breath of air and dabbed at her eyes. Lucinda unwrapped the bandanna from around her neck and handed it to Caroline.

"Thank you," Caroline said and began to wipe the moisture from her face.

"You have the sickness?" Lucinda asked.

"No, I—I'm fine, it's just that . . ." But Caroline could not put her feelings into words. She had tried to talk to Martin about what happened to her each time she went out to the barn in the morning, but each time she started to say something, the words sounded silly in her head. Martin might think her mad if she told him these things. He might think she was a crazy woman. So, too, would Lucinda, she thought.

"I—I'll be all right," Caroline said, taking in another deep breath. Gradually the fields steadied and came into alignment. "I—I'm going to walk around the barn and open the front doors."

"Why do you not just walk through the barn?" Lucinda asked.

Caroline frowned, deepening the lines in her forehead,

rumpling the flesh beneath her eyes. "Because," was all that she said.

"I will go with you," Lucinda said.

"If you wish," Caroline replied, without intonation. She drew in a deep breath and started walking to the side of the barn, not looking at it, stepping gingerly as if not wanting to make any noise that might arouse the nameless presence inside the building.

Lucinda trailed after her mistress with short, choppy steps, hiking her skirt once again, which she had vowed to hem if she ever had a free moment.

Caroline turned the corner at the front of the barn, her heart hammering in her chest, her ears pulsing like a blacksmith's bellows. Summoning up her courage, she strode to the latch and lifted it with both hands, let the two-by-six fall to the ground on the loose end. She jumped when the board struck and listened with a growing panic as the door squeaked open slightly.

Lucinda stopped, stared at Caroline. "Do you wish me to open the door?" she asked.

Caroline turned and looked at the woman, a veiled look of bewilderment shadowing her eyes. "What?" she asked.

"The barn door, it is not yet open."

Caroline grabbed the door and swung it wide defiantly. "There," she said. "It's open."

"Do you go inside?" Lucinda asked.

Caroline stared into the dark bowels of the barn. Shafts of sunlight slanted through the cracks in the walls and a massive cube lighted the back doorway, glistened in the straw on the floor. Rose whickered softly and stirred in her stall.

A beam of sunlight struck another object off to the left side and Caroline shuddered as if ice water had been poured down her back.

"I thought I had covered it," Caroline said.

"What do you say?" Lucinda asked in Spanish.

Caroline did not answer. Instead, she walked into the

cool barn, through columns of sunlight, stirring up dancing motes of dust that swirled in the light like tiny fire-
flies. She strode to the object against the wall and
grabbed a corner of the tarp and jerked it smartly over
the exposed part.

"The cannon?" Lucinda asked. She had followed Caroline into the barn like a shadow. "It was covered. I saw
you do it last week."

"Someone's always uncovering it," Caroline said, her
voice sounding to her as if it were coming from a hollow
place. "Anson, maybe. Martin? But, why?"

"I do not know," Lucinda said before she realized that
Caroline was not speaking to her, but to herself.

"It—it should not even be here," Caroline said softly.
"Damn it, damn it to hell." Her voice rose in pitch and
she closed her eyes as if to shut it out, to shut everything
out. "Damn him. Damn Martin."

"Eh?" Lucinda asked.

"Why does he keep it?" Caroline asked of no one. And
then, the images began to surface in her mind, unbidden.
She saw it all again, heard the shrieking, yipping Apaches
charging down toward the barn from the ridge above La
Loma de Sombra, the little hill where the house sat. She
heard the deep throaty boom of the cannon, felt the con-
cussive explosion, heard the terrible whistle of the nails
and chunks of iron hurtling through the air. She saw the
Apache braves sliced and stabbed and shredded to pieces
by the whistling metal, saw them fall and writhe and convulse like hideous painted dolls. She heard their screams
of agony and saw the blood gush from necks and heads
and torsos. She saw herself lighting the candle and holding the flame to the touch hole of the four pounder and
then heard it roar again with the thunder of death. And
Martin yelling in her ears and Anson loading more shot,
and felt the sweat running down her legs and her chest
and between her breasts and heard again the crackle of
rifle fire, the whispering hiss of arrows in flight and the
screams rising in a crescendo as more Apaches fell and

writhed in the blood-soaked dirt and the horses screaming too, the ponies staggering away with broken knees
and ankles and falling down, spurting blood, gushing it
from gaping wounds in their chests and necks, and always the snapping crackle of the Mexican rifles and Anson shooting, too, and Roy Killian, and Martin, his face
a raging mask of fury, blackened by smoke and blown
back powder and death spewing from that gleaming
brass muzzle every time she shot flame into its small
hole and the stench of black powder still strong in her
nostrils after all this time, the acrid sting and stink of it
clogging her nose and throat and the white smoke bil-
lowing from the cannon's maw and filling the barn until
she could no longer see the carnage outside, could no
longer see her husband and son and the looks on their
murderous faces, and the rifle fire dying away until it
sounded like air pockets popping in a fireplace log.

Once again in the silence of the barn, she saw herself
stumbling after Martin to go outside and see the slain
and the wounded Apaches lying around like shattered
rag dolls, and the Mexicans dispatching them one by one
with pistols and rifles until the wounded no longer struggled or kicked or spasmed and the quietness of death
descended upon her and she stood there numb, trying to
understand it all, trying to understand those moments
between life and death when all reason was suspended,
all thoughts frozen like insects caught in amber and the
horror of it was too monstrous to comprehend at that
moment and so she had closed her eyes and gone deep
inside herself where it was safe and calm and the
screams faded into a solemn silence and the dead disappeared like the smoke blowing from the barn and
shredding to tatters in the breeze.

But the dead had not gone away and she had watched
as the Mexican hands dragged them away, one by one,
to a burial place beyond sight of the house and she had
whimpered at the sight and turned away so that she could
forget what those brave men had looked like in death

and the Mexican dogs eating the pieces of bodies like savage wolves, gulping down hands and feet and arms, and carrying away bloody bones still covered with flesh and the Mexican women praying for the dead souls even as they swept up the blood and raked the killing place clean and made off with the souvenirs of the battle, the bows and arrows and clothing of the dead Indians.

Caroline had lived with those memories ever since that terrible time and had never spoken of it to either Martin or Anson, but she now knew why she hated to go into the barn, hated to open the doors of her mind to that terrible day of death.

"Oh my God," Caroline said, and Lucinda crossed herself even though her face waxed blank in puzzlement. "I've got to get it out of here."

"What do you say?" Lucinda asked.

Caroline turned and stared at the Mexican woman. "Do you hear me? Martin has to take it away."

Lucinda nodded dumbly.

"Feed my horse and take her outside," Caroline ordered. "I must speak to Martin right away."

"Yes," Lucinda said in Spanish as Caroline stumbled away, heading for the front of the barn like a woman swimming through drowning waters. Lucinda crossed herself again and mumbled a prayer for Caroline's soul. She saw the Baron woman disappear and turned toward the stall when Rose nickered.

"That poor woman," Lucinda said. "*Pobrecita.*"

She walked to the stall, shaking her head in bewilderment. "*Loca,*" she whispered, as if that word explained everything.

Rose, a large bay mare, snorted and poked her head over the stall gate. She bobbed her head up and down, shaking her mane. Lucinda froze and blessed herself once again.

She was terrified of horses.

5

MICKEY BONE, A Lipan Apache, rode slowly up to the Rocking A ranch house, which seemed deserted. None had challenged him on his long ride over the ranch; he had not seen a vaquero in ten miles, even though he had seen many cattle, all bearing the Rocking A brand of Matteo Miguelito Aguilar. He had thought it strange and he could summon no explanation from his mind. He knew that Matteo was a very suspicious man. It was not like him to let anyone ride up unchallenged like this. Yet he had ridden in from the south without seeing a soul once he passed through the main gate.

It was as if the ranch was deserted and Mickey knew that could not be so.

"*Hola, la casa,*" he called out as he rode up to the hitchrail.

There was no answer.

Mickey touched his right hand to the butt of his pistol. He rode around to the back of the house, his senses at full alert. He loosened the pistol in its holster, kept his thumb on the hammer.

Bone edged his horse toward the side of the house. Some faint sound caught his ears as he rounded the building, but he would take no chances. When he cleared the rear corner, he slid his pistol halfway out of its holster.

Matteo's woman did not look up from her washing as Bone rode toward her. She stood over a large washtub sitting on a two-by-eight board straddling two small barrels. An even larger iron tub sat in a ring of stones where a fire was blazing. Hot steam rose in the air from the fired tub, swirling in the air like some specter of a dancing dervish. Bone smelled the acrid aroma of lye soap and the pungent odor of wet dirty clothes.

Luz Aguilar looked up as Mickey rode around the corner of the house. She was still young and beautiful, Mickey thought, but like most of the Mexican women in their teens and twenties, and Apache, too, she would grow old before her time. Too much work, too many children in a short span of time, too much trouble with their men—all these things served to age the women on the frontier or away from civilization. Luz was probably no more than eighteen, but already there were shadows under her beautiful brown eyes and little spider marks where she frowned.

Luz did not speak to him as he rode up close to her, nor did she stop what she was doing. Instead, she continued to scrub the clothes in her hands, dipping them into water bubbly with lye soap and raking them across a board that had been glued with small battens to make the surface rough.

"Where is Matteo?" Mickey asked.

"Miguelito has gone to the brasada, to El Rincón," Luz said. She moved her head to indicate where her husband was. Mickey had forgotten that Luz called him by his middle name, Miguelito.

"And the vaqueros? Where are they?"

"They are with Miguelito."

"Who is watching over the cattle?"

"The men come back in the evening. Miguelito, he stays out there. The young boys should be watching the cattle. Did you not see them?"

"No, I did not see them."

"Well, they were probably asleep. They are lazy boys. Like their mothers."

"Why does Matteo not come back with the men?" Mickey asked.

"He stays out there to be with God," she said.

Mickey did not know what to say. From Luz's tone she did not like her husband to be away. He wondered why Matteo had gone to that wild brush country, the brasada, and why he took the men there and why he did not return with them in the evenings.

"Miguelito wants to see you," Luz said, unexpectedly.

"I have just returned from Mexico," Mickey said.

"You are to go over to the brasada right away."

"How will I find him? Out there?"

"You will see where he has gone. He left signs."

Mickey nodded and looked off in the distance. The brasada was a desolate place, a maze of mesquite and swampy ground where a man could get lost and never come out. He had seen some of that brush before, with his people, the Lipan, who considered it a sacred place. Some of his people had seen visions while inside there, and some had never returned after venturing deep inside the labyrinth. Was this what Matteo was looking for as well? But why were all the hands there, too? Had Aguilar gone crazy?

Luz startled him again when she asked: "Where is your wife? Dawn."

"She is with the People, down in Mexico. She waits for my return."

"That is good that she waits for you," Luz said, and Bone thought she meant more than she had spoken about.

"Yes," he said. "I will ride over to El Rincón and look for Matte—Miguelito."

"Go with God," Luz said.

Mickey Bone nodded and spurred his horse, headed away from the house. He looked back once, but Luz was hanging more clothes up and it was as if he had never been there.

He passed more cattle grazing on the prairie's sparse grasses. These were part of the herd Aguilar had brought up from Mexico when he claimed the Rocking A Ranch from his uncle, Benito. This had been Matteo's plan and Bone had agreed to work for him. Matteo had killed Benito and Benito's wife, Pilar, Matteo's own mother. Since that day, Bone had gone back to Mexico to sell some horses for cash and he carried that money with him now.

There were some boys watching the herd. They had truly been asleep, but when they saw him, they rose out of the grasses in their white trousers and shirts looking like diminutive wraiths and picked up their sticks and tried to look busy and responsible. They shaded their eyes and watched Bone as he rode past, but they did not wave, nor did he give them any sign that he had noticed them.

Dogs emerged from the brush, chased after the boys, and wagged their tails. One or two barked at Bone, but did not chase after him. They sniffed him over a long distance and then turned tail and ran back to their young masters. Soon, Bone left the pasture and rode the sloping land as the mesquite got thicker, following a wide path that was marred with horses' hoofprints.

The trail was bordered by mesquite stumps and the pathways littered with the bark of dead trees, some rotting to dust, others so old they were turning to stone. Bone felt as if he were riding through a graveyard. After a time, he could no longer see the cleared ranch land, and the concourse of trails and roads intersected and intertwined into a bewildering maze. But he followed the tracks of horses that were most recently engraved in the soil and these led him to the top of a low hill where he could see the surrounding terrain.

As Bone rode up to the thick mesquite forest known as the brasada, he heard voices in the distance.

The trail disappeared into the dense thicket of trees and brush. The voices he heard were muffled and he could not determine their directional source. As he rode toward the dark opening, a rider appeared carrying a rifle. Bone did not recognize him.

"What do you want?" the vaquero asked.

"I am Bone. I come to see Matteo."

"Follow me," the man said.

"What are you called?" Bone asked, in Spanish.

"I am called Isidro," the man said.

Isidro followed a twisting course through the brasada, ducking under the mesquite branches, crossing small sloughs, over dry packed ground where the sun shone like a beacon through the green leaves. Along the way, Bone heard rifle fire that startled his horse, single shots and volleys, and the occasional bark of a command.

Presently, Isidro rode into a wide clearing on high ground, a place that stirred some primordial memory in Bone's mind as he looked at the remnants of adobe structures, little crumbling dwellings and the stark detritus of jacals that had rotted away.

At the far end of the clearing, Bone saw the vaqueros gathered in a cricle. As he rode closer, he heard the stern voice of Matteo giving orders to fire. Isidro melted away, back into the brush. One moment he was in front of Bone, and then he was gone.

Another Mexican rode out to see who Bone was, challenged him in Spanish.

"I am Bone. I have come to see Matteo."

"Come, then," the rider said, and Mickey saw that the man was heavily armed, with two pistols, two rifles, powder bags, horns and shot pouches hanging over his chest.

As Bone rode closer, following the sentry rider, he

noticed that some of the men were performing military maneuvers. One line of men would fire their rifles and then kneel down, while a second phalanx would step up and fire theirs as the first shooters reloaded their rifles. Puffs of white smoke billowed from the muzzles and settled in the grasses so that there was a pall of smoke yards wide in front of the riflemen.

"There is Matteo," the sentry said to Bone. "Over there." He pointed to the man standing off from the shooters.

"I see him," Bone said. The sentry nodded and rode back to watch the road. Bone rode across the meadow, dismounted, let his reins trail. His dun horse began to graze. Matteo looked over at Bone, barked an order to the shooters. They broke up ranks and walked to the shade of a clump of mesquite and started building smokes.

Matteo started walking toward Bone.

Bone noticed that some of the men started packing up their rifles, saddling their horses. He saw that there were flattened places where they sat, probably to rest and eat their lunches during the day. It was as if they did not want to be near the crumbled adobes and the decayed remains of the jacals.

"You have returned from Mexico," Matteo said. It was not a question.

Bone nodded.

"Good. You can stay here with me tonight. We will talk."

As Matteo and Bone stood there, the men in the mesquite finished their smokes and walked off into the woods. They returned a few moments later riding their horses. Small groups began to ride off toward the woodcutter's trail. None of them waved, none spoke as they passed Matteo and Bone.

"It is good you do not ask questions," Matteo said. "But I will tell you everything when they have all gone."

"It is your business, Matteo."

"And you are a part of it, my friend."

Matteo's face, as always, was a mask. Bone knew that
Aguilar was a man who thought things through before
he spoke and that he had big plans for himself, a pur-
pose, always, and he would tell what was on his mind
when it suited him. He was a man who commanded respect, although he was still young. There was something
inside him that was strong, like iron, and people sensed
that about him. He seldom smiled. He was a serious man
and Bone liked that about him.

When all the men had left the meadow, it was very
quiet. Matteo brought out the makings, built a smoke.
He handed the papers and tobacco to Bone. Bone rolled
a cigarette. Matteo held up his burning glass and lit their
smokes.

"Bring your horse, Mickey," Matteo said. "We'll put
him up and feed him. There is a corral in the brasada,
out of sight."

Bone caught up the dun and followed Aguilar across
the clearing. The sun was on its descending arc in the
western sky and drew the long shadows from the trees,
striped the grass. Matteo slapped Bone's bedroll,
squeezed one of the saddlebags.

"You do not have much food with you," Aguilar said.

"Some hardtack, jerky."

"We will eat and drink some wine. You will tell me
how you did with the horses you took to Mexico."

"I have the money for you."

"I will get it from you later. I am training my men to
fight. To shoot, to follow orders. My little army."

Bone said nothing.

The two men came to a clump of tightly packed mesquite trees. Beyond, a corral stretched in a U shape,
formed by mesquite logs and boughs. Just past the growing trees, there was an opening. Across this opening,
there were fresh-cut logs, a makeshift gate to the large
corral. Aguilar's horse whinnied and trotted out to the
gate. There were buckets inside with water and feed.

Matteo opened the gate as Bone unsaddled the dun. A moment later, he slapped his horse on the rump and it ran inside past the gate. Aguilar's horse sniffed noses with the dun and laid back its ears as Bone's horse drank from one of the water buckets.

Matteo led Bone to his camp which was invisible from a few yards away, since it, too, lay inside a massive half circle of adobe bricks. Trees growing above the campsite served to break up the smoke from Aguilar's fire. Over a supper of quail and rabbit, stale tortillas, fiery salsa, frijoles, the two men talked.

"There is trouble again with the Apaches. Cuchillo's son, Culebra," Aguilar said, chuckling. "Baron made a big mistake when he killed Cuchillo."

"You are still friends with Culebra?"

"Yes. I buy horses from him, horses that he steals from Baron."

"And cattle?"

"We do not need cattle. We need to sell what we have."

"When? How?"

"I am watching, and waiting. This Martin will lead us to the markets. But I do not trust him. I think he is stealing some of my land."

"Do you fear him?" Bone asked.

"I have some respect for him. I watch him."

"It is not Martin that you should be watching, Matteo. It is the son, Anson."

"The boy? Why, that one is still suckling at his mother's breast. He is no older than I am."

"Do you remember Juanito Salazar? He says that the young Baron is very strong. Even Culebra says this."

"Anson Baron is a boy. And, yes, I remember Juanito Salazar. He was more dangerous to me than any of the Barons. He was a smart man. *Muy sabio.* Very wise."

Bone did not add or subtract from what Matteo had said. He knew Anson better than Matteo did. He had liked the boy when he worked for Baron. Anson had wanted to go away with Bone when he left that place. He would have gone, too, if Bone had not sneaked away in the night.

Matteo looked at Bone a long time as he sucked the marrow from a rabbit bone. He pondered his face in the firelight, trying to read his eyes, trying to discern what Bone was thinking.

"You do not say much about the Baron boy, Mickey. Do you fear him as well?"

"I am not afraid of him."

"But, you what?"

"I respect him, as you respect his father," Bone said.

"That boy? Respect? Why?"

"He is stronger than the father, but the father is a strong man, too. Anson could be an Apache himself except for his birth."

"What in the devil do you mean by that? He is a gringo."

"There is something in him that is Apache, I think," Bone said. "He is of the land more than he is of his parents."

"I do not know what you mean," Matteo said, a note of irritation in his voice.

"Maybe I do not know either."

"You know. You tell me. If Anson Baron is to be my enemy, I want to know all about him."

Bone looked away from the fire, into the sunset sky, at long thin clouds painted salmon and purple, all silver rimmed and tinged with gold patches. He daubed a tortilla in the grease of a clay bowl, his slender fingers roiling it around as if plucking some instrument of divination.

"When I went away from the Baron rancho to be with my people, Anson wanted to go with me. There was something in his eyes that almost made me take him. A wildness, maybe, the look of a wolf that wants to be free of the trap."

"That does not tell me anything. Just that the boy is stupid."

"He is very smart. He learns quick. I think he will run the Baron rancho better than his father. I think he will make a very bad enemy for you."

"Why? What makes him so strong?"

Bone swallowed bites of the grease-soaked tortilla before he answered. He drank from the goatskin of wine and took a deep breath.

"Why?" Bone replied. "Because Anson is not afraid of death."

"How do you know this, Mickey?"

All Bone said was: "I just know."

Matteo sat back and set his bowl aside. He reached for the bota and tipped it to his lips. He squeezed the skin and a stream of wine poured into his throat.

"We will see what young Baron is afraid of," Matteo said. "If it is not death, it will be another thing, eh?"

Bone was silent, looking once again at the sky to the west, already turning black as a raven's wing.

6

JORGE WINCED EACH time Anson plucked a spine from his back. Peebo Elves, a rifle in his hand, stood by the open door, looking and listening for any sign of Apaches. Tumbleweeds rolled across his line of vision, some coming to rest against the corral where his horses continued to eat. When he wasn't doing that, he was watching each quiver of the Mexican's flesh with obvious enjoyment.

"Seems to me," Peebo said, "that if you pulled off his shirt, you'd get most of the stickers out."

"No, no," Jorge protested.

"I thought of that," Anson said. "If you don't stop shakin', I might just do that."

"This Culebra, how come he didn't just cut your throat and lift your scalp?" Peebo asked the Mexican.

"He say it is a warning," Jorge said. "He say to tell you he will make war on you, Anson."

"Hell, looks to me like he already has," Peebo said.

"It's just talk," Anson said. "We killed his daddy and he's riled up."

"I had the fear," Jorge said in Spanish. He cried out as Anson pulled two thorns at once.

"Let me spell you, Anson," Peebo said. "I think I can make better time."

"No, no," Jorge said again. "Anson, he does it good."

Anson jerked a clump of spines from the small of Jorge's back and the Mexican almost jumped off the bed. Then, Anson stood up. He looked at Jorge. There were spines still sticking in his legs and rump.

"Jorge, you got to take off your clothes and let Peebo do this for a while. I'm plumb tuckered out."

Peebo grinned. "Get naked, Jorge. I'll get them stickers out in no time at all."

Jorge looked up at Peebo in dismay. Peebo smiled at him like some impish elf. Jorge shuddered.

"Come on, Jorge," Anson said. "We ain't got all day."

Jorge unbuttoned his shirt. Peebo grabbed the collar and skinned the shirt down Jorge's arms and jerked the shirt clean. Jorge let out a cry of pain. But, several spines came off with the shirt.

"Now, your trousers," Peebo said.

Jorge looked sheepish as he reached for his belt. Anson nodded to him that he should continue.

Jorge untied the thong that held his pants up and slid them down off his legs, wincing at each inch of travel. He stepped out of them.

"Christ," Peebo said. "He does look like a porkypine for danged sure." Then, he began pulling spines from Jorge's back and legs, his hands working smooth and swift. It was all Jorge could do to keep from dancing with the sharp pain. His body was so peppered with tiny drops of blood it looked as if he had the measles.

Anson watched Peebo work in fascination. Jorge's eyes were closed and his flesh quivered like jelly each time a thorn came out.

"You know, Peebo," Anson said, "we probably can't pay you for a while. Money's real scarce on the Box B."

"Oh yeah?"

"That's why me and Jorge been gatherin' up strays without no help. We have only a few hands to take care of the herds."

"Well, me and your daddy can work somethin' out."

"You and me, you mean," Anson said.

"I reckon."

"It's kind of embarrassin'."

"Well, your daddy said I could go to work for him. We never did talk pay."

"Well, this might be a good time."

"How do you figger to raise cash?" Peebo asked.

"The army needs beef, and we've sold some in New Orleans. Charlie Goodnight thinks that one day soon the market will open up back east."

"How would you get beef back east?"

"Goodnight says there'll be shippers in Kansas right soon."

Peebo continued to jerk the barbed spines from Jorge's legs and arms. He followed no particular pattern, but just grabbed from an arm or a leg or on Jorge's back. Jorge hung his head down over his chest as if he was some condemned prisoner about to be hanged.

"People back east don't have no taste for beef," Peebo said.

"Not yet. But, they will." Anson moved suddenly, bringing his rifle halfway up to his shoulder. Peebo stopped plucking spines and Jorge lifted his head.

"What do you see?" Peebo asked.

"I saw something move," Anson said.

"Apache?"

"I don't know." Anson scanned the land beyond the window. "I'm wonderin' just what it was I saw. Something moving."

"A jackrabbit?" Peebo ventured.

"No. More like a coyote," Anson said. "Or a small deer."

"Maybe we better take a look," Peebo said.

Jorge turned to Anson. "Culebra."

"What makes you say that, Jorge?" Anson asked.

"He say he will be back. He say he will be like your shadow, Anson."

"What else did he say?" Anson asked.

"He say he is like the snake. You do not see him until he strikes. He say you might step on him he will be so close."

"Shit," Peebo said. "He's just tryin' to throw a scare into you, Anson."

Anson continued to peer intently out the door. Now, however, he was not sure he had seen anything. But, the hairs on his neck stiffened and prickled his skin. He cleared his throat of the lump that had gathered there. "Well, he's doin' a pretty good job of it."

"Hell, ain't one lone Apache a-goin' to jump three men," Peebo said.

"Two," Jorge said, without humor.

"You ain't got far to go," Peebo said. "Couple more pricklers, that's all."

With that, Peebo jerked another five spines from Jorge's back and grabbed up his rifle. He joined Anson near the doorway. Jorge started scratching the undersides of both arms and found two more spines near his armpit. He pulled these and began to get dressed.

"See anything?" Anson asked Peebo.

"I see a lot, boyo, but that's not what bothers me."

"What, then?"

"Is what I see out there what's supposed to be there, for one thing. And, for another, what am I not seeing that is there?"

"I don't understand," Anson said.

"See that clump of tumbleweed yonder?" Peebo pointed to a dried weed some sixty yards away.

"I see it."

"Was it there when we rode up here?"

"I don't know," Anson said.

The two men stared at the tumbleweed. It did not move. Peebo licked his right index finger and stuck it outside the doorway. He held it there for several seconds. Then, he brought his hand back inside.

"Breeze blowin' from left to right," Peebo said. "Stiff enough to move that tumbleweed, maybe."

Anson stared at the brushy clump. Another, a smaller weed, bounced past it on some aimless course. The small one kept moving.

"I see what you mean," Anson said. "That big one's stuck."

"Stuck, or somethin's holdin' it."

"What something?" Anson asked.

"Let's go inside," Peebo replied. "Don't look at it for a couple of minutes."

Anson nodded and turned his back on the door. Jorge had just finished tying the rope around his waist that served as a belt. He continued to scratch himself, dipping down to get to the backs of his legs.

"You'll claw yourself raw, you keep that up," Peebo said to the Mexican.

"It is the itching," Jorge said, wriggling inside his clothes.

"Better not scratch it, Jorge," Anson told him. "You might get infected."

"*Ay de mí,*" Jorge said.

Peebo rolled a smoke. He walked to the back window and stuck his head out, held a glass just above the tip of the cigarette. A thin spiral of smoke lazed up from the tobacco and Peebo drew air through it with a loud sucking sound. He filled his lungs with smoke, then blew a plume of blue-gray smoke from his mouth. He saw more tumbleweeds out back, some motionless, one or two more rolling slowly under the push of the slight breeze. A large clump of weeds that had clustered together sat near the corral.

"Now, let's take another look-see out yonder," he said softly. "Don't make much of it. Just amble over to the door with me."

Jorge stood watching the two men as they sneaked up to straddle the doorway.

"What you see?" Jorge asked.

"Some of those weeds bunched up since we last saw 'em," Peebo said.

"Maybe," Anson said. "That one hasn't moved, though."

"No, I reckon not."

"Looks natural to me," Anson said, after a moment. Jorge walked over and stood behind Anson. He stuck his head past the door frame and looked out.

"Just tumbleweeds," Jorge said.

"Don't see no coyote, neither," Peebo said.

The three men continued to look out the door. Small weeds moved slowly, stopping and turning with every whiff of air.

Peebo stepped back, rubbed his eyes. He looked out the doorway again. Anson cleared his throat. Jorge scratched his left underarm. A tumbleweed broke loose from the large cluster and rolled erratically toward the line shack. It stopped when it struck a clump of dirt upturned by a horse's hoof.

"Shit," Anson said. He closed his eyes and turned around, walked away from the doorway. "I guess I really didn't see anything move but a dadgummed tumbleweed."

Jorge shrugged and scratched another spot on his spine-riddled body.

Peebo sighed and left the doorway. "Spooky, ain't it?" He grinned. "We could shoot tumbleweeds until we ran out of powder and lead."

Jorge and Anson both laughed.

"Funny how one Apache can get on your nerves," Anson said.

"*Verdad,*" Jorge said.

"I reckon that Culebra done lit a shuck," Peebo said.

"It looks that way," Anson said. "Maybe we ought to

get after them strays and put some iron to 'em while we got daylight."

"How many you figure?" Peebo asked.

Anson looked at Jorge. Jorge shrugged. "Maybe twenty," he said, "twenty-five."

"Hell, we ought to finish up in an hour or two," Peebo said.

"Make that more like three days," Anson said. "Those wild cattle are scattered from hell to breakfast."

"I got a suggestion," Peebo said.

"What's that?" Anson asked.

"Put them all in the corral as we make the gather, then do the branding."

Anson's face ashed over with a sheepish look. "I figured to do that," he said. "I was just goin' to brand that one cow to get him out of my hair. He was ornery all the way."

"I know," Peebo said.

"First, we must find my horse, no?" Jorge asked.

"Shit," Anson said. "I forgot about your horse."

"We ought to track him pretty easy," Peebo said. "Can't be far."

Jorge smiled with relief. "He will come when I call him, I think."

"What do you call him?" Peebo asked.

"I call him *Burrito*."

Anson laughed. "Jorge says he works like a burro."

"Hell of a name for a horse," Peebo said.

"He does not care what his name is," Jorge said.

"Okay, let's go look for him," Peebo said, and started for the door.

Something caught the corner of Anson's eye as he was about to follow Peebo outside. He looked out the back window and saw a raft of tumbleweeds scooting toward the corral and the line shack.

"Hold on," Anson said. He walked to the window and looked out.

Peebo stopped just outside the front door, then he

slowly started backing toward the house. He fingered the trigger of his rifle. Jorge looked from Anson to Peebo, a look of confusion on his face.

"*Qué pasa?*" he asked.

Peebo stepped back inside, let out a breath. "Those tumbleweeds out front have bunched up and moved right close."

Anson, in a very soft voice, said, "Peebo, come here. Quick."

Peebo dashed to the window. Anson pointed outside. Peebo's lips pursed in stern reaction to what he saw. Tumbleweeds lay pushed up against the corral and close to the shack, so thick and high that the slight breeze could not account for the arrangement.

"Boyo, we got seven kinds of shit pilin' up on us," Peebo said.

Jorge, looking out the front door, cried out. "Apache," he shouted.

Anson looked toward the door. A raft of tumbleweeds moved swiftly toward the shack, pushed there by something or someone he could not see.

"Christ," Anson swore.

The horses in the corral began to mill and whinny in low notes that suddenly turned shrill.

Anson heard an odd sound, a hissing that was like a loud whisper. Out of the corner of his eye, he saw an orange light. His stomach knotted and he felt a cold finger brush down the back of his neck. Then, he heard the same sound again and saw the arcing arrow glide slowly toward the pile of tumbleweeds now bunched up around the front of the line shack.

"Get the hell out," Anson shouted.

Peebo hesitated for a moment as he, too, saw a flaming arrow arch toward the corral. Then, two Apaches appeared out of nowhere, from behind the mass of tumbleweeds, running, not toward the shack, but toward the corral gate.

"Sons of bitches," Peebo cursed, and headed for the door.

Jorge jumped outside, right behind Anson. Around them, the dry tumbleweeds crackled as flames licked at their branches from deep inside the pile. Three Apaches leaped up just beyond and ran to the left, toward the corral.

Peebo cleared the doorway and started to follow Jorge and Anson who were tossing tumbleweeds aside as smoke billowed out of the cluster of weeds and the fire, quickened by a wind of its own making, sped through the brush with a snapping and crackling sound that was like far-off rifle fire.

The horses screamed and the Apaches yipped. As Anson fought his way from the house, he saw a stream of Peebo's horses running from the corral, Apaches flanking them on foot.

Jorge cried out and Anson turned to see him clutching his throat.

An Apache arrow jutted from Jorge's neck and blood streamed from the wound even as he stumbled into a mound of blazing tumbleweeds that erupted all around him.

Anson choked on the smoke and began swinging his rifle to clear a path into the open. Behind him, Peebo gasped as smoke filled his lungs and he staggered like a man become drunken on strong spirits.

And the high-pitched barks and yips of the Apaches could be heard above the roar of the wind-fanned flames.

7

DAVE WILHOIT SHOULDERED his transit and started walking toward the Killian house. He waved to the Mexicans whom he had ordered to quit for the day and return to camp. He knew that Ursula's son, Roy, was not at home, and that she had not gone with him. The buckboard was still out back, its tongue lolling in the dirt, giving it the appearance of a tired skeleton of some boxy beast.

There were few single women in Baronsville and those who were not married were well sparked by the local swains. Baronsville wasn't much of a town yet, but it was getting a newspaper and there was talk of a bank coming in. Now it consisted of one mercantile store, a homely tavern, a hotel, a livery stable and a feed and implement store that also sold hardware and tack. Not much there for a single man unless he wanted to gamble at cards or visit the Mexican boarding house that fooled no one.

Dave didn't have to knock on the door. It opened as

he approached from the front. Ursula Killian stood there, her figure partially revealed, a close-fitting gingham dress of magenta and blue clinging to her leg and thigh. There was enough of her leg showing to send a rush of blood through Dave's veins as his heart pumped fast enough so that he could feel his right temple throb.

"Good evening, Mrs. Killian," he said, a slow lazy smile breaking on his face.

"Mr. Wilhoit," she said, not without a slight blush and a wispy trace of coyness in her soft voice. "Whatever brings you over here at this time of day?"

"I come calling," Dave said, "if I'm not presuming too much, ma'am." He took off his hat, held it in front of him with steady sun-browned hands. A lock of his hair slid down his forehead, arched in a slight wave.

"Why no, sir, I'm flattered, I really am, and I hope you'll call me Ursula now that we're better acquainted."

"If you'll call me Dave," he said, the smile breaking into a wide grin.

"Dave, won't you come in? Would you like some coffee?"

"Yes, that sounds good."

Dave stepped toward the door as Ursula opened it wide. She held the door for him as he entered, then closed it gently, leaving the latchkey inside. Dave glanced at the room quickly, then turned back to gaze at Ursula. Her light hair was neatly coifed with a single graceful curl falling to her cheek like a wavelet of meringue. Her merry blue eyes danced with light.

"Not very commodious, I'm afraid, but will you take a chair, Dave? I'll get us both some coffee while you get settled."

"Yes'm." Dave sat in one of the chairs by the window. There was a small table between both chairs with a large muslin doily atop it. Dave set his hat on the floor beneath his chair and watched Ursula as she set out cups and saucers, lifted the coffeepot from the stove and poured the cups nearly full. She set them both on a tray, along with two cloth napkins, and brought them to the table.

"Thank goodness my things arrived from Fort Worth," she said. "Roy and I lived quite primitively for a day or so."

"You've fixed up this place very nicely," Dave said.

"Did you see it before I moved in?"

"No, I just gathered that it was lacking the feminine touch."

"How very nice of you to say so, Dave."

Ursula sat down primly and handed Dave a cup and saucer. Dave took them and held them chest high. He did not take a sip until Ursula picked up her own cup and saucer and held the cup to her lips, looking at him over the rim with batting eyelashes.

"Good coffee," Dave said.

"Umm, I'm glad you like it. It's Arbuckle's."

"I can taste the cinnamon a little."

"Yes, I like that."

There arose one of those silences that come between two people who do not know each other well, a silence between comparative strangers that is like smoke from a smoldering fire that needs more than a single breath to reignite it. There was an invisible, but palpable tug that Dave felt, but for the moment he was tongue-tied. He sipped the coffee, sipped it slow so that it would last a long time, and Ursula mimicked him, it seemed, barely touching her cup to her lips and smiling in between as if to encourage him to speak.

When the silence was broken, they both spoke at once.

"Would you—" Dave started to say, while Ursula said, "How long—"

And they both laughed nervously.

"You first," Dave said, glad to know that some of the ice was broken.

"No, I was just wondering . . ."

"What?" he asked.

"I—I wondered how long you would be surveying our—my son's—land."

"I don't know," he said. He had finished the survey, but wanted an excuse to come back to see Ursula.

"And, have you found out that we are trespassers?" She arched her eyebrows as if daring him to accuse her of such a crime.

Dave laughed softly as if to reassure her and set his cup down on the saucer as if it were fine china and sacred to him. "I don't really know much at this point. I will take my measurements back to the Aguilar ranch and go over the deeds and plats and let Matteo make any decisions."

"What if we are trespassing?"

Dave shook his head. "Oh, I doubt if it will come to that. Those old Spanish land grant deeds are difficult to interpret. Landmarks change, measurements were not exact nor even very accurate. I generally make a recommendation to the client who pays my salary and they usually go along with me."

"But, if Mr. Aguilar does not follow your recommendation?"

Dave sighed. "I don't know, Ursula. Sometimes these land disputes are not worth the bother. If a mistake was made in the original deed, or land grant, then sometimes it takes a court, a judge, to decide whose land is whose. I wouldn't worry about it," he added lightly.

"I won't," she said. "I just hope there's no trouble. My son prides himself on owning this piece of land. He wants to build a large ranch."

"I'm sure everything will work out," Dave said.

"So, you came to see me," she said, changing the subject. "Not about the land, I gather."

"No'm. I just wanted to get to know you better. I thought you might like to go into town this evening, have some supper with me. I've a buggy at the Rocking A and I'd like to call on you if you've a mind to get out of the house and see some of Baronsville."

"Why, that's very nice of you, Dave. I believe I would like that. What time would you come for me?"

"Would eight o'clock be all right? It should be a pleasant evening and my horse is right gentle, the buggy comfortable."

"Eight o'clock would be just fine," she said. "More coffee?"

"No'm, not just now."

She set her own cup down as if in approval and leaned back to regard Dave. He felt as if she was inspecting him, but he didn't mind.

"Were you in the army?" she asked suddenly, catching Dave by surprise.

"Why, no, I wasn't," he said. "Why do you ask?"

"The army uses a lot of surveyors. I thought perhaps you might have been a soldier."

"From what I hear soldiers don't get paid much."

"That's true," she said. "There was a lot of talk at Fort Worth about war when I left."

"War?"

"If President Lincoln frees the slaves. The Southerners say they will leave the Union, form a new country."

"That's nonsense," David said.

"Maybe, but there are some soldiers ready to desert the Union and join the Southern forces if there is secession."

David rubbed his forehead. "I hadn't thought about slavery much. Have you?"

"I think it should be abolished."

"It would be an economic disaster to the South."

"Do you hold with keeping slaves, David?"

"Not personally. But I've met some slaveholders. They treat their slaves kindly."

"But a man owning another . . ."

"It doesn't sound right, you put it that way, Ursula."

"No, it doesn't. Jack, my husband, he hated slavery. Roy does too, I think."

"Well, I doubt if Lincoln would go so far as to grant full freedom to slaves bought and paid for."

"Well, he's a Yankee, isn't he?"

"That's just a term. He's our president."

"I think it would be just terrible if the Union split up. If it came to war, it would be even worse."

"Slavery's not worth fighting for," David said. "I doubt if it would come to that if Lincoln does free the slaves."

"That's not what the soldiers at Fort Worth think."

"Well," David said, with a shrug, "soldiers are always looking for a fight, aren't they?"

Ursula did not laugh. She arose from her chair and brought the coffeepot from the stove. She poured their cups full and returned the pot to a cool place on the stove.

David cleared his throat during the awkward silence that had clouded up between them. Ursula sat back down, picked up her cup and blew on the surface of the hot coffee.

"I hope I haven't said something wrong," David said.

"No. You may be right. I am not so sure. I would hate it dreadfully if Roy had to choose sides and fight in a war here in Texas."

"I pray he does not, Ursula. He seems a fine young man."

"I tried to teach him right from wrong while he was growing up."

"I'm sure he'll make you proud someday," David said, relieved to be on safer ground.

"He already does," she said.

David smiled. Ursula was proud of her son. All he had to do was show her that he liked Roy and she would warm to him. He drank the fresh coffee with relish now that he had the woman all figured out in his mind. All he had to do was avoid talk of war and slavery and concentrate on praising her son. Ursula was a fine-looking widow woman and she seemed to like him. He was glad he had walked over from the field to call on her.

David was smiling warmly to himself when Ursula surprised him.

"Which side would you fight on if it came to a war between the Yankees and the Southerners?" Ursula asked.

David choked on his coffee and spluttered droplets all over his shirt and the table as Ursula scooted her chair away. He gasped for breath and set his cup down, then tried to clean up his mess, frantically searching for the correct answer to Ursula's question.

"Never mind," she said, "I'll clean that up. Are you all right?"

"Yes'm," David said, hoping she would have forgotten what she had asked him. "I'm fine. Coffee just went down the wrong pipe, that's all."

"Maybe my question upset you," she said.

"No'm, I just . . . I mean, I didn't . . . wasn't . . . well, it just surprised me is all."

"And?"

David aligned his shoulders and sat straight in his chair.

Ursula looked at him, a querulous expression on her face.

"I guess I'd fight on whichever side wanted me to," he said. "Well, I mean, since I live in Texas I'd fight with the Texans."

Ursula smiled and lifted her cup to her lips.

"Me, too," she said, after a moment.

David looked at her, a feeling of respect building in his mind. Ursula wasn't at all what he had expected. She was a strong woman with a mind of her own. He would have to be careful, he thought. She was the kind of woman who could eat a man alive. She could be dangerous, he felt, and he was intrigued by her. He sensed the ferocity in her heart, the fearlessness of a tigress beating in her chest, uplifting those proud breasts of hers.

The danger she promised made her all the more desirable to him. He wanted to hold her and subdue her at that moment, but he knew that this was not the time. Thinking of it summoned up little tremors inside him. He wondered if he could lift his coffee cup up again without showing his desire with hands that threatened to tremble as he gazed at her across the table.

He cleared his throat. "Perhaps I'd better be going," he said. "It's a long ride both ways and I don't want to be late picking you up."

"Finish your coffee," she said as she dabbed at the spillage with one of the napkins. "You mustn't rush off when we're having such a delightful conversation."

"No'm," he said, and picked up his cup. His hands were steady. He drank slowly, hoping she would not surprise him again.

"You're not afraid of me, are you?" she asked bluntly.

"No, no, of course not," David said quickly while admiring Ursula's perception.

The truth of it was that he was afraid of her at that moment. Afraid of losing her before he had even known her, and afraid of her overwhelming womanness. It was something he was not used to and didn't know if he could handle. Ursula was no spring chicken. She was a full-blown woman and he could almost feel the heat of her across the table. He felt a stirring in his loins that told him positively of the power this woman already had over him.

Yes, he thought, she was dangerous, and he wanted her very much. He pulled one of the napkins from the table and set it on his lap in a wad.

"That won't help," Ursula said, husky throated. "I've already seen what I do to you, David."

David swallowed, unable to speak. He felt his face flush hot and cursed himself for allowing his emotions such free rein.

"It's all right," Ursula said, a patronizing tone to her voice. "I've seen such things before."

And then she smiled knowingly at him and David felt

her heat melting him and the napkin rose in his lap like some ragged, unkempt tent on a scorching plain.

"My, my," she said. "I had no idea you were so impetuous, Dave."

"Ma'am, I—I'm not, I mean, I couldn't help . . ."

"Now, don't apologize. I'm flattered. I just didn't know I had such an effect on a feller, that's all."

"Yes'm. I mean, no'm, I mean, it's not you—"

"Not me, Dave? Were you thinking of someone else?"

David blushed and his collar seemed to tighten around his neck. He felt as if he were digging himself a deeper hole every time he opened his mouth. And, it was embarrassing to have her notice his ardor this way.

"No'm, I wasn't thinking of anything."

"Then, your little man must have a mind of his own," Ursula said.

"What?"

Ursula came over to him, knelt by his side. She touched his neck lightly with her fingertips. The hairs on the back of his head bristled as if electrified.

Ursula didn't answer. Instead, she rubbed his neck with soothing delicacy and his arousal became more apparent despite his trying to will his manhood to soften and shrink back to a harmless glob of flesh.

"I think you're a very sweet man, Dave. But I don't want to make you uncomfortable."

"No'm."

Ursula broke off contact with David and stood up with an abruptness that surprised him. He looked up at her. She was looking down at his lap and smiling.

"It's nice to know that a woman my age can still interest a man."

"Oh, yes'm, you're not old. In your prime, I'd say."

Ursula fluffed the back of her hair and walked back to her chair. She stood there for a moment, gazing wistfully out the window. David crossed his legs, recrossed them.

"I don't feel old," she said. "But I am a widowed woman, after all."

"Yes'm. I'm sorry about that."

"Sorry that I'm a widow?"

"Sorry that you lost your husband, I mean." David began to breathe easier.

"I hope you don't think I'm looking for a man, Dave."

"No'm. I mean, I just think you're nice and I'd like to get to know you better."

"We'll see, David, we'll see. Perhaps you should leave now and pick me up later. We'll go to town."

David got up, feeling much better. He set his coffee cup on the table, smoothed the front of his trousers. "Yes, I—I look forward to that, Ursula. I'll hurry on home and change clothes."

Ursula turned and looked at him. He could feel the heat from her eyes, the radiance she projected with the rapturous expression on her face. She looked almost beatific, but there was something else, too, the look of a wanton. Her breasts seemed to have swelled, making her even more desirable, and he thought of how close she had been to him, how very close and he could still feel her finger touching his neck, burning into his flesh, leaving an invisible mark that he knew must be there, indelible, permanent.

"I look forward to seeing you at eight o'clock," Ursula said, starting toward the front door.

"I won't be late, ma'am."

She opened the door, held it for him as he approached. As he was leaving, her hand touched his arm. He felt it burn through his skin as if she had dipped her hand in fire.

"I'll be ready," she said, and stepped back so that he could pass. He stumbled outside, feeling foolish and not a little bewildered.

"Good-bye, Ursula," he said, tossing her a wave.

"Good-bye, Dave."

He walked around the house quickly, wanting to be

out of her sight so that he could breathe, could think. When he was well past the house and headed for his camp, he began to relax, suddenly realizing that he had been wound up like a watch spring.

Nothing had happened, he told himself, yet something had happened. He could feel Ursula's closeness even now, could feel how close she had come to him and how much he had wanted her. Yet, she had done nothing remonstrable, nothing bad. In fact, he decided, she had done nothing at all.

But it felt as if she had done something. And, worse, it felt as if he had done something, something shameful, perhaps. But what? Now he wondered if he had not imagined her nearness, the way she had looked at him, the effect she had on him. He wiped his forehead. His face was bathed in sweat and he could hear his pulse racing in his ears.

Ursula, he thought, was surely a most dangerous woman. An exciting woman. He wondered what the evening would bring. His pulse raced even faster at the thought and he tried to scrub his mind of such sinful thoughts.

But, he wanted Ursula. The idea that she was a widow excited him, too. There was something wicked about a widow woman he believed. As a boy, the widow in the town was a subject of great mystery. And Ursula was a most mysterious woman. Of that he was certain. A very mysterious and exciting and desirable woman.

He skipped lightly the rest of the way to his camp, feeling like a young boy who had just seen a pretty girl smile at him.

8

PEEBO STAGGERED AWAY from the smoke, gasping and choking. Anson slapped at sparks attached to his trousers and beat at those mired in his hair. He held his breath and followed Peebo away from the flames, stomping at patches of fire curdling the grass under his feet.

When they were clear of the smoke and rasping flames, Peebo and Anson kicked their smoldering boots into the dirt to put out the sparks, wiped their blackened faces and drew in lungfuls of clean sweet air.

"Them sonsofbitches," Peebo muttered.

"Tricky bastards. Caught us with our pants down." Anson gingerly touched his singed eyebrows, flaking off small motes of fried hair that fell to the earth like the husks of tiny dead flies.

The two men stood and watched the flimsy jacal blaze like a torch. The roof was a sheet of flame before disappearing in a puff of smoke, then the walls became engulfed in lashing tongues of fire that quickly consumed every square inch of fuel right before their eyes.

The heat from the conflagration drove the two men further away from the dwelling. A thin and ragged column of smoke rose in the sky, twisting upward on invisible currents of air until the top fanned out and left a smoky pall that stretched for a hundred yards before the breeze nibbled at its edges and twisted it out of shape until it resembled a torn and tattered shroud.

Anson muttered a low curse, kicked at a dirt clod with the disconsolate air of one who has lost everything in the world. His mouth sagged into a surly frown and he blinked his fire-seared eyes as if fighting back tears.

"Damned sonsofbitches," Anson said aloud.

"Them Apaches done boogered us for fair," Peebo said, his blond bangs plastered against his sweaty forehead, his hat miraculously still stuck to the back of his head, the dirt on it sooted over as if huge thumbprints had left their indelible marks on brim and crown. "I'd like to skin each one of 'em with a paring knife."

"Well, they took all your horses, Peebo, and mine, too. It's a damned long walk to La Loma de Sombra."

"Where's that?"

"The house at the main ranch."

"How far?"

"Hell, I don't know. Thirty miles. Forty."

Peebo laughed drily, started walking a circle around the burning jacal, looking at the ground.

"Whatcha doin', Peebo?" Anson asked.

"Seein' if I can find our canteens."

"Hell, they burnt up."

"Maybe not. Mine was nigh full of water. What about yours?"

"Hell, I don't know. Don't even know where I left it. Might still be on my horse."

"I took mine off to keep it in the cool," Peebo said.

The blaze was yet too hot for Peebo to walk close to the jacal, but he peered hard into the inferno to see if he could spot his canteen. When he had completed a full circle, he shook his head and ambled back over to where

Anson still stood, watching in fascination the fire consume everything in its rabid grasp.

"Shit," Peebo said.

"No canteen?"

"Oh, it's in there, somewhere. I can find it easy."

"How?"

"Just listen for the sound of boiling water," Peebo said, a grin magically risen on his face as if it had been there all the time and by some unknown power had flashed into being like a sudden sunrise.

"Yeah, sure," Anson said. "Well, we can't wait around here to see if your goddamned canteen's boiling."

"Oh, it's boiling all right. If I get to it before it all evaporates into steam, we'll have us some water to carry us on our journey."

"Back to La Loma."

"Hell no."

"What do you mean 'hell no?' "

"I mean to get my steeds back."

"How?" Anson asked. That interminable grin was still plastered to Peebo's face like a swatch of barn paint. "We're afoot, or didn't you notice?"

Peebo's nose wrinkled up and he made a face, squint eyed and all. The grin was twisted some, but it was still there, teeth bared to the raw gums of the man.

"Anson, did you ever walk down a man on horseback?"

"No. And didn't nobody else neither."

"That's where you're wrong, pilgrim. I done it."

"When?"

"When a Comanche stole a horse of mine. He come in on foot just to get him a free ride and got away before I could throw down on him."

"And you walked him down?"

"I sure as hell did, son. Slick as grease on shit. He liked to rode that horse into the ground a-tryin' to get away from me and I just kept on a-goin' and kept on until he run out of horse and time."

Anson shook his head in mock disbelief. He was almost sure that Peebo wasn't lying, but he thought he might be stretching a story beyond its regular boundaries. He tried to picture it in his mind, Peebo walking after a lone Comanche warrior on horseback. It was common knowledge that Comanches and horses were one and the same. They were like those centaurs his pa had told him about when he read him old stories out of a book he had kept at sea. Half man, half horse, a Comanche was, and scrawny little Peebo with his bow legs and bandy feet wasn't going to walk down any such critter.

"The horse must have been lame," Anson said.

"Sound as a twenty-dollar gold piece."

"Sheeeit, Peebo."

"Shit, my ass. A man can walk farther than a horse any day. Might not be able to outrun him, but a horse is packing a lot of weight, and he needs grass and water to keep going. A man can fill his belly with water and just keep going with not so much as a hardtack biscuit to waller in his mouth."

"I'd damn sure have to see that, Peebo."

"And, by the gods, you will, me bucko."

"Well, walkin' down one Comanche ain't the same as takin' after a passle of Apaches."

"One or a dozen, we can do it."

"We'd be outnumbered if we do catch up to Culebra and his bunch."

Peebo laughed and pointed a finger at a spot just above his right temple. "Not here, we ain't, Anson. We've got powder and ball. They've got arrows and spears. You leave it to me. We'll get those horses back."

Anson heaved a sigh as he looked askance at the grinning Peebo. "You're crazy," he said.

Peebo laughed. Then, he began walking around the smoking rubble of the jacal, kicking aside burning faggots that might conceal a canteen. Something caught his eye and he ran through the cinders and snatched something from a heap and kept on running as tiny flames licked at his boots.

"Find it?" Anson asked.

Peebo flung the object five feet through the air and skidded it across bare ground. Sparks flew from the canteen's edges, but Anson could hear the water slosh inside it.

"Hot," Peebo said, flicking his scorched fingers. He danced around, stamping his feet to put out the sparks that had attached to his boots and the bottom of his trousers.

"I'm damned," Anson said. "You found it."

"I'll spit on it to cool it down and it'll be good as new."

"You *are* crazy," Anson said, dipping his head. He could not stand to look at that grin he knew was on Peebo's face. But, he could still see it in his mind.

"Scared?" Peebo asked.

Anson did not feel compelled to answer.

"I didn't think so," Peebo said. "Come on. Let's see if I can tote this canteen to the creek. We'll fill our bellies and the canteen."

"What we ought to do is look for Burrito," Anson said.

"Burrito?"

"Jorge's horse. If the Apaches didn't get him, Burrito's still around somewhere."

"Anson, we could track the rest of the day and not find that horse in this brush."

"Well, let's keep our eyes open, in case we run across his tracks."

Peebo picked up the canteen, juggled it between his hands, spit on it, blew on it, until finally it was cool enough to carry. The two men started walking toward the creek, both checking their rifles and pistols as they went.

Anson walked with difficulty, his feet wobbling on heels built high to keep his feet from going clear through the stirrups. Peebo was wearing a different kind of boot, more like a moccasin.

"You might want to cut some off them heels," Peebo said. "Be easier walkin'."

"Yeah, I just might," Anson said, trying to walk without toppling to one side or the other.

They reached the creek, finally, both sweating salt and liquid out of their pores in profusion. Peebo emptied the hot water out of the canteen, filled it with the cool stream waters, drank a third of it and filled it again.

"Here, you drink all you can swaller," Peebo said, handing the wooden canteen to Anson. The wood was charred on the edges, but the hot water had swelled the wood tight so that the vessel didn't leak.

Anson took the canteen and drank thirstily, gulping down the sweet water until he could hold no more. He handed the canteen back to Peebo, who filled it again and drank some more.

"Can you swaller any more, Anson?"

"I reckon not."

"This'll be all we have until we find another creek or water hole."

"I don't want to get any sicker than I already am, Peebo."

"Let's go back, then, and pick up them Apache tracks."

"We ought to look for Jorge's horse."

"We oughter be at siesta right about now, too, but we ain't got time to dawdle. Them was prime steeds those red rascals took offen us."

Anson looked up at the sky, shading his eyes from the sun. It was still blazing high in the sky and they had a lot of daylight left to burn. He didn't relish walking in high-heeled boots through some of the roughest country on the Box B just to wind up empty-handed.

"I don't think we stand a chance in hell of catching up to those Apaches today or tomorrow or the next day," Anson said.

"You say it's thirty mile or more to the ranch house, what'd you call it, La Loma somethin', well, we ain't goin' to make that today, neither, Anson me bucko, so might as well walk toward somethin' we can catch. That ranch house ain't goin' to come lookin' for us."

"Nor your damned horses, either, Peebo."

Peebo grinned wide and it was hard to argue with someone like that, Anson decided.

"Let's cut them heels down to size," Peebo said, "and see where those boots can take you."

"Shit on you, Peebo. Those Apaches are five or ten miles away by now."

"Well, we can do that in a couple of hours, don't you think?"

Anson looked up at the sun again, felt its heat on his face. He sat down and shucked off his boots in the shade of a mesquite tree. Peebo drew his knife and sat down across from Anson.

"You keep grinnin' like that, Peebo," Anson said, "and your face is goin' to freeze that way permanent."

"Why, it already has, son, don't you know?"

Anson shook his head, trying not to smile.

"I grin even in my sleep," Peebo said.

Ten minutes later, Anson was walking on short heels, following Peebo, who was stepping out as if going on a short stroll down to the well in the cool of an evening.

Anson was too worn out to curse his friend. His eyes stung from dripping sweat and his clothes were plastered to his body like sodden wallpaper.

And every time Peebo looked back at him, Anson groaned inwardly to see that Peebo's infernal grin was still intact.

9

MARTIN BARON HAD a deep sinking feeling in the pit of his stomach as he watched the three vaqueros trying to drive the small bunch of unbanded strays toward the corrals they had finished building the week before. Tito Lucero was chasing two of the unbranded longhorn yearlings that had broken away from the bunch with pathetic futility.

Chamaco, Tito's awkward son, had lost four more at the rear and was yelling at them while his ungainly horse balked at every head that strayed across his path. Chamaco had no control over his mount and the cattle were running back toward cover like pups chasing a ball.

The other vaquero, Pedro Amador, was trying to keep what was left of the gather together, but it was clear to Martin that he neither knew what he was doing nor had the ability to manage his horse.

There was nothing wrong with the horses, Martin knew, they were all good mounts, had been trained to work cattle, were responsive, quick, agile, good in brush.

But, the Mexican vaqueros were just too inexperienced, too unwilling to take command. They had drifted onto the Box B a month ago, on foot, and begged for work, saying that they were truly vaqueros from Sonora and swore they knew cattle and horses as well as they knew their mothers' sacred names.

Martin glanced toward a distant speck on the horizon, a rider, slowly making his way across the open plain. Puzzled, Martin unconsciously touched his pistol butt, the .44 caliber Navy Colt six-shot cap and ball pistol he carried with him at all times when he was away from La Loma de Sombra, along with his .50 caliber caplock rifle jutting from a scabbard attached to his saddle.

"Pedro," Martin called. "Hurry up," he said in Spanish. "Drive those cattle into the corral."

Pedro did not reply as he tried to turn the strays back into the herd. A swirl of dust arose from the flashing hooves of those longhorns trying to escape and run back into the brush. For a moment, Martin could no longer see either Pedro or the strays he was trying to recapture.

The speck on the horizon grew larger and Martin kept one eye fixed on the rider while he tried to monitor the progress of the three inept vaqueros.

Tito chased a lone bull into a clump of thick mesquite brush higher than a man's head. The Mexican yelled out a sacrilegious stream of curses. Martin turned just as the rump of the bull disappeared into the thicket. Tito jerked the reins of his horse hard and the animal skidded to a stop. Martin devoted his full attention to the scene, forgetting, momentarily, about the rider heading his way.

To Martin's horror, Tito lifted his right leg to swing it over the high cantle of the Mexican saddle and dismount.

"Tito, no," Martin yelled, but he was too late.

Tito jumped down from the horse, snatching the lariat coiled around the large saddle horn as he hit the ground.

"Don't go in there," Martin hollered out in English, before realizing that Tito spoke no more than eight or ten words in that language. "*No vaya adentro,*" Martin cried.

But, either Tito hadn't heard him, hadn't understood him, or was just disobeying, because the Mexican ran into the thicket. Pedro and Chamaco stopped trying to round up the wild strays and watched their companion disappear into the brush.

Martin saw Tito's horse prick its ears and start to back away.

"God damn!" Martin yelled.

He had warned all of his Mexican wranglers not to get off their horses when they were rounding up wild longhorns. It was very dangerous, for many reasons.

"Tito, *cuidado,*" Pedro called out.

Chamaco's face blanched and he turned his horse to ride over to the mesquite clump.

"Stay away, Chamaco," Martin warned.

"*Mi padre, muy peligroso,*" Chamaco muttered, and kept on riding toward the spot where his father had vanished.

"Chamaco," Martin warned as he turned his horse in a tight circle. But he knew the boy wasn't listening and was probably going to do something foolish, as his father had just done.

Pedro sat his motionless horse as if stupefied while Chamaco whipped his own mount toward the balking horse Tito had left behind. Tito's horse was backing away from the brush, his ears tipped toward the dark thicket, the hairs bristling as if electrified.

"Goddamm it, Chamaco, get the hell away from there," Martin said in English as he rode toward the boy.

Chamaco rode up to the brush and his horse balked, humping his spine as if to buck the young Mexican off. Martin saw the saddle rise up as if a wave had run under it. Chamaco, confused, strapped the horse's rump with the trailing end of his reins. That was all it took. The horse twisted to the left and went stiff-legged as it began to buck.

"Shit," Martin exclaimed.

Chamaco had sense enough to grab the apple knob of his saddle horn as his horse bounded away in jolting, stiff-legged hops. The saddle flopped up and down on its back so high Martin could see daylight under it and under Chamaco's butt when he rose above the cradle, airborne.

Pedro yelled something Martin could not hear as Chamaco's horse stopped bucking and ran toward a lone oak to try and brush its rider off its back.

"Hang on," Martin said in English, knowing the boy could not understand him. But, he did not know the Spanish for such a situation and used the only words he could think of as the boy's horse began to buck again, now close to the tree.

Chamaco screamed as the horse slammed him into the tree and twisted away, still bucking. The boy lost his grip on the saddle horn and left the saddle in wingless flight as the horse kicked out with both hind hooves and sped away, reins trailing, saddle sliding back and forth on its back, the cinch loosened a good four inches in girth.

The horse kept bucking until the saddle swung over its side and hung underneath its belly like a planter box. This only made the horse wilder. It tried to kick the offending baggage away and got its left hind foot caught on the underside of the saddle. It hopped along on three legs as Chamaco arose from the ground, one side of his face scratched and bleeding.

"Stay there, Chamaco," Martin said in Spanish as he rode off to rescue Tito. Chamaco leaned against the tree that had scraped the hide off his face, groggy as any drunken cowhand on a three-day bender.

Martin rode into the brush, digging spurs with short, soft rowels into his horse's flanks to head him where he didn't want to go. He rode a sorrel gelding, sixteen hands high, as jittery a horse as he could find to work the brush, a good cutter, but wary of the wide deadly sweep of the long horns of the wild cattle, just as Martin wanted him to be.

"Cap'n," Martin said, speaking to the sorrel, "you watch it now, go on in, go on now. That's the boy."

Cap'n's ears swept back flat on his skull, but the horse went into the brush. Limbs brushed against Martin's chaparejos, scratching white lines in the leather that protected his legs. The brush opened up, but not much, and Martin saw that he had entered a thicket with a warren of cow and deer trails leading in every direction.

Cap'n stopped abruptly, and Martin didn't fight him to keep on going. He, too, heard the noise, the crunch of dry branches, the rustle of leaves, the pounding of heavy hoofbeats.

He also heard Tito's yell, a yell full of the kind of mortal fear that Martin dreaded. Seconds later, Tito came running out of one of the dark warren trails, his eyes wide, sweat gleaming on his bronzed face. He saw Martin and screamed a string of Spanish cusswords that blistered the air.

Cap'n turned just as a maddened longhorn bull boiled out of the thicket, his horns knocking down branches right and left, shredding wood and leaves, leaving a wide swatch of desolation behind him.

"Run, Tito," Martin yelled, as if Tito needed any prodding, and Cap'n scrambled out of the bull's path just in time. The longhorn was bent on destroying Tito and never swerved in its path as it bolted toward the hapless Mexican vaquero.

Tito made it through the tunnel that he had entered, but the bull smashed a path right behind him. Martin turned Cap'n to try and head off the longhorn, and put the spurs to his flanks.

Cap'n bolted through the opening in the wake of the rampaging bull and Martin saw Tito running on short bandy legs eight or ten yards ahead of the snorting longhorn. Tito ran a zigzag pattern, which, while slowing him down, also made the bull change its course.

Out of the corner of his eye Martin saw Pedro shake loose his lariat and begin to build a loop as he kicked his horse in the flanks. Pedro held his reins in his teeth as his horse charged toward the bull and Tito.

Pedro began to twirl the loop over his head as he drew closer to the bull. His horse lowered its head and followed the path of the longhorn with surprising finesse and agility.

Tito looked back over his shoulder, eyes wide in fear, his face a daub of bloodless flesh. At that moment, the bull lowered its head in preparation for a full-blown butt just as Pedro closed the distance and threw his loop just in front of the charging animal. The loop was wide enough to clear the horns and fell gracefully over the longhorn's neck.

Pedro pulled the reins from his teeth and hauled in on them. His horse dug in its rear hooves and skidded to a stop as Pedro took up slack in the rope.

The rope tightened around the bull's neck. Pedro put his mount into a twisting turn, putting more pressure on the lariat. The bull's head jerked sideways as its neck bowed upward in the grip of the noose.

Pedro kept the rope taut as he spoke to his horse. The horse backed away expertly, keeping the tension on the lariat. Martin could see the strain in the animal's muscles as it fought to bring the huge longhorn down, halt its forward motion.

Martin jerked his own lariat from his saddle and built a loop as he rode up to the struggling bull. The longhorn pawed the ground and shook its head trying to break away from the rope. Martin threw his own loop over the cow's horns and started jerking when it dropped parallel to the boss. He halted his horse and it began to hunch down and back away as it had been trained to do.

Tito was still running, his legs pumping even faster than before, even though he was yards away from danger. Chamaco staggered away from the tree, still dazed, and headed toward the bull. The longhorn bawled loudly and flung snot from its nostrils as it shook its head trying to escape the pair of lariats.

Martin spurred his horse away from the bull at an angle, pulling in the opposite direction of Pedro's rope. The longhorn, exhausted from its struggle, dropped to its knees, slobbering foam and gobbets of spittle from its mouth, its long tongue lolling over its teeth like a slab of raw liver.

"Ho," Martin yelled. "We got him, Pedro."

Pedro, who understood some English and could speak several words, said, "Jess, Jess, we got him, big son-ofabitch bull."

Martin spoke to Cap'n and swung his leg over the cantle, stepped down from the saddle. He grabbed the tail end of his lariat and ran to the bull, taking up slack as he shortened the rope. He knelt down and quickly looped the end around the bull's hind legs, jerked it tight, then grabbed a front leg and tied a loop around the ankle, pulled the rope tight so that he had three legs bound together. He knotted it with a bowline on a bight and stood up, breathing fast and shallow. Sweat dripped down his forehead, sheened his stubbled cheeks and jaw.

Pedro sat his horse. Martin turned to him, saw that he was shaking from shoulder to hip, including his hands.

"What passes, Pedro?" Martin asked in Spanish.

"That is a very big bull."

"Where did you learn to throw a rope like that?" Martin asked.

"When I was a boy, I watched the vaqueros from a nearby village. I practiced the roping."

"Too bad that is all you learned from the vaqueros."

"That is all that I saw them do."

"You and Tito never worked the cattle before?"

Pedro shook his head. "No, we did not have cattle where I lived."

"But, you saw vaqueros who knew how to work cattle?"

"Oh, yes, the vaqueros I saw were very good with the

cattle. But I just learned how to throw the lariat."

Martin pulled a bandanna from his pocket, dabbed at his forehead.

"I would like to hire those vaqueros, Pedro. Can you show me where they can be found?"

"They live south of the Río Bravo. There are many of them."

Tito walked over to the bull, but kept his distance. He seemed dumbstruck by the size of the animal. The longhorn had tired of kicking and lay there, panting, his tongue touching the dirt.

"He is very big," Tito said.

"Better see to Chamaco, Tito," Martin said. "He used his head to mash a tree."

"Someone is coming, I think," Tito said.

Martin remembered the lone rider. He looked in the direction Tito was facing and saw the boy.

"That is the son of Lucinda Madera," Pedro said.

"I see," Martin said in English, more to himself than to Pedro. "What does he call himself?"

"He calls himself Julio."

"Tito," Martin said, turning his attention to the man who had nearly been killed by the bull, "if you ever get off your horse again when you're rounding up strays in the brush I will shoot you myself."

"Yes, *patrón*."

"Now, see what passes with Chamaco and leave that bull alone."

"I will shoot the bull," Pedro said.

"You will not shoot the bull, Pedro," Martin said. "That is a good bull. He has the balls, he has the heart. He will make a fine sire."

"Who will brand this big bull?" Pedro asked, as Tito shuffled off to see after his son.

"I will give you the honor," Martin said. "You caught him."

"I think you should do the honor, *patrón*. You tied him so that he could not cause damage."

"No, you will put the Box B brand on this bull. And, you will take me to that village where the good vaqueros live. I will hire them all to work on this ranch."

"Yes, I will do that," Pedro said, his voice trembling. He looked up. "Here is Julio already."

Martin turned to see the boy ride up.

"Julio?"

"Yes, sir," the boy said in Spanish.

"Why do you ride to Golondrina?"

"I have a message from my mother."

"What passes? Is my wife sick? Is your mother sick?"

"My mother says to tell you to come back to La Loma de Sombra quick and take the cannon away."

"What?"

Julio repeated the message he had been given to deliver.

Martin quelled his rage, smiled at the boy.

"You ride on back, Julio, and tell your mother that you gave me the message. Tell her I will be back soon and remove the cannon."

The boy nodded, smiling. Then, he turned and started the long journey back to the main house where the Baron family lived.

"Pedro," Martin said, "what do you suppose Lucinda meant by that message?"

Pedro, who was still on his horse, shook his head. "I do not know, but if Lucinda told you to take the cannon away, then your wife told her to do it."

"That's what I think," Martin said. "Either Caroline has gone crazy or Lucinda has been drinking too much aguardiente."

Pedro did not say anything. He had heard that there was trouble in the Baron house. Everyone had heard that. And, some said that it was true, the wife of Martin Baron was *loca,* crazy. But, he, like his boss, was puzzled by the message. The cannon was in the barn, covered up with a canvas. It was not in the way of anything. Why would Lucinda send her son on such a long ride to tell

Martin to take the cannon away? It did not make sense to Pedro.

"Pedro," Martin said, abruptly shattering the vaquero's thoughts. "Get Tito and Chamaco. We've got to round up every head that you let get loose. Before dark."

"Yes."

"And you'd better hope that this bull here doesn't have a big brother."

Pedro did not laugh.

MICKEY BONE CARRIED things in his heart that he wished would go away. Feelings he no longer had any use for, affections he could no longer afford. Riding back to the Aguilar rancho, he fought with those feelings, tried to bury them in that same place in his heart where he carried hatred, but their tendrils kept writhing and breaking back out like the tentacles of a strong vine, whipping and lashing at his senses like demonic arms.

While he had no affection for Martin Baron, he did not like doing what he was doing with Anson, Martin's son. He bore no malice toward Anson. But this had been Matteo Aguilar's wish, to send Culebra after Anson, to steal from him, to kill him, if the Apache had the chance.

He had watched as Culebra and his braves had stolen the horses, marveling at the cunning of the Apaches, almost wishing he were one of them, instead of being an outcast, forced to drift like a tumbleweed between two worlds, perhaps three, if he included Aguilar and the *mexicanos*. He was part Lipan Apache, but he had lived in the white man's world and now was working for Matteo Miguelito Aguilar, not as an equal, but as a hired man.

The hard angles of the Aguilar rancho house loomed on the horizon, just beyond the shimmers of heat waves that arose from small dancing lakes of silver, mirages that vanished like ghost smoke into thin air as he neared them.

Bone had stayed behind long enough to know that the Apaches had gotten away with the horses. They would drive them down into Mexico, sell them, and nobody would know that Culebra had any connection to Matteo Aguilar. Or to Bone, for that matter.

What bothered Bone now was that Anson and that other gringo, he did not know his name, were following Culebra on foot. It might be that Anson would catch up to Culebra and his braves. It might be that Anson and his friend would be killed, their scalps taken to hang from an Apache lance. But, Anson would not be easy to kill. That one had uncommon courage and stamina. Bone knew. Once they had been friends and he often wondered how it would have turned out if he had let Anson go with him when he left the Box B. Perhaps he and Anson would be riding together now, not here, not in Texas, but south of the Río Bravo, in the mountains of Mexico. Perhaps they would be with the Lipan Apache, fathering children, hunting, fishing, living as his people had lived for centuries.

Bone shook all those thoughts from his head. He would not think of Anson Baron again. Not so long as he worked for Matteo. Not so long as he carried the hate in his heart for Martin Baron.

Matteo Aguilar was waiting for Bone. The rancher stood in the shade at the side of the house, hatless, a pipe in his mouth. He beckoned to Bone to follow him as he turned and walked behind the house toward the stables. Bone saw no sign of Luz, Aguilar's wife.

Bone could almost smell the blood on the house where

Matteo lived. The Mexican had taken the house and all the land in blood and the reek was still there, although all traces had long since been washed away. He could still see the bodies of Matteo's family, could almost hear the crack of gunfire, smell the acrid aroma of burnt black powder.

"You come back so soon," Aguilar said. "What do you know, my friend?"

Bone saw the strange horse tied to one of the stalls. It was a fine horse and bore a saddle that had silver on it, a graceful rifle in a scabbard and two pearl-handled Colt revolvers hanging in holsters from the ornate saddle horn. He knew the horse did not belong to Matteo. There was sweat on its black hide and its four white stockings were flecked with mud. This horse had come from far away and not too long ago.

Bone swung down from the saddle in a single, smooth motion, as if part of his horse had separated and detached itself, the human from the equine, in some primitive, mythical sense.

Matteo blinked as if his eyes were playing tricks on him. He blew a plume of pipe smoke out of the side of his mouth.

"A man came from the east with horses," Bone said. "I do not know his name. Culebra killed the Mexican working for the Baron boy, stole the horses. Baron and the stranger are following the Apaches on foot."

"On foot?"

"I think the stranger wants his horses back."

"Smoke?" Aguilar asked.

Bone shook his head.

"Why did you not kill the young Baron?"

"You did not ask me to do that, Matteo."

"No, I did not. I want the boy to suffer as I have suffered. I want the father to lose all the land he stole from my family."

Bone said nothing. He knew how deep Matteo's hatred went, but he also knew that Martin Baron had bought the Box B land fair and square. When he looked into Aguilar's eyes, he could almost see the eyes of the demon spirit that possessed him.

"Put your horse up, Mickey. I have someone I want you to meet. Then I will tell you what I'm going to do with Martin Baron. Did you see him?"

"No, I did not see Martin. Why?"

"I have plans for him."

Bone walked his horse to the stables. Aguilar went into the house through the back door. The door did not slam. It was as if a ghost had passed through the wall of the house.

Bone could not follow the twists in Matteo's mind. He seemed not so much a rancher, bent on building a good herd of cattle, improving his lands, as a man who was breathing a fire of his own making, a man who hated the Barons more than he loved the land he tended. Aguilar had plenty of land, but he wanted Baron's as well, as if he could manage it with the small army of Mexicans he had trained like soldiers.

Bone entered the back door. He heard conversation in another room as he passed into the kitchen. Matteo called to him from the front room.

"Come on in, Mickey."

Bone walked down a hall that led to the living room. He took off his hat when he saw Luz sitting in a chair that faced him. Aguilar was facing a man whose back was to Bone.

Bone did not speak. Luz did not smile. Matteo beckoned to Bone and stood up. The man stood up, too, but he did not turn around.

"Mickey, I want you to meet a compadre of mine. From Mexico. He just got in a few minutes ago."

Bone walked around the couch and faced the man standing there. He did not know him, but from his clothes, the way he stood, Bone knew what kind of man he was. The man wore tight-fitting trousers, cut from fine cloth, a satin sash, polished kidskin boots, a full-sleeved shirt of blue silk, with gold cuff links and bright brass buttons. He did not wear a gun, but Bone saw a bulge in his sash that probably held a small derringer pistol. He was a swarthy man, thin, but muscular, with a pencil moustache and twin swaths of sideburns curving down the upper reaches of his jaws.

Before Aguilar could make the introductions, Luz got up and left the room. Mickey tried to read her eyes, but they were vacant, her face drawn and tight, as if she had just heard bad news. Aguilar did not seem to notice that his wife was leaving. He was smiling as though he had a secret he was about to reveal, a secret that he thought was wonderful.

"Mickey, I want you to meet Jules Reynaud, from New Orleans. He is a Frenchman who has known Martin Baron since he was a young man selling his fish to the merchants on the docks. He has told me a very interesting story about Baron."

Reynaud did not offer his hand, but stared at Bone with eyes that seemed sculpted out of polished obsidian; they were as black as coals, shiny as a crow's wing.

"You are an Indian," Jules said, without emphasis.

Bone said nothing. There was something oily and smooth about the man who did not have a French accent, only a slow drawl that reeked of black swamp water and muskrat scent. His hair was slicked down, black, smooth as rubbed mahogany.

"Tell Mickey about your sister, Rey," Aguilar said.

"Ah, my sister, Camille," Reynaud said, sitting down. "My sweet, sweet sister."

"Mickey, take a chair," Aguilar said, sitting down himself.

Bone sat where Luz had been seated, a feeling of edginess creeping upon him like the green slime of a fetid bayou. He had been to Louisiana once, had not liked its steamy air, its dank smell, its moss-dripping cypress trees, the snakes that swam its bayous, mouths whose insides were like cotton.

"Tell him about Martin and Camille," Aguilar urged, his eyes blazing with a frantic light.

"There is not much to tell, really," Reynaud said. "Martin was a young man when he came to New Orleans, a ragged runaway, with no home, no money. This was years ago, right after the Alamo fell, or just before. He was a mere boy. My father sold him an old boat, let him pay for it with fish he caught."

Bone said nothing. He tried to imagine Martin as a youth, could not picture him that way.

"Martin seduced my little sister," Reynaud said, looking directly at Bone. "Do you understand the meaning of 'seduce'?"

Bone shook his head.

"My sister was a virgin. She had not been with a man. Martin deflowered her and left her with child. When my father found out, he was furious. He wanted Martin to marry Camille. Martin refused. My father wanted to kill Martin. He challenged him to a pistol duel."

Reynaud paused.

"Does he understand me?" Jules asked Aguilar.

"I understand," Bone said.

"Martin accepted the challenge. His second was a man named Richman. The duel was at dawn, on Lake Ponchartrain. Martin shot my father dead before my eyes. My father, Emile, did not have a chance. His powder was fouled and did not ignite."

Bone made no comment.

"It was not fair and square," Reynaud continued. "I think Martin's friend somehow squeezed water into the barrel of my father's pistol. Martin did not attend the funeral, nor did he speak to Camille after that."

"That was a long time ago," Bone said.

"No, Mickey, it was two years ago that this happened. Camille has a daughter and no husband. Martin knows about her, but he does not see her."

"I thought you knew Martin when he was a boy," Bone said.

"I did. He did not deflower my sister until she was mature, sixteen years of age. He stopped to pay his respects to my father, and stayed the night. He went into Camille's bedroom after my father was drunk. I was away on business in Baton Rouge. When I returned, Camille told me of her seduction."

"Did she have proof?" Bone asked.

"I did not need proof. I saw the way Martin looked at my sister. He told her he had left his wife and family."

"You do not believe Jules, Bone?" Aguilar asked.

"This does not sound like Martin Baron."

"Do you mean the seduction or the duel?"

"The seduction," Bone said.

Aguilar laughed.

"He was the only one who could have made Camille pregnant," Reynaud said.

"Why did you come here?" Bone asked.

"Ah, don't you know? I have come to kill Martin Baron. And Matteo here tells me you will help me."

Bone looked at Aguilar. Matteo nodded in agreement.

"Martin will not be easy to kill," Bone said.

"I will challenge him to a duel of honor."

"What if Martin does not accept?" Aguilar asked.

"I will shoot him dead on the spot," Jules said. "And you, Mr. Bone, will make sure that I kill Martin, even if you have to shoot him in the back."

"Bone, you take Jules to Baronsville. I believe the second he spoke of was Martin's friend, Ken Richman. Richman will see to it that Martin comes into town. Then, Jules will challenge him to a duel."

"I do not like to do this," Bone said.

Jules and Matteo exchanged looks.

"Do you work for me, Mickey?" Aguilar asked.

"I have done work for you, Matteo. This is not work I do. This is, how do you say it? In back of the face."

"Treachery," Jules said.

"I do not know," Bone said. "You say that this duel you fight is of honor. I see no honor in this."

"Are you on Baron's side?" Aguilar asked, his tone tinged with anger.

"I am on no side," Bone said. "I would not kill an enemy this way. It is the way of the fox, the snake, not the way of a man."

Reynaud drew himself up, his thin lips tightened in a frown of indignation.

"You talk of honor," Reynaud said. "Martin showed no honor when he deflowered my sister and left her without so much as a farewell."

"That is what you believe," Bone said.

"And you do not believe him, Mickey?" Aguilar asked.

"I do not believe Martin was a snake in this. He fought a duel with this man's father. He did not owe this man's sister anything. She gave herself to him. She opened the blankets to him."

"Why you—" Reynaud started.

"*Calmate*," Aguilar said. "Do not get angry, Jules. Bone does not understand civilized ways. Do you, Mickey?"

"I have seen civilized ways," Bone said. "I have stolen cattle and horses and I have helped my people kill to get back the land that was taken from them. But, I have shown my face to my enemies. I have not talked behind their backs and told them one thing when I was going to do another."

"I don't need this man," Reynaud said. "I know where to find Richman. I know how to bring Martin to justice."

"Mickey, do not go against me," Aguilar said, an ominous tone to his voice.

Bone looked at Aguilar for a long moment before he spoke. Matteo had given him a home and paid him money. Now, it was time to go back to his wife, to his family, to his people. If he did this thing that Matteo wanted, he would be asked to do another, perhaps to rub out Anson Baron. And, he did not want to do that. He did not care about Martin, but he did not like Jules Reynaud. And now, he did not like Matteo Aguilar, who had brought a snake into his house to kill rats. If Matteo was not careful, the snake would turn on him and fill him with poison.

"Matteo," Bone said. "I am going back to my people in the mountains. I will see my wife and I will make sons to take my place in this world. I do not help this man. I do not have a taste for the blood of any Baron."

"A curse on you, Mickey Bone," Aguilar said. "And a curse on your family, your people. Get out, get out of my sight, you bastard."

"I will be gone within a day," Bone said. "I will help you with the horses and then I will leave."

Bone turned to leave. He was stopped by the lash of Jules Reynaud's words.

"If you warn Martin I'm coming after him, Bone, I'll kill you, too."

Bone turned and looked at the Frenchman.

"Be careful you do not try to kill too many. This is Texas, not Louisiana. We do not buy and sell slaves here."

Bone left the room, walked out the back door without making noise. He was not angry. He was relieved that he would soon be leaving this place where snakes writhed and coiled and hissed in the bushes. If he stayed with Matteo, worked for him, one day, he was sure, he would be bitten by him or one of his friends.

Bone looked once more at the black horse that he now knew belonged to Jules Reynaud. He wondered if he ought to steal it when he left. No, he decided, Matteo would hunt him down if it took all the days of his life.

Bone wanted no shadows following him when he left Texas, a place that had once been his home, but was no longer. Perhaps his people would take him back. Perhaps his woman would forgive him for leaving her to go with Matteo Aguilar. Perhaps he would no longer be an outcast, as he had been all his life.

B ARONSVILLE, TEXAS, WAS just a scrub of a town, barely out of its early childhood in that year of our Lord, 1861. Martin Baron had not had much to do with the creation of the budding hamlet, lending only his family name as his contribution. But, Martin did derive an income from Ken's sale of land and city plots, money he desperately needed to survive.

Rather, Ken Richman had nurtured Martin's dream of a cattle empire, realizing that, with such vast holdings of land, Baron needed a city to bring in workers and builders, breeding families who would help the region grow. While there was still no great market for cattle, both Martin and Ken believed that someday the Box B would be the king of ranches, providing beef for the entire nation.

Richman had laid out the plat of Baronsville, had lured the first settlers, the first merchants, brought in commerce, a newspaper, a preacher to found a church, a freight hauler, a banker, a saloon keeper. He was a man completely devoted to Martin Baron and Baron's interests. Some called him an idealist and Ken did not deny that. Few, except for Martin and his son Anson, knew what Richman's ideals were. While Martin had the vision that was based on the country, Ken's vision included all of Texas, and even the world beyond.

Ken's office on Main Street was the hub of Baronsville business. It was in a small building next to the Longhorn Saloon. The Baronsville bank flanked it on the other side. Richman wanted to do business at street level, and he liked to take his lunch in the saloon and be close to the bank where he could take new residents and businessmen to open up accounts.

The sign on the front door read: LAND OFFICE. Below it on a smaller sign were the words: WALK IN. Ed Wales read both legends and opened the door. He expected to enter an outer office and see a clerk or secretary seated at the front desk. Instead, he stepped into a large room with several chairs around a potbelly stove, and in one corner a single, large desk piled high with documents. A man stood with his back turned, staring at a large map. Next to the map was a sign with another legend that read: *It is not enough to know how to ride a horse; one must also know how to fall off of one.* Beneath it was a name painted in flowing script: Juanito Salazar.

The man at the map turned around at the sound of footsteps on the hardwood floor.

"Richman?" asked Wales.

"I'm Ken Richman."

"I'm Ed Wales. I wrote you about starting a newspaper here in Baronsville."

"Yes, have a chair, Mr. Wales."

Wales sat down. "I've a lot of experience," he began.

"You're from the east," Richman said, "worked in New York, Boston."

"And Philadelphia. But I read your ad in Austin. Lot going on there. I didn't bite then, until I saw your ad in San Antonio and talked to some folks who told me a lot of stories about the Baron family and the Aguilars. But, Austin is boiling over with news that hasn't even reached San Antonio. Or here, I gather."

"Secession, you mean."

"Well, even though Houston fought it, Texas is now mixed in with the other states that voted to secede."

"Hell, Mr. Lincoln wasn't even on the ballot here, Mr. Wales."

"I know. There's going to be hell to pay. That's why I was attracted by your offer to start up a newspaper out here. From what I gathered, news is slow in coming and not very reliable this far west."

"Yes. But, I think you misunderstood my advertisement."

"Huh?"

"We already have a newspaper. You said you were interested in starting one here."

"Yes, I thought, that is, it was my understanding that you had no newspaper here."

"Oh, we have one, Mr. Wales. And, we've had three editors who said they had experience. None of them were worth a tinker's damn as a publisher. I need a publisher."

"Well, I have published a newspaper," Wales said.

"Yes, I know. Someone came out here and brought me a copy of *The Fort Worth Gazette*. That's why I paid for an ad in it. To get your eye."

"Well, it sure as hell did," Wales said.

"I wonder if you can make *The Baronsville Messenger* into a paper like that one."

"First thing I'd do is change the name. Make an alliteration of the banner."

"How's that?" Ken asked.

Wales smiled. He was a balding keg of a man with a frazzle of beard stubble on his face, crackling blue eyes, tobacco-stained teeth. The string of a sack of makings dangled from one pocket of his shirt.

"Change it to some name people can remember. *Mes-*

senger makes it sound like you're preaching to them. You've got to knock people down. I was thinking of changing the name of *The Gazette* in fact."

"To what?"

"Maybe *The Fort Worth Sentinel*. You know, troops on guard, that sort of thing."

"Because of the army," Ken said.

"Exactly. Mr. Lincoln, you know, offered Sam Houston fifty thousand Union troops to keep down any insurrection, help keep Texas in the Union. Didn't work. Those troops aren't down here. But, they will be and it won't be for Texas's benefit."

"What would you call our paper?"

"Our paper?"

"Yours and mine. I'd want a hand in it."

"Then, you'd be the publisher, Mr. Richman. And I'd be the editor."

"No. I want you to publish it. Hire your own editor if need be. I just want to be able to give you a story now and then."

"Or a bias on a story?"

"Bias?"

"The slant. The direction. The bullshit beneath the bullshit, so to speak."

Richman cocked a baleful eye at Wales.

"Look, Mr. Wales, I'll shoot straight with you. There is only one business here in this part of Texas. That's the cattle business. And there's only one man with the guts and brains to put his brand on every head of cattle between the Rio Grande and the Nueces. And that's Martin Baron. Baron and his Box B Ranch are the reason I'm here and if you stay, they'll be the reason you're here. Have you got that?"

"Clear as a bell. Will you call me Ed? And should I call you Mr. Richman?"

Ken laughed.

"You can call me Ken, Ed. And I hope that's all you'll call me."

"I'd like to see the shop. But, first, maybe you can explain that saying you've got on your wall there. Who's Juanito Salazar? I never heard of him."

"He worked for Martin Baron."

"A greaser?"

Ken's jaw hardened. "Juanito was an Argentinian. He knew cattle better than any gringo."

"I meant no offense."

"We don't call Mexicans *greasers* in Baron country, Ed. We respect them. If it weren't for Mexico, there wouldn't be any Texas. And we depend on Mexican vaqueros to take care of the cattle and other stock."

"Sorry Ken, I thought the term was in widespread use."

"Not on the Baron range, it isn't."

"So, was this Salazar some kind of philosopher?"

"He was, but he was more than that. He was a man who knew the meaning of loyalty. He knew cattle, but he also knew men. I wish you could have known him."

"So do I," Wales said. "Now, how about a look at the newspaper shop?"

"First, we'll go next door to the Longhorn and see what Paddy's got set out to eat. Do you drink spirits, Ed?"

"I drink what the boss drinks."

Ken stood up and extended his arm and hand across the table. "We'll get along, Ed."

"I'm sure we will."

"One thing."

"What's that, Ken?"

"Since you mentioned putting a new name on the newspaper, it struck me that you're right. We need another name. *Messenger* just doesn't cut the mustard."

"No."

"Anything in mind?" Ken asked.

"I'll give it some thought."

"I had a thought. Do you think Texas might have to fight the Union?"

"Yes, Ken, I think we will."

"Then, we ought to have a militant banner for the newspaper. A name that has some warning to it."

"I agree."

"How does *The Baronsville Bugle* sound?"

"Hell, Ken, it sounds just fine. Perfect, I think."

"Good. You put it in type and we'll send a man to Austin and have him get us the news before San Antonio does."

"I've already got a man there, Ken. And, better than that. I've got one in Washington. If you've got a post rider, we'll get the news in here."

"Damn, Ed. We think along the same lines, I reckon. By God, we'll put Baronsville on the goddamned map "

"It already is," Ed said.

"God, I wish Juanito was here. You two would get along."

The two men shook hands.

Ed Wales wondered if he and Ken Richman would really get along. He sensed that he was being measured against the character of a dead man, Juanito Salazar. He vowed to learn more about the Argentinian if he stayed in Baronsville. Evidently, Salazar had cast a long shadow.

12

◼

PEEBO SEEMED SURE of himself. He took the lead as if born to it, walking at a steady gait, following the horse tracks on the churned-up ground. Anson followed, not because he was unable to read the wide swatch of hoofprints left by the Apaches and the herd they had stolen, but because it was Peebo's business, mostly; all but one horse belonged to him, and besides, it was his idea to walk down the Apaches and get their stock back.

"They'll slow 'em down soon," Peebo said.

Anson looked at the ground. It was plain that the horses had still been running at the place where they were now, less than a mile from the jacal the Indians had burned down. "Yeah, or they'll wear 'em out quick."

"Bastards," Peebo said.

"You reckon they know we're following them?" Anson asked.

"I reckon."

Within another half mile, the tracks changed. The ground was not so roughed up, the space between forehooves and hind ones had lessened. Anson studied the tracks carefully. The Apaches had flanked the stolen horses and had them walking in a straight line. A half hour later, the tracks began to curve toward the south, toward Mexico.

Anson's feet began to chafe and he knew he was growing a blister on his right foot. The ground was rough, uneven, strewn with small pebbles. Small islands of grass became treacherous lumps underfoot. Peebo didn't seem to be bothered by his boots or the terrain, so Anson did not complain.

An hour later, Peebo stopped. Anson drew up behind him. As he watched, Peebo studied the ground, walking around in little circles. He picked up a small stone, then another. He rubbed both on his pants leg, handed one to Anson. He popped the other in his mouth, rolled it around like a chunk of hard candy.

"Keep you from gettin' too thirsty," Peebo said.

Anson looked at the pebble. It had dirt on it, was oval shaped, with a small indentation in it. "Are you touched, Peebo?"

"Try it, son."

Without waiting, Peebo set off again, following the horse tracks. Anson rubbed the small stone some more and then gingerly put it into his mouth. He tasted the dirt, the iron in it. As the stone became salivated, he rolled it inside his mouth as he had seen Peebo do, then tucked it into one cheek. The rock did seem to take away some of his thirst. As he walked, he shifted the stone from cheek to cheek until it lost its earthy savor.

After the best part of another hour, Peebo stopped again, resting in the shade of a mesquite tree. His face glistened with sweat, but he made no move to wipe it off. Anson pulled out his bandanna, started to touch it to his forehead.

"Be a lot cooler if you leave the sweat on," Peebo said.

"What?" Anson stopped the motion of his hand in midair.

"You leave the sweat on, it'll help cool you down."

"You are crazy," Anson said.

"Look, son, when I started ranchin', I took off my shirt when the sun got hot. I wiped sweat offen my forehead and my hatband. Then, an old hand told me what sweat was for."

"What's it for?"

"Why, for coolin' down the body, same as shiverin' in the cold makes you warm. You leave that sweat on you and you won't burn up in the heat."

"I never heard such," Anson said.

Peebo laughed. "What in hell did you think sweat was for? Makin' you stink to high heaven?"

"I never thought about it much."

"Well, son, it's nature's way of givin' you a cool bath in the heat of the day. Sweat is good. Damned good."

Anson cocked his head, stared at Peebo with a quizzical look on his face. "Are you funnin' me?" he asked.

"No, I ain't. I'm just as hot as you are. And, I've got me a bandanna in my pocket. My feet hurt like twenty kinds of hell and my back's burnin' like it was scalded. But, I ain't wipin' my sweat off and I ain't takin' my shirt off so's I can blister like a roasted crawdad."

Anson stuffed the bandanna back in his pocket, flashed Peebo a sheepish grin.

Peebo made the pebble in his mouth click against his teeth as he grinned at Anson. "You learn quick, son."

"Why do you keep callin' me son?" Anson asked. "You and me are 'bout the same age."

"It's just a way of talkin'. It don't have nothin' to do with how old you are."

"It makes me feel like I'm a kid. Or like you're treatin' me like a kid."

"Well, I don't know you well enough to call you by your Christian name. And, besides, Anson ain't an easy name to remember."

"Neither is Peebo."

Peebo laughed. "Well, call me son, then, if you want to."

"I'll call you by your name," Anson said. "And I wish you'd learn mine."

"Aw," Peebo said, "you take all the fun out of conversation. I call you son 'cause I like you, see? If I didn't, I'd call you Baron or boy."

"You'd better not call me boy," Anson said, and he was serious.

"No, son, I won't," Peebo said, and his grin made Anson's anger melt like candle wax under a flame.

"Let's be gettin'," Peebo said, and he lurched away from the trunk of the mesquite. "Feet hurt?"

"Like fire," Anson said.

"We come to a crick, we'll stick us some mud in our boots and maybe we won't be walkin' on blisters."

"I already am."

"They'll turn to callous soon enough."

"Not soon enough," Anson said, and Peebo touched a finger to the brim of his hat in mock salute.

Peebo picked up the pace as the day wore on, but Anson could not tell if the horse tracks were any fresher than when they had first started out. He felt as if they were walking in a giant maze. Everything looked the same, the mesquite, the brush, the land, the sky, and the sun bore down hotter on them with each wearying step. Peebo seemed bent on winning a race and did not look back to see how Anson was doing. If anything, Anson would have sworn that Peebo's stride kept lengthening. The man showed no signs of letting up.

Anson's side began to ache and the stone in his mouth had dried out, leaving him with a powerful thirst. He wondered if the Apaches were headed for water. Surely they must be thirsty, too, and they would have to water the horses or the animals would start foundering, one by one.

Peebo finally looked back at Anson, just after they

broke into the open plain after wandering through a labyrinth of mesquite and cactus that left Anson with the feeling that they would never find their way out.

"We're gainin' on 'em," Peebo said when Anson caught up to him. "Look at them fresh horse droppings."

"They're still steaming," Anson said.

"I'd say them Apaches ain't more'n a half hour ahead of us."

"The horses must need water," Anson said.

"They been drinkin'," Peebo said.

"How?" Anson's heart felt as if it had fallen a foot through his chest.

"They got water bags or gourds or somethin'," Peebo said. "Didn't you notice where they been stoppin'?"

"No," Anson said, feeling foolish.

"Well, they been stoppin' long enough to give the horses some of the water they was carryin'."

"I never noticed."

"Hard to see, if you ain't lookin' for it. But them horses have been takin' on water."

"Shit," Anson said.

"If you're hopin' for a drink, son, you're gonna have to kill an Injun for it."

"What do you mean?"

"I mean these bastards are stayin' away from water holes and cricks. They know we're chasin' after them."

"How do you know?"

"Every so often I seen a set of tracks where one of the bunch pulls away and waits awhile, a-lookin' down their back trail."

Anson felt the bottom go out of his stomach. "Damn," he said.

"A 'course they don't know if we got water or not."

"I'll bet they do," Anson said.

"You might be right. Well, we'd better pick up the pace if we're gonna catch 'em this day."

"I don't think we have a chance," Anson said.

"Why, son, we're right close."

"That's what worries me, Peebo. Even if we do catch up to them, they're more than we can handle. Those Apaches could be waiting in ambush for us. We'd never see them until it was too late."

Peebo frowned. "I been keepin' a careful eye out for any such."

"You can walk right up on 'em and not see 'em."

"I know," Peebo said. "I mean I heard such tales."

"It's true."

"Well, we got to get them horses back. They're all I got in the world."

"I'd like to get my horse back, too. He's a pretty nice gelding."

"You break him?"

"No," Anson said. "A—a friend of mine, Juanito, he broke him. The horse means a lot to me."

"What's his name?"

"The horse? Oh, I call him Sal, short for Salvador. That was Juanito's middle name."

"So, you got a personal feeling for this horse. Sal."

"Yeah," Anson said.

"Well, I damned sure love ever' one of mine, so let's keep after them thievin' Apaches."

"Just be careful, Peebo. Go slow."

Peebo looked at Anson with a quizzical expression on his face, but said nothing. Instead, he hitched his pants and continued following the horse tracks. Anson sighed and fell into step behind Peebo.

Anson lost all track of time. His throat and mouth were dry, his shirt clung to his back, glued down by sweat. The stitch in his side had gone away and was now replaced by pains in his calves. His feet felt wooden, becoming more numb with each step.

"Peebo," Anson called. "Whoa up."

Peebo turned around. "Huh?"

Anson halted in his tracks. "We have to talk."

"We're wasting time, son. You can talk while you walk."

"No, I think we've gone far enough. This is crazy. We're not going to catch up with Culebra and his bunch. He's probably laughing at us right now."

Peebo turned and walked back to where Anson stood. He waited a moment before he spoke. "Look," he said, "I know it's hot and we're thirsty, but the way to walk down these Injuns is to keep on after them."

"They know we're following them, Peebo. They're not going to let us catch them."

"Well, that's true. But, we're goin' to catch 'em anyways."

"Damm it, Peebo, I'm sayin' we need to get to the ranch, get some help. We're walking into trouble."

"If you're scared—"

"I'm not scared," Anson said.

"Go on, then. Go back to the damned ranch. I aim to get my stock back."

"Peebo, if you want to work for the Box B, you'll damned sure learn to take orders."

"From who?"

"From me, for one."

"You ain't the boss," Peebo said.

"Until another one comes along, I am."

"Sheeeit."

Anson stalked up to Peebo and stood square facing him. His eyes turned hard as black agates. Peebo stood his ground, but a few flickers of worry ticked at the corners of his eyes.

"What you aimin' to do?" Peebo asked.

"Talk sense into you, if I can. If not, then you can go your own way. You won't ride for the Box B."

"You didn't offer me the job here, Anson. Your pa did."

"A lot's happened since then, Peebo. Make up your mind."

"By damn, Anson, you caught me plumb by surprise. I didn't know you was the ramrod of the Box B."

"It don't make no difference. You can't take orders

here, no ranch worth its salt will take you on."

Peebo took off his hat, slapped it against his leg, spangling dust particles into miniature clouds.

Anson watched and waited to see what Peebo would do. His gaze did not flicker or waver as he skewered Peebo with a hard look that showed his resolve to hold the new hand in check.

"Well, doggone it, Anson, I just hate to lose them horses."

"I know. Sometimes we have to take what we're given and let it go at that."

"I hate to have a bunch of ignorant red savages get the best of me."

"Well, they only got some horses from you. They took Jorge's life."

"Yeah, I know. Cut you a deal, Anson."

"What's that?"

"We go on another couple of miles so I can get a fix on where they're heading for sure, then I'll walk back to the Box B with you."

"They're headin' for Mexico."

"I know. I just want to make sure."

"All right, Peebo," Anson said, a sigh in his voice, "we'll go a little farther. But, when I say quit, I mean quit."

"Yes sir," Peebo said, slamming his hat back on his head and flashing that wide grin of his. "You bet."

Anson was not deceived. Peebo was not broke to the halter yet. He would buck again. "I've got a funny feeling about this whole thing," he said.

Peebo did not say anything as he started walking down the horse tracks again. Ten minutes later, he came to a stop, looked back at Anson.

"Find something?" Anson asked.

"Anson, you might have been right, them feelin's of yours. Take a look at the tracks."

Anson bent down, then straightened up. He walked around in a circle, shaking his head the entire time.

When he came back to Peebo, his eyes narrowed to slits.

"Well?" Peebo asked. "What do you make of them tracks?"

"They had this figured right down to the nub, Peebo. Now, they've got riders for every horse they stole."

"Looks that way to me, too. The boys on foot just waited here and now they're a-horseback."

"We'll never catch them now," Anson said.

"Not this day, we won't."

Anson let out a long breath, looked around. He tilted his head back and looked up at the sun, shading his eyes. "Well, Peebo, one thing's in our favor."

"What's that?"

"We can follow a while longer. This is the way to the Box B."

"Be a long walk."

"At least I know where we can find water."

"I'll bet them Apaches do, too."

Anson frowned. Culebra knew the country better than any living man. The Rio Grande Valley was his home, where he had grown up, where his father and ancestors were buried. Yes, the Apache would know where the creeks and water holes were, and they might be waiting for him and Peebo to come to the nearest one. It was something to consider as they walked their way toward the ranch.

Less than ten minutes later, Peebo and Anson both heard the horse scream. The sound began as a high-pitched whinny, then dissolved into a terror-stricken series of shrieks that tore at their senses.

"Horse in trouble," Peebo said.

"Sounded like my horse."

Both men cocked their rifles and hunched over, twisting their heads to see what might be at either side of the trail. They walked, bent over like hunchbacks, toward the place where they had first heard the horse.

The screaming stopped and the silence seemed leaden, heavier than the thick air the two men breathed. Anson felt the skin on the back of his neck prickle. In the eerie quiet, he gestured for Peebo to follow him.

Anson held his breath as he stepped toward the source of the scream. He ducked under a mesquite branch, waited, listening for any sound.

Ahead, a horse lay in a clearing, its hide twitching as if trying to shake off flies. Anson looked all around to see if any Apache might be nearby. Peebo came up behind him, breathing fast.

"See anything?" Peebo whispered.

"That's my horse yonder. He looks hurt."

"Looks like blood on his hind legs."

Anson sucked in a breath, winced at the sight. "Wait here," he said.

Peebo started to say something, but kept his silence. He moved into Anson's spot and kept watch.

Anson reached the horse, knelt down beside it. The horse moved its head, looked at him with liquid brown eyes.

"Oh, no," Anson breathed. Then, he turned, beckoned to Peebo, urging him to come quickly.

Peebo ran to Anson's side, knelt down.

"Jesus," Peebo breathed. "Look what they done to your horse."

Anson fought back tears. The Apaches had slashed all four legs, cutting the tendons so that the horse would never walk again. Blood still oozed from the wounds, stained the ground. Flies clung to the open wounds like thick mats of hair.

"You got to put him out of his misery," Peebo said softly.

"I—I can't," Anson said, and the tears broke from their ducts. He crumpled up as the sobs shook him. "Oh, God, how could they do this?"

"Son, you walk on ahead. I'll take care of it."

Anson lifted his head, looked at Peebo. "No," he said, "I'll do it. He's my horse. I hate to see him suffer."

"Do it quick, then," Peebo said, rising to his feet.

Anson looked into the horse's eyes, saw the pain flitting. The horse whimpered and that's when Anson saw that its throat was slit, the wound so small he could hardly see it.

He stood up, cocked his rifle. He put the muzzle behind the gelding's ear and squeezed the trigger. The explosion deafened him as the horse shuddered, then lay still under a blanket of white smoke.

Anson doubled over and began vomiting. He turned away from the dead horse and coughed up phlegm and liquid and remnants of food, staining the earth with the contents of his stomach. He staggered away, sicker than he had ever been, a rage boiling in him, choking off his ragged tears, blinding him to all danger, all that was around him.

Anson gulped in air, stopped throwing up, and walked toward the waiting Peebo. With mechanical motions, he began to reload his rifle, pouring powder down the barrel, fishing for a patch and ball in his possibles pouch, the stench of acrid smoke and blood and death clogging his nostrils.

"Home?" Peebo asked, as Anson drew near.

"No, by God, we're going to walk that sonofabitch down."

"Who?"

"Culebra," Anson swore, the very name a curse on his lips.

13

CAROLINE STALKED THROUGH the house in her white gown like a haunting wraith in the darkness. She stopped at unshuttered windows and peered out toward the stables and the barn, then crept away to wring her hands and dab her brow with a fluttering handkerchief.

She passed the kitchen where Esperanza was still working, but said nothing, gliding by in ghostly silence to haunt the front room and peer through a window at the gray pewter yard so empty and lifeless at that hour, dimly lit by a fingernail sliver of moon, desolate and silent, not a creature stirring. Lazaro, she knew, was asleep in his room at the far end of the cavernous house, his blind eyes closed to the night he could not see. She was glad that Esperanza had brought Lazaro to her after the blind boy's parents had been killed. He was someone to love, someone to love her. And she desperately needed that.

She turned from the window and drifted into the den lit by an oil lamp turned low, its furniture shrouded in darkness, the desk, the chair, the table, the small settee where Martin often sat while she went over the books with him. She sat in the settee now and waited, listening to the soft sibilant creak of the house as the outside temperature fell. There was a window there, too, and she could see the treetops in the orchard, the scarves of clouds streaming across the velvet black sky, the pinholes of light where the stars blinked like faraway beacons, like ships she imagined on the sea, harboring sleeping sailors as Martin had once been, dreaming their secrets of the deep in rocking slumber.

The silence of the room billowed around her, punctuated only by the soft clatter of dishes as Esperanza dried and put away the supper dishes, the soft whine of cupboard doors opening and closing on leather hinges and the purr of the breeze against the windowpanes.

Caroline's body jerked as she heard the back door slam shut. The sound startled her, even though she had been almost expecting it. She heard Esperanza's muffled voice, then the boom of Martin's timbral greeting to the *criada*.

"She is in the little office room, I think," Esperanza said, in Spanish, and Caroline held her breath, tried to will her suddenly fluttering heart to stillness.

Boots boomed on the hardwood flooring, coming ever closer and Caroline braced herself for her husband's entrance.

"Caroline?"

"In here," she said, her voice almost a squeak.

The footfalls sounded outside the door and then Martin was inside, squinting to see through the dimness. He came over to her and stood staring down at her face. Her lips quivered slightly, and she folded her hands to halt their trembling.

"What in hell did you call me out of the field for?" he asked, his voice booming in the hollow quiet of the study.

"Martin, don't be loud," she said.

"I damned sure want to know why I had to drop everything and ride a dozen hard miles to see you sitting here in the dark like a mouse."

"Please, Martin," she said, fighting back her tears.

"Well?" His voice softened.

"I—I'm frightened," she said.

"Of what?"

She tried to avert her eyes from his. She felt his stare boring into her and now that he was here, she could not form the words she had said over and over in her mind all day long.

"Martin, it—it's that cannon. I can't stand to see it out there anymore."

"The cannon?" He sounded genuinely puzzled.

"The cannon. So much blood on it. So many dead. Such cruelty. You must take it away. Take it away tonight."

"Tonight? Caroline, have you lost your senses?" His voice was loud again, querulous.

"Y-yes," she whimpered. "I—I think I have lost my senses."

She looked up at him again, her eyes wet with tears, her lips quivering. He reached down and took her hands, pulled her up.

"Caroline," he said softly, "what in hell's happened to you? That cannon can't hurt you. Can't hurt anyone. It's not loaded. It's just sitting there."

"No," she said, an urgency in her voice, "I can hear it. I can hear it roar and I can see the torn bodies, the pieces of flesh, and the screams, always the screams."

She shivered and shook against him. Martin held her tightly to him, smoothing her hair with one hand. She began to feel calm, but the visions of terror were still there.

"I'll sell the cannon," he said.

Caroline looked up at him. "Will you? Promise?"

"I promise. Tomorrow. Get it out of your mind."

"I—I can't. . . ."

"You must," he said, and she crumpled against him, weeping softly, her trembling rippling in every fiber of her body. Her sobs grew louder and she felt Martin's body stiffen as if he wanted to flee from her arms.

"Now, now," he said. "It's not that bad. Just don't worry about it no more, darling. I'll get some hands to haul it out of the barn in the morning."

"No," Caroline said. "You must do it now. They come back, you know."

"They come back? Who?"

"The savages. At night. They come back and I can hear the cannon boom, like thunder, and the screams. They're all out there, all over again. In the morning. They're there, lying in blood, their eyes . . . their eyes."

"Caroline. Stop it."

She whimpered and the tears burst forth from her eyes again and wet her face until it was shiny in the lamplight, shiny and wet as blood and she was sure that it was blood on her face and when she touched a hand to her cheek, it came away bloody, like always, and she could see the faces of the dead Apaches, painted hideously, the eyes vacant, staring into the sky.

Martin shook his wife, held her away from him, stared into her weeping eyes and he could see the look of horror and disbelief on her face.

"Please, Martin," she whispered, "please do it now. Take the cannon away. I—I can't stand it anymore."

"Caroline, what in hell's wrong with you?"

They both heard the swish-glide of sandals on the floor, a susurrant intrusion on their private world. Caroline turned, looked toward the doorway. Martin released his grip on her arms and she almost collapsed, but steadied herself, swayed there as he turned toward the door.

Esperanza stood there, a dim figure, faceless, like a statue, a carving of wood that loomed there in silence, like some large *bulto*, the carving of a saint.

"Esperanza? What do you know about this?" Martin asked, in Spanish.

"She is like that every night when you are gone," Esperanza said. "She sees the ghosts."

"There are no ghosts."

"For the señora, there are ghosts."

"Jesus," Martin said.

Esperanza crossed herself and turned away, shuffling off into the darkness, leaving the two Barons alone.

"Jesus," Martin said again.

"He can't help," Caroline said, and her voice was soft and lost, like that of a child.

The lamp flickered as if a wind had slipped into the room and it sputtered as if trying to speak, its hot oil hissing an unintelligible message in the darkness.

14

L UZ AGUILAR FELT the piercing glare of the man's
eyes burning into her flesh as if he were probing for
her heart, or for another place that was not so secret, but
every bit as private. Her fingers dug into the mass of
dough as if that were his flesh, the fat of his neck, and
her rage transformed her fingers into iron daggers
plumbing for the windpipe, squeezing off his air supply,
choking the life out of him as she would wring the neck
of a chicken.

But she did not turn around to look at Reynaud. Instead, her eyes flickered with the burning hatred inside
her, smoldered with the loathing she felt, the loathing
that was like a clammy sweat between her legs, like the
musky dew on her pubic hairs. For she knew that Reynaud was trying to peer through the thin cotton of the
dress that clung to her naked body, trying to penetrate
the cloth and feed his filthy mind with her image. She
had seen the looks of such men before, before Matteo
had gazed upon her with a look that was different from

those lusting men of the Mexican earth south of the border.

Her companion, working the *harina de maíz* in another clay bowl, Conchita Morales, was hidden from the man's view, sitting as she was directly opposite Luz at the kitchen table of butcher block, lifted her head and saw the look in Luz's eyes.

"What passes?" Conchita whispered in Spanish.

"That man, that *feo cabrón,* behind me. I do not like him. I do not like what is in his mind."

"And what is in his mind that you can see it?" Conchita asked lightly, for she could see part of the man's body, the top of his head, from where she sat.

"Do not make a joke of it, Conchita. You know what he is thinking. He is always looking at me."

"You are beautiful to look at, señora. Any man might look at you that way."

"He is different, this one, this filthy one. He knows my husband is out in the back working, and he stays around here like a fly hoping to drink the honey."

"He does not look at me that way."

"You are a child with no breasts, Conchita. He does not want a flat-chested girl."

Conchita flushed with embarrassment. She had only little more than a dozen years, but already she was growing pips on her chest and she was self-conscious about them. "I did not mean to compare myself with you, señora. I just meant that he probably means no harm."

Luz squeezed the dough between her fingers until it oozed like flesh from between them. Her dark eyes blazed with a liquid fire that Conchita could almost feel. She sat a little lower on the stool so that the man could not see her even if he came close.

"Luz," Reynaud said, "are you whispering about me?"

Luz did not turn around.

"What do you want?" Luz asked, a pleasantness in her voice that was forced.

"I wanted to talk to Matteo," he said, and both women

could hear his footfalls on the board flooring, the tap of his high polished heels on the rubbed wood like little mallets.

"He is not here," she said. "He left before you awoke. He is working. If you look out the back window, you will see him and Mickey Bone with the horses."

Reynaud came close, peered over Luz's shoulder. Conchita scrunched down, but she knew he had seen her. "Umm, smells good in here," he said. "What are you making?"

He was so close behind her, Luz could almost feel the heat of his body and she imagined that he was aroused and might rub against her with his manhood so that she would take notice of him. She turned as if to ward him off, as if to warn him with her look that he was to come no closer.

"We make the flour for the tortillas," Luz said, and there was no welcome or kindness in her voice.

"My mouth waters at the thought of eating your tortillas," he said.

Conchita suppressed a giggle.

Reynaud moved away, walked to the side of the large table so that he could see both women. He looked at Conchita. She lowered her head and cowled her eyes against the shame she might feel. Luz attacked Reynaud with her stare, her gaze boring into his eyes as if they were the loaded barrels of guns.

He smiled at Luz, a disarming smile meant to melt her heart. But, she did not smile in return. Her fingers contracted once again, delving into the lump of ochre dough and she lifted the brain-sized chunk from the bowl. Tendons rippled in her arms as she applied pressure and then she dropped the dough back into the bowl. It landed with a plopping sound.

"Hard work," he said.

"And you are keeping us from it," Luz said. "A man should not be in the kitchen. You should be out working with Matteo."

"I am a guest," Reynaud said.

"Only when my husband is here," she said.

"Oh? I thought his hospitality extended to me no matter where he was."

"You are wrong, señor. You are Matteo's guest, not mine."

Reynaud strode to the window over the counter and looked outside. "I do not think that Bone likes me," he said.

"No, he does not," Luz said, more quickly than she would have liked.

"He likes Martin Baron, I think."

"It is not Martin that is the friend of Bone, but his son, Anson."

"I do not know this Anson. A boy, you say?"

"He is a man. You asked Bone to help you kill Martin Baron. He would not do that, even for Matteo. Matteo respects such loyalty."

"Loyalty," Reynaud spat. "To a coward, a dog like Martin Baron? That is ridiculous."

Reynaud turned from the window, looked at Luz. Conchita hunched over the table, kneading the corn flour in the bowl.

"I have heard what you told my husband about Martin Baron," Luz said, glaring at Reynaud. "He did not molest your sister. He is not that kind."

"So, you like the Barons yourself, eh? That is quite amusing, considering that Matteo hates them all with a passion."

Luz pushed the ball of dough down into the bowl and stood up. She shoved the bowl away, toward Conchita. "Matteo does not hate the Barons," she said. "He is angry that they have so much land that once belonged to the Aguilar family. He wants the land back."

"But, he would kill for the land," Reynaud said.

"Not if he has someone do it for him," Luz said, an accusing tone in her voice.

"Matteo is a smart man. I think he would kill Martin Baron himself if I did not do it."

Luz tossed her head. Her black mane of hair swirled in the air, settled on her shoulders and back. "He is not afraid of the Barons," she said. "He prefers to drive them off the land. There has already been too much blood spilled."

"What do you mean?"

"That is none of your business, señor. Now I think you had better go and see Matteo. But I will warn you that Mickey Bone is as loyal to my husband as he is to Anson Baron. If you harm any of the Baron family, I think he would kill you."

"And Matteo would not mind?"

"Matteo would not care," Luz said, and she sat back down at the table, dismissing Reynaud as if he were one of the Rocking A field hands.

Reynaud snorted and stalked to the back door. Luz heard it slam behind him. She looked up at Conchita and smiled. "I would not think anything of killing that Frenchman myself," she said.

"Why do you hate him so?" Conchita asked.

"He will cause my husband much trouble if he tries to kill Martin Baron. There has been enough killing. There is blood on this house."

Conchita winced. "But your husband wants the Frenchman to kill Martin Baron, does he not?"

"I do not know. Sometimes, I think my husband wants to kill everyone. He has the anger inside him. I think if Reynaud does not kill Martin that Matteo will take his men and kill all of the Barons."

"But you told Reynaud—"

"I know, I lied. I do not like Reynaud. I hope Martin kills him."

"But then your husband might fight Martin Baron and—"

"And Matteo might be killed?"

"Yes, pardon, he might be killed."

Luz smiled the smile of someone with a dark secret.

"Yes, that might happen," Luz said softly. "And then there might be peace here in the valley."

"But you do not want Matteo to be killed," Conchita said, her voice rising in pitch.

Luz picked up the wad of dough and scrunched it in her hands as if she meant to tear it apart. She sighed and looked beyond Conchita into empty space.

"No," Luz breathed. "I want my child to have a father. But Matteo was born under an unlucky star. He was born to be killed."

Conchita shivered at the thought. She looked at Luz with eyes full of puzzlement.

"And Bone is the same way. They both are men of destiny. But it is a bad destiny. I think maybe that Reynaud might be the man sent to see that both my husband and Bone are finally killed."

"Do not say such things, my mistress," Conchita said. "It makes me afraid."

"Yes, yes, I know. I, too, am afraid. I have the fear in my heart and it hurts so much I want to scream."

Conchita fell silent. She averted her gaze from Luz because there was a look on her face that she did not understand.

Luz felt the darkness inside her blossom and grow into a cloud like the black thunderhead preceding a storm. Her fingers began to slowly work through the dough and a tear spilled from one eye and trickled down her cheek. She touched her slightly bulging stomach and patted the child inside.

Then, to herself, she began to pray silently to God.

15

MATTEO AGUILAR SWORE softly as the rope burned his fingers, peeled the brown skin back until the rosy flesh was exposed. Blood seeped from the raw wound and the hemp fibers stung like salt as they stuck to the gooey mass. Matteo shifted his hand and dug his boot heels into the ground as the rope tautened once again.

The horse at the other end of the rope kept backing up, its eyes flaring wildly in their sockets, its ears flattened like a cur's, its rubbery nostrils twitching in anger.

"*Pendejo,*" Matteo swore again. "Whoa up, you bastard." The last phrase uttered in English.

Mickey Bone pulled on the other rope, making it tight, jerking the horse in the opposite direction. "You get burned?" he asked.

"That son of a whore," Matteo said.

Bone laughed.

"It is not funny," Aguilar said.

"It is funny if the horse can understand you."

"He understands me. I am going to kill him."

"That is what is wrong with you, Matteo. You want to kill everything. What is it that burns inside you? You have a ranch, a nice wife who is with child. You have good horses and cattle and plenty to eat."

"That is none of your business, Mickey," Aguilar snapped.

"I am just curious, my friend."

The horse stood its ground, not moving, caught between two tight ropes. But, from the look in its eyes, it was ready to bolt if either man allowed any slack.

"That is true," Bone said. "I will keep my distance."

"I did not mean that, my friend."

"Yes, you did."

"I do not know what to think of you, Mickey. You seem loyal to me, yet you will not help Reynaud."

"I do not like Reynaud."

"Why not?"

"He is a coward."

Aguilar bent the rope around his waist as the horse tried to step away. He dug his heels in harder, leaned backwards to keep the tension on the rope.

"Why do you say this?" Aguilar asked. "You do not know the man."

"He says he comes to kill Martin Baron, but he asks for your help. I think he is afraid of Martin."

"Are you afraid of Baron?"

"I am not afraid of him," Bone said. "I just do not want to kill him."

"Reynaud would kill him."

"I would not help Reynaud to kill a rat or a snake."

Matteo laughed harshly, swallowing in a dry mouth. "You have said you would help me in a fight with Martin Baron."

"If it came to that, I would fight at your side, Matteo."

"If you help Reynaud, we will not have to fight Baron."

"We would have to fight Anson."

"And you would not fight the son?"

"I would have to think a long time about doing that."

Matteo savagely released his grip on the rope and the line went slack. He began to whip the loose end as he charged toward the startled horse, driving it in Bone's direction. Bone pulled on the rope instinctively and fell backwards as the slack went out of it. He lay on the ground as the wild horse bolted toward him.

Bone rolled out of the way, but the horse reared up and flailed its forelegs in the air as if boxing, its eyes flared wide, its ears laid back flat against its head. Bone drew his pistol, cocked it as it cleared the holster and fired it at the horse. The lead ball whistled past the horse's ear and the stubborn animal came down on its forelegs with a jolt, then turned away and began to gallop toward the open field, the ropes trailing in the dirt, snapping and undulating like angry serpents.

"Are you trying to kill my horse?" Aguilar snapped.

"If I had wanted to kill it, I would have shot its eye out."

"Now, we have to catch it and start all over," Aguilar said, as if musing to himself.

"You show anger to the horse, Matteo, but the anger is for me," Bone said.

Aguilar walked over as Bone stood up. He glared at Bone in a silent rage. Bone thumbed the broken percussion cap off the nipple of his cap and ball Colt and spun the cylinder until the hammer rested on a loaded chamber.

"I do not understand what it is between you and Anson Baron, that is all," Aguilar said.

"There is nothing between me and him."

"There is something," Aguilar insisted.

"I was once his friend."

"But you are no longer?"

"No, I am no longer Anson's friend."

"But you do not treat him as my enemy."

"He is your enemy, Matteo, not mine."

"If a man is loyal, his enemies are his friend's enemies."

"Anson has never done anything to me. He has never done anything to you."

Aguilar stomped the heel of his boot hard against the ground as Bone holstered his pistol after checking the unfired caps. Matteo ground his heel into the dirt as if crushing an insect and his face clouded up with anger.

Bone said nothing. His black eyes held Aguilar's gaze as if they were granite, empty of feeling, impervious to any assault of wind or rain or sun.

"His family has stolen some of my land," Aguilar said, his words measured and venomous.

"Martin paid your family for every hectare he owns."

"Damn you, Mickey, do not argue with me."

"I do not argue with you, Matteo. But I was there. Martin bought the land. You do not need it. You cannot work the land you have."

"What do you know about owning land? You have no land. You will never have any land."

Bone did not move; his gaze did not waver. "That is true, Matteo. My people do not believe in owning land. They say the land and everything on it belongs to the Great Father in the sky."

"That is a heathen belief."

"It is my belief."

Aguilar opened his mouth as if to say something else, but just then they both heard the back door of the house slam shut. Matteo turned and saw Reynaud coming down the steps of the porch, heading toward them as if he were out for a Sunday stroll.

"We will speak of this later, Mickey," Aguilar said.

"If that is what you want to do, Matteo. I am already tired of speaking this way."

"What way?"

"About things we cannot change, about land that my people once rode upon and left their blood on and now your people have left their blood here and when we are gone someone else will claim it and our blood will be on it."

"Shut your mouth, Mickey."

"I will catch the horse while you talk with the Frenchman," Bone said. "Tomorrow I will go to Mexico and bring my woman back to this ranch."

"Tomorrow?"

"Yes, Matteo. I have been too long without my woman. This makes my temper grow short."

Bone walked away and Aguilar cursed under his breath in two languages. He kicked the ground again and the veins in his neck stood out like purple cords. He turned away and watched Reynaud as he came closer, a smile on his face.

He did not want to admit it to himself, but he was beginning to dislike Reynaud himself. The man had been there for two days and had made no move to go after Martin Baron. And, his appetite for food could break a man.

And, another thing, Aguilar thought, if Bone were right and Reynaud was a coward, then he had no use for such a man. For all his faults, Bone was not a coward.

And, neither was Martin Baron.

16

THE TREBLE KEYS of the piano rippled with tinkling arpeggios while the bass keys clunked in a driving rhythm that nearly drowned out the clank of glasses and the drone of conversation at the bar and tables set for dining. The player, a rotund man whose bottom lapped over the rounded edge of the stool, tapped his feet in rhythm with his flying fingers, one foot stepping on the damper pedals, the other rapping leather on the hardwood floor. A sodden cigarette dangled from his corpulent lips, a tendril of bluish smoke snaking into a thin cloud above his balding, sweat-glistened head. A drink jiggled on a wooden ledge at one side of the keyboard, the amber liquid electrified into a miniature sea by the percussive shaking of the entire piano.

Men stood at the long bar, or sat on tall stools, drinking and smoking, talking loud enough for their voices to be heard above the sound of the rollicking music. A lone bartender, sleeves bound by royal purple garters just above the elbows, poured whiskey into tumblers and slid

them on the polished bar top toward those who had ordered them.

Two or three tables were already occupied with diners,
as new arrivals streamed through the batwing doors of
the Longhorn Saloon, wearing clothes freshly laundered
and pressed for evening. A waiter emerged from the
kitchen, bearing a large tray heaped with plates of steaming beef, potatoes, biscuits, turnips and beans.

Ken Richman and Ed Wales sat at a far table, en-
grossed in conversation, drinking whiskeys and flicking
ashes from their cigarettes onto the floor instead of in
the ashtray. They both looked toward the doors as David
Wilhoit and Ursula Killian entered, looking like bewildered children. At the bar, Roy Killian turned around to
stare at his mother who was blinking her eyes to accus-
tom them to the light in the saloon.

Roy frowned and the man sitting next to him punched
him in the ribs. Roy turned to him and, a look of anger
flooding his face, jabbed out his cigarette in a *cenicero*
made of clay that sat atop the bar.

"Hey," said the man next to Roy, "ain't that your
ma?"

"So what?" Roy said, his eyes ablaze with a lambent
light.

"Aw, nothin', it's just I ain't never seen her out at
night before."

"Well, you ain't seen a whole hell of a lot," Roy said,
turning his back to his mother and Wilhoit.

"Christ, Roy, what you so hot about? I was just
sayin'—"

"I ain't hot about nothin', Will. Just shut your damned
trap."

Will Harrison grabbed his drink, downed it as if to
still his already thickened tongue. Roy sat there, fuming,
and began to roll another cigarette.

"There's a fine-looking woman," Ed Wales said, nodding in Ursula's direction.

Ken nodded. "Widow woman. Seems like she's got herself a beau already."

"That man? He doesn't look as if he could hold a candle to her spark."

"Maybe not," Ken said, a musing tone to his voice.

"Who is he?"

"Surveyor. Works for Aguilar."

"Oh yeah." All day long Ken had filled Ed Wales in on the inhabitants of the vast Rio Grande Valley, and the name Aguilar had come up.

"What's he surveying?" Ed asked.

"Land that's not any of his damned business."

"Oh?" The newsman sensed something worth delving into behind Richman's words.

"Matteo Aguilar is a bitter man. Killed almost his whole family to get back the Rocking A and now he wants to run Martin Baron off of land he bought legally from the family."

"Aguilar must have owned the original Spanish land grants," Wales said.

Ken looked at the newsman with a startled gaze. "You know about land, then."

"Land is the basis for all wealth."

"True."

"Then Martin Baron must be a very rich man."

"In many ways. Cash poor, but rich. Potentially."

"Potentially," Wales said. "And what man isn't?"

"True, also," Ken said.

Wilhoit escorted Ursula to a table in the opposite corner where the lamps were dim. He made sure Ursula sat facing the room. In the flickering glow of the coal oil flame, she was a striking woman; the light was kind to her and it appeared David knew it. He smiled and took his chair, beckoned to a waiter.

"You going to talk to that man?" Ed asked.

Ken shook his head. "Now is not the time. I expect we'll hear from Aguilar one of these days if the survey appears to be in his favor."

"Appears to be?"

"Land can be juggled like tenpins," Ken said.

"You think Aguilar might try to pull something?"

"Like wool over my eyes?"

"Yes."

"He might. He is not beneath any form of behavior to get what he wants. He's already proven that."

"Is that so?"

"I suspect, and Martin does as well, that Matteo is behind some of the Apache raids on the Box B."

Ed pursed his lips, spewed a low whistle. "That's something serious."

"It is."

"You have proof?"

"Talk. Suspicion. No real proof. Out here, proof is not needed, Ed. If one of our vaqueros found Culebra's band of Apaches camped at Aguilar's ranch, that would be reason enough to go against Matteo."

"Is that likely?"

"No," Ken sighed, "Aguilar is not that stupid. There's a man who works for him who does all his dirty work."

"Who is that? The surveyor?"

"No. A half-breed named Mickey Bone. At least we think he's a half-breed. He's pure Indian, I suspect. Used to work for Martin."

"A traitor, so to speak."

"So to speak," Ken said.

"I can see a range war developing," Ed said.

"Oh, I don't think so. This isn't sheepmen against cattlemen, after all. There's plenty of land and some of it may be in dispute. Matteo Aguilar wants something else. He's just using the land as an excuse."

"What does he want?" Ed asked.

"God only knows," Ken said.

"And may the best man win, huh?"

"That could be it."

"Well, the newspaper could be a powerful weapon, Ken."

"That's so. People take sides easily. It just depends, sometimes, on who has the loudest voice."

"Right," Ed said.

"You just make sure you know which side you're on and we'll get along."

"Noted."

Both men laughed and the waiter brought a tray with their evening meal and began setting plates down on the table. Steaming tortillas, beans, beefsteak, hot chili peppers soon graced their table and the two men ordered wine and began to eat.

Roy Killian kept glancing toward the back table where his mother sat with David Wilhoit. He was careful not to draw attention to himself and sulked privately as he drank watered whiskey as if it were cold milk.

"You better watch that stuff, Roy," Harrison said. "It can cut a man's legs right out from under him."

"Mind your own business, Will."

"Aw, Roy, I thought we came here to have some fun."

"I came here to get drunk," Roy said. "I don't know about you."

"Well, that, too."

"So, go on and get drunk, Will."

"Say, what's a-gnawin' at you, anyways, Roy? You keep lookin' over at that feller with your ma?"

"That's a damned survey man who works for Aguilar. I don't like him."

"How come?"

"He ain't got no business with my mother. He's a snoop for Aguilar, buttin' into our lives like he was one of us. He's tryin' to take my land away from me."

"He is?"

"Yeah, I think so. I ought to go over there and punch him in the snoot."

"Well, before you do, look what's a-comin' through them doors," Will said.

"Stage's in," a man yelled from the front. A group of Mexicans strained their necks to see who was coming through the batwing doors and the piano player stopped thumping the keys and swung around on his chair to look at the disembarking passengers entering the saloon.

A small, wizened, bowlegged man entered first and politely stepped aside to hold one door for the women who followed, all wide-eyed and bewildered looking, as if they had been ushered into a den of thieves.

First to step through the doors was a small, finely featured young lady in her late teens, with reddish curly hair, wearing a blue dress and bonnet that partially shielded her face. Behind her, a square-jawed woman, deeply tanned, with black straight hair braided into a single pigtail, wearing a blue shawl and a red comb in her hair, dressed in a one-piece gingham dress and wearing high-topped shoes, stepped delicately as if walking on eggs. She swept the room with a steely gaze, giving the impression that beneath her frock beat the heart of a strong-willed woman with a spine forged of high-grade Damascus steel.

The flint-eyed woman was followed by a petite blonde lady in her twenties, a small pillbox hat laced to her head with velvet green ribbons. She wore a pale yellow dress that hid her feet, but she was dainty from head to toe and wore a serene quizzical smile on her comely face. She carried a small valise in one hand, and a folded fan in the other.

Ken stared at the young blonde woman with a bold intensity that gave him the appearance of a man who had been struck by a bolt of lightning. Ed Wales noticed the expression on Ken's face, but said nothing.

Two more men tramped through the doors and the small, wizened man made for the bar, rubbing his throat like a man who had crossed a desert without water. The last two men glanced around the room and headed for Ken's table as one of them waved and smiled in recognition.

"Who're they?" Ed asked, as the two men approached.

"Hawks," Ken said, a cryptic edge to his voice.

Roy Killian could not avert his gaze from the young girl with the red curly hair. She moved with a confidence that belied her years and when she glanced his way, she did not turn away from his stare, but held her head proudly and fixed him with a frank stare of her own.

Roy felt his pulse race and a lump formed in his throat that blocked any chance for him to speak, even if he could have found his voice. The older woman behind her, evidently her mother, guided the young lady to a table near the center of the room. Roy noticed that the girl took a seat facing in his direction. Her mother sat beside her and scanned the room with sharp dark eyes.

"Roy," Will said. "What you lookin' at?"

"That girl there, the one with the red hair. Isn't she beautiful?"

"Not to my mind. Homely is more like it."

Roy, in a state of rapture, paid little mind to his companion's comment. His gaze remained fixed on the young lady. She suddenly stopped looking at Roy and he felt as if he had been erased from her mind.

The two men stopped at Ken's table and looked at Ed Wales for a long moment without speaking.

"It's okay, Tom," Ken said. "You and Cullie sit down and tell me what you know."

"Ken," Tom said. Cullie said nothing, but looked at Wales as if ready to pounce on him. Ed squirmed in his chair. Both men sat down and Ken motioned to one of the waiters.

"Order what you like, gentlemen," Ken said. "And shake hands with our new newspaper publisher, Ed Wales. Ed, this is Tom Harris and Seth Culbertson. We call him Cullie."

The three men shook hands as the waiter stood waiting for Ken's order.

"Lonnie," Ken said, "bring these gentlemen something to drink. Something strong, I imagine."

"Whiskey," Tom said. Cullie nodded.

"Two whiskeys," Lon Visser said in a monotone. "Anything else?"

"We're fine for the moment," Ken said.

Tom reached inside his shirt, pulled out a sheaf of papers wrapped in oilskin. He laid them on the table in front of Ken. Cullie took a sack of makings from his pocket and began to build a cigarette. Neither man said a word. Ken did not pick up the packet of papers.

"You can speak freely in front of Ed," Ken said. "What have you got to tell me? That bunch on the stage, for starters."

Cullie cleared his throat, licked the thin cigarette paper to seal it around the tobacco he had thumbed into an even layer. Tom glanced at the table where the women sat.

"That pigtailed gal didn't give out her name," Tom said. "That's her daughter sitting beside her, the red-headed one. She calls her Wanda. The other gal, the blonde, is named Nancy Grant. She's the schoolteacher you sent me to fetch from Galveston."

"Nancy Grant."

"Single. Spinster, I reckon," Tom said.

"The pigtailed woman says her last name's Fancher," Cullie said, a tinge of sarcasm edging his voice. "Won't tell us her given name."

"Fancher?" Ken asked.

"That's the name she give," Cullie said.

"From Arkansas," volunteered Wales.

Cullie shrugged.

"Wild country," Ken said. He turned to Tom. "What about the cattle?"

Tom shoved the sheaf of papers toward Richman. "Orders there for several head in New Orleans, a hundred here, a couple hundred there."

"How many all tolled?" Ken asked.

"Five hundred head," Tom said.

"We could double that, I think," Cullie added.

Ken's eyebrows arched. "How?" he asked.

"Some people we talked to said they'd like to see how the beef sale goes. If you doubled the herd, you might be able to sell the ones we didn't get nailed down."

"I agree," Tom said.

"Sounds right," Ken said. "But just as easy to drive a thousand head as five hundred. Easier, maybe."

"I think we might have a buyer for that cannon of Martin's," Tom said.

"Oh?" Ken brightened.

"Cullie talked to a man who said he had a buyer up-river."

"He said he'd take it if the price was right," Cullie said.

"Well," Ken said, "you boys seem to have done your work and then some."

"Problem is, in New Orleans, at least," Tom said, "there ain't much market for beef. The Mexicans and South Americans are all tryin' to sell there."

"We'll just have to give 'em a better price," Ken said.

"Price ain't the point," Cullie said. "People just don't hanker for beef much over yonder. They eat fish and crawdads and goddamned mutton."

"Did you find out who is bringing the merchandise into Texas?" Richman asked Cullie.

"A man out of New Orleans," Cullie said. "He is here now, in fact."

Ed Wales shot Ken a questioning look.

"Later, Ed. Now is not the time."

"Your friend Aguilar is in on it," Tom said.

"Who's his partner?"

"A Frenchie named Reynaud. He's a pretty cagey feller."

"How does he do it?" Ken asked.

"He off-loads the cargo in New Orleans, reloads 'em onto ships heading for Corpus Christi and Galveston. Then he picks them up there and carts them overland to Aguilar's ranch. He hasn't gotten that far, but he's down there now."

"Where? Corpus Christi?"

"No. Far as we know, he's at Aguilar's."

Ken whistled.

"There's more," Tom said.

"More?"

"Yep. This Reynaud is an old pard of Baron's. But, there ain't no love lost between 'em. Word is that Reynaud come out here to put a frog-sticker between Baron's shoulder blades."

"Or a bullet in his back," Cullie said.

Ken let out a breath. He shook his head in disbelief.

"What's this 'merchandise' you keep talking about?" Ed asked, looking at the faces of the two nighthawks.

Cullie and Tom both looked at Ken without speaking. Ken shrugged and let out a deep breath. Then he leaned over the table and spoke in a soft voice so his words would not carry.

"I guess it won't be a secret much longer," Ken said, "but I got word that Negro slaves were being smuggled into New Orleans for later transport to Texas, more specifically, to the Rio Grande Valley. I asked Tom and Cullie to look into it."

"And you think Aguilar is smuggling slaves onto his ranch?" Wales asked.

"I do now. Like most of the ranchers out here, money is in short supply. Now we have word that Mr. Lincoln has freed the slaves and that the South might secede from the Union. It was only a matter of time before someone tried to illegally sell slaves to Southerners who want to break loose from the federal government."

Ed Wales let out a low whistle.

"Do you get the idea?" Ken asked.

"I never thought it would go this far," Ed said.

"Oh?"

"I mean, I've heard talk about secession, and of course, there's a lot of animosity from slave owners against Honest Abe, but I never thought it would go this far."

"Do you think the South will secede?" Ken asked.

Ed shook his head. "I don't know. I just don't know."

"Well, what if Texas didn't join in? What if Texas wanted to throw its lot in with the Union?"

"Are you talking about war?"

"There sure as hell could be a war," Ken said.

"That's the talk," Tom said. " 'Bout ever'where we been. Right, Cullie?"

"We saw a lot of guns comin' in to N'Orleans, Corpus, Galveston," Cullie replied.

"Shit," Wales said.

"Exactly," Ken said. "And that bastard Aguilar is probably just waiting to see which side he'll fight on. And, making him some money while the wrangling's going on in Washington and Austin and every other capital city."

"Where does Martin Baron stand in all this?" Ed asked.

"He hasn't paid much attention yet. He doesn't get much news out at the Box B." Ken finished his drink. "Tom, you and Cullie get yourselves rooms at the hotel. I'll take care of it. See you in the morning. Eat what you like. Ed, you keep all this under your hat, hear?"

"But, if it's news . . ."

"It will be news," Ken said. "But only when I say it is."

"I understand." Ed nodded and stared into his drink as if divining tea leaves in a cup.

Ken looked at the light-haired woman again. She, in turn, was looking at him with bold, sparkling eyes. He felt something inside him melt.

"So that's the new schoolm'arm yonder," Ken said. "The one looking over here."

"That's her," Tom said. "Nancy Grant. And she don't have no husband."

"Not yet she doesn't," Ken said, scooting his chair back from the table.

"Where you goin'?" Cullie asked.

"You boys get some grub in your bellies. I'm going to talk to Miss Grant."

Ken left the table. Wales stared after him. Cullie looked at Tom. "I'll bet that ain't all he's goin' to do," he said.

"Cullie," Tom said, "you got the dirtiest mind in Texas."

Cullie grinned and downed his drink without shedding a tear.

17

THE HUNGER STARTED in his belly soon after the sun went down. So, too, the chill that crept over the darkening land with no more breath than a whisper. Anson grunted at Peebo a few yards ahead of him and Peebo stopped and turned around.

"Yeah?"

"No use in goin' on," Anson said. "In another ten minutes, we won't be able to see the ground, much less a track."

"I can see well enough. We can go another hour."

"No," Anson said. "We've gone far enough. We won't catch anything tonight but a damned cold."

"We'll likely catch one quicker if we stop now, son."

"Peebo, you got a hard head, you know that?"

"If you mean I got sense in it, you're right, Anson. Sun ain't been down more'n ten minutes and it's sure as hell light enough to see for a while longer."

"I'm hungry," Anson admitted.

"Stoppin' ain't goin' to fill your belly, son."

"My feet are wore out."

"Shit, what else?" Peebo asked.

"I don't like trackin' Apaches in the damned dark, that's all. They could be waitin' up ahead in the shadows."

Peebo walked over to Anson and set his rifle butt on the ground. He took off his hat and rubbed fingers through his blond locks. Anson held his rifle with both hands, stretching it across his legs just above his knees, his thumb on the hammer.

"You scared of gettin' kilt, son?"

"No. I'm scared of being stupid, Peebo."

"Fair enough. You think it's stupid to go on trackin'. I don't, comes to that. But, we got a problem here, the way I see it."

"No problem. It's dark and we ought to get some rest. Be fresh in the morning."

"Well, like I was goin' to say, you may be the boss of the Box B, and, as far as I know, I'm workin' for you. Right?"

"Right, so far," Anson said.

"But, them horses are mine and I got a stake in 'em, sure enough."

"So?"

"So, if they're my horses, and they are, I should say whether or not we keep goin', fair enough?"

"I don't see it that way, Peebo. Your horses, yes. But, it's my land and I don't work for you. So, you can go on by yourself and I'll just turn my feet toward home tomorrow." Anson paused a moment. "And fire you before I go."

"Fire me?"

"Without pay."

"Shit," Peebo said.

"Shit is right. So, what's it going to be?"

Peebo grinned, shifted his weight on his feet. "Okay. We camp here. Leave early in the morning."

"That's better," Anson said. "Smarter, too."

"Well, I don't know about smart. But, the way I figure it, them Apaches are holed up, too. They can keep a while longer."

"Good. Now, let's find a place to bed down before it gets too damned dark."

Peebo threw a hand up in the air as a sign of surrender and the two men began to seek out a place to lie down. Anson led Peebo well off the trail and they cleared a spot surrounded by mesquite trees. They couldn't see very far, but Anson knew they couldn't be seen very easily, either.

"You ever camped out by your lonesome before, Anson?"

"Some."

" 'Thouten bedroll or blankets?"

"I reckon not."

"You got yourself a knife?" Peebo asked.

"Yeah."

"Well, dig out them rocks until you got a soft sandy bed. Like this."

Peebo hollowed out a shallow depression on a perpendicular line to a mesquite tree. Then, he began to cut boughs from trees and laid them in the dug-out pock. Anson followed suit, stacking the limbs up.

"Looks like a grave filled with tree limbs," Anson said.

"We ain't finished yet, son."

Peebo began to stack cut limbs next to the bed he had made and Anson did the same, without argument.

"Them branches'll give you a springy bed after you get used to it. You put them other cut limbs over you after you lie down. Keep you warm and out of sight."

"You've done this before?" Anson asked.

"Yep. An old-timer taught me the trick. He could build a shelter out of dirt or sticks or old boxes. A man could live in such, he said, until hell froze over."

"It looks like lying on a bed of nails," Anson said.

"Crawl in there, and I'll pile up your limbs. Next time, you can do your own."

"I hope to hell there ain't no next time."

Anson lay down in the burrow and Peebo piled leaves and brush over him. Peebo walked away, leaving Anson alone, staring through the limbs and leaves at the night sky, the stars. He loosened his cap and ball pistol in its holster, moved it so that it did not press against the side of his leg. He knew he would have a better chance with the .44 caliber pistol at close range than he would with the rifle. A feeling of aloneness and claustrophobia swept over Anson until he closed his eyes and calmed his thoughts. His rifle lay at his side, but he wondered if he could bring it to bear if an Apache appeared standing above him. It almost felt as if he had been put in his own grave and he was just waiting for someone to throw dirt over him and bury him for eternity.

He heard Peebo lie down and pull brush over his own bedding ground and then it was silent except for the occasional swick of a leaf or limb as Peebo changed position. Anson opened his eyes again and glimpsed the few stars visible through his canopy of vegetation.

He forgot about Peebo and the horses as he lay suspended in a lassitude between wakefulness and sleep, a state he had nurtured before, when Juanito Salazar had been alive, and told him how to shut out the worries of the world and just let his mind drift off into space where all was calm and peaceful.

Juanito had taught him so many things, but they were not easy to explain. Mostly they were things he kept inside him and did not talk about. That was how it was with Juanito. Anson could talk to him about feelings he did not understand himself and Juanito would know what he was talking about. Not only that, but Juanito knew so much more than Anson ever would. Yet, when he thought about the Argentinian, he would remember the important things.

Juanito had told him that each man and woman had a

center, and that when troubles arose, a man could go inside himself, to that deep center and find peace and calm and great knowledge.

Anson let himself sink into that place and his weariness drifted away, along with his wild thoughts as his thoughts became calm, orderly and in his mind, with his eyes closed, he saw bright lights, like stars, but he knew they were not stars. They were what stars had once been, balls of energy blazing silver flames, fires that shot through the heavens and created other shapes and images that his mind could traverse while his body lay on the ground in a state that was like death, but powerfully alive.

It was odd, but Anson could still hear the night sounds, the frogs, the crickets, the sizzling insects, the very rhythm of the stars pulsing in the velvet black sky, and yet he was away from all of that and in his own quiet secret place where no harm could come to him.

There was still turmoil in his mind and Anson knew the reason. Peebo. Peebo didn't have any quit in him. He sensed that Peebo would track the devil himself into hell if he thought something had been taken from him. But, he also sensed that Peebo didn't know much about the Apache, did not know how hopeless it was to go on foot after a band of savages on horseback.

"Settle down," he told himself, and he tried to shut out the images of death that swarmed in his brain like moths to firelight. It seemed he could still hear the cannon's roar, see it spew flame and iron and tin at charging Apaches, see them twist grotesquely as they fell, see arms and legs flying everywhere, all spewing blood, heads ripped open, chopped off, smashed. And, now the son of Cuchillo had returned to avenge the death of his father, his uncles, his brothers. Culebra, the snake, hissing and gliding in the grass, almost invisible, his face painted with the signs of death, his heart beating with the blood lust of revenge.

Gradually, the cyclone in Anson's mind began to subside. He opened his eyes once to let the light of stars inside and closed them again, wishing for sleep to wipe away the rush of mortal images. He peered at the afterglow of stars in his mind and felt something inside him float off into space and he saw worlds beyond worlds, clouds of cosmic dust glowing like the pulsing coals in a furnace, caverns illuminated by unseen torches that closed and opened like the petals of a blooming flower, and in that floating, he wafted into a peaceful region of his mind and self and left the things of the earth behind.

He fell into a dreaming sleep that made no sense, but seemed real inside the hypnotic slow-motion imagery of senses buried so deep they could not be summoned once he awakened and behind it all was a threnodic hum that reminded him of water flowing over mossy stones and sandy creek beds in fall.

Sometime later, when there were no more dreams, Anson heard a gruff whisper and felt something grab his shirt and pull him upward and he was fighting brush and flicking away leaves and branches that scratched his cheeks and when he opened his eyes, he saw a terrible apparition in the dark that was wild-eyed and grinning like some jack-o'-lantern skull carved out of alabaster.

"Wake up, Anson," Peebo husked. "Goddamm it, wake up."

"Peebo?"

"Shh," Peebo warned.

"What the hell . . ."

"They've come back. The Apaches. Get your rifle."

Anson fought off the dregs of sleep that weighted his brain and fogged it to dullness and Peebo's words gradually crept into his consciousness.

"Apaches?" Anson muttered.

"You're goddamned right, son. Apaches. I got one of 'em and there's more out there. Get your rifle. Quick."

As Anson shook off the last wisps of the mists that smothered his thoughts, he bent down to retrieve his rifle from the hollow that had been his bed.

Then, he heard a terrible sound close by and the pad of running feet and before he could touch the stock of the flintlock, he saw, out of the corner of his eye, a dark shape hurtling toward him and he felt the air rush out of his chest and saw the stars spin in the sky like silver whirligigs blowing in a dark soundless wind.

18
—

THE BLIND BOY listened to the sunrise. He stood in front of the window and felt the coolness of the soil on his face as the sun pulled the heat out of the ground. He heard the crow of the rooster, the soft clucks of the hens in the henhouse. He heard the whippoorwill go silent and the chirp of the wrens, the trill of the meadowlark.

He always tried to put shapes to the sounds, make pictures of what he heard and smelled. Then, he would ask Esperanza questions, and she would tell him how a thing looked. But, he sometimes didn't tell her what he saw in his mind, not only because he wanted to keep it secret, but because sometimes it was hard to explain to her what he saw. And, he knew that she could not tell him what colors looked like, but he knew he could tell her the shape of blue and yellow, the way purple looked and what red tasted and looked like.

He knew it was difficult for Esperanza to explain the color of rain, the shape of a roadrunner, the difference between white and black. But, she was good about it, and she tried. She would let him touch a rabbit's fur, feel its dead eyes, its ears and rub its soft belly and she would tell him the shades of color in a sunset, the shapes of clouds, the noises of different things.

So, he had learned a lot from Esperanza, but he wanted to know more. He had touched her face hundreds of times and wondered if her eyes looked like the eyes of a rabbit or a quail, and she would try and tell him the differences. He knew what water tasted like, and the smell of an apple or a persimmon, but he could not see the color blue in his mind, nor could he see anger on his mother's face, nor did he know exactly what a smile or a frown looked like, other than the mouth was shaped differently and Esperanza would take his hand and let him draw in the dirt, then retrace the curvature of what he had drawn.

He knew something about his mother, Caroline, but he had never touched the face of don Martin and nobody would let him get close to the man. He could feel his anger, could feel don Martin's eyes on him, but he could not read his face and did not know if he was smiling or frowning. Esperanza had made him freeze his own face and touch his mouth and teeth so that he knew more than drawing smiles and frowns in the dirt, but he could not freeze another's face so that he could see if his or her countenances were like his own.

Some things that Esperanza could not describe to him were very real and visible. Lazaro could see words in his mind, and they all had shapes and colors to go with their sounds. He could see fat words, thin words, words that were liquid or solid, blue or red or white or green. While he did not know if the names he put to the colors were right, he knew that they were colors because he could see them in his mind. Grass was a green word, and sky was a blue word. Thin was a very slender and white word, while fat was round and red and had a belly like the one Esperanza said belonged to Francisco Garcia, one of the Box B hands. Water was a liquid word and flashed silvery in his mind, while dry was a brown word like a dead thrush, and thirst was reddish and razor sharp like a knife with blood on it.

So, in some ways, Lazaro created his own world and while he felt safe and secure in that world when he was alone, he liked for Esperanza to read to him. When she read from a book, he could see all the words dancing, flying, walking, running, tumbling, falling, rising, staggering, hissing, laughing, giggling, spraying, spouting, leaking, breaking, stumbling, soaring, diving, swimming, jumping as they poured from her lips and into his ear like sweet honey or warm milk.

During the night he had heard his mother arguing with the man who lived there, her husband, Esperanza said he was, and then he had heard voices outside and the creak of the barn doors opening. He had tried to make sense of the sounds, but he could only understand the curse words of the men, in both Spanish and English, and then the rumbling noise that sounded like a wagon. He knew it wasn't a wagon, but something heavy being moved out of the barn and then it was quiet for a long time until the husband, Martin, came into the house. And then he had heard voices from his mother's room and then the husband had left, with his boots still on, and had gone into the living room. Lazaro had strained to hear more, but the house had gone quiet again and he was once more blind to what was happening in the house.

Later, Lazaro had awakened and heard Esperanza making that funny sound through her nose that his mother, Caroline, called snoring and he wondered if Esperanza could hear her own sounds. He called out to her once, but she had not answered and she had not awakened when the husband had gone out to the barn and taken something away and come back without it.

Lazaro stepped away from the window and tiptoed to the door. He groped for the latch and when he found it, he fumbled to slip it from its notch so that he could open the door.

"Do not leave the room," Esperanza whispered and Lazaro's blood jumped in his veins.

He turned and bore down on Esperanza with sightless eyes.

"I want to go out," he said, his voice soft, delicate.

"*El patrón* is still asleep."

"I know. I will be quiet."

"No, *el patrón* will be very angry when he awakens."

"Why?" Lazaro asked. He could hear Esperanza shift her weight on the bed and knew she was rising.

"Because he had to take the cannon away last night."

"Where did he take it?"

"I do not know. Far away."

"Not too far away. He came back."

The two were speaking English which Caroline had insisted they do. But, when they were away from the house, and alone, or with one of the ranch families, they conversed in Spanish, which Lazaro preferred. It was a more flowing language and it had stronger colors than English. He could hear melodies in Spanish that he could not detect in the English tongue.

"Esperanza? What does the word *hate* mean?"

"It means that you do not like something very much. Why do you ask this?"

"I heard Mama Caroline say to don Martin that she hated him."

"That was just talk. It is nothing for you to worry about."

"Why does don Martin hate me?"

"He does not hate you, Lazaro."

"He never speaks to me."

"Don Martin has many things on his mind. Now, you must get dressed. Can you find your clothes? Do you want me to help you?"

"I can find my clothes." Thin to the point of being

skeletal, Lazaro was wearing his cotton nightshirt and shorts, was barefoot.

He padded over to the wardrobe closet, a freestanding container that was large enough for his clothing and Esperanza's. He dressed quickly, deftly, as Esperanza watched him, ever fascinated by Lazaro's agility even though he was blind. It was difficult for her to explain to him who he was, and she had never used the word *bastard* in front of him. But, that's what he was, the bastard child of Pilar Aguilar and Pilar's brother-in-law, Augustino Aguilar. Lazaro was afflicted with syphilis, as were both of his dead parents. She wondered when Lazaro would begin showing the signs of madness that afflicted people who possessed the horrible disease.

"I want to talk to don Martin," Lazaro said. "I want to ask him where he took the cannon."

"You must not speak to him."

"If I cannot talk to don Martin, then he does hate me, Esperanza, doesn't he?"

"No, he does not hate you."

"Is he my father?"

"In a way," she said.

"I do not understand."

"It is not an easy thing to explain to a young boy." Lazaro was still a boy, almost five, yet sometimes she thought he acted older than he was. He was wiser than most boys his age, she thought. He certainly asked questions that would have been more appropriate from an older boy.

Lazaro went to his pallet, sat down and put on his sandals. He looked up at the place where Esperanza was sitting, tipping his head back.

"Come here," she laughed, "and I will comb your hair."

Lazaro arose with alacrity and clomped over to the bed. He listened as she rummaged beneath it for the big comb. He liked for her to comb his hair. He heard her pour water from the pitcher into a bowl and splash her fingers in it. She wet his hair as she did with the clothes when she was ironing, sprinkling water on his dry locks until they were damp enough to manage. Then, she began running the comb through his hair, stimulating his scalp, smoothing his unruly black hair down flat against his skull. She dabbed at the water with a cloth and patted his cheeks when she was finished.

"There. You can go outside and pee now. But do not disturb don Martín."

"Esperanza, will you teach me to shoot a gun?"

"A gun? Why?"

"I want to learn how to shoot."

"But, you cannot see. You would not be able to shoot a rabbit or a deer."

"Oh yes, I would. I could shoot at the sound."

"You might miss and hurt someone. You might even hurt yourself."

"Please. Please teach me."

"I do not know how," she said, a frown on her face that Lazaro could not see, but knew was there.

"Then, get me a gun, a pistol or a rifle, and I will teach myself."

"You are much too young to own a gun," she said.

"But, when I am old enough I would be able to shoot. Please, please."

"No. Your mother would not allow it. And, neither would I."

"I will get a gun myself," he said, and there was a disturbing tone to his voice that alarmed Esperanza.

"Why are you so eager to have a gun?" she asked.

"Because then I would be able to shoot those people I hate."

"What? You, a boy, dare say such things?"

"I know what hate is now," he said, his voice soft. "And when you hate someone, like the Apaches, you need a gun to kill them."

"That is a terrible thing to say, Jesus, Mary and Joseph. You must not think such things. You must not talk that way, Lazaro. I wish we could go to the priest right now so that you could confess such a sin."

Esperanza had spoken to him many times about sin, about bad thoughts, and bad deeds, but he still did not understand what she meant.

"Besides," she said, "you are too young to hate anything. God loves you and you must love everyone."

"I know what hate is," Lazaro said. "Now that you told me. And if someone I love very much hates someone, I will kill that person."

"What person?"

"The person who I hate."

"But you do not hate anyone, Lazaro. You are too young."

"Oh, yes I do," he said, and skipped across the floor and was through the door before she could call him back.

"Such a child," she said in Spanish. "Perhaps he will not live long enough to bring harm to anyone." She blessed herself and her lips moved in prayer. "My God," she breathed, "protect us all from this child who does not know what he says."

But, something in her heart told her that Lazaro understood hate and that one day he would strike someone down. She thought it might be Martin Baron who disliked Lazaro. Martin did not beat the boy, nor mistreat him, but he did something far more cruel, she knew. Don Martin ignored the boy, and that was the harshest punishment of all for a boy who so desperately wanted his love.

19

ROY KILLIAN HEARD the voice through clogged ears
filled with thick paste, heard it echo in his anvil-
heavy brain. His head throbbed like a sore toe, and he
knew it must be swollen as big as a watermelon. He
fought off the vocal intrusion, but then he felt a hand on
his shoulder and the shaking made the pain shoot from
his head to his ankles and he opened boil-sore eyes to
sunlight and a shadowy person standing over him, saying
words he couldn't understand and that hurt to hear.

"Wake up, Roy, wake up now," his mother was saying. "Wake up so I can kill you."

"Ma? Jesus."

"I ought to wash your mouth out with soap."

"Wha? What's goin' on?"

"I threw that Will out an hour ago, the lazy lout. Now,
you get up so's I can whup your miserable hide."

"Ma? What's wrong? What did I do?"

Roy felt himself being jerked out of bed by his right
arm and then he fell three feet to the hard floor and the

jarring pain coursed through his head as if someone were driving a twenty penny nail straight through the top of his skull.

"Godamighty," he exclaimed, and the cobwebs of sleep began to crumple and drift away in milky wisps.

"I ought to beat you within an inch of your life," Ursula said.

Roy looked up to see his mother standing over him, both hands on her hips, her hair straggling down the sides of her face, her eyes blazing with a caustic rage.

"Ma, what's got into you? I ain't done nothin'."

"Roy, you're one sorry excuse for a son. You don't remember last night? At the Longhorn?"

Roy scratched his head, tried to clear it of the throb that blocked all thought. He blinked his eyes and even that slight movement hurt. There was pain deep in his eye sockets, pain that stabbed in all directions.

"I 'member some of it."

"You were drunk, Roy. You said terrible things to David. And, you got into a fight. Oh, it was horrible. You were horrible, Roy Killian, worse than your father Jack ever was."

"I guess I don't remember that much, Ma."

"Get up. You look like you've been sleeping in a hog wallow."

"Yes'm," Roy said, and he grabbed the side of his bunk and tried to get up on his feet. Ursula had to help him. He stood there, his head reeling, the room, his mother, all a blur, out of focus, all the images wavy and undulating.

Roy could smell himself. He looked down at his shirt front and saw the remains of vomitus and his stomach rebelled, roiling and contracting as if bound to the coils of a snake. He tried to remember where he had been, what he had done.

"Well?" Ursula asked. "What have you got to say for yourself?"

"Ma, I—I don't remember much. Let me think."

"You made a fool of yourself, of me, insulted Dave, and you got into a stupid, senseless brawl."

Roy rubbed his right hand over his chin. It was sore as a swollen boil. He had a crick in his neck and his ribs felt as if they had been pummeled with bricks. He felt woozy and unsteady on his feet as he tried to recall the events of the night before.

"I—I got into a fight?" he asked.

"Oh, I wouldn't call it a fight," his mother said. "It was more like one of Jack's donnybrooks at the alehouse in Fort Worth. You even tried to hit me."

"I did?" Roy fought to clear his brain. He remembered sitting at the bar with Will. Then, he remembered the girl, the half-Indian girl and the other women sitting at the table in the center of the room.

He remembered seeing Ken Richman walk over to the center table and lean down to talk to one of the women. After that, his mind was a slate wiped clean of chalk.

"If it weren't for that half-breed gal," Ursula said.

"What half-breed gal?" Roy's heartbeat stumbled and tripped, seemed to leap up into the gutter of his throat.

"Oh, some wastrel who came off the stage. She ran over and grabbed you. My, I never saw a little bit of a thing with so much gumption and strength. She pulled you away from David and turned you around, marched you across the room before I could gather my wits about me."

Roy strained to remember. He wondered if the girl his mother was talking about was the same one who had caught his eye. He remembered her, all right.

But he remembered her through a haze of smoke and strong whiskey, through waves of raucous laughter and the clink of glasses, the scrape of chairs, the scuff of shoes, and the interminable babble of the Longhorn Saloon.

He remembered her sad wise eyes and the wild scuff of dark hair poking out from her bonnet and the rustle of her skirts as she walked into the saloon, and her bearing, the air of poise and femininity she carried with her like a royal shawl.

And he remembered her smiling at him, and glancing in his direction out of the corner of her eye, hypnotizing him with her dark looks, that maddening smile, so old on one so young, yet so understanding, so soft and warm, he could feel it now as if it were a summer breeze on his face, or light fingers riffling through his shock of reddish hair.

"Wha—where did the girl take me?" Roy asked.

"To her table, of course. But, you angered David so much, he got mad and came after you. He hit you with his fist, knocked you down. Oh, it wasn't a hard blow and I must say you deserved it. Then, Mr. Richman had to restrain David, and that gal cleaned the blood off your mouth and David and I left. What happened after that, I don't know. You were lying in your bed when David dropped me off, and Will was sprawled out in the front room, half naked and stinking of whiskey. It was all so terrible and it was all your fault."

"I don't like David Wilhoit," Roy said.

"Well, you've no call to dislike him. He's never done anything to you."

"He works for Matteo Aguilar, that's enough."

"That's no reason to dislike him. He works for whomever pays him."

"Aguilar murdered his whole family," Roy said lamely.

"You don't know that."

"Anson told me."

"Oh, Anson. Those Barons think they're so high and mighty. I wouldn't put a penny on what they tell you."

"Well, it's thanks to Martin Baron that we have this land, a roof over our heads."

"Grub land, not worth a tinker's damn. Charity, to boot."

"Who told you this? Wilhoit?"

Ursula dipped her head, batted her eyes. She seemed

to struggle with the answer. "Well, he did sort of say the land wasn't worth much."

"Because he means to take it away."

"He wouldn't do that," Ursula said in a temper. "Besides, he doesn't want the land."

"No, but Matteo Aguilar sure as hell does."

"You don't know that."

"What did Wilhoit say? About his damned survey?"

"Why, ah, nothing. It's not his say."

"I don't believe you, Ma."

"Don't you call me a liar." She lifted a hand as if to strike her son, but held it suspended as Roy glared at her in defiance.

"I'm not calling you a liar. I think Wilhoit has a blanket over your head. He's using you, Ma. He gets his pay from Aguilar."

"Roy, listen to me." She put both hands on his cheeks, brought her face close to his. "I don't want you to be hurt, but I've got to talk to you."

"What about?" he asked, a surly tone in his voice.

"David has asked me to marry him."

Roy blinked. A stunned expression froze on his face as if she had slapped him. He opened his mouth, but no words came out.

"I'm lonely. Since your father died, I haven't had a man. David is kind and has some means. This place . . . it just doesn't feel right to me. You and Will haven't finished the cistern yet and there's really no market for cattle even if you had a herd to tend."

"Ma, Ma, don't talk that way. I'll fix the place up, make it bigger. Me and Will, we ain't got much more to do on the cistern. We just need to haul in some more wood and buy some nails. It won't take but a week or two."

"Roy, it's not just the cistern. It's just hard for me to stay out here all alone every day."

"You hardly know this Wilhoit feller, Ma. He—he's just after you because . . . because . . ."

"Don't say anything that would make me ashamed of you, Roy. David's not like that. He would never take advantage of me."

"Ma, that's just what he's a-doin'. I wouldn't put it past him to throw in whole hog with Aguilar and get this land back by fixin' his survey figures."

"He doesn't like this part of Texas, he told me."

"I don't believe him," Roy said. "He's got somethin' up his sleeve."

"Well, I'm not going to discuss it now. He's coming by here and I don't want you here when he comes."

"This is my house, too."

Ursula sighed. "Yes, it is, and I feel like an unwelcome guest. All that's going to change. Roy, I'm going away with David."

"What?" Her statement jolted Roy into full wakefulness. He stared at her in disbelief, speechless from shock.

"David is coming by with his wagon. I'm all packed. I just wanted to tell you good-bye before I left."

"Where are you going?"

"Back to Fort Worth. David has a home there and I'm going to marry him."

"Jesus H. Christ."

Ursula stepped forward and gave Roy a hug. She wiped away a tear when she broke away.

"I love you, Roy. You take care of yourself."

"But . . . you . . . you just can't . . ."

Ursula turned away from her son, her body shaking with sobs.

Then, they both heard the creak of a wagon out front, the slap and flat crack of leather harness. Roy followed his mother from the room and saw her bags by the door.

Ursula picked up her two bags and turned to her son. "Good-bye, Roy. I'll write you."

Then, she stepped through the open door and Roy saw the wagon standing out by the hitchrail. He padded to the door on bare feet and looked outside as David was setting the hand brake. He watched as the surveyor took his mother's carpetbags and helped her up onto the wagon seat.

Ursula waved to Roy. David nodded at the young man, then released the brake and turned the wagon around.

Roy lifted his hand to wave good-bye, but his mother's back was facing him. He dropped his hand in disconsolate failure and blinked his eyes as the tears broke from their wells and spilled onto his face.

"Good-bye, Ma," he said, and choked as the sobs began to wrack his body.

Then, he saw her turn and wave farewell one last time. He lifted his hand again, but she turned away before he could wave good-bye.

Roy watched the wagon until it disappeared from sight. Then, it was quiet, and he was all alone. The tears stopped and he drew a deep breath. He went back inside the house and looked out the back window at the cistern. The large wooden vat was finished and it was on its supports. But it still lacked braces and he would have to drill a hole and set a spout for the water to drain.

He put on his socks and boots and walked out back to the unfinished cistern, wondering if he'd ever see his mother again. He picked up a hammer, looked at it for a long time, then hurled it as far as he could out into the field. He watched it twirl and tumble and heard it hit the ground with a dull thud. He kicked at a clod and turned back to go inside the empty house.

Then, he saw another wagon in the distance. For a moment, he thought it was his mother and David returning. But, no, this wagon was smaller and was coming from the direction of Baronsville. He squinted into the sun to see who was coming to call, but they were too far away.

"Shit," he said, and went to the water trough to scrub his face, dampen his hair so he could comb it. His mouth tasted of iron and copper and he felt a queasiness in his stomach.

When he looked at the wagon again, he saw the shapes of two figures in it.

"I wonder who in hell that is," he said aloud.

And, for a moment, he thought it might be some Aguilar hands coming to throw him off his land. He walked inside to strap on his pistol and check the priming of his rifle. It would be another fifteen minutes before the wagon arrived and he wanted to be ready to defend his property—no matter who wanted to take it away from him.

20

A NSON BRACED HIMSELF, grabbed for his knife as the shadowy figure barreled down on him again. He heard Peebo grunt and the sound of something falling, hitting the ground. Anson had just grasped the handle of his knife when the man struck him in the belly, drove him backwards. He could smell the sweat, the oil of flesh. He went down, his breath knocked out of him and, instinctively, he rolled away and kicked out with both feet.

Still half asleep, Anson felt his feet strike flesh and bone, which jarred him out of his stupor. He scrambled away, rose to a crouch and sought his attacker in the darkness. He saw the Apache sit up, then struggle to regain his footing.

A thin strip of cream signalled the dawning, as Anson gripped his knife, prepared to meet his attacker. He heard sounds behind him, but far enough away so that he knew he need not worry for a moment.

The Apache stood up, glared at Anson, then turned

and ran off into the mesquite. Anson turned and saw Peebo wrestling with a man, each gripping the other like wrestlers trying to throw the other down.

Anson rushed over to help Peebo, keeping his knife low, ready to jab. In the eerie half light of dawn, the trees around him seemed like enemies, taller and mightier than he, their arms raised to strike. Peebo was grunting and struggling against his adversary and Anson had to sidestep to avoid Peebo's back. As Peebo and the Apache twisted again, Anson dashed in close and rammed his knife into the Indian's back, closing his eyes at the last moment because it was something he did not want to do, had never done before.

He heard the blade strike flesh and bone, felt the jarring in his wrist. The Indian let out a low grunt and Anson twisted the knife. He felt a gush of blood drench his knife hand and he reacted by drawing the blade back out. He saw the Apache sag as Peebo stepped away, panting for breath.

"Jesus, God," Peebo gasped.

The Apache twisted on the ground, a knife in his hands. He swept the air in a futile swipe of his knife, made a choking sound in his throat and then writhed into a knot as he expelled one last breath.

"You okay?" Anson asked in a breathless voice.

"Just barely, goddammit."

"Any more around?"

"I don't know."

"One come after me, then run off," Anson said.

"We better get our rifles and find some cover, Anson. We could be up to our asses in Apaches any minute."

Anson struggled to bite in a deep breath. His senses were scrambling with images. He knew the Apache was dead and it gave him a feeling of deep guilt and a peculiar kind of sorrow. He forced himself to look at the dead Indian lying all balled up on the ground and then he felt his stomach convulse in a sudden spasm.

Life was such a quick and uncertain thing, he thought.

One minute, the Apache had been alive, his heart beating, his blood running in his veins, his mouth gulping air into his lungs, and now he was nothing but a rotting corpse, wiped off the face of the earth in a twinkling as if he had never been there at all. It was an awesome moment for Anson, much like the time he had first killed a man, but different, somehow, filled with a deeper meaning.

He thought of Juanito, so full of life, an eternal man, destined to live forever, but now dead. And gone. The loss of Juanito wrenched at him now and he fought back the tears of self-pity. He drew in air to fill him with life and quell the nausea he felt.

"Better move, boy," Peebo said softly and Anson realized that he was still rooted to that spot, frozen there, witless, unable to control movement, to make himself step away from the lifeless hulk on the ground and grab up his rifle.

For a long moment, he didn't care. He almost hoped the fallen Apache would rise up and strike him dead and erase all the guilt he felt. But, he cleared his head of the dark shrouds of grief and self-blame and tore himself away from the killing spot and stumbled toward his bed, so like a grave now, an open hollow in the earth, filled with leaves and branches. A tomb that had opened up and released him from an eternity of sleep, and the worms that ate to the bones and removed all traces of life.

Anson slid his knife back in its sheath and picked up his rifle, felt the pan to see if the powder still was there and it was damp and he rubbed the gummy residue away and reached for his small powder horn. He dried the pan well and poured more powder on it and blew away the excess and closed the frizzen.

"You comin'?" Peebo called from somewhere in the half dark, a voice from a tree shadow, disembodied, without form or visible breath.

"Yeah," Anson said, and his voice sounded strange to him, a voice from someone who was near death, or lost and bewildered. Not his own voice, but a man's gravel groan in the early morning before he had drunk water to wash away the clog of night.

"You hear anything, son?" Peebo asked.

Anson listened for several seconds.

"Just my own breathing," he said, and this time his voice sounded more like his own.

"Keep your eyes open and step light," Peebo said and emerged from the silhouette of a tree as if he had been part of it and was now separated. Anson had never seen him until Peebo moved.

Anson hesitated when he passed the body of the slain Apache, but willed himself to go on, to catch up with Peebo and leave that place of death. He did not look back, but the dead Indian lay still in his mind, lifeless and yet a part of him, if not forever, certainly for a long time to come.

"What now?" Anson asked as he fell into step with Peebo.

"There's at least one what got away," Peebo said, "and we have to step careful. You look left and I'll look right."

"The whole bunch could be waiting for us."

"Might," Peebo said. "I don't reckon, though."

"Why not?"

"You get a good look at that Injun you kilt?"

"No."

"Well, he didn't have no paint on him. I figure them two just stumbled on us. Fact is, the one you knifed stepped into my hole and I come up like a snake at him. He liked to jumped out of his skin. Scared the living shit out of him."

"How do you know? I didn't hear him yell."

"He jumped a foot straight up and about a yard sideways, son. He was plumb scairt all right."

"Why didn't you shoot him?"

"How come you didn't shoot the one what jumped you?"

"He ran off," Anson said, his words lame as they came out of his mouth.

Peebo and Anson crept along, stopped and listened, cupped their ears, breathed slow and quiet, heading away from the lightening horizon where the sun was already burning away the mist of morning.

Anson shivered in the chill dawn air, heard his teeth clack together, cursed himself silently as his hands and arms shook. He wondered if Peebo was as cold as he was, but when he looked at him, he saw no sign.

It was quiet, quiet and eerie, and he heard no bird singing, which alarmed him because he knew he should have heard some natural sounds at that time of day. The silence hung like a long cloak between them until Anson thought his ears would burst. He could almost feel it falling over his head and shoulders. He felt closed in, trapped. Mesquite trees were all around them, and beyond, a heavy mist blocked the view in any direction.

Anson felt like he was suffocating. Peebo just stood there, not saying anything, crouched with his rifle ready to bring to his shoulder. He looked like a statue, Anson thought. He could not even tell if Peebo was breathing.

"Peebo," Anson whispered.

Peebo turned around. He held a finger to his lips as his eyebrows arched.

"Something funny here," Anson said.

"What?"

"Listen. No birds. Nothing."

Peebo shook his head, but he stood there and turned his head to the left, then to the right. Then, he slowly cocked his rifle, bringing it up to his waist. His finger curled inside the trigger guard.

Anson's heart seemed to stiffen in his chest. He could hear the pulsebeat in his ear, a steady throb in the silence.

"Anson," called a voice and the voice sounded familiar. "Over here."

"Who's that?" Peebo asked in a loud whisper.

Anson shook his head.

"Anson," the man called again.

Peebo jerked around, swinging his rifle at his waist.

"Mickey?" Anson asked in a querulous voice.

"Tell your friend to take his rifle off cock."

"Peebo," Anson said, a sternness in his voice.

Peebo eased the hammer down, but left the frizzen pitched.

"Who is it?" Peebo asked.

"Mickey Bone," Anson replied. "Mickey, come on out. We won't shoot."

Mickey Bone rode out from behind a mesquite tree. He was armed, but did not have his rifle or pistol at the ready. He looked tired and his clothes were covered with dust.

"Mickey, is that really you?" Anson stood, slack jawed, his rifle drooping in his hands. Peebo stood rigid as a post.

Bone laughed. "You ride a dangerous trail," he said.

"Where are the Apaches?" Anson asked.

"Hell, Bone looks like an Apache to me," Peebo said, an accusatory tone to his voice.

"He's a friend, Peebo." Anson paused. "I think."

"I am your friend, Anson."

"What happened to that Apache that snuck off?" Peebo asked.

"He is gone," Bone said. "But, Culebra waits just ahead for you."

"Where?" Peebo asked, still suspicious.

"There is a deep draw about a mile ahead of you," Bone said. "He waits there where you cannot see him. Those two braves are not of his band, but he made them find you."

"How come you know all this?" Peebo asked. "How do we know you ain't just trickin' us?"

"Shut up, Peebo," Anson said.

"I come to warn you, Anson. I have tracked you from the place of the fire."

"Why?" Anson asked.

"I am going to Mexico to bring my family to Texas. I did not know about Culebra, but Matteo Aguilar wants to kill you."

"He sent Culebra after me?"

"Yes. And, there is another who would kill your father. *Ten cuidado.*"

"Who is this man?"

"His name is Reynaud. He is a slave trader, but he bears a grudge against Martin."

"I never heard of him," Anson said.

"Go back to your ranch. Tell your father that I have warned him."

Anson let out a breath. His eyes narrowed as he mulled over what Bone had said.

"Why did you come to tell me all this?" Anson asked.

"It is no matter. I was riding this way."

"No," Anson said. "Mexico is south of where the Apaches burned us out."

"You do not believe me," Bone said. It was a flat statement. "*No importa.*"

"You run off once," Anson said, remembering when Bone had left in the night. "I never expected to see you again."

"Sometimes trails cross when we do not know that they will."

"We can take them Apaches," Peebo said.

Bone turned to look at Peebo. His eyes crackled with a lambent fire. "No, not Culebra. Not this time. He waits for you, and you will not see him until just before you die."

"Bullshit," Peebo said. "He stole my horses. I aim to get them back."

"You do not know the Apache," Bone said. "Anson, if you want to see the sun another day, you will take your friend away from this place. Now, I must go."

"To Mexico?"

"Yes."

"Why do you work for Aguilar?" Anson asked.

"Because he pays me," Bone said.

"How do I know you won't come and try to kill my father?"

"Because I told Matteo that I would not."

Bone turned his horse and before either Peebo or Anson could say anything, he had disappeared into the brush. They did not even hear his horse's feet, even though they were shod. It was as if he had turned to smoke, or become part of the mist.

"What do you make of that shit?" Peebo asked.

"I believe Mickey."

"A damned Apache?"

"He once rode for the Box B, Peebo."

"And now he rides for your enemy, this Aguilar feller."

"Yes. But Bone doesn't lie."

"Well, now we got us a full crock, ain't we, son?" Peebo stomped the ground in helpless anger.

"I think we better head west, to the ranch, Peebo."

"Well, shit fire, that damned cuss Culebra's gonna get away with my horses."

"We can catch horses or buy them, Peebo. I'm glad we saw Bone."

"I ain't," Peebo said.

"He probably saved our lives."

"Or he cut himself in for some of them horses."

"No," Anson said. "Bone wouldn't do that. I know him."

But, he wondered if he really did know Mickey Bone. He had not seen him in a long time, and his father hated him. I should hate him, too, Anson thought.

But, he could not. In a way, he wished he had ridden off to Mexico with Bone. It would be like it was when he was a kid and followed the Apache around like a shadow, like a puppy wagging its tail.

But, he was a boy no longer and Bone, he realized, no matter his warning, was no longer a friend.

21

K EN RICHMAN NUDGED Ed Wales in the side with his elbow as the wagon rumbled into Baronsville from the southwest, a Mexican driving the team of horses. Whatever was in the wagon was covered by a tarp, and it looked heavy from the strain on the shock flanges bulging underneath. Behind the team rode a tall man on a tall horse with four white stockings, flax mane and tail, a horse with spirit even though its flanks glistened with the sheen of sweat.

"What, a wagon?" Ed said.

"Nope. Coming up behind it. That's Martin Baron himself, Eduardo, and he seldom comes to town."

"What's in the wagon?"

"I don't know. But, I've got a pretty good idea."

Ed held a copy of *The Baronsville Bugle* in his hand. The ink was still wet. Behind them, in the newspaper office, a printer was pulling levers and gears were grinding as people gathered up the pages and assembled them. The headline read: CIVIL WAR LOOMS in seventy-two-point Bodoni Bold.

Martin Baron rode up to the driver of the wagon, leaned over and spoke a few words, then rode on ahead. He pulled up a few yards from where Ken and Ed stood, swung down from the saddle and wrapped one rein around the hitchrail. The horse stood hipshot and switched its tail at the flies that swarmed over its sweaty hide.

"Martin," Ken said.

"Ken."

"What brings you to town?"

Martin didn't answer as he looked over Ed Wales, his glance raking him from balding pate to dusty boots. He took in the newspaper, too, pausing for a second in his visual survey to read the headline. The wagon stopped a few yards away and the Mexican drover set the brake and sat there, seemingly impervious to the blazing sun that hammered his straw sombrero.

"Ken, I need a favor," Martin said. He pointed to the wagon. "I got that four-pounder there and it needs a place to sleep."

"The brass cannon?"

Martin nodded.

"Why, I guess we could store it in the livery. How come?"

"Just so it's no place Caroline can set eyes on it. She's plumb spooked about that cannon."

Ken nodded. "Consider it done. Drink?"

"No, I got to get back. See that boy on the wagon there?"

Ken shaded his eyes, peered intently at the Mexican on the wagon seat. "Don't recognize him right off. One of your hands?"

"One that Anson hired for branding over on the Nueces side of the Box B. Name's Jose Hidalgo. He and three other Mexican hands come back to the ranch with their tails tucked between their legs."

"Trouble?"

"I don't know," Martin said. "They said Anson was

all right. One hand stayed with him. They said they were about finished with the branding, anyway."

"What made them come back like that?" Ken asked.

Martin slid his Stetson over the back of his head. His forehead glistened with beads of sweat. "I couldn't make a whole hell of a lot of sense of it. Something about a great big old longhorn bull. El Blanco, they called it. One called it El Blanco Diablo. Scared the living shit out of them."

"Chased after them, did it?" Ken asked.

"I reckon. One of them had a horse gored, plumb reamed its guts out. They're a superstitious bunch."

"Well," Ken said, "there is a superstition about white steers, bulls too, I imagine."

"Yeah, I know. Some say a white steer's the first to bolt in a stampede. Might be something to it."

"But, you're worried about Anson."

"I am some," Martin admitted. "He ought to have better control over the hands, him grown and all."

Ken detected a note of bitterness in Martin's tone, but he suspected the real problem was Caroline. She had not been quite right since the Apache attack, when Martin had used the four-pounder on them, had left more than one man and woman pretty badly shaken.

Still, this was not the time to press it, Ken reasoned. Martin had his hands full and he seemed in no mood to talk any of it out. Let sleeping dogs lie, Ken thought. But, the Caroline thing worried him more than Martin's obvious irritation with his son, Anson.

"You could have a cup of coffee with us, couldn't you, Martin? While I get that cannon put away."

Martin squared his hat on his head and nodded. "I reckon," he said. "Long as it's not public. I'm in no mood for a lot of gossipy chatter from the womenfolk in this town."

Ken suppressed the urge to laugh. Martin didn't come to town too often and when he did he was the object of stares from all of the women, and some of them were married. Stares and whispers. Baron was still a handsome man, young enough to attract the pretty girls, old enough to set the older women's hearts aflutter, their tongues to stutter.

"I know just the place," Ken said. "Besides, I want you to meet the new schoolmarm."

"Oh, no," Martin said.

"Be quiet," Ken said. "I've already staked my claim to her. She'll make us coffee, then disappear. You won't even know she's there."

"Why in hell isn't she teaching school?" Martin asked.

"You'll see," Ken said, a cryptic tone to his voice. "Come on, Ed, bring that paper with you."

"I should really stay until the run's finished."

"If you trained your people right, they can do it," Ken said.

Ed shrugged, his face lighting up with a grin. "You've got me there," he said.

Martin took a longer look at Ed Wales as the three men passed the wagon. Ken gave instructions in Spanish to the Mexican cowhand. The wagon creaked as the horse took up the slack in the traces.

Ed walked slightly ahead of Martin on his right, while Ken took the lead on Martin's left. Martin saw a man with his shirtsleeves rolled up, ink on his hands, hair that was thinning fast on his head. A flask jutted from Ed's hip pocket and Martin knew it didn't hold apple juice.

He sized the man up as a hard drinker, but a hard worker, just the kind of man Ken would pick to run his newspaper. Ken had insisted that the town of Baronsville start with a newspaper and Martin had agreed, although he hadn't seen the use of it at the time.

But, *The Bugle* had brought in settlers, merchants, farriers, blacksmiths, people of imagination and gumption. To Martin's amazement, the town had grown into something more permanent than a tumbleweed, and seemed still to be growing. As they walked along, he could hear the sizzle of a handsaw, the ring of hammers on iron nails, the clap of fresh lumber and people were moving about the town as if they meant to stay.

Ken turned off Main Street and ambled down one he had named Poplar, although Martin saw no such trees. There were shops on both sides of the street, some finished, some still under construction, and he liked the feel of the shade thrown by the false fronts. At the end of the block, there was, indeed, a small tree growing that he thought might be a poplar, but he knew little about trees.

Ed folded up the newspaper, tucked it under his arm. Ken turned on a street he had named Baron Lane, and in a few minutes, the three men had walked to the edge of town, where a man could see for miles. In the center of their view, however, was a small frame house, and next to it, a building that was not quite finished, but, from its bell tower, Martin knew it was a schoolhouse.

"Nice," Martin said.

"It will hold fifty children," Ken said.

Martin laughed. "Back east, we never had more than ten kids at a time."

"Baronsville is growing," Ken said. "We only have a dozen or so children who want to go to school, but in a year or so, I expect we'll be crowded."

"You're a dreamer," Martin said.

Two Mexicans were working on the schoolhouse, and as they approached, Martin saw a young woman, her dress hiked up, her sleeves bunched, hammering a board on what would be the front porch.

"Hey, Grant," Ken called, and the woman stood up. Two or three nails protruded from her mouth and a wisp of hair raked her face gently in the breeze.

"Ho, there, Richman," the woman said, pulling the nails from her mouth. "Coffee's all boiled, a-setting on the stove. It'll positively grow hair on your chest. Or remove it, one."

The men laughed.

"Who's the tall one?" Miss Grant asked. "He looks like one of our nighthawks."

Ken said nothing. The woman laid down her hammer and approached the men, a faint smile on her face. "Hello, Ed," she said, stretching out her hand. "My name is Nancy Grant," she said. "Pleased to meet you. Any friend of Ken's is a friend of mine."

"Nancy, hon, meet Martin Baron."

"Pleased to meet you, Mr. Baron. Don't you own some cows or have a ranch around here?"

"Call me Martin, Miss Grant. And, yes, I have a few head of cattle."

"And you must call me Nancy," she said lightly. "Well, Ken, you and your friends go on inside. I'll be there directly."

Ken led the two men inside the small house, which was neatly appointed. They went to the modest kitchen where they could smell the coffee as soon as they entered. Martin saw that there were four chairs and he was surprised. He and Ed sat down while Ken got out tin cups and poured the coffee.

"What's that about war?" Martin asked Ed. "I read your headline."

Ed set the paper down on the table and unrolled it to reveal the headline. Martin stared at it for several seconds. "Civil?" he asked.

"Nothing civil about war, of course," Ed said, "but that's the term being bandied about in Washington and Austin."

"Meaning?"

"Meaning the South has seceded from the North and each side means to fight over the issue of slavery. Honest Abe has signed a proclamation declaring slavery illegal."

"That so?" Martin asked, as Ken set cups of steaming coffee before the two men, then turned to get his own cup.

"Sam Houston was ousted from his office as governor," Ed said, "and President Lincoln himself sent some emissaries down to Austin offering Sam troops to get him back at his desk."

"And?"

"Sam refused. Fact is, he and his family have already moved down to Cedar Point."

"Down to Galveston," Martin said.

Ed nodded. "He tried to get the South to hold together, putting out proclamations and such, but they all failed. I'm afraid it's too late to do anything now."

Ken sat down, blew on his coffee.

"How come?" Martin asked.

"Ten days ago, on April twelfth, Confederate forces fired on Fort Sumter."

"Where's that?"

"Charleston. South Carolina."

"What's Confederate forces?"

"The South has an army. Texas will probably get into it. At least that's what Houston was trying to prevent."

"Meaning?" Martin asked.

"Meaning, we might have to fight the North. You and your son might be wearing uniforms before long."

Martin took a sip of the hot coffee. He fixed Ed in a stare that did not waver.

"The state legislature ratified an amendment that puts Texas smack dab among the Confederate states bucking Lincoln," Ken said.

"And Lincoln called up seventy-five thousand troops to fight those of us who broke away from the Union," Ed added.

Martin let out a low whistle. "Jesus," he said.

"It looks pretty bad," Ed said.

"Bad? It smells to high heaven," Martin said. "You mean Texas is going to fight to keep slaves? Not this boy."

Ed looked sheepish as he bowed his head to bring the coffee cup to his lips. Ken took in a breath, let it out in a deep sigh.

"You may have to fight someone," Ken said.

"What in hell do you mean by that?" Martin asked.

"Slavery in this country's a big issue," Ken said. "A burr under the blanket of a lot of folks."

"Well, I don't cotton to slavery," Martin said.

"Those nighthawks Nancy mentioned. Thought you was one of 'em."

"Yeah?"

"They work for me."

"Gunslingers?"

"Not in that way, Martin." Ken leaned over the table, his elbows bracketing his coffee cup. "There are some who want to make a lot of money over this disruption in the government. I got word that slaves were being brought into the Rio Grande Valley illegally."

"Huh?"

Ken nodded. "Our friend Aguilar is out to get him some cash. He hired a man from New Orleans to smuggle slaves up to his ranch. Aguilar plans to sell 'em on the open market."

"Who's the man in New Orleans?"

"Reynaud."

"I know the sonofabitch," Martin said.

At that moment, Nancy entered the room. Her face was damp where she had washed off at the pump and her hands were clean.

"What sonofabitch would that be, Martin?" she asked, a lilt to her voice.

But none of the men said a word and Martin stared at her in wonder. She returned his gaze and there was a crooked little smile bending her lips as if they shared some secret together. Martin held his breath, then broke into a smile. He turned to Ken and cracked an even wider grin.

"Well, Ken, you sure hired yourself one hell of a schoolmarm. She's top notch in my tally book."

Ken smiled and the tension in the room was broken.

"Sit down, Nancy," Ken said, "and get to know Martin

Baron a little better. I think you'll find him refreshing after the louts you met in town."

"I'm beginning to see that, Ken," she said. She took a cup from the sideboard where Ken had placed it and poured coffee into it. Ken arose and pulled out a chair for her.

"I'm sure glad you aren't one of those nighthawks, Martin," Nancy said. "Now, what kind of cattle do you raise and how damned big is your little old ranch?"

22

·━·

A WHIPPOORWILL CALLED from the tree line beyond the thicket behind the Aguilar house and barn on the Rocking A Ranch. Matteo listened to the plaintive ripple of throaty notes and watched the western sky fade from a pale turquoise into a gray pall brimmed with a faint light from the dying sun.

A lantern sat on the ground, its shortened wick flickering feebly. A thin tendrill of black smoke floated from the tin chimney, just barely visible in the dim light of dusk. Matteo drew a breath and let out a satisfied *ahhh* sound.

"Do you hear that bird, David?" Matteo asked.

"I hear it," Wilhoit said, his voice soft as a whisper. "Reminds me of home."

"This is your home now. Did you have any trouble with the boy? Roy?"

"No, Ursula told him we were moving to Fort Worth."

"Good. We do not want Martin Baron to know too much."

"Ursula and I don't want the boy hurt."

"No. Do not worry. One day he will want to be close to his mother. I will give him land and that will be one less friend for Martin to rely on."

"Better than trying to run him off the land. Roy, I mean. He's a pistol, that one. Strong as a bull and with a temper Ursula says he got from his father."

"His father was a mean bastard. He had no heart."

"I did not know him."

"No, and you are better off for it. Your Ursula did not suit him. He had no love for her."

David said nothing, for he did not know the truth of it. Ursula did not talk much about Jack Killian and Roy never spoke about his father, to him, at least.

Matteo stepped out a foot or two and peered into the gathering darkness, toward the impenetrable brasada that he knew was out there, at the south end of the Rocking A spread. "Anytime, now, they should be coming," he said.

"If you say so."

"It will mean money for you."

"I know."

"But you do not like it much."

"No. Do you?"

"It is nothing to me," Matteo said.

"Then, I hope it will be nothing for me, as well."

"Ursula. She is a good woman for you?" Matteo asked.

"I could ask for no better."

"She has fire in her, no?"

"Matteo, you embarrass me."

"A man is not embarrassed by passion, *amigo mío*. If the woman has no fire in her, she is worthless."

"Ursula has more fire than I can handle."

Matteo laughed softly. David shifted his feet, either from nervousness, or because one of them was going to sleep. Matteo often talked of intimate things and it bothered David because he wanted his private life with Ursula to be private. But, he knew from the first that she was a passionate woman, lustful, even, and it was something that he was not used to. But, he liked her boldness because he had never been good with women, not smooth and wily as many men he knew were. He was shy, and Ursula complemented that shyness by teaching him ways to make love that he had never even dreamed of and that left him with a feeling of wonder.

Even after David's survey had shown that Roy Killian's acreage was not on Rocking A land, Matteo had offered him two thousand acres and help in building a house if he would stay on, live there, do other survey work. David had accepted because he needed the money, especially now that he had a wife. He had never imagined that Ursula would accept his offer to marry him and move away with him so quickly. He had made sure that the land given to him was properly surveyed, recorded and the deed in his hands showing his ownership free and clear.

"I read all of your report last night, David," Matteo said.

"I'm glad you did."

"I was disappointed that the deed did not show Killian was on my land."

"That couldn't be helped."

"But, you wrote something that caught my eye."

"The creek," David said.

"Ah, you know, then."

"Bandera Creek. It could be a problem."

"But it is not a problem now."

"No. But waterways change course, rivers erode banks, creeks run rampant after rainstorms."

"So, what can I do about this Bandera Creek?"

"Nothing, at the moment. But, I walked it, and it is very close to Roy Killian's property. And, it could eventually even come on to the Baron range."

"We could dam it," Matteo said.

"It would do no good if there was a flash flood. I

marked the creek so that you would know, could keep an eye on its course."

"That is good, David. You mention water much in your report."

"Yes."

"Why did you do that? If it is not a problem now, perhaps it will never be a problem."

David swallowed a wad of phlegm in his throat. He was no longer listening for the sounds of the deer in the thicket. "Because, since man was put on this earth, water has always been a bone of contention between neighbors."

"A bone of contention?"

"Wars have been started over water rights. Murders have been committed. Friendships have been destroyed."

"I did not know that."

"In fact, water may have been one of the reasons Cain killed Abel. In the Bible."

"I know the story in the Bible."

"Abel was a tender of sheep. Cain, a farmer."

"So?"

"So, perhaps they both had to use the same water source and they may have fought over a creek, or a river. Abel's sheep would have needed water to drink and Cain may have diverted the same stream to irrigate his crops."

"But Cain did not kill Abel over water."

"No. He killed his brother because he was angry at God."

"So, why do you mention the water?"

"Cain may have already hated his brother over land and water rights. God just gave him a better reason to kill his brother."

"Interesting," Matteo said.

"Just remember, water is essential to all life. If you can't get any, and your neighbor has some, you will first ask for water, and then you will try and buy it, and then you will fight for it."

"And kill for it, eh, David?"

"Yes, you would kill for water if your neighbor had plenty and would not give you any."

"Then, we must see that this does not happen, do you not think?"

"That is why I wrote it down in my report," David said.

"Good. I will keep my eyes open."

Just what Matteo wanted of him, David was not yet sure. But, Matteo asked him a lot of questions about surveying and geology and the legality of Spanish land grants. Some of the questions were beyond David's expertise, but he answered as best he could and offered to find out whatever Matteo wanted to know.

So, the two men had formed a tenuous friendship and Matteo had promised that David could earn a living off the land if he stayed with Matteo, helped him expand his ranching and other activities.

The good part was that Ursula didn't care how he made his living. She loved him and wanted him and he was happy to comply with so generous a woman. David wanted to earn money, and Matteo had paid him generously for his survey work. But, the business of this night had left him with a fluttering in his stomach, a weak feeling in his knees. What Matteo was doing was well beyond David's field and he was almost certain that it was not legal. But, in this case, he did not want to know too much, not anymore, really, than Matteo wished to tell him.

Matteo dug out the makings, offered the sack of tobacco to David, who shook his head. David was too nervous to roll a cigarette and he did not want to have a pipe in his hand when the wagon rolled up.

"This is a good time of the day," Matteo said as he spread the thin paper and made a trough with his finger. He shook tobacco onto the paper, spread it evenly with a single finger. Then, he pulled the string on the sack with his teeth and closed it, put it away. He finished rolling the cigarette and licked the flap so that it stuck tight. He produced a box of matches and struck one on the sandpaper side, bursting the head into flame. He lit the cigarette, inhaled deeply. "So quiet you can hear the deer down in the brush."

David could not hear them.

"They sound like squirrels," Matteo said, "but not so noisy."

"I can't hear them."

"It is only a little rustling sound."

David tried to hear the sounds, but he could not hear anything above the pounding of his heart. Then, he did hear something, but it was far off, and was not a deer.

"I think I hear a wagon," David said.

"Yes, it is coming. That will be the Frenchman, Reynaud."

"You mentioned him. Something bad between him and Baron."

"He wants to kill Martin Baron."

"And, you don't care," David said.

"Reynaud is a man of many, what do you say? Skills? Purposes?"

David wanted to say "scoundrel," but he didn't. He wondered if Matteo meant to pay Reynaud to kill Martin Baron. He would not put it past him.

"Why does Reynaud want to kill Baron?"

"Martin raped his sister. She is with child."

"I see," David said, but he did not understand any of it. He was still somewhat wary of Matteo, even though he had been treated well by the rancher. It was just that he felt uncomfortable around Mexicans because he knew very little of their language. When he was doing the survey on Killian's land, he would hear the Mexicans speak in their native tongue and it bothered him because he could not understand. He always felt as if they were talking about him. And, now that he thought about it, he felt as if all Mexicans were secretive and that was why he did not always feel comfortable around Matteo.

"You must not worry about these things, David," Matteo said. "Reynaud might kill Martin. Martin might kill him. Did you meet the son, Anson?"

"No," David said. "I only saw Martin once, briefly."

"How did he strike you?"

David thought about it for a few seconds. Martin had ridden by and stopped to talk to Roy. He had not been able to hear what they were saying, but Roy pointed at him, and a moment later Martin Baron rode up to David and introduced himself. He asked how the survey was going, David remembered, and then had ridden away without comment.

"I only spoke to him for a moment. He did not say much. It's hard to figure a man so quickly."

"Martin is a dreamer, but he has a feel for the land. He is a sailor at heart, though, and I do not think he will do well with cattle. He has learned much, but he was not born to the land as I was."

"I see," David said, and he was beginning to understand Matteo from what he had just said. He probably resented Martin as a latecomer to what once had been Spanish, and then Mexican, land. He had seen such feelings before with other surveys he had done. Resentment between neighboring landowners. It always ran deep and was sometimes murderous.

"There," Matteo said. "There is the wagon. See it?"

"Yes, I see it," David said.

The wagon had emerged from the trees and was headed their way. Three outriders flanked it and carried rifles that glinted faintly in the starlight. Matteo reached down and turned the wick up on the lantern.

As the wagon drew closer, David saw that there were people in it, all huddled together so that he could not count them. But, he could see bobbing heads. He heard no voices and thought that was odd.

The wagon pulled to a stop and the driver set the brake and stepped down. He was well dressed, David noted, wearing a flat-crowned hat, polished boots that gleamed in the lantern glow, and a well-fitted suit.

"Matteo."

"Reynaud. How many?"

"A dozen. Do you want to see them?"

"Yes. We have a place for them in the barn."

David felt his scalp prickle as Matteo spoke in Spanish to the outriders. Matteo had not told him what cargo Reynaud was bringing, but he was beginning to get a queasy feeling in the pit of his stomach.

Two of the outriders grabbed hands and dragged people from the wagon. The other pushed them toward the lantern light where Matteo could take a look at them. Matteo lifted the lantern and held it high, looking into the faces of the people. David counted them, an even dozen, all black people, ranging in age from about twelve, he figured, to men in their thirties.

The contraband slaves were all barefoot, and some wore clothing made of burlap or cotton. They appeared sheepish as Matteo shone the light in their eyes. He looked at each one.

"All good?" Matteo asked Reynaud.

"All sound. They'll bring top dollar."

"Where?"

"I have an auction set up in San Antonio."

"You'll have to feed them and haul them up there," Matteo said.

"Tomorrow night, I will leave."

David looked at the hapless Negroes lined up. He didn't know how sound they were, but he knew they were tired and sleepy. They were so quiet, he wondered if their tongues had been cut out.

There was something eerie about seeing the dark people lined up like cattle or sheep, silent, unmoving, awaiting an uncertain fate. He could not look any of them in the eye and he had the sudden inclination to take a bath, scrub away the feeling of dirtiness.

"Reynaud, this is David Wilhoit. David, you will accompany Reynaud to San Antonio? As my agent?"

"I don't know," David said.

"Do you not trust me, Matteo?" Reynaud asked. He did not offer his hand to David.

"I trust you. But, I wish David to act as my agent and report to me the results of the auction. He may have to make the next trip to New Orleans."

"These people were brought in to Corpus Christi," Reynaud said. "I have friends there."

"Well, David, will you go with Reynaud?"

David looked again at the slaves, chattel for sale on the auction block. He knew his decision would affect his future, Ursula's. If he refused, Matteo would hold him in disfavor. If he accepted, he would be bound to the man, and he would be guilty of dealing in contraband. He wished he could discuss it with Ursula first, but he knew Matteo was waiting for an immediate answer.

"I'll go," David said, his voice so soft, Matteo had to strain to hear him.

"Good," Matteo said. "Then it is settled. David, you will be paid along with Reynaud. I think you will like the money these people will bring."

Reynaud smiled and David had the strong urge to slap his face and wipe the smirk from it. But, he only nodded and turned away, his stomach suddenly the enemy, roiling with a foul bile that threatened to burst and surge up his throat and embarrass him in front of everyone there.

"Take the people to the barn," Matteo told Reynaud. "There is a place to lock them up. My men will feed them. David, come to the house with me and we will have a drink with Reynaud when he is finished."

"I—I'm sorry, Matteo. I don't feel well. I want to go home."

Matteo's expression shifted from benign to hostile in an instant. David felt the heat of his anger and tried to think of something to say.

"It seems David does not share our enthusiasm," Reynaud said.

"Take the people away," Matteo barked. "I will walk a ways with David. This is all new to him."

David felt relief. Reynaud turned away and David took one last look at the forlorn group of Negroes. One of the boys clung to one of the women and a young girl clung to the boy. He watched them shuffle away, prodded by the Mexicans with rifles. Reynaud picked up the lantern and followed after them.

Then, it was dark, and he and Matteo were alone.

"You must not show your weakness to Reynaud," Matteo said. "He will bear watching when you go to San Antonio."

"I'll be careful," David said, and his heart sank deep into a place where it was even darker than the night. He knew that he had stepped beyond a place to which he would never be able to return.

And, even though he walked with Matteo back toward the house, he felt all alone.

23

＋

A HUSH SEEMED to fall over the land after Bone rode away. Anson stared after him for a long moment, then heard Peebo clear his throat as if impatient to move on.

"You don't trust that Injun, do you, son?" Peebo asked.

"I don't know." The truth was, Anson didn't know what to make of Bone's visit, his help. He was still startled at seeing him, bewildered that this emergence from his past had appeared so suddenly, and so suddenly disappeared again. He felt that same compulsion he had felt before, when Bone had left the Box B, to chase after him, go wherever he would go.

But, he had grown since that dark night, and he no longer felt the same about Bone. Yet, in a way, he did. He envied Bone's free life, the secrets of his race he carried with him. He had always been fascinated by the Apaches, and, despite their troubles with them, he held a kind of grudging respect for them. He knew, deep down, that the Apaches were the true owners of the land, and that he and his father and the other ranchers had somehow taken the land away from them.

But, he wasn't about to give any of it up over sentiment. He had learned that much from his father. The land belonged, Martin had told him, to whomever was the strongest, to the man who could fight for it and keep it.

"We gonna stay around here all goddamned day, son?" Peebo asked.

"No, we'd better keep going. One close call was enough."

"You figure we got another day of walking to the ranch?"

"A long day," Anson said.

Just then, as the two started to walk away from that place of danger and death, they heard a noise that froze the marrow in their bones. It sounded like a roar, a roar like neither one had ever heard before.

"What in hell was that?" Peebo asked.

Anson shook his head. "Damned if I know. But, it scared the hell out of me."

Then, they heard the sound again, a deep bellowing, almost a roar, that made the hackles rise on the backs of their necks, the hairs on their arms stiffen as if from a sudden chill.

A half second later, they heard a human scream, almost unidentifiable in its tortured agony. The scream split the air with a raging series of notes that curdled their blood. Then, the sounds of thrashing and yelling, and hoofbeats, all jumbled together and both men ducked instinctively as if about to be smothered by a wild stampede.

"Jesus," Peebo said.

"Come on," Anson yelled, jerking his rifle off the ground. "Somebody's in a hell of a fix."

Peebo didn't need much urging. He sprang after Anson and the two raced toward the sound of the commotion. They dashed past a clump of mesquite trees and came to a small open plain and what they saw next turned their stomachs as they came to a sudden halt.

There, on the edge of the open meadow, a huge long-horn bull swung its massive horns from left to right, and up and down. Impaled on one huge horn was part of a human carcass, red with blood, jagged with flesh torn asunder.

Apaches ran in all directions, leaving their horses behind as they fled on foot. Peebo's horses fought against ropes and hobbles, bucking and kicking, screaming with terror. A bunch of smaller longhorns watched from the trees in silence, some chewing their cuds, others switching their tails disconsolately.

The huge bull kicked up a cloud of dust as it pawed the ground with its forehooves, circled and swung its horns to rid itself of the bloody carcass. On the ground, nearby, an Apache head sat upright, wide-eyed, mouth slack, and a pair of legs and the bottom part of the Apache twitched and kicked spasmodically, a disembodied horror that made the two men blink and lose all power of speech.

Anson felt his stomach retch and buck and he doubled over, fought for air to keep from vomiting. Peebo turned ghost-white, fingered the trigger guard of his rifle as if struck dumb by the horrible sight.

Then, they heard another scream and saw a thrashing among the mesquite trees. When they looked, they saw a wounded Apache brave trying to crawl away, half of his entrails in one hand, the other trailing after him like coiled blue snakes.

Peebo swore and Anson doubled over to vomit, but nothing came up, for he had no food. He struggled with the dry heaves until his eyes watered and then gulped in air and stood straight to clear his lungs of the foul air he had created.

The big white bull swung its head in a mighty arc and the blood-soaked torso flew off his horn and landed a few yards away with a sickening thump. Peebo brought his rifle to his shoulder, but he was shaking so bad, he could not get a bead on the errant bull.

Hearing the sound, the bull turned their way and bellowed a loud roar at them. Peebo brought his rifle down. Anson squeaked a warning: "Run, Peebo."

Peebo turned and ran toward the safety of the trees. Anson waited but a second, then began to chase after him. The bull roared again and pawed the ground, stirring up dust. Then, the two men stopped and looked back.

The white bull had heard the Apache in the trees and charged after him. The Apache rose up and let his entrails fall to his lap. He shot out his right arm, held it rigid as if to ward off the bull's charge.

"Godamighty," Peebo breathed.

"Damn," Anson muttered.

The bull charged the wounded Apache and swung its head left, sweeping its right horn in an arc with terrible force. The blow struck the Apache on the left shoulder and broke it before the horn struck his head and smashed it like a pumpkin. Blood spurted and sprayed from the gory opening between the Apache's shoulder blades and his head flew off a foot or two and rolled sickeningly out into the open.

Anson could still hear the Apache's screams although he knew there was no sound coming from that broken head. The white bull turned and began to stomp the Apache's remains into a bloody pulp, roaring and bellowing its rage as it ripped and tore with its horns and cloven hooves.

"Sonofabitch," Peebo whispered.

"That's one mean bastard," Anson said, breathing freely now, but feeling the rawness of his stomach lining, the swirling sickness within.

Then, the bull gave a last smash of its boss to the ragged corpse and, bellowing loudly, disappeared into the brush. The other cattle ran after its leader and a great silence settled over the crimson-stained battlefield.

Peebo and Anson listened for a long time as the hoof-beats faded. They watched the hobbled horses blow and snort, shake their heads as they tried to escape the smell of death that hung over the meadow.

Peebo turned to Anson, who seemed to be still in shock. "Well, what do you think, son?"

"I—I think we better get the hell out of here. I never saw anything like that in my life."

"Me, neither. But, them are my horses yonder and we been walkin' too godamned long."

"What if that bull comes back?" Anson asked.

"Then, we got several kinds of trouble."

"Some of your horses ran off, I think."

"I'm not going to catch those, but there are five over yonder all yarned up like Christmas presents. We just as well take them."

"Are they broke?" Anson asked.

"Hell, no. But we can sure as hell halterbreak 'em and ride off before that white bull comes back and makes 'em into glue and hide."

Anson drew in a deep breath, let it out in a sigh. "Well, let's do it damned quick, Peebo."

Peebo grinned and the two started across the meadow, rifles held at the ready, looking all around, listening for any alien sound. Anson looked at the torso of the Apache that had been impaled on the bull's horn and got sick all over again, but he kept going.

Peebo walked up to a dun and grabbed the rope around its neck. The horse pulled away from him and started backing down on its haunches. Peebo lifted his rifle with one hand and rammed the butt into the horse's ribs, cursed it.

The hobbles kept the dun from running off and before the horse could recover, Peebo had jumped onto its back. The horse began to buck and Peebo held onto the rope with one hand while he beat the horse in the flanks with the rifle stock.

"Go on, Anson. Jump on one and enjoy the ride."

Anson approached a lean sorrel with rolling eyes that flickered danger in their depths. The horse was quivering all over as Anson got close to him. Carefully, Anson stepped slowly up to it as it backed away. He grabbed the rope, then began to speak to the horse in a calm voice. "Easy, boy, easy."

The horse was wild-eyed and skittery, but Anson walked up to its head, playing out rope until he had it snubbed close to the knot. He kept talking to the animal and realized he was shaking as much as the horse.

"Steady, boy, easy," Anson said.

Anson pressed his upper body against the horse's flank, kept speaking to it. "Just hold on, boy. Stay steady. We'll get along."

Slowly, Anson began to inch his way upward until he was draped over its back. Then, he edged his right foot up over its rump and slid forward. As soon as he raised up, the sorrel began to buck, nearly jarring Anson loose from his perch.

He held on, continued speaking to the animal as it twisted and fishtailed around the meadow, landing each time it bucked with hard stiff legs that shook Anson to his bones.

Finally, the horse lost heart in bucking and slowed down. Anson patted its neck and rubbed it with a gentle hand until it calmed down. He leaned over and looped the bitter end of the rope around through the other loop and tied it in a loose knot. The rope didn't make a perfect halter, but gave him two places to hold and he thought he might rope break the horse in time.

"About set?" Peebo asked a few moments later.

"We can try it."

"I'm going to lead those other horses. Maybe it'll quiet ours down some."

"I can take one," Anson said.

"Good. Then, maybe that sorrel won't feel so much like a prisoner."

Peebo caught up two of his horses and Anson picked up the rope of the third one. The horses were skittery, and they kept eyeing the pieces of dead Apache, but as Peebo took the lead, they followed, seemingly happy to leave that place of terror. Their rubbery nostrils quivered until the two men and the horses were well past the smell.

"Which way?" Peebo asked.

Anson pointed westward. Peebo nodded.

"Be there tonight, if we keep up this pace," Anson said.

"Good. Ain't none of these steeds worth a damn riding bareback."

Anson chuckled. Already, he could feel the bones in his butt beginning to ache. But, it felt good to be on horseback again after walking his feet to blisters. He breathed the air and looked at the high blue sky.

And, he thought about that white longhorn bull, the one the Mexicans called El Blanco. Someday, he thought, he would have to run it down and put a rope on the beast. He would take great pleasure in planting the Box B brand on its mean old white hide.

24

ROY STEPPED OUT of the house as the wagon rolled up, came to a stop. He recognized the two women on the seat. The hard-eyed woman and the rusty-haired gal. Neither of them waved or smiled. The taciturn woman set the hand brake and sat there as the young girl climbed down. She was as agile and graceful as a deer.

"Hello, Roy," the girl said. "Do you remember me?"

"Yes'm."

"Are you going to invite me and my mother in?"

"Well, yes'm, I reckon." He did not know her name and as she drew close, his heart began to thrum a bit faster, throbbing enough so that he could hear it and thought she might be hearing it too.

The girl turned to the woman on the wagon and beckoned for her to get down. Roy saw that they had carpetbags and sacks of something in the wagon and wondered why they had come all the way out here. He knew he hadn't invited them.

"You're quite a fighter, Roy," the girl said.

"Ho-how did you know my name?"

"Oh, everyone knows your name at the Longhorn Saloon. That was all they talked about last night."

"I, uh, I don't know your name, ma'am."

"I'm Wanda Fancher, and this is my mother, Hattie."

"Yes'm," Roy said, slightly overwhelmed by the two women. He was about to turn and wave them into the house, but Wanda swept past him, followed by her mother. He went inside behind them, a sheepish pallor to his pasty face. He felt guilty about what he had done at the Longhorn and thought maybe the two women were there seeking damages. He might have caused Wanda harm, but he couldn't remember.

"Do you have tea?" Wanda asked. "If not, we brought some. I like tea, do you?"

"Yes'm. I think there's tea. There might be some fire left in the stove."

Wanda spoke to her mother in low tones, just above a whisper. Roy could not hear what she said. The stolid woman went to the stove and opened the firebox. She took a stick of kindling and poked the morning fire into a blaze and added kindling. Wanda looked around as Roy stood there, dumbfounded, incapable of speech.

Hattie said something to Wanda. Wanda replied in the same lazy drawl. The two women walked around the small house, looking in and under things, lifting a pot, opening a cupboard, as the pot on the stove began to rattle with heat. Hattie set out three cups and rummaged around until she found the tin of tea. She spooned leaves into the cups as Wanda returned to confront Roy.

"I had a long talk with your mother last night, Roy," Wanda said. "She told us she was leaving to get married and that you needed looking after."

"Huh?" Roy said.

"I agree with her."

"Look, ma'am, who are you?"

"Why don't you sit down on that settee there? We can talk while my mother prepares the tea."

Wanda's speech seemed refined, but carried an accent Roy was unfamiliar with, a slanted tang that was not Texan, but seemed liquid and smooth, even cultured, as if it might be from back east.

Roy allowed Wanda to lead him to the small couch. And he did not resist when she gently pushed him down on it and took a chair nearby. He stared at Wanda and thought she was even more beautiful in the daylight than she had seemed in the saloon the night before.

Hattie walked past them, out the front door. Roy stared after her, saw her walk to the back of the wagon, reach in and pull some valises from it. She returned, carrying what he figured were purses and satchels. She set the carpetbags on the floor, then handed Wanda one of the purses.

Wanda smiled at Roy and set the purse on her lap.

"What are you doing?" Roy asked.

"Wait a minute," Wanda said, as Hattie returned to the stove. "Ah, here it is," she said, as she pulled a piece of paper from her purse. "There. Can you read, Roy?"

"Sure I can read."

"This ought to explain why we're here," she said, handing him the sheet of paper.

Roy took it with slightly trembling hands. He began to read the writing, which he recognized as his mother's. When he got to the bottom, there was his mother's signature and two others. He could only make out one of them, Wanda Fancher.

"What the hell is this?" he asked, looking up at Wanda.

"Your mother took David Wilhoit's survey maps to the Land Office in Baronsville and laid claim to the land this house is on."

"What?"

"That's what she told me. After you got into that fight, she leased the land to me for a year."

Roy read over the papers. Wanda Fancher did indeed have a lease on the land Martin Baron had given him. For this she had paid the sum of fifty dollars. The document further stated that at the end of the year, if she was married to her son, one Roy Armstrong Killian, she would be granted full title, free and clear.

"Well, I'll be a sonofabitch," Roy muttered.

"That's no way to talk about your mother, Roy." Wanda reached over and snatched the papers from Roy's hand. When he looked up at her, she wore a curious smile, a maddening smile that he could not fathom. He did not know if she was laughing at him or merely gloating.

"You mean I got to move out? Offen my own land?"

"No, not at all," Wanda said. "I plan to build on this place, make the house larger, build a barn, a guest house, stables, corrals for the cattle you and I will raise. Within a week, Mr. Richman will see to it that the lumber I ordered is delivered. Lumber, nails, hammer, saws, all bought at the mercantile in town."

"Lady, I don't even know you."

"Oh, but I know you. That is, I knew your father, Jack Killian. He came to the Ozarks once to trade horses. He told me a lot about you."

Roy began to squirm. He looked again at the enigmatic Wanda Fancher and she was still wearing that half smile, that irritating, grating little smile on her pretty face.

"Where in hell are you going to get the money to do all this?"

"We already have the money," Wanda said with a smug smile.

"Oh?"

"That's right," Hattie said as she emerged from the other room carrying a tray with steaming cups of tea atop it, complete with napkins, spoons, and sugar. "My husband was a good man, but a very miserly man. Until he died last year, I had no idea that he was stashing away some of his money. He has provided a comfortable life for Wanda and me, God bless his soul."

Roy shook his head. "I—I just don't know what to make of all this. I mean, my mother left real sudden, and then you show up and tell me you got a lease on this place and that you're going to make all these changes. I got to see Martin Baron about all this."

"It won't do you any good. My lease is legal. Mr. Richman assured me that I have every right to live here. And, that's what we're going to do. If you're the man I think you are, we can build a wonderful ranch here. In time, I will talk to Mr. Baron and see if we can purchase more land from him."

"Jesus God Almighty," Roy said.

"I think we're going to like it here, don't you, Mother?" Wanda said, ignoring Roy's outburst.

"Yes, it is a very nice house. We will make it a mite more liveable," Hattie said, in a drawl Roy had never heard before.

Roy looked around the room, feeling trapped. When his gaze stopped on Hattie, she wore that same puzzling little smile and his heart sank like a stone in his chest. It seemed to him that the bottom of the floor had dropped out from under him and he was falling straight down into the very bowels of the earth.

25

MARTIN HAD DIFFICULTY in keeping his gaze from lingering on Nancy Grant. Every time he looked at her, their eyes met and he turned away, feeling the heat of her, and the heat rising in him, burning his neck, scorching his loins. But, it was obvious to him that Ken had staked Nancy out for himself. The way Ken looked at her, with something like adoration on his face, told him that much.

Yet Nancy seemed to pay no more attention to Ken than she did to Ed Wales or himself. She seemed the perfect hostess, engaging in light banter, smiling, laughing at Ken's jokes, attentive to the silent Ed, but trying to draw him into the conversation.

"Ed, let me take a look at your paper," she said.

Ed handed it to her and the conversation halted as she perused the headline, scanned the copy of the main article. "It's very well written," she said. "Did you write this?"

"Yes, ma'am," Ed said.

"Ominous, too. Do you really think the North and South will take up arms against each other?"

"That's the talk in Austin and Washington," Ed replied.

Nancy handed the newspaper back to Ed. "I dread it," she said. "Civil war. It's such a terrible prospect."

"Yes'm," Ed said.

"Maybe it won't come to that," Ken said.

"All over the issue of slavery," Nancy said.

"Well, there's more to it than that," Ed said. "States' rights seems to be the main issue."

"Then, why have a united statehood?" Nancy asked, and Martin was impressed with her intelligence. He listened to her every word, hung on each phrase, watched her mouth form the words and the way her throat quivered, her delicate clean throat, when she spoke. He felt warm and the coffee was not helping any.

During those moments of fascination with Nancy, Martin began to think about Caroline, and a deep longing stirred within him, a longing for the Caroline he had once known, and loved, and married, and the dark abyss that lay between them now, a chasm so huge he could no longer cross it, no longer desired to bridge the vast distance between them.

In Nancy's lilting voice, he heard echoes of a Caroline that once was, a happy woman who was warm and giving and caring and had since turned into a barren creature with no affection for him, hardly any civility. And, he supposed, a lot of that was his fault. But, since she had been raped and he had made the terrible mistake of wrongly accusing Juanito, he could hardly bear to look her in the eye. He could scarcely bear to look himself in the eye, for that matter.

The talk at the table drifted around him as Martin withdrew inside himself, and he forgot about Nancy, his thoughts dwelling on Caroline and Anson, and the terrible mistakes he had made in his life. But, as he looked at the fresh young woman again, he thought of the emp-

tiness in his life, and his loins ached for a woman, not
Nancy, but a woman he could care for and who would
understand him. It was something he had never thought
much about before, and he felt guilty every time he did.
Caroline was dependent on him, but he knew there was
no longer any love between them. There was hardly even
any companionship. She was just someone who lived in
the big house and who thought only of the blind boy,
Lazaro, and, of course, Anson, whom neither of them
hardly ever saw during spring roundup.

"A penny, Mr. Baron," Nancy said.

Martin heard her say the words, but did not know she
was talking to him.

"Martin?" Ken said.

"Oh, huh? What?"

"A penny for your thoughts, Mr. Baron," Nancy said.
"My goodness. I must be boring you all to death."

"Oh, no," Martin said. "Just thinkin'."

He drank from his cup to hide his embarrassment. He
looked around the table and saw that Ed, Ken and Nancy
were all staring at him.

"I—I should get back, I reckon."

"What's your hurry?" Ken asked.

Just then, before Martin could answer, they all heard
hoofbeats. Horses were coming at a pretty good clip.
Ken was the first to rise from his chair and go to the
window. He looked out, then turned to face Martin.

"You can't go just yet, Marty," Ken said. "Here come
the two nighthawks I told you about."

"Oh," Nancy said, "Cullie and Tom. My, they seem
in such a hurry."

"Nancy," Ken said, "we're going to have to leave you
now. Thanks for the coffee and all . . ."

"But, can't they come in?"

"No, it's business, I'm afraid. Ed, Martin. Let's go
outside."

"Sorry, ma'am," Ed said. "Hate to rush off. I'll leave
the paper with you."

"Thanks, Ed," she said.

Martin arose from his chair, nodded to Nancy. He was interested in meeting the men Ken had told him about, but was at a loss for words to say good-bye to Nancy. He tipped his hat to her and was out the door before she could say anything.

Cullie and Tom rode up in a hurry and reined in just in front of the house. Their clothes and horses were covered with dust and the sweat on their horses was turning to mud. Rifles jutted from boots attached to their saddles, and both men were wearing cap and ball six-guns.

Tom swung down from his horse, left the reins dangling. Cullie slid out of the saddle to join him as Tom approached Ken Richman. The horses stayed where they were, reins touching the ground.

"Reynaud's got them slaves up at Aguilar's."

"When?" Ken asked.

"Last night."

"What's Aguilar going to do with them?"

"Damned if I know. He's got 'em in his barn for now."

"They won't move 'em at night," Cullie said. "We thought we'd go back up when the sun falls and find out what's what."

The horses wheezed and blew, their sides bellowing out as they sucked in air. They switched their tails, whisking at flies and shook their heads to rid themselves of the pests.

Cullie's eyes were red rimmed from lack of sleep, as were Tom's. It was obvious to Martin that the two men had ridden a long way. If they had been at the Rocking A the night before, they must have ridden all night to get to Baronsville.

"I'll go with you," Ken said.

Martin looked at his friend. "Why are you getting into this, Ken?"

"If we let Aguilar practice slave trading, we risk some of the blame rubbing off on us."

"That makes sense," Martin said. "So, what do you plan to do?"

"Take those slaves away from him once Reynaud tries to take them someplace to sell them."

"And, then what?" Martin asked. "What are you going to do with the slaves?"

"I don't know," Ken said.

"There are an even dozen of 'em," Tom said. "Men, women and kids."

"Seems to me you're buying into more trouble than you can handle, Ken. Where did Jules Reynaud get the slaves? Off the boat? Or did he steal them? Which is more likely."

"I don't know," Ken said, his brow knitted in thought.

The hammering next door stopped, and there was a silence in the group of men. Martin could hear Nancy talking to the Mexican laborers. Her voice barely carried, but he was pleased to hear her speaking in Spanish, telling the men they could stop work for five minutes.

The horses blew again and one of them nickered.

"We got to walk them horses before we water them, Cullie," Tom said. "Ken, we thought we'd get a bite to eat at the Longhorn, then head back. You just say the word."

Cullie walked away, picked up the reins of the two horses, started walking them away to cool them down.

"Cullie, do you want to meet Mr. Baron?" Ken called after him.

"I know who he is," Cullie said.

"Tom Harris, shake hands with Martin Baron," Ken said.

"Pleased to meet you, Baron."

"Equally," Martin said, thinking in Spanish as he pondered the idea of Aguilar smuggling slaves into the Rio Grande Valley. It could present a problem for him and the other ranchers.

"Well, Martin, Cullie and Tom are waiting for me to

give them the word," Ken said. "What do you want to do about those slaves?"

Ed Wales cleared his throat. Martin and Ken both looked at him. Tom was studying his sweaty hands, the grime in the lifelines, caked in the fissures like black worms.

"You have something to say, Ed?" Martin asked.

"It may not be my place, but I was thinking . . ."

"Go ahead."

"Well," Ed said, "seems to me that you could kill a couple of birds with one stone."

"How's that?" Martin asked.

"If you were to obtain those slaves from Aguilar, or Reynaud, and you didn't know what to do with them, you could grant them their freedom."

"What?" Ken exclaimed.

"Wait a minute," Martin said. "Let's hear him out."

Ken nodded to Ed.

"Well, sir, if you were to grant the slaves their freedom, you couldn't be accused of keeping slaves, if Texas should vote later on to be a free state. And, if not, you'd still be all right. You could just turn the slaves loose, or put an ad in some papers—"

"Wait a minute," Martin said. "If I gave the slaves their freedom, they'd be free to go where they wanted to, right?"

"Well, I suppose . . ." Ed said.

"But, if they wanted to stay here, say, and work for me, they could do that, too."

"Sure," Ed said, "I guess they could do that. You'd be harboring stolen slaves, though."

"He's right, Martin," Ken said.

Tom hawked up a gob of phlegm and spat into the dirt. He appeared to be disinterested in the conversation and kept looking up at the sun to mark its course across the sky.

"If I gave these Negroes jobs on my ranch, that would be legal, wouldn't it?" Martin asked.

"You wouldn't want to do that, Baron," Tom said.

"Why in hell not?"

"You don't want a bunch of raggedy-ass niggers on your spread . . ."

"Look, Harris," Martin said. "I don't give a damn about your religion, your politics or whether you're a goddamned bigot or not, but I've been thinking about this slave problem a long time. No man has any right to own another human being. And, those Negroes are human beings."

"If you say so," Tom said, a sullen tone to his voice.

Martin ignored him and turned to Ken.

"I say we get those slaves away from Aguilar any way we can and set them free. I'll give them a choice. If they want to work for an honest dollar on the Box B, I'll give them shelter, food and found. That sound all right to you?"

"Christ, Martin. I don't know."

"Do you have a better idea, Ken?"

Ken dropped his head. He wore a sheepish look on his face. Ed smiled. Tom turned away and spat again into the dirt, stirring up a tiny cloud of dust. At the end of the street, Cullie turned, leading the horses back to Nancy's house and the unfinished school building.

"Look, it makes no never mind to me," Tom said. "But, unless we get to going, we'll never find out where Reynaud takes them niggers."

"Tell you what, Tom," Martin said. "I'll stake you and Cullie to some grub and I'll ride out to the Rocking A with you."

"Ain't no need for that, Baron."

"There is if I plan to free those slaves—if we get them away from Reynaud. I'll ride along with you."

"You're not packin' iron, Baron."

"Ken can give me a rifle and pistol, can't you, Ken?"

"Can do," Ken said.

"Let's do it. I'll meet you and Cullie at the Longhorn. Okay?"

"Sure, Baron, if that's what you want."

"Maybe we can clear some of those stumps between us over some grub, Tom," Martin said, looking Harris straight in the eyes.

"I reckon maybe we can," Tom said.

Martin waited as Tom walked away toward Cullie.

"You sure you want to do this, Martin?" Ken asked.

"You worried?"

"No. It's just that . . ."

"Ken, let me tell you something. I've let you have your head pretty much in my business. Maybe you ought to back off some, and let me handle some of it."

Ken stepped back a couple of paces, his face drawn and colorless.

"You don't like what I've done for Baronsville?"

"No, you've done a hell of a job," Martin said. "But, sometimes a man can get too much leather in his hand and pull a hard rein. I don't know those two fellers you hired on, but I know saddle trash when I see it. You might trust 'em, but I wouldn't hire gunnies like them if my life was on the line."

"They're hard men doing a hard job, Martin. I bought 'em with tax money. Didn't cost you a dime."

"You stick to town business, Ken," Martin said, and started walking back to the saloon, leaving Ed and Ken standing there. When he was out of earshot, Ed spoke up.

"Trouble?" he asked.

"I don't know, Ed. Martin's got something in his craw."

"I noticed him looking Nancy over pretty good."

"No, that's not it. Martin is quick to judge a man. Let's just hope he makes his peace with Tom and Cullie. Those men work for me and they don't know Martin like I do. They might not take to him."

"And?" Ed asked.

"Ed, either one of those men would kill Martin in the blink of an eye and never think a thing of it."

"Don't you think you ought to warn Martin?"

Ken shook his head. "Nope. Martin knows it, same as I. And, he never was one to back away from a hornet's nest if there was honey in it."

"But, slaves?"

"Yeah, he's got a burr under his blanket about those slaves, that's for sure. I wonder why."

Ed sighed. "He seems a very complex man, Martin Baron."

"Oh, he's a tangle, all right, like a big thicket. You think he's going one way and he goes another."

"Well, I hope it all works out," Ed said.

Ken turned toward the house as something caught the corner of his eye. Nancy stood at the door. He waved to her and tipped his hat. She waved back.

"Come on, Ed," Ken said, "I'll have to get a rifle, pistol, powder and ball for Martin. Some grub for the trail."

Ed looked back at Nancy, who was still standing in the doorway. She smiled. He wondered if she was trying to figure out where Martin had gone or if she was just looking after Ken.

Martin was married, he knew, but he had also heard there was something wrong with his wife. He wondered if Baron was the type of man to stray. It was a situation that might bear watching, he thought.

"Don't even think it, Ed," Ken said. "Nancy's not Martin's type."

Startled, Ed spluttered for a moment. "Do you read minds, Ken?"

"I read some minds real well," Ken said affably.

26

THEY SPOKE SOFTLY in a dialect of the Bantu language. In the darkness, they seemed to the Mexican guards like invisible people. Huddled together in the makeshift cell in the Aguilar barn, they complained of hunger and thirst among themselves. Claude, a boy of thirteen, lay next to a pile of straw, gripping his belly. He had not eaten in three days.

The Mexicans listened to them for a few moments, then found soft places to sit and lean against the boards of the barn where they could doze.

"Are they going to kill us, M'buta?" the young woman nearest the older man asked.

"I do not know," M'buta said. He was a big man, of thirty-five years, as near as he could figure. On the white plantation, he had been called Socrates. The young woman was named Sarah by the family who had owned her. But, they still remembered their real names and when they spoke, they used those appellations rather than their slave names.

"My stomach hurts," Sarah said.

"At least you are not being beaten," Caesar said. He was a young man of only eighteen who bore ridged scars on his back from being whipped. "Your stomach does not bleed."

"Do not be so mean," Sarah said. "I know we are all hungry. Maybe the Boss Man will come after us and take us back to our homes."

"Ha," muttered a slave called Rastus, a married man of twenty-five years, tall and slender, handsome, with thick black hair like wire. "Boss Man don't care about us."

They never used the white man's real name when they spoke of him among themselves. They considered it an evil name that could do them harm to speak it. They did not use the term *Boss Man* in their native tongue because they had no such words. The nearest they could come to it would be *chief man* and they hated him too much to call him that. So, they used the English term, *Boss Man,* because that was what he had told them to call him and they knew it was not his real name.

The woman lying next to a young man whom Boss Man called Fidelius stirred. She poked her husband in the ribs, a gentle nudge that served to flip open his sleep-heavy eyelids. "Water," she said, in English, and he straightened, sat up.

"Petunia, you have to get it yourself. Ain't no cup."

"Tired," she said.

The small wooden bucket sat in a corner by the padlocked gate, no ladle, nor spoon with which to dip into it and bring forth water. Petunia struggled to rise and Fidelius leaned over and helped her get to her feet. She stood there, wobbly, a thin, twenty-year-old woman aged beyond her years. She hobbled over to the bucket and knelt down, dipped her head like some dark fawn and sipped the straw-flecked water, straining it through her teeth to keep the dirt and straw from entering her mouth.

Fidelius watched her drink and felt the hot tears well

up in his eyes. He could almost see the bones of her back beneath the thin worn dress that clung to her like a burial shroud. They might have been in a thatched hut on some night-blackened savannah in Africa, he thought, listening to the he-lion's cough as it waited in the high grasses for its mate to kill the kudu, free to go with the sun to the river where the crocodiles basked like sunken logs on copper water. He often went back to Africa in his mind to glimpse the high grasses waving gently in the breeze as gazelles fed or bounded away from him, looking like graceful porpoises leaping from a tawny sea.

"Don't you drink it all, girl," the old man chided. He was called Socrates by the Boss Man and the other slaves liked the sound of the word, saying it sounded like the African grasshopper feeding on the grasses of the plain in high summer when they all lived like the water buffalo and the hippopotamus down at the river where they could stay cool while the boys laughed and chased away the crocodiles or teased the waterbirds by throwing sticks and stones at them.

"No, sir," Petunia said obediently and stopped drinking.

"You're hungry, aren't you, girl?" Socrates said in a kindly voice.

"Yes, sir, I'se hongry."

"Maybe they will feed us in the morning," a young man called Pluto said. He was nineteen, his skin black as polished ebony, with high cheekbones and pretty eyes like a girl's or a sable's, and white even teeth that made people smile when he grinned, for it was as bright as the moon over the veldt on a clear spring night.

Lucius, who was only seventeen, arose to squat in the corner. He made sounds as he voided the small amount of waste in his system, grunted softly, then rubbed straw on his bottom. He stood up, a tall, slender young man, and stretched his wiry arms over his head. Talia, who was but a girl of sixteen, looked up at him in admiration. She was tall, too, and her hair was beribboned with faded pieces of cloth that set off her comely, pear-shaped face, her beautiful dark eyes. She purred softly and patted the empty place next to her and Lucius grinned, walked over and sat down.

"Aren't you hungry?" Talia asked him.

"I could eat a warthog," he said, "but I do not think about it."

"I want to cry I'm so hungry."

"Must not let the massa see you cry."

"There ain't no massa no more."

"There's always a massa," he said.

The two grew quiet and she nudged up against him, stroked his bare arm for comfort in the darkness.

Buelah, a childless mother of thirty-one, looked over at the two young people and sighed. Her son and daughter, twins, had been taken from her when they were only six years old, when the slave ship came for her, and she had never seen them since. But, she saw them in every child still. They would have been about the age of Talia by now and she hoped they were still alive and safe. She had seen babies die in their mothers' arms while waiting for the slave ship to pick them up, and she had once seen a white massa grab an infant by the feet and dash its head against a tree while its mother watched in horror.

Buelah had seen the scars on Lucius's back and longed to soothe them with a caress of her hand, but she had kept her feelings to herself. She had scars of her own that she could not bear to look at or touch, not the thorn scars she had gotten as a child in the bush, but whip scars on her breasts and legs. She had been a slave for ten years and was resigned to dying a slave, for she knew there was no hope for any of them. They were all so far from home and none of them knew how to return.

But, Buelah had been making a quilt at the plantation before they were taken away by their captor, a quilt that contained secret signs that pointed to the North Star and the road north where she had been told there was freedom for Negroes, and she had learned, from another

slave, the secret hiding places, and the rivers along the
way, and she had sewn all of those into her quilt. And
the quilt was back at the plantation hidden under her
pallet, not quite finished.

She heard a sound outside the barn, footsteps, voices,
and the Mexicans began talking. They arose and she
heard the clickings of their rifles and the swishing sound
of their feet as they moved toward the doors.

"*Quién es?*" one of the Mexicans asked, and Buelah
did not know what it meant.

"David," came the answer, and she heard the door
creak open and when she craned her neck, she saw two
stars in the sky and then she heard a woman's voice
soft and low, and then the door closed and she heard the
people walking toward them, their shoes scuffing the
straw and dirt.

Then, a man looked in on them, and a woman, a white
woman.

"We brought food for them," David said, in Spanish.
Buelah could not understand his words, but she smelled
the scents in the large basket the woman carried. She
stirred and got to her feet.

"Poor dears, haven't they eaten?" Ursula asked, in English.

"No," David said.

There was more talk in Spanish and then the Mexicans
stepped back. But, they held their rifles up so all the
slaves could see them. The white woman lifted a cloth
from the basket and David opened the door a crack. She
pushed the basket inside, and Buelah smelled fresh
bread. She rushed to the door just as it slammed shut.

"Thank you," Buelah said. "Bless you."

"You're welcome," Ursula said. "Please see that each
one of you gets something to eat. There isn't much, but
it was all we had."

"Yes'm, yes'm," Buelah said, and she plucked a loaf
of bread from the basket and stuck the end of it in her
mouth and bit off a large chunk. The others arose and

urried to where the basket lay and began pushing and
hoving to get at the food.

"Look at them, poor things," Ursula said. "They're
tarving. How can you stand to see them treated this
vay, David?"

"There's nothing I can do about it, Ursula. They be-
ong to Matteo."

"Why didn't he feed them?"

"I don't know."

Socrates established order and handed out the food,
read, turnips, dried beans, potatoes, dried beef, a dozen
pieces, at least, and a bag of cracked corn. He did not
hank the white people for the food, but went to the
arthest wall and sat down, began eating.

For a long time, that was the only sound in the locked
oom as Ursula and David looked through the large
cracks in the door. Ursula began to weep, but she made
no sound. Tears trickled down her face as she watched
he young ones gobble down the food like starving
peasts.

Then, she turned away and pulled on David's hand.

"Tell the Mexicans to set the basket out when they
are finished and I'll pick it up in the morning."

David spoke to the two guards, who grunted without
assent. Then, Ursula and David left the barn and one of
he Mexicans closed the door behind them.

"An angel," Buelah said to Socrates. "Did you see the
white woman?"

"I saw her," Socrates said. "She ain't no angel."

"But, she brought us food."

"She brought us garbage she would not eat. It is dry
and tasteless."

"She wasn't no slaver," Buelah said.

"She was white."

"You have no gratitude."

"No beggar has gratitude," Socrates said.

"I did not beg. Neither did you."

"Do you pray, Buelah? That is begging. Did you beg the white man's god to bring you food?"

"You mean old bastard," Buelah said.

Socrates laughed and chewed a potato to shreds with white gleaming teeth. The others made sounds as they ate and Sarah was crying because the food made her stomach stretch and hurt. Elmo, another man, sat near the door by himself, pouring cracked corn into his mouth and mashing the grains to a pulp before he swallowed.

"*Animales,*" one of the Mexicans said.

"*Por seguro,*" the other replied.

"Tomorrow, we will take them north and sell them for much money."

"I will be happy to be rid of them."

"I would like to try that young black one first."

"Don Matteo would kill you."

"I would die happy."

Elmo, who had been a slave on an island before he was brought to the United States, understood Spanish and when he was through eating, he crawled over to Talia and slept near her. He had found a nail on the floor of the barn, and it was a large enough nail to pierce a man's neck if he drove it hard enough and he thought of how he would do it if the door ever opened again that night.

27

━

CULEBRA SAT CROSS-LEGGED and stoic in the umber bloom of the mesquite tree shading his bronzed skin from the sun, sniffing the smoke from the sacred tobacco as it rose like a smoky vine from the coals of the fire in the center of the gathering.

The others, Pajaro, Ferro, Conejo, Oso, Tecolote, and Dedo, sat with him, staring into the smoke, some with blood streaming down their legs and arms, others still covered with patches of soot and dirt that had stuck to their skin like stains.

"We have lost the horses we caught," Culebra said. "We have lost brothers who are now with the Great Spirit. Now, we are few, when we were many."

"We are scattered, that is all," Oso said, the large fat one with big lips and small eyes like those of the javelina.

"Where is our brother Cicatriz?" asked Conejo. "I did not see him go down when the white bull attacked us."

"And where is our brother Hormiga?" Pajaro asked.

"I saw him running away, but he did not come to my call."

"The devil white bull killed them all, I think," Ferro said. He scowled, and touched the many scars on his body, scars from the pieces of iron thrown by the cannon in the fight when Cuchillo had died at the Baron ranch.

"Do you think the white bull is a spirit on the side of the Baron child, the one they call Anson?" Oso asked, and he was looking at Culebra.

"I do not know. It is a thing to think about. The white bull gored our brother Humo and tore him to pieces."

Culebra passed the pipe to Conejo, who drew the smoke into his lungs and blew it out in the four directions. He looked up at the sky and saw faces and visions in the clouds, in the smoke from the pipe and the others knew he was trying to divine something from what he saw and they were silent.

When Conejo finished, he passed the pipe to the next man, Tecolote, and he spoke. "If we kill the Baron whelp, perhaps the white bull will die too."

"What did you see, Conejo?" Culebra asked.

"I saw the smoke of battle and the faces of our brothers who have gone to the place of the Great Spirit, who are traveling along the star path in the sky. I saw the face of Anson, the one we call Anda Lejos, the white boy who is a man, the friend of Hueso, the one who walks far."

"And did you see Anda Lejos die?" Culebra asked.

A shadow seemed to pass across Conejo's eyes. "No, I did not see this. I saw men fighting, white men fighting white men."

"What does that mean?" asked Ferro.

"I think it means Aguilar will fight Baron."

"And will they rub each other out?"

"I do not know. The clouds blew into the smoke and they changed shape and I could not read the shapes."

"Pah," Oso exclaimed, "I do not believe in visions. I think we must rub out Anda Lejos and his companion, the one who brought the horses. I want to cut their faces and slice off their balls and make them swallow their penises."

The others grunted in assent. All but Culebra, who stared up at the little streamers and puffs of clouds and tried to make sense of them. He believed that clouds were part of the mysterious spirit world and he often saw visions in them, like Conejo.

"I am thinking of my father, who was killed by Anda Lejos and his father," Culebra said. "The spirits tell me I must kill them and Matteo says he will pay me for the scalps if I bring him their hair."

"Yes," Oso said. "That is what we must do."

"But," Culebra said, "we must speak with Matteo and ask him about these visions. And, there is another we must kill, the man who came to help Anda Lejos."

"Hueso," Conejo said. "Bone."

"That one," Culebra said.

"But he has the favor of Matteo," Tecolote said, handing the pipe to the man next to him. "Will Matteo not be angry?"

Culebra wiped a streak of blood on his leg into a smear that he studied for several seconds. His horse had been gored by the big white bull and it was the horse's blood that stained his leg. The horse was limping badly and they would probably eat him before their journey was over.

"Maybe the whites will kill Bone, too," Conejo said. "When they fight with each other."

A quail piped in the ensuing silence, a sweet, plaintive call that reminded those seated there that they were part of the earth, part of all that walked, swam, or flew over the land.

"No, I must have blood for blood," Culebra said, after a few moments. "I hear the blood of my father calling out to me. I hear the voices of my ancestors telling me that I must spill the blood of Anda Lejos and his father, *el marinero.*"

"And, what of Bone?" Oso asked. "What do your fathers say of this outcast, this man who calls Anda Lejos friend?"

"I will drink the blood of Bone, too," Culebra said. "I will carry his hair on my lance for all to see. I will speak of his death to my sons and they will tell of it to their sons."

"I swear I will help you kill these men," Oso said.

And the others nodded and swore their oaths and the quail went silent and the clouds passed over the sun and cast down a giant shadow that made for the men a small darkness in the day and then one of the horses whickered and Culebra heard its call, grunted, and rose to his feet.

"Come, we will ride to a place where we can gather more arrows and food and talk some more of these things. Then, we will take up the war club and hunt down these men and spill their blood on the earth."

"We will go to the brasada," Conejo said. "That is the sacred place for warriors."

"Yes," Culebra said. "And we will pass by the house of Matteo and tell him what has passed this day and see what words he has in his mouth."

The others rose to their feet.

"Yes," Tecolote said. "Perhaps Matteo will need to know about the white bull and know whose spirit breathes through its nose."

As they mounted up, the Apaches saw Culebra draw his knife and step up to his gored horse and put one arm over its neck. Then, he spoke softly to the horse: "I am sorry, my brother," he said, "but you will carry me on your back no more. You will feed the grasses this day and our brothers will grow on your brave spirit."

Then, Culebra jabbed the tip of his blade at the base of the horse's neck and twisted it hard and drew it up to its throat. Blood poured out of the wound like the water of a fountain and covered Culebra's loins and he caressed the horse as its front legs buckled and it sank to its haunches. He lay atop its quivering body and drew his knife free and wiped the bloody blade across his lips. When the horse was still, Culebra stood up and beckoned to Oso, who rode over to him.

"I will ride with you, Oso. We will go to the brasada and cut the arrows and make the fires and hunt the rabbit and the pig and the turkey."

Culebra climbed up behind Oso and the two rode ahead of the others who followed after, silent as holy men at chapel and the cloud shadow followed after them with a deep silence that seemed like the quiet voice of the Great Spirit in their hearts.

And, each of them thought of the great white longhorn bull and wondered if their days were numbered like the leaves on the oak tree in autumn.

28

CAROLINE SUMMONED UP all her courage to go out to the barn. Esperanza had assured her that the cannon was gone, but Caroline was not sure. She had to know. And, since Martin was gone to town, when he had left, she did not know, this seemed the perfect time. She had wanted Esperanza and Lazaro to go with her, but they were nowhere to be seen.

"It's gone, it's gone," she chanted to herself as she walked across the backyard, toward the outbuildings. She saw men working in the field and three or four were herding a few head of cattle from one pasture to another. They stopped to look at her, but she did not wave. "I pray it's gone," she said to herself.

She heard the crows cawing from the trees that edged one pasture and one of the cows bawled and one of the Mexican hands called out something that she couldn't hear. From the field came the scent of manure and the aroma of grasses giving off their dew as the sun warmed them.

She was trembling inside, with fear, but she swallowed hard and steeled herself to finish her small journey, the task she had set for herself after talking to Esperanza.

When she arrived at the back door of the barn, she saw that it was partially open. And, she heard soft voices from inside. With caution, she leaned against the door and peeked around it.

Then, she heard another sound, and for a moment could not isolate it in her mind, could not put a name to it. *Pringgggg*. Then, another, *pranggggg*. It was a strange sound, but she knew she had heard something like it before. But where? Then, another pair of notes, more highly pitched than the first two and then, a *plungggggg,* and a full three-note chord sounded.

"Esperanza?" she called.

"Señora? *Entra, entra.*"

Caroline stepped from behind the door and entered the barn. Sunlight seeped through cracks in the board walls and streamed in slanted columns that danced with flickering dust motes that looked like tiny insects.

"Where are you?" Caroline asked in Spanish.

"Here," Esperanza replied and Caroline saw her and Lazaro seated next to some nail barrels in the far corner. Quickly, she looked around. The cannon was gone. She breathed a lazy sigh of utter relief. She felt as if a great weight had been lifted from her shoulders and the swirling wings in her stomach melted into harmless dust.

"What are you doing?" Caroline asked.

"I am teaching Lazaro to play the guitar."

Caroline came closer and looked at the guitar in Lazaro's small hands. It was an old, badly scarred instrument, with deep gouges in the wood and scratches where someone's fingers had marred its surface. But, it had six catgut strings on it and appeared to be serviceable.

"But, how . . . ?"

"I put Lazaro's fingers on the upraised wood, the frets, and told him how that shortened the strings to make notes. I do not know all the notes, but he seems to know which ones make the chords."

"When I was a little girl," Caroline said, "my mother taught me to play the piano. I didn't like it, at first, but when I learned to play one song, I loved it. I loved what I could do with my fingers."

"My father and my brother played the guitar," Esperanza said. "This one belonged to my brother, Antonio. I have kept it since he died and now Lazaro will learn how to play it."

Lazaro began to move his fingers on the strings and he played single notes that were disjointed, not connected, but there was a glow on his face that Caroline recognized. She thought of her mother and father now, and how she used to play for them when they were all gathered together in the living room after supper. Tears welled up in her eyes when she thought of those lost gone days when she had been innocent and happy and nurtured by the love of her mother and father. And then Martin had come along and taken her away from all that. She still had the piano, but she rarely played it anymore. Martin never had time to spend with her, since she had betrayed him. Now, she thought of the piano with its silent keys and wondered if it was still in tune.

"Perhaps we will play together one day, Lazaro," she said, "with me on the piano and you with your guitar."

"Would you play for me sometime, Mama?" he asked.

"Yes, one day. Not today."

Caroline looked away from Lazaro, from his sad blind eyes that had been scrubbed of the detritus of sleep by Esperanza, and the tears started to flow again despite her resolve not to be sad that day and not to let either Esperanza or Lazaro know that she was weeping. But, something tugged at her heart when she talked about playing the piano again because it reminded her of home, the home she had lost, and the life she had given up so long ago when she had fallen in love with Martin. Martin, who was now a stranger, a man whose heart was cold toward her, who never showed her affection any-more, nor kissed her, nor cared for her. Caroline sat down next to them. It was cool inside the barn, and she realized she had been perspiring. She breathed deeply and looked closely at Lazaro, whose fingers were poised over the strings at the top of the neck.

"Can you play something for me, Lazaro?" Caroline asked. "A song, maybe."

"I cannot play a song yet, but I have one in my mind and when I hear the notes, I will be able to play it."

"Play her a chord, Lazaro," Esperanza said.

Caroline watched as Lazaro bent his fingers and pressed them against the strings. Then, he plucked them with his right hand, over the round hole in the guitar. The guitar resonated with a musical sound, a full chord.

"That's a G," Caroline said.

"A G?" Lazaro said.

"I learned that when I used to play the piano," Caroline said, dreamily. "That is one of the chords in G. If you can learn more chords, you can play any song that you can think of."

Lazaro smiled.

"He will have to find his way," Esperanza said. "We have to give him time."

What had happened, Caroline thought, to the little innocent girl who had once played the piano to her parents' delight? What had happened to the young woman who had fallen in love with the sailor from the sea, the strong man with the tender touch and the good heart? She could barely remember those days at home, the mornings in spring when the wisteria bloomed and filled the air with a fragrance like fine wine. Those days when her mother let her help with the baking, when they made pies together, cutting up the apples, ladling sugar on the fruit, and the aroma that came from the oven, mingled with the acrid scent of wood smoke. Her heart filled up with the thoughts and ached for the loss she felt at that moment, with the hot tears burning her eyes even as she choked back the sobs that threatened to burst forth if she did not stifle her feelings.

"What passes?" Esperanza asked, as Caroline sniffled, pulled a kerchief from her sleeve.

"Nothing, Esperanza. I was just thinking about when I was a little girl."

"I think about such times myself. It is good to remember."

"Sometimes," Caroline said, a wistful slide to her voice. "Sometimes I think about how lonely I was as a girl. We lived far from anywhere and my father was gone all day and my mother and I scrubbed and cleaned and cooked and I felt like a prisoner."

"I did not feel that way. In our village there were always many people. We did the scrubbing and the cooking, but we laughed and told stories and joked with each other. And, on Sundays we went to the Catholic church when the priest would ride there to say mass and when he did not, we listened to music and flirted and danced with the boys."

"I didn't have any of that," Caroline said. "I was lonely. Like Lazaro must be."

"I'm not lonely, Mama." And, there was his bright smile again, the smile that melted Caroline's heart and seemed to belie the blackness of his blind world, but never failed to cause her heart to miss a beat and feel as if he were squeezing it in his hand.

"No, of course not, Lazaro. I just meant that you don't have any children your own age to play with. I am sorry about that."

"Esperanza plays with me. And, she teaches me things. I am very happy she is teaching me to play the guitar."

"Yes, yes, that is good, Lazaro. Esperanza is good to teach you things, and to read to you."

"I am going to grow up and help Anson with the cattle, am I not, Esperanza?"

"*Por seguro,*" Esperanza lied.

"I can ride a horse, Mama," he said.

"You can? Did you teach him, Esperanza?"

Esperanza was silent for several seconds. A look of panic arose in her eyes like sudden clouds over a still horizon. "I—I think he goes out by himself and rides the horse," she said.

"You do not go with him?" Caroline asked.

"He goes alone."

"Lazaro, you must not do that. You could be hurt."

"I am not afraid," he said.

Caroline stood up and looked down at Lazaro. "Practice," she said. "Can you teach him, Esperanza?"

"No, I cannot teach him much. But, I can hum the songs and teach him the words of the *son huastecos,* the folk songs of my people. He will learn. He will learn quickly."

"Good," Caroline said. "I can't wait to hear you play and sing a Mexican song, Lazaro. And, maybe someday I will teach you some American songs. Would you like that?"

"Yes, I would like that," the boy said. He looked up at his adoptive mother with sightless eyes and smiled.

Caroline looked around the barn again.

"I am glad to see that the cannon is gone," she said.

"Don Martin took it away early this morning," Esperanza said.

"Where did he take it?"

"I do not know."

"I never want to see it again," Caroline said, a hard cast to her jaw. "Never."

Esperanza said nothing.

Caroline walked out of the barn, humming to herself. As soon as she was outside, she heard Lazaro strum the old guitar again and this time she heard him strike G minor and it seemed to set something in her heart humming with that same threnodic chord and she carried the sound with her back up to the house.

As she was starting to go toward the back door, she

heard hoofbeats and someone shouting. Curious, she walked around to the front of the house and saw a lone rider on a saddleless horse. She shaded her eyes from the sun and peered intently at them as the horseman approached.

"Help, help," he called.

Caroline did not recognize the man who rode up to her. His face was sweaty and covered with dirt and his arms were smudged with soot. He looked, she thought, like an outlaw.

"Can you help me, ma'am?"

"Who are you?"

"Name's Peebo Elves. I'm a friend of Anson Baron's. Are you his ma?"

"Anson? Yes, he's my son. What's wrong?"

"Horse threw him. He's knocked out cold, I reckon. I need a wagon to bring him here. You got a wagon?"

"Yes. But, how do I know this isn't some trick?"

"Ma'am, you got to believe me. I think Anson's hurt real bad. I can't drag him here and I can't put him on this half-wild horse."

"Take me to him," Caroline said.

"But, ma'am, you can't do no good for him by yourself. He needs to get to some shade and get some water in him."

Caroline looked hard at Peebo, scanned his eyes with a fierce intensity. Peebo returned her stare, but squirmed as if he were on fire.

"Is my son alive?"

"Ma'am, I don't rightly know. He was barely breathing when I left him. I knowed we was close to the ranch, 'cause he told me so. We thought we'd be here last night, but we been fighting these horses all the way."

"You take me to him, whatever your name is."

"Yes'm, but I got to get me some water, first. We ain't had no grub nor water in three days. I'm near stove up."

"Just a minute," she said. "You wait here."

As Peebo stood there, Caroline turned and ran into the

house. She returned a few moments later with a tin cup of water and a pistol in her hand.

"Now," she said, "you drink this real quick and then you take me to my son or so help me I'll shoot you right off the back of that horse."

"Ma'am, ain't no call for that. I'm just tryin' to help."

"You ran off and left Anson to die. If he's not alive when we get to him, you won't be either."

She leveled the pistol at Peebo, and he saw that she knew how to use it. It was a .44 caliber Navy Colt and he could see the copper caps when she pulled it up to level at him. He started to open his mouth to say something, but she cocked the hammer and her hands didn't shake. He could see that the blade front sight was lined up straight at his heart.

Peebo turned the horse around and started back from where he had come. He looked over his shoulder and saw Anson's mother traipsing after him with the pistol held high, aimed at his back.

"Mothers," he said to himself.

A moment later, he heard a strange sound and it took him a few seconds to realize that Anson's mother was sobbing out loud.

That's when he knew Caroline Baron was a crazy woman and began to fear for his life if Anson was not still alive.

29

◼

MILLICENT COLLINS FINISHED wiping the table and looked up as a shadow fell across the gleaming surface. Startled, she backed up a step, clutching the wipecloth to her breast.

"Didn't mean to scare you, ma'am," Martin said.

"Oh, Mr. Baron," Millie said. "You just caught me by surprise, that's all."

"You know me?"

Millie smiled and looked at the man standing next to Martin. Tom did not smile back. "Well, I know who you are, Mr. Baron. I mean, everybody does."

"I don't believe I've seen you before."

"No, I suppose not. Ken had me working nights until last week."

"What's your name?"

"Millicent. But, everybody calls me Millie."

"All right. We're waiting for another man, then we'll order," he said as he sat down at an empty table.

"I'll bring you some water and table settings, Mr. Baron."

"Martin."

Millie blushed. Martin stared at her as she walked away. He figured she was in her mid or late twenties. She wore a starched skirt and a pretty yellow blouse and seemed perfectly proportioned. He had scarcely noticed any of the local women since his return to the Box B, was seldom in town. He didn't feel guilty about it now. He no longer had strong feelings for Caroline, not in a sexual way, and he had not thought much about looking for another woman in months. But, when he had met Nancy Grant, he thought about it. But Nancy was Ken's gal, and he wouldn't horn in on him. Now, though, Millie had caught his eye and he wondered if he might not be taking a fancy to her.

"You've got a roving eye, Baron," Tom said.

Martin snapped out of his brief reverie and looked at the man across the table. "Huh?" he said.

"You got eyes for every damned woman you see?"

"Tom, are you just curious, or do you have a habit of tending to other people's business?"

They spoke with the din of clattering plates and tinkling glasses in the background as people ate and drank. The other conversations were like the sawing of insects, the drum of swamp frogs at eventide.

"I just wondered. I heard you had a woman. A wife, I mean."

"So?"

"It's none of my business."

"That's right," Martin said.

An uncomfortable silence settled between the two men. Millie set three glasses of water on the table, put silverware rolled up in napkins beside three places.

"Did I interrupt something?" she asked.

"No," Martin said. "Tom and I just have nothing to say to each other right now."

"Well, do you want to see the bill of fare?"

"Steak and beans," Tom said.

"And you, Mr. Baron?"

"Call me Martin. I'll have the same."

Millie looked up just as Cullie entered the saloon and walked toward the table where Martin and Tom were sitting.

"Here's your friend," Millie said.

"He'll have the same," Tom said.

Martin looked at Tom closely, as if to tell him silently that he knew he was arrogant, used to being the boss. Cullie grunted and sat down in the empty chair, picked up his glass of water and downed half of it in one long swallow.

"What's a-goin' on?" Cullie asked after Millie left.

"Mr. Baron and I were just having a discussion, Cullie."

" 'Bout them slaves?"

"No, we haven't gotten to that, yet," Tom said.

Both nighthawks looked at Martin, who smiled using only his lips.

"Let's get something straight right off," Martin said. "You two work for Ken Richman, right?"

"He hired us," Tom said.

"And Ken works for me," Martin said, looking at each man in turn. "So, any arguments about that before we go on?"

Cullie looked at Tom. Tom shrugged and looked at Martin. "I reckon that suits us, Mr. Baron. Long as you pay us, it makes me no never mind."

"Good," Martin said. "As long as we understand each other, we'll get along fine."

"Well, Ken always did say you was the boss," Cullie said. "Ain't that right, Tom?"

"Not in so many words. But, we knew where the money was coming from."

"You ever wonder where Ken heard of you, why he hired you two to be his eyes and ears in New Orleans and other places?" Martin asked.

"He mentioned a name or two, as I recollect," Tom said.

"Did he mention Charlie Goodnight to you?"

"No, can't say as he did."

"Charlie told me you two were running brands and doing some nighthawk work on herds here and there. He warned me about you boys."

"Be damned," Cullie said. "Now, why would he want to do that, you reckon?"

"Shut up, Cullie," Tom said, coming to a boil. His neck swelled like a bull elk in heat and his face started to turn crimson.

"No need to get riled up," Martin said. "He had some good things to say about you two. Said if I ever needed a couple of men who weren't afraid of the devil himself and who could keep their mouths shut, you were the boys to ride with."

"He said that?" Tom said.

"Well, he wouldn't buy any of our cattle we . . . we had," Cullie said.

Martin laughed.

"No, he said he wouldn't hire you to have anything to do with cattle, but said if he ever needed a gun, he'd put you two on his payroll."

"We don't do killin' for pay," Cullie said, a sullen tone to his voice.

"And Charlie never said that," Martin said, smiling. "He said you might ride shotgun for me on a cattle drive if I was desperate."

"We might," Tom said. "But you ain't asked us to do that."

Millie carried the food out on a tray, began setting the plates down. The men watched her. She tended to Martin last and lingered close to him, catching his eyes with hers, bumping into him, rubbing her thigh against one arm. Tom didn't miss any of that business, but said nothing.

"Anything else I can bring you, Martin?" Millie asked.

"Not for me. Tom? Cullie?"

"More water," Cullie said.

"I don't need nothing," Tom said, and he emphasized the personal pronoun.

"You just holler if you need anything," Millie said. Then, "Martin," looking at him point-blank.

"I will," Martin said, and Millie loped away slowly, her hips undulating under the starched skirt that fit her like a second skin.

The men ate in silence, except for Cullie's lame attempts to start up a conversation. Millie kept filling up their water glasses, and Martin made sure his was kept nearly empty.

"You sure do drink a lot of water, Baron," Tom said, as he sopped up the last of the drippings from his steak. There was an edge of sarcasm to his voice.

Martin ignored him. "I'll pay the bill, meet you boys outside."

Neither man thanked him for the lunch. Tom and Cullie walked outside, although Tom seemed to be in no hurry. Martin got up from the table, walked over to the bar.

"How much do I owe you, Charlie?" he asked. Charlie Stonecipher was the jack-of-all-trades at the Longhorn, tending bar, cooking, cleaning up during the day. But, he also managed the place in Ken's absence.

"I'll give Millie a holler, Mr. Baron."

Charlie went to the door that led to the kitchen, opened it a crack. "Millie," he called. "Mr. Baron wants to pay his bill."

Millie emerged seconds later, a small notepad in her hand. She smiled at Martin, stood at the bar and did her addition. Then, she handed the bill to Martin.

"Thank you," he said, and signed it with his name. Then, he dug in his pocket and took out a handful of silver, laid it on the bar. "That's for you, Millie."

"Why, thank you, Martin," she said. "Will that be all?"

"For now," Martin said, and started for the door.

"I'll walk you to the door," Millie said, almost brazenly, and Charlie turned away, suddenly finding a spot on the bar that he might not have polished to a high sheen long since.

"First time a lady ever walked me anywhere," Martin said.

"You're a special guest, Martin. Folks in town have a lot of respect for you."

"Why?"

"Ken Richman says you're a man who knows where he's going, that you are making this wild country into a good place for people to live."

"Ken said that?"

"Oh, a lot more than that, but I don't want to embarrass you."

Martin stopped to look at Millie closely. "Where do you hail from?" he asked.

The hum of voices in the background rose and fell like the tides of a sea, and the occasional chip and clack of utensils on plates set up a contrapuntal patter to the faint din of the diners.

"Why, I come here from a little old place called Shreveport over in Louisiana."

"What brought you to Texas?"

"I like the open spaces, and not too many people always coming and going, never staying put."

"Do you have a family?" he asked, seemingly not in any hurry to leave.

"Nope. My family run off from Tennessee two years ago."

"And left you?"

"I didn't want to go with 'em," she said. "They went back to stay with relatives in Virginia, kin I never did take a cotton to."

"How old are you, if you don't mind me askin'?"

"I'm twenty-three, going on twenty-four."

Martin could smell the faint musk of her perfume, not lilac water, but something different, and not like flowers, either, more like the scent of mint and honeysuckle growing by a cistern. He liked the smell. It was a clean smell, like spring fields, or the early mornings at the beginning of summer. Her aroma reminded him of his boyhood, and the newly plowed fields of home, a home dimly remembered now, but far from the sea, far from the fish oil, crawdad, snake and alligator smell of New Orleans.

"You seem mighty independent for being a girl so young," he said, and wondered at himself speaking of such things to a woman he had just met.

"I'm not a girl, Martin," she said, and there was a soft purr to her voice, a melodic curl to it that seemed to wind into him like music. "And I guess I'm pretty independent, in a way."

"Meaning?"

"Meaning, I don't have no man nor anything and I really haven't been looking that much."

Millie moved closer to him and he started to back off, but did not take a step, as if wishing to see how close she would come and how much courage he had to call her bluff. If that's what it was.

"Where do you stay?" he asked, and there was something in his throat that made his voice rasp.

"I got a room at the boardinghouse. Just around the corner on Oak Street. It's run by Mrs. Lomax, the widder woman."

"I don't know her, I reckon."

"She's only been here two months and I've been two weeks. She's still got her two empty rooms. But, she says they'll fill up once people find out about Baronsville and how nice it is."

"Well, Millie, I'd sure like to talk to you more about that. I—I have those men waiting for me."

"You come back soon, you hear?" she said, and he heard the soft Louisiana drawl in her voice, not New Orleans, exactly, but a river drawl, for sure.

"I will, Millie. You can count on it," and he surprised himself with his boldness.

She touched his hand, then, and he didn't know if it was accidental or not, but she set his blood to tingling and he knew he wanted to see her again and just talk to her, if nothing else, and learn more about her.

"I'll see you soon," she said, as he walked toward the door.

"Good-bye, Millie. It's been real nice talking to you."

"Yes, Martin, real nice."

And he looked back to see her still standing there, looking at him and he saw an invitation in her gaze that set up a deep longing in him that he didn't know he still had and there was no shame to it which surprised him even more.

He walked outside into the sunlight to see the two nighthawks standing by their horses in the shade of the overhanging roof of the Longhorn, smoking rolled cigarettes.

"Ready, boys?" Martin said.

"Way behind ready, Baron," Tom said. "We got a long-ass ride ahead of us."

"I know how far it is," Martin said, and walked to his horse. He checked the soogan tied in back of the cantle and patted the saddlebags which he knew were packed with food, jerky, hardtack and dried beans, and canteens of water. "It's just a good stretch of the legs."

"You'll hope your damned legs still work after we get there," Tom said, and Martin knew he was going to have trouble with that man sooner or later. Harris had a chip on his shoulder as big as a hickory stump and he seemed to be begging for someone to come up and try to knock it off.

"Tom, you ain't got no manners," Cullie said.

Tom put out his cigarette on the heel of his boot and climbed into the saddle.

"Oh, I got manners, Cullie," Tom said, "and they're as bad as any you're likely to see."

"That's for sure, Tom," Cullie said, "that's for damned sure."

Martin mounted his horse and let out a sigh.

He adjusted the pistol on his hip, and checked the rifle in its boot. He wondered if he'd have to use either of them on Tom Harris before they finished their business at the Rocking A that night.

30

ROY FELT AS if he was immersed in sweat, even with his shirt off and his wide-brimmed hat shading his face from the sun. His bare torso glistened under a sheen of perspiration and the bandanna around his neck was soaked through. He licked the salt residue from his upper lip and glared at Wanda, who seemed impervious to the heat as she set another board in place atop the one he had just finished hammering to the studs that formed one wall of the addition to his house.

"Roy, come on," Wanda said, "I can't hold this board in place all day."

"Woman, you test every peck of a man's patience. Ain't you got no heart? It's nine hunnert degrees in the sun and not a scrap of shade and all you can do is lay up another board for me to pound nails into."

"Roy," Wanda said, her voice silken and low, "you'll thank me when you can have your own room and a little privacy."

"I had plenty of privacy before you and Hattie barged in on me."

He glanced at Hattie, who was hoeing what she had laid out as a garden big enough to feed the three of them and a dozen ranch hands. There hadn't been a moment's peace since the two women had descended on him like a pair of crows to a cornfield.

But, both women fascinated him, and he even had to admit to himself that Wanda was a most beautiful and capable woman, seeing to it that he ate well, that his clothes were clean and ironed, that his boots were polished. Hattie had cleaned the house and arranged the furniture to make it comfortable. He still resented their intrusion, and was still angry at his mother at having deserted him. He was even angrier that she had gotten married to David Wilhoit and was living on the Rocking A. He considered that a traitorous act, for he knew that Aguilar was an enemy of his friends, the Barons.

Hattie stopped hoeing and stood up, looking off into the distance. He could not see what she was looking at because the house blocked his view, but Hattie took a few steps, shaded her eyes and continued to stare to the east, in the direction of the adjoining Box B.

"Someone is coming," Hattie said.

"Who?" Wanda yelled.

"Three riders. Three men. Very fast."

"You'd better strap on your pistol, Roy," Wanda said.

Roy looked at his pistol and holster lying a few feet away atop a stack of lumber. He walked over and picked it up by the belt. Wanda ran over to her mother and they both looked toward the east. Roy tightened his belt, checked the cap and ball pistol, saw that it was loaded and capped.

By the time he reached the place where the women were watching the oncoming riders, he saw that Hattie had picked up a rifle that she had left leaning against the house. She looked ready for war. Wanda seemed unperturbed.

"They're in a hurry," Wanda said.

Roy shaded his eyes and looked at the three riders.

One of them he recognized; the other two were strangers.

"That's Martin Baron himself ridin' up," Roy said.

"He rides his horse like an angry man," Hattie said.

"He's just in a hurry, I reckon," Roy said. "Something must be up. Put that rifle away, Hattie."

"I wanted to meet Mr. Baron," Wanda said. "Let's walk out and make him feel welcome."

Hattie set her rifle down at her feet and did not move from her spot. Roy almost smiled at her behavior. She was a woman who did not take chances, he thought. Nor did she trust anyone she did not know, apparently.

Wanda and Roy walked around the house and Roy waved at the riders. They slowed when they saw him. Martin waved back. The other two riders gave no sign of recognition. Spools of dust floated in the air behind the horses, and gradually disintegrated. Roy surmised that they had been coming from town from the pall of dust far away in their wake.

"I will wait here," Hattie said, after Roy and Wanda disappeared around the house. She said it in a loud voice, so that the two heard her. Wanda smiled and grasped Roy's hand with hers. He was surprised at the intimacy, but he did not resist.

"Our first callers," Wanda said, a proud lilt to her voice.

"I wonder what Martin wants and why he's in such an all-fired hurry."

"We'll soon see," Wanda said airily.

In a few moments, the three riders pulled up a few feet from Roy and Wanda. Martin touched a finger to the brim of his hat. Roy noticed that all the riders were carrying rifles and pistols, slickers tied to their saddles behind the cantles. Neither of the strangers smiled as Wanda curtsied.

"Mr. Baron," she said, "won't you set down and come inside out of this barely tolerable heat?"

"No'm," Martin said. "I don't believe we've met. Roy?"

"Martin, this here is Wanda Fancher. Her mother's out back spadin' the garden. They—they're uh, stayin' here for a spell."

"Mighty glad to meet you, ma'am," Martin said.

"The pleasure is all mine, sir."

"Roy, thought you might want to ride along with Tom and Cullie here," Martin said, cocking a thumb toward his two companions. "Might be something in it for you."

"Where you going?" Roy asked.

"A ways," Martin said.

"Is this business, Mr. Baron?" Wanda asked.

"You might say that, ma'am. I can't say too much right now, but we sure could use Roy if you can spare him."

Martin looked directly into Wanda's eyes and it seemed to Roy that she stood right up to him, returning his gaze and no sign of a blink.

"Roy's his own man," she said. "If he wants to ride with you, I'm right sure he will."

"Yes'm," Martin said. "Roy?"

Roy did not hesitate. He thought about the boards waiting to be nailed up, the two women watching over him like hawks, the scrutiny he would undergo at suppertime when the two ladies had him cornered between them, picking over him like birds over spilt corn, questioning him from both directions as if he had been caught with his hand in Hattie's purse.

"I'll saddle up."

"We got enough grub for you," Martin said. "Bring a rifle and pistol with you, too." He said it almost casually, but Wanda's eyebrows arched slightly and when she turned to catch Roy's eye, he was already trotting toward the lean-to barn where the horses were getting some afternoon shade.

Hattie came around the corner of the house a moment after Roy passed her. She was holding the hoe, not the rifle. The men on horseback looked at her with curious gazes.

"This is my mother, Hattie, Mr. Baron," Wanda said. "Mother, meet Mr. Martin Baron."

"Pleased to meet you, ma'am," Martin said.

Hattie did not curtsy, but stared at Cullie and Tom, who did not tip their hats or acknowledge the introduction.

"I know you two from the stage coach," she said.

"Yeah," Tom mumbled.

"Where are you going with Roy?" Hattie asked.

"Ranch business," Martin said.

"You will hire him to work for you?"

"In a way, yes."

"Will you hire me?"

Martin looked at Hattie. Her face was well tanned and she obviously spent a lot of time outside. And, although she looked strong enough to do a man's job, he didn't want any women on this trip.

"No, ma'am, I don't reckon," Martin said. "It's not hardly a regular job and a lot of riding to boot."

"Maybe some shooting, too," Wanda said.

"I hope not," Martin said.

"You and your men look as if you're chasing after someone."

Martin squirmed in the saddle. He slipped the bandanna off his neck and wiped the sweat from his forehead. His horse switched its tail and kicked one leg out to dislodge a biting fly on its rump.

"We're not chasing anyone."

"But, it's a dangerous job you have for him," Wanda persisted.

"This is dangerous country, ma'am."

"You must have confidence in Roy, then."

"I do," Martin said.

"Then, I will leave him in your good hands, Mr. Baron. Come, Mother, we have work to do."

Martin watched the two women as they walked to the back of the house. Cullie cleared his throat. Tom rode up alongside Martin, a faint smile on his lips.

"Either one of them might could do this job, I figger," Tom said.

"You may be right. They don't look like they scare easy."

"I don't reckon," Tom said.

Roy appeared a few seconds later, riding a dappled gray gelding. Martin noticed that he had a slicker tied to his saddle and a rifle jutted out of a leather boot. There was an extra cap and ball pistol dangling from his saddle horn, as well.

"The son knows what he's doin'," Tom said.

"He'll do to ride the river with," Martin replied.

Roy joined the three riders as they passed him on the way back to the road. "Where we going, Martin?" he asked.

"Over to the Rocking A."

"Hell, it'll be plumb dark by the time we get there."

"That's the idea," Martin said.

The four men rode in silence for a time, until they were well away from the house and out in the range country that was dotted with mesquite and oak trees, sage and cactus.

Martin was the first to speak, after motioning for Tom and Cullie to ride behind him. He leaned over toward Roy so that his voice would not carry.

"How do you feel about holding slaves?" Martin asked.

"I never thought about it none. Why?"

"Matteo Aguilar's bringing slaves into the country. Aims to sell 'em."

"That where we're going? You're going to buy some slaves from Aguilar?"

"What if I was?"

"I'd say that's your business, Martin," Roy said, a tightness to his lips that made the words spit out like an epithet.

"But, you wouldn't like it much, eh?"

"I wouldn't think much about it," Roy said, but he

began to look at Martin oddly, as if the older man had lost his senses.

"I think you would, Roy."

"What are you aimin' at, Martin?"

"There's talk in town of a war between the states, North against South. Over slavery."

"I've heard that. Seems crazy to me. Dumb, maybe."

"Texas has already voted to secede from the Union. Did you know that?"

"No. But, it seems like we'd be goin' backwards, you ask me."

"How's that?"

"Well, we just got our statehood not long ago, fought the Mexicans and all, and now here we are ready to break away. Might as well give Texas back to the Mexicans."

"Yeah, I see what you mean. If Matteo brings slaves in here, we'd be just like those other states holding a gun to President Lincoln's head. If a man keeps slaves, he's bound to get pretty lazy, maybe."

"Maybe. I don't hold with owning another man, black or white."

"You don't?" Martin asked.

"I don't think it's right," Roy said lamely, and looked away, as if he thought he had said the wrong thing. "But, if you want to . . ."

Martin laughed.

"Hey, hold on, Roy. I didn't say I was going to buy any slaves from Matteo Aguilar."

"No, sir, you didn't."

"Fact is, we're going to take those slaves away from Aguilar, by God, and set 'em free."

"Huh?"

Martin laughed again, slapped Roy on the back good-naturedly.

"You think I'm crazy?"

"I, well, I—I just don't rightly understand what it is

you aim to do. After you take the slaves I mean. Just cut 'em loose in the brush?"

Martin laughed more loudly this time and doubled up in the saddle.

Roy looked askance at Martin, his eyebrows elevated.

"Here's my idea, Roy," Martin said. "When we get the slaves, and they were stolen anyway, I'm going to make them offers, each and every one."

"Offers?"

"Sure. They can come to work for you and me at regular wages, or they can go back where they came from or head north. Just whatever they want to do."

"Sure enough?"

"Yes, and I brought you along in case you might want to hire some hands to help you with that land I gave you. Seems to me you're building a family and getting yourself some new muscles breaking your back to get started."

"Well, I don't know. I did have plans to build me a herd and there's one hell of a lot to do, like building fence and putting up a regular barn and corrals and such."

"So, you might be able to use a black man or two to help you."

"I guess so."

"I'm not going to ask you about those women you have there. I figure you'll tell me when you're ready. But, it seems to me that Wanda has her eye on you, and Ken told me as much, and her mother looks like she can work right alongside any man in the field."

"Yes, sir," Roy said, meekly.

"There are a dozen slaves at the Rocking A. I can't use but a half dozen or so. If you could maybe hire you one or two, or two or three, I'd help you with the cash until you could pay me back."

"I am short on cash."

"Who isn't?" Martin said. "Well, what do you think?"

"Give me a minute, will you?"

Martin said nothing.

Roy thought about the land Martin had given him, the cattle and horses he wanted to raise. Wanda had talked about getting a dairy herd and selling milk in town to raise some cash and Hattie wanted to grow a big enough garden so she could sell her crops in Baronsville. It all seemed possible, but he could use help. He had thought to hire some Mexicans when he could afford to, but that would take time. Martin's offer was beginning to sound pretty good, especially if Martin would help him with the wages.

"I reckon we could try it," Roy said, after a while. "But, seems to me, Matteo ain't goin' to give up them slaves without a fight."

"No, I don't expect he will," Martin said.

"You figure there'll be some shooting tonight?"

Martin chuckled. "I wouldn't be a bit surprised."

Roy said nothing, but he was thinking about his mother and David Wilhoit, and hoped she wouldn't be around if there was any shooting.

But, he wouldn't mind if David got in the way of a lead ball if he was stupid enough to back Matteo Aguilar.

It was something to think about, all right.

31

CAROLINE GAZED DOWN at her unconscious son. Anson's eyes were closed and there was a large bump and a bruise on his forehead. Nearby, a smear of blood marred the surface of a large rock. She shivered in the sun and the water splashed over the sides of the vessel.

"I-is he dead?" Caroline asked.

"No'm, just knocked cold," Peebo said.

A few yards away, the horses were strung to a mesquite bush with rope. One stood hipshot, the others eyed the humans warily, their ears pricked to pick up any warning sound. Peebo glared at the horse that had thrown Anson and then turned away to look at Anson's mother.

Caroline knelt down and cradled Anson's head in her arm. She lifted it gently and poured a little water onto the wound, then pressed the glass against his lips, bending his neck. The water spilled over his mouth, but did not enter. She set the glass of water on the ground.

"I reckon we better carry him down to the house, get Anson in some shade," Peebo said.

"Yes, yes," she said. "Anson, can you hear me, son?"
Anson did not move.

"I'll get his shoulders, if you can lift his feet, ma'am."

Caroline laid her son's head back down on the ground and scooted to his feet. Peebo walked over to Anson, leaned over and grabbed his shoulders. "Okay, lift his feet," he said.

Caroline stood in a crouch and grabbed Anson's legs just above the ankles as Peebo lifted him by the shoulders. "We'll walk sideways, be quicker," Peebo said.

"What happened?" Caroline asked, and Peebo heard the croak in her voice, the gravelly sound that told him she was weeping.

"Rattlesnake."

"It bit Anson?"

"No'm, the horse he was riding. On the leg. I've got to go back and cut some and suck out the poison."

"You both look like you've been in a fight. What's all that black stuff on Anson's clothes and face?"

Peebo told her about the fire, the Apaches stealing the horses. He did not tell her about Bone or the white bull. They walked down the slope toward the house. Caroline was puffing for breath, but kept on, and Peebo tried not to walk too fast.

Waiting in front of the house were Esperanza and Lazaro. Peebo saw the Mexican woman bend down and say something to the boy, then she left him there and started running toward them.

"*Qué pasa?*" Esperanza asked as she came close.

"Anson is hurt," Caroline said in English.

Esperanza crossed herself and uttered a sacred oath, then looked down at the face of Anson. His complexion was drained of blood but his face and neck were tanned from the sun. He had smudges of soot on his face and clothes.

"I will go back and open the door for you," Esperanza said in Spanish.

A few moments later, Caroline and Peebo carried Anson inside the house. They laid him on the couch in the front room. Lazaro was silent, waiting patiently as if sorting out the sounds before he asked any questions. Esperanza went to the kitchen, returned a few minutes later with towels and a bowl of cold well water. Caroline knelt by her son, wiping the sweat from his brow, careful not to touch the lump on his forehead.

She spoke to him in near whispers, coaxing him to wake up, but Anson lay there without moving, his breathing shallow, his face wan, almost colorless.

"I better get them horses before they run off, ma'am. Is there a place I can put 'em?"

"In the barn," Caroline said, not looking at Peebo, but only at Anson. Esperanza began cleaning up the blood, using care, wiping around the bump, laving his face, wiping away the smoke smudges.

Peebo left without another word and did not slam the front door.

"What is the matter?" Lazaro asked.

Esperanza explained to him that Anson was hurt. Caroline said that he had fallen from his horse after a snake bit the animal in the leg.

"Will Anson die?" Lazaro asked.

"No, no," Caroline said, and then broke into tears.

Esperanza soothed her with soft words and patted her back. Then, she leaned closer to Anson and began to whisper into his ear, speaking English.

"Wake up, Anson," she said. "Rise. Open your eyes. We will take care of you."

"Let me speak to him," Caroline said.

Esperanza stepped away, her features wooden, impassive. Lazaro stood like a sentinel, frozen in place, his closed eyelids twitching as if he was trying to blink, or open his eyes.

"Anson, son," Caroline said, gently shaking his right arm, "please wake up. It's your mother. Please wake up."

"He sleeps," Esperanza said.

"He must wake up," Caroline said.

"I want to touch his face," Lazaro said. "Let me touch him."

Caroline sighed and stepped away. "You might as well," she said.

Esperanza led Lazaro over to Anson and put his right hand on Anson's cheek. Lazaro lightly moved his fingers over the nose and eyes, to the forehead and back down to the mouth and chin. Then, he laid his palm flat against Anson's left cheek.

"He does not have the fever," Lazaro said. "Maybe he is only asleep." His fingers touched both of Anson's eyes. He did not try to open the eyelids, but kept his fingers there. His lips moved slightly, but Lazaro did not speak for several moments.

"You can do nothing, Lazaro," Caroline said.

"He can feel my fingers, my mother. I am talking to him in my mind. I am telling him to wake up. He can hear me in his mind."

"No, he can't," Caroline said.

"Wait," Esperanza said. "Maybe the boy has the gift."

"Gift?" Caroline asked. "What gift?"

"The gift of the curandero. Sometimes God takes away one sense from a person and grants another. Perhaps Lazaro can heal Anson with his touch."

"That is silly superstition," Caroline said. "You should not say such things to Lazaro."

Lazaro lifted his left hand, put a finger to his lips, calling for silence. Caroline and Esperanza watched the blind boy, whose lips quivered as if trying to form speech.

"*Abre los ojos*," Lazaro whispered. "Open your eyes."

As Caroline watched, Anson's eyelids quivered beneath Lazaro's fingertips. He withdrew his hand and Anson's eyelids fluttered, then opened. Caroline gasped; Esperanza crossed herself.

Anson stared upward until the image came into focus: Lazaro's face. Lazaro stood there, unmoving. Anson blinked his eyes twice, then kept them open.

"What are you doing here?" Anson asked.

"Me?" Lazaro said.

"Yes. Did you touch me? Did you touch my face?"

"Yes," Lazaro said.

"Then, get the hell away from me," Anson said.

"Anson," his mother said sharply. "What's got into you? You've never spoken to Lazaro that way before."

"He never put his goddamned hands on me before."

Lazaro backed away. Esperanza came up behind him and touched his shoulders with both hands. Lazaro started whimpering, and tears leaked from his closed eyelids, seeped down his cheeks. Esperanza whispered something inaudible to the others into his ear.

"Now, you've gone and hurt Lazaro's feelings, Anson," Caroline said. "Tell him you're sorry."

Anson lay there, an expression of annoyance on his face.

"I'm sorry, Lazaro. I didn't want to hurt your feelings. But, don't you ever put your hands on me again."

Lazaro did not reply. He tried to stifle his sobs, and Esperanza slipped a handkerchief from inside her sleeve and wiped his face. He turned to her and she led him away, out of the room.

"There, you've gone and done it now, Anson," Caroline said. "How cruel. Why did you ever say such things to that poor boy?"

"Because he's filthy, that's why. Did you see the sores around his crotch? Jesus."

"Be quiet," Caroline said quickly. "That's not nice."

"He's got the pox, that blind boy," Anson said. "And I don't want to get it."

"You can't get it that way," she said.

"No, I reckon not."

"What do you mean by that?" Caroline was defensive.

"Nothing."

"Must I pay for one mistake the rest of my life?"

"Some of us have to. Ma, how'd I get here? Where's Peebo?"

"Don't change the subject. It's about time you and I thrashed this out."

"Ma, my head hurts like fire."

"I imagine it does. Anson, we must talk about this now. You've broken Lazaro's poor heart and you're breaking mine."

"Ma, I'm sorry. It just struck me all wrong, that's all, Lazaro putting his hands on me like that. He ain't no doctor."

"Isn't. Haven't I taught you to speak correct English?"

"Sure, but it's easier, sometimes, to just talk like everybody else."

"I want to know what you mean by how one gets the pox."

"I was talking to someone about it."

"About me?" she asked, her tone sharp as a nail.

"No'm, not about you, in particular. Just about . . ."

"About what you saw on Lazaro?"

"Yes'm."

"And what did you tell this—this Peebo?"

"Ma, I told him about them sores on Lazaro's pecker and on his balls."

Caroline stiffened as if stung.

"That's an ugly thing to talk about. To a complete stranger at that."

Anson put a hand to his head and sat up. His body swayed as if he was off balance.

"You're dizzy?"

"Yes'm. Some."

"Well, it's no wonder. Getting thrown from your horse like that."

"I don't remember much about it. I heard this rattling sound and the horse bucked and next I knew I was flying through the air. Then, everything went black I guess."

"Well, you had a nasty fall. Anson, who told you how Lazaro got that—that disease?"

"I don't rightly want to talk about it right now, Ma. Where's Peebo, anyhow?"

"He went to fetch his horses. Anson, please. We must discuss this. I—I don't want you to hate your own mother. I don't want you to hate me."

Anson shook his head gently as if to clear it, and looked everywhere in the room except at his mother. She sat down beside him, wringing her hands. "Oh, Ma," he said. "Don't worry about it. It was just talk between Peebo and me."

"Peebo told you what?"

Anson stiffened both arms, set his hands on the divan to steady himself. He drew in a deep breath and let it out, moved his head as if to clear out the cobwebs and see if he was all right.

Caroline rubbed the arm closest to her, stroked it up and down with soothing motions.

"Are you afraid of me touching you?" she asked, her voice just above a whisper.

"No'm, I reckon not."

"I have the same disease as Lazaro. He got it when he was inside his mother's womb. I got it from my indiscretion, I guess."

Anson shut his eyes. "Ma, please."

"No. If I tell you about this, maybe you'll tell me what your friend Peebo told you."

"Ma, I don't want to talk about it none."

"I have the same sores as Lazaro has. Only mine are worse. They're all over my privates, eating at me, eating me up. I think they're eating inside my body. In other places, I mean. Sometimes, I think there must be sores in my brain. I—I—"

Anson turned to her, grabbed the hand that was stroking his arm. "Ma, you don't have to . . . you don't have to tell me nothing."

"Anything," she said. "I don't have to tell you anything."

"That's what I mean."

"You can't treat Lazaro as if he were a leper. Not unless you treat me the same way."

Anson looked into his mother's eyes for the first time. He saw the pain there, saw the deep sorrow that made him hurt inside as he had never hurt before. As he looked at her, he saw the tears well up in her eyes and trickle over the edges, and her pain struck even deeper inside him and he squeezed her hand and felt the tears strain at his own eyes.

"Ma, I—I can't think of you that way."

"It's horrible, isn't it?" she said, her voice almost a croak. "Just horrible. I can't look at myself anymore. I put salve on the sores and Esperanza has brought herbs for Lazaro and me and she says she prays for me and—"

"Ma, don't. . . ."

"Well, it's from my sinning, you know. I made a terrible mistake and I don't know why I let Bone do that to me, but I didn't stop him and God has seen fit to punish me for that sinning."

"Jesus, Ma."

"Wha-what did Peebo tell you?"

"It—it wasn't only Peebo. I heard some men talking about it in New Orleans when we took the herd there that time."

"What did they say?" Caroline's voice was husky with penitence and regret, husky with the weight of sin and eternal punishment in the fires of hell.

Anson felt his heart breaking and he could no longer stay the tears. They bubbled out of his eyes and rolled down his cheeks and he saw that his mother was quietly weeping, not sobbing, just letting the tears flow down her cheeks and make her sallow skin glisten as if she had been in the rain.

"Peebo, he said, well, he said it was something the whores got from sailors."

"And, where did the sailors get it?"

"Ma."

"Tell me."

"Peebo said the sailors got it from humping animals in Africa and other places."

Caroline sighed deeply and squeezed Anson's arm until the blood drained from the skin and left chevrons where her fingers had been. Then, she arose from the divan and wiped her face with both hands.

"Thank you for telling me," she said. "Now, I know why your father looks at me the way he does. When he looks at me. Now I know why he doesn't want to be with me. Why he does not sleep in my bed."

"Pa was a sailor," Anson said, a pleading for forgiveness in his eyes.

"But he did not go to Africa and he does not mate with animals."

Just then, Peebo entered the front door and Caroline whirled and left the front room, openly sobbing, her sadness ripping into Anson's heart and leaving him sad and confused.

"What's wrong?" Peebo asked.

"Just shut your fucking mouth, Peebo," Anson said. "Just don't say a goddamned fucking word."

32

MARTIN AND THE other three men rode along the old road that he and Juanito had cut many years before, and it had seen enough use to keep from being overgrown, but was nearly invisible in places where flash floods had razed the land. Riding it brought back many memories to Martin and some he harbored with regret and a certain amount of sadness. The road was not straight, and it had taken a long time for it to be a road. It had started out as a game trail and the wild longhorn cattle had used it as a line of least resistance, as had Martin and Juanito. Over the years, wagons had rutted it and the rains had scrubbed it, and he and the Mexicans who worked for him had widened it, pulled its stumps and hacked back the mesquite trees. The road led through the brasada clear to the Matagorda on the Gulf.

Martin had caught glimpses of roadrunners, jackrabbits startled from their motionless shadows, and coyotes slinking off into the brush like gray wraiths, and small deer rising from their beds. The country was still wild and he loved it, could feel it draw at him, hold him, slip into him like the first taste of wine from a glass and make him as giddy as if he'd drunk a quart of mescal.

In the light zephyrs, he could pick up the scent of the sea and the aroma stirred his senses back to that time when he roamed the Gulf of Mexico like a gypsy, free as the gulls that wheeled above his stern when he was on a bite, dragging red snappers, groupers, sea bass, jewfish from the depths, gutting them until the decks ran with blood and slime and the gulls descended onto the decks like a snowfall and, when the bite was finished, he tossed entrails into the sky and watched in amazement the acrobatics of those birds of the sea, dazzled by their skill and aptitude for thievery.

And, the breezes shifted and blew their wending ways from the west and there was a tang to those airs, too, tasting of wildness and the unknown, the grasslands yet to be grazed and beeves not yet harvested with the rope and the gate, beeves yet unbranded, moving across the savannah like ancient herds not yet tamed by man.

The scent of chaparral wafted to his nostrils and the grit of the old trail they now called a road had its own appeal, its special aroma like a strong-willed woman in season, like a five-gaited gal who never closed her eyes and never lost her smile and rode with a man to the very end of the road, and beyond.

It was good to be riding again, though. He loved raising cattle and building the brand, but he hated being confined to the main house, having to avoid Caroline because he no longer had feelings for her that were not seasoned with a bitter root. He could not look at her without thinking of Mickey Bone and what he had done. What they both had done, and that blind kid, Lazaro, he was a constant reminder that Caroline had let Bone have his way with her while he had thought that his friend Juanito Salazar had done the deed. He scattered those thoughts from his mind through the sheer power of will and set it on the task ahead, and the men he rode with, two of whom he knew not at all, and one who was the son of a man he had once hated when he was alive.

Martin told Roy Killian all about the slaves and Reynaud, as they rode toward Aguilar's Rocking A Ranch that long afternoon. Roy tried to explain to Martin about Wanda Fancher and her mother, Hattie, but he didn't understand the situation that well himself. He was on firmer ground when he explained to Martin about his mother, Ursula, taking off with David Wilhoit and now living on the Rocking A.

Cullie and Tom set the pace, taking the lead on their long-legged horses. Late in the day, the four men stopped at a creek to water their horses and build their smokes.

Tom walked over to Martin at a casual pace, as if what he had to say was of no particular importance. He scraped a hand across one of his wiry muttonchops as if to smooth it. He might have been preening himself, Martin thought, so he had something to say, all right, and it wasn't just offhand.

"Baron."

"Tom."

"What you said before. About there bein' some stumps between us we had to get cleared away."

"Yeah?"

"Well, I been wantin' to clear one or two of 'em away."

"I'm listening," Martin said.

"I didn't mean no harm by what I said back at the Longhorn. I had somethin' else in mind when I saw you eyein' that serving gal."

"It's not important, Tom. Already forgotten."

"Not by me. I guess I didn't get it out right. I'd like to say it straight. Right now."

"Go ahead."

"Well, sir, Ken Richman, he asked me and Cullie to do something else for him when we went through Galveston, and if we didn't find out what he wanted to know there, we was to have a look-see in Corpus."

"About the smuggled slaves?"

"No, about a sawbones. A doc. Ken, he said your wife was real sick and he asked us to find a doctor who would ride to Baronsville and take a look at your missus."

"You found such a doctor?" Martin asked.

"Name of Purvis. Pat Purvis."

"He's not a barber, is he?"

"No, he's genuine, got him a certificate and all. Says he's a surgeon."

"What did Ken tell you about my wife? About what her sickness was?"

"He didn't. Just said she was always feeling poorly."

"He didn't tell you what ails her? What did you tell the doc, this Purvis?"

"I didn't have to tell him anything. Ken gave me a letter written in Latin. He told me to show it to every doc I talked to and if they didn't understand it, he wasn't interested."

"And, this Purvis could read Latin?"

"Yes. He seemed surprised, but he said he would take a look at Mrs. Baron, see what he could do."

Tom drew on his rolled cigarette and held the smoke in his lungs until most of it had diffused into his bloodstream, then blew out the blue fumes not absorbed by his lungs.

"Well, you did what Ken asked you to. Beyond that, my wife's none of your business."

"I know that. Reason I asked what I did back there, is that I thought maybe your wife had already died."

"That's a hell of a thing."

"I know. Jumped to a conclusion, I reckon."

"My wife is not dead," Martin said.

"I reckon I got me some crow to swaller."

Martin waited for Tom to walk away, but he didn't. "Roy," he said, "don't let your horse drink too much."

Roy pulled his horse away from the creek. Cullie had already put his horse to grass, but was watching him.

"You got something else to say, Harris?"

"Do you know the Rocking A layout?"

"I've been there."

"They got them slaves in the barn. I figure after dark they'll load 'em back in the wagon and head north."

"What's on your mind?" Martin asked.

"There'll be the two Mexes, and the Frenchie, and I don't know about Aguilar."

"Matteo won't go," Martin said. "He lets other people do his dirty work."

"Well, that's only three men and we got four."

"There might be another man," Martin said.

"Oh?"

"There's a surveyor living on the Rocking A and I think he might be Matteo's eyes and ears on this expedition."

"I don't know the man," Tom said.

"No. I reckon nobody does."

"So, it's four against four."

"Unless . . ."

"Unless what?"

"Nobody knows which way the slaves will jump. I'd like to do this without any killing."

"Those Mexes are armed. Heavy armed, and the Frenchie, he was packin' a rifle and a pair of horse pistols. Single shots, but big bore sonsofbitches."

"Reynaud will fight," Martin said.

"And this surveyor?"

"I don't know. He might. But, he's got the most to lose. Just took him a bride and I've got a hunch his woman has a snapper hold on him."

"I know what you mean," Tom said.

Cullie finished his cigarette, stomped it out, ground it into the dirt. Roy stood by his horse, its hair moth-eaten from summer shedding.

"Let's follow the wagon from a distance," Martin said. "Let it get far enough away from the ranch house so that Matteo won't hear any noise we make."

"Then, what?" Tom asked.

"One man in front to stop the horses pulling the wagon. Roy, there, maybe. Cullie over there come up from behind, and you and I come in on the flanks."

"We might have to drop the two Mexicans right off," Tom said.

"We might." Martin kept his smoke going, cupping it from the light wind so that the air wouldn't fan the sparks.

"Then there's the Frenchie, and the surveyor. We might have to drop them, too." Tom rolled his short cigarette up between his fingers, snuffing it out as he made a ball of it. He let the ball drop from his hand, paid it no more mind.

Martin finished his cigarette, lifted his right leg and ground the stub out under the heel of his boot. He let out the spent smoke and breathed in fresh air.

"We'll talk some more about this when we see what Matteo's up to," Martin said. "But, if we shoot the horses out from under the Mexicans, they probably won't give us any trouble. If the surveyor is on horseback, we'll shoot his horse while we're at it."

"What about the Frenchie?"

"Reynaud is used to riding stables and English saddles. We'll let him stay on his horse and make sure we give his mount something to worry about."

"Make it run?"

"Run, buck, anything to keep Reynaud busy."

"I forgot about the Mexican drover. The one in the wagon."

"I'll tell Roy to point his rifle at the man's face when he stops the team. We'll see if he wants to give up his life for a bunch of stolen slaves."

"Lots of ifs in this plan."

"It isn't set in baked clay, Harris. These things go best set loose and leave the figuring to each man when the popping starts."

"Might work," Tom said.

"What works is what works." Martin turned to walk over to his horse.

Tom walked away, caught up his horse. Martin nodded to Roy, who climbed on the dappled gray.

The sun fell away in the afternoon sky and shadows began to stripe the land, form puddles of gray on the eastern edges of trees. It would be getting on to full dark by the time the four men rode up to the Rocking A main house and the barn where the slaves were kept.

The birds disappeared and the nighthawks began to appear, silent, flapping rags silhouetted against the raging western sky. Martin felt his stomach go squirrelly as he thought about the business ahead.

"Better check your rifles and pistols while it's still light," he told the others. He jerked his flintlock from its scabbard and poured fresh fine powder into the pan, blew away the excess and folded back the frizzen. He heard the snap of locks as the others checked their rifles and cap and ball six-shooters.

The breeze stiffened, and it was from the south, balmy, fresh-warmed in the Gulf and carried with it the scent of sea and the huff against his shirt like the first tug of a sail filling up with wind for a stretch of sailing close-hauled.

Martin felt good just then. He went over the basic plan in his mind and could find no fault in it. But, then, everything depended on the actions of men under pressure, on both sides, and there was no way to figure that out or write it down on paper or cast in clay.

"It won't be long now," Cullie said.

"Yeah, like what the cat said when it caught its tail under the ripsaw," Tom replied.

No one laughed.

33

◼︎

URSULA KILLIAN PUT away the early supper dishes, a melancholy droop to her face adding years to her visage. The twilight always brought her a twinge of sadness, but it was worse tonight. Moments before, the western horizon had blazed like a prairie fire frozen in time. Now that the sun had set, leaving gray shrouds streaming across the sky, she was filled with a feeling of dread, and, as always, she missed Roy, wondered what he was doing at every close of day. She listened to the noises in the next room, knowing David was packing clothes for a long trip, several days he said, and she knew that the journey might also be dangerous. She closed the last cupboard, sighed, and walked into the next room of the adobe house, trying to affix a smile to her face so that David would not see what was boiling inside her, what thoughts skulked in her mind. But the minute she saw him, she knew she could not hold her tongue, for that would be against her nature.

"I'm just about ready," David said.

"I don't want you to go," Ursula said.

"Urs, we've gone over this. I have to go."

"Are you a slave to Matteo like those poor people out in the barn?"

David finished tying the thong around his soogan, his slicker, and stood up. He looked at Ursula, framed in silhouette at the center of the doorway. She had not yet lighted the lamps, so she was just a shadow, but no less powerful, appealing.

"I'm beholden to Matteo. When he asks me for a favor, it is in my character to grant it."

"You're beholden to me, too, I thought," she said, and stepped toward him, out of the fading light from the kitchen and into the dark of the front room.

"It's not the same thing," David said.

"It's wicked to sell those people. Like cattle."

"I know it's not exactly legal."

"It's not legal at all. I lived in Fort Worth, you know. I heard a lot of talk about smuggling slaves. Contraband, the soldiers called it. It's immoral, that's what it is."

"Ursula, we're in no position to judge what Matteo does."

She walked close to him and David sighed as she drew near. She folded her arms around his neck, closing her hands like the clasp of a locket. "All you have to do is say no," she said. "Turn your back on it. Stay home with me."

"I don't think we'd have a home here if I backed out now."

"We can always go somewhere else."

She pressed her breasts against his chest, and tugged on the back of his neck to bend it toward her.

"I—I think we're better off here. There's lots of opportunity. Matteo has big plans."

"David, please. I—I have a bad feeling about you leaving tonight."

He resisted her and grabbed her wrists, brought her

arms back down to her sides. He held them there, pushed her away.

"Don't worry, Ursula. I'll be back in a couple of days. All I'm doing is going along to make sure that Reynaud doesn't cheat Matteo."

The darkness seeped into the room, cloaking them in secrecy while Mexican voices outside rose up like croaks from the grasses, crackling phrases that invaded their privacy with insistent staccato signals.

"*Andale, pues.*"

"*Abre la puerta.*"

"*'Onde está aquel chingado, Paco?*"

David heard his name called.

"I have to go, Urs."

"Damn you," she husked.

"Don't make it any worse than it is."

"Me make it worse? How can you do this to me? I'm begging you to stay."

"Urs, don't," he said, and picked up his slicker, rifle, possibles pouch, and powder horns. He almost left the food she had prepared for him, wrapped in a cloth. At the last minute, he picked it up and tucked it under his arm.

"Kiss me good-bye," she said, her voice suddenly changed into a purr.

He leaned down and kissed her. She put a hand inside his belt, tugged him toward her.

"Good-bye, Urs," he said. "Be a good girl."

"You bastard," she hissed and he walked away from her and out the door. She did not follow after him, but walked to the window and looked at the swinging lantern one of the Mexican hands carried as he walked to the barn. The darkness became a strangling thing and she turned away to light a lamp.

But, she could not dispel the black shades inside her mind, nor stem the tears that burned her eyes and slaked her hot cheeks as they cooled in the night breeze that crept through the house in vague, uncertain whispers.

34

⬛

ANSON LOOKED AT the leg of the horse as Peebo lifted it and cocked it to show him the snakebite. The wound, twin punctures, was still suppurating slightly.

"You sucked all the poison out?" he asked Peebo.

"Much as I could. Horse kicked that snake so far and quick, I don't think it pumped much juice into him."

Peebo let the leg back down. The horse nickered and Peebo patted its neck and walked out of the stall. "I'll keep an eye on him next day or two. If I'm still around."

"Peebo, I'm sorry," Anson said. "Tomorrow we can start all over. I didn't mean to climb all over you."

"Oh, I figured you were out of your head some, or maybe you and your ma had words. If they were about me, I'll mosey on."

"No, it wasn't about you."

"I think your ma blamed me for you getting your noggin cracked."

"No, she did not."

"All right."

The two walked out of the barn. They had checked all the horses, grained them, rubbed them down and now the sun was setting, the sky afire to the west. Flaming clouds spread across the horizon like molten bars of iron snatched from the furnace and stacked haphazardly as if they were ingots waiting for the alchemist's arcane art to turn them into gold.

The adobe was one of several that sat like outbuildings in a semicircle behind the main house and barn. Unlike most of the others, this one had no flowers growing outside or in pots on the windowsills. The shadows were eating it up as the two stopped just outside.

"Here's where you'll stay," Anson said.

"I could stay in the bunkhouse," Peebo said.

Anson opened the door, pushed Peebo inside. The leather hinges did not creak; Anson had oiled them recently.

"No, I don't want you bunking with the other hands. The men who stay there are mostly drifters. They come and go with the seasons, don't have no particular loyalty to the Box B."

"You've got loyal people working here?"

"Most of the hands are married and they live in adobes like this one."

"Looks like someone still lives here," Peebo said, looking around the room.

Clothes hung on pegs driven into the wall; there was a burnt coffeepot, a pair of tin cups and a cold cooking pot on the sideboard near the small cookstove, an old pair of shoes under the bunk, with holes in their soles, some tobacco and rolling papers on a table, an old rusty knife with a bone handle, an old Bible written in Spanish, and a couple of plates covered with a thin patina of dust, with spoons and forks lying atop them.

"This is where Jorge Camacho lived," Anson said.

"Oh."

"I'll get Esperanza to come down and pick up his

clothes. You can eat with us in the big house. We'll give you a holler."

"That Esperanza makes a mighty fine supper," Peebo said an hour later, rubbing his full belly.

"Don't get too used to it. We won't be here that long."

"More branding?"

"We have to go back and get those irons I left at the jacal those Apaches burnt to the ground."

"Then what?"

"Then, we brand every head of beef we come across, wild or tame."

"Jesus. There must be millions of acres in this part of the country."

"Millions upon millions," Anson said.

"And how many head of cattle?"

"Thousands."

"And none claimed."

"Few claimed."

"But, no roundup," Peebo said.

"No roundup yet. We have men planting grass, clearing fields, building corrals. It all takes time."

"A lifetime, maybe."

"Maybe," Anson said.

"Christ."

Anson headed for the door. "I'll be back," he said. "Something I got to do."

"Your head feel all right?"

"Feels like it's full of feathers," Anson said.

"You might have got concussed."

"Concussed?"

"Scrambled brains."

Anson laughed, but not loudly. His head still hurt. He walked outside, headed toward the big house. The flames had died on the western horizon, leaving only ashes hanging in the sky, the clouds transformed from gold back to lead. He went in through the back door, into the kitchen. The lamp was still lit. Esperanza was wiping the counters. All the cupboards were closed, the hanging pots and pans glancing light as if they were treasures.

"Where is Lazaro?" Anson asked, in Spanish.

"Listen," she said.

The faint chords of a guitar drifted into the kitchen. They were not unmusical, but had no discernible pattern.

"Lazaro?"

"Yes. He plays."

"He is trying to play. *No toca. No todavía.*"

"No, not yet. He is in his room."

"I will speak to him," Anson said.

"You will not strike him?"

"No. *Cuanto lamento lo que ha pasado entre nosotros.*"

"He is playing his sadness now," she said. "I think your mother weeps in her room."

"I will not speak to her this night."

"You will do what you will do."

The guitar chords sounded sad. They were all in a minor key, like the darkness.

Anson left the kitchen, walked to Lazaro and Esperanza's room. The door was open. It was dark inside. Lazaro needed no light. It was eerie, listening to the strings of the guitar vibrate and not seeing either the guitar or the player.

"Lazaro."

The guitar went silent.

"*Quién es?*"

"Anson."

"Oh. Did my playing disturb you? I am just learning."

"No. You play well."

"A million of thanks. I can hear the music, but I cannot yet play it."

"I want to tell you something."

Anson heard Lazaro put the guitar down, heard his feet shuffling as he made his way to the door. When he got close the boy stopped and Anson could see him, not his eyes, but his shape, the outline of his face and body.

"What is it that you want to tell me?"

"I am sorry I treated you badly today. I am sorry I cursed you."

"It imports nothing."

"I was angry at being thrown from the horse."

"No es necesario para explicar."

"Well, I am sorry, Lazaro. Good night."

"Good night, Anson. *Ten cuidado.*"

"You take care, too, Lazaro. Keep playing. You'll find the music."

Lazaro did not answer. Anson walked through the silent house. By the time he reached the kitchen, he heard the guitar strike up again, single notes, this time, in some kind of order, a tune springing from Lazaro's mind. Anson felt a pang in his heart.

"Good night, Esperanza."

"Good night, Anson."

He walked back to Camacho's house where Peebo was bunking and knocked on the door.

"It's open."

Anson went in.

Peebo was shucking off his boots. He sat on the edge of the cot where Camacho had once slept.

"What do you want for that horse that threw me?" Anson asked.

Peebo looked up in surprise. "I don't know. It's going to be all right, you know. That bite will heal."

"I know."

"Thirty bucks?"

"I'll give you thirty dollars tomorrow."

"What do you want with that horse?" Peebo asked.

"I'm going to kill it."

"Jesus. Why?"

"I won't have a horse on this ranch that throws its rider."

"Hell, it was an accident, Anson. It could have been any horse. You'd throw somebody if you got rattlesnake bit."

"I'll see you in the morning, Peebo. Early."

"Goddammit, Anson. Just like that? What if I don't want to sell the horse?"

"Then, I'll shoot it anyway."

"God damn."

" 'Night, Peebo."

"You are some kind of bastard, Anson."

"You want to work for me?"

"Why, hell yes, I guess so."

"When we go back for those branding irons tomorrow, be set for a long ride. We're going to take rope and catch cows and put the Box B brand on them. But, there's something else, too."

"What's that?" Peebo asked.

"I'm going after that white bull. I mean to have him hump some of my cows or . . ."

"Or what?"

"Or, I'll kill him, too."

Anson left the adobe without another word. Peebo sat there on the side of the bunk, shaking his head.

"Jesus the Christ," he said as he got up and walked to the lamp. He blew it out and the night came into the room and stayed there in the silence.

35
▄▌

SOCRATES WAITED UNTIL he heard the Mexican guard begin to snore with a regular rhythm. He had listened to the man fighting off sleep as the night slipped into deeper waters with an agonizing slowness. Most of the others were already asleep, young Fancy chirping softly, the boy Claude whimpering in his dreams, and Sarah moaning through some visions of the dark dreaming country she roamed.

Only he and Elmo were still awake, staring at each other, making signs, pointing in the guard's direction, not speaking, but knowing there was much to say when they could speak freely. Still, Socrates waited, wanting to make sure the guard descended to a level where he would float without ears to hear, without eyes to see, without mouth to sound an alarm.

He breathed the heavy musk of the barn, mingled with the honeysuckle breath of summer wafting through the cracks in the barn, and the heavy scent of the hayricks, the spoor of horses and mules thick as the night itself and he knew these creatures slept too, their breathing a faint hum in the air, like the sighs of lions napping after feeding on a fresh kill in the high grasses of the African savannah.

Finally, Socrates spoke in a whisper to Elmo, sliding close to him so only his ears could hear. "Awaken Sarah and Buelah. Let the young ones sleep. I will awaken Caesar, Pluto and Fidelius. We will gather close and talk of what we must do."

Elmo nodded and crawled to Sarah's side. He leaned down and blew into her ear. She slapped at the touch as if it were an insect and Elmo caught her wrist and put a hand over her mouth so that she would not cry out. "Go to the corner where Socrates waits," he whispered.

Sarah blinked and saw that it was still full dark. She could see the pinholes of stars through small fissures in the roof of the barn. She got up quietly and scooted to the corner where Socrates had been sitting. She saw that he was awakening some others as Elmo gently shook Buelah while he spoke so softly in the woman's ear that Sarah could not hear his words.

Socrates awakened the others and they slid and slithered through the straw on all fours to his corner. He sat in the center and spoke to them, each in turn so that his voice would not carry to the guard's ears.

"When it becomes night again, the Mexicans and the Frenchman will take us to a place and sell us."

Those in the circle nodded. Buelah rubbed her eyes and shook her head to throw off the sleepiness that bore down on her.

"That is when we will try to escape. I will tell you all what you must do when that time comes."

"This is a strange country," Lucius said. "If we run away, we will be lost. They will hunt us down."

"You must trust me, son," Socrates said. "I have been thinking long and hard about how we can gain our freedom. Do you want to be a slave all your life and pick cotton, clean the stalls of horseshit, slop the hogs and eat scraps at the back door of the white man?"

"No," Lucius breathed.

"Then, we must act as one. We must be as the stalking lion, the silent leopard. We must become the night when we run from these Mexicans and the Frenchman, and I will tell you how to do it and when."

"The Frenchman will shoot us all," Pluto said.

"We cannot outrun the lead ball, even at night," Lucius said.

"They cannot shoot that which they cannot see," Socrates said.

"We will do it," Buelah said, looking over at her daughter, Fancy. "We will follow you, Socrates."

"Are you all in agreement?" Socrates asked.

All of them nodded, each in turn, some after a brief hesitation, some quickly and with eagerness.

"Now, go back to sleep. We wait one more day and then in the night to come we will run for our freedom. Freedom. Is it not a sweet word?"

"We go north?" Elmo asked.

"Yes. We will follow the big stars in the sky. We will follow the drinking gourd as we have heard in the songs of our people."

"The drinking gourd," Sarah said, and looked up beyond the rafters to the winking stars.

Socrates shooed them all back to their sleeping places.

"I cannot sleep," Elmo said, as the others settled down. "My blood is running hot."

"You must sleep, and so must I. If you dream, dream of freedom."

"I will dream of the drinking gourd."

"Yes, yes," Socrates hissed, and lay down and let the night cloak him and claim him as he drifted away on the flowing ribbon of the whippoorwill's plaintive cry.

And finally, Elmo, too, went to sleep while staring up at the fractions of stars he could see through the rifts in the roof and it seemed to him he was looking into a river and seeing reflections of lights that would lead him to a sunny happy land where the black people still laughed and danced and sang the good songs of his long-ago boyhood.

36

■

A THICK FOG hugged the ground, surrounded the big house and masked all that lay beyond in all directions. Anson let himself out the back door and stepped soft on the steps. As he walked through the brume, wisps of gauzy moisture wafted away from him, closed in behind him. He could not see five feet ahead of him, but he knew the way to the adobe beyond the barn.

The adobe lurked behind a thick scrim of fog, but he thought he saw a scrap of orange light coming through one of the windows as he approached. As he stepped up to the door, he confirmed that a lantern burned inside, its feeble light dissipated to a smear on the brumous cloud that cloaked the dwelling.

Anson was surprised to see that Peebo was already awake and dressed. The dawn had just barely broken when he walked from the house to the adobe where he had put Peebo up. The old rooster had not yet crowed and shreds of darkness still lingered around La Loma de Sombra, in the mist of the fields, in the silence of the night birds.

"We got coffee at the house," Anson said.

"I could drink me some."

"Lucinda makes some mean eggs and beef and salsa. Can you smell 'em?"

"Yeah," Peebo said. "Like twistin' a knife in my innards, that smell. I thought I'd done died and gone to heaven."

"Well, come on and we'll get some of her *huevos y carne asado y tortillas de harina y salsa.*"

"That's pretty damned easy for you to say."

The two men laughed and walked toward the house.

"I got your money in my pocket," Anson said.

"Don't want it," Peebo said.

"You ain't givin' me that horse?"

"No. I ain't givin' you nothin'."

"What do you mean?"

"I ain't selling that horse what threw you."

"We made a deal."

"No, you made a deal. I never did."

Anson stopped, his anger stretching crimson fingers up his neck.

"That horse in the barn?"

"Nope, it ain't," Peebo said.

"Where is it?"

"I put it out to pasture until you cool down."

"Well, I ain't cooled down none."

"Then, it looks like that old crowbait might live another day."

"Aren't you the smart son of a buck, though."

"My horses trust me."

"Well, I sure as hell don't."

Anson still stood there, shrouded in fog. Peebo could feel his glare on him, like a candle down in a deep cave. Cold as wet clay.

"Does this mean I don't get no breakfast?"

"Shit," Anson said, and turned toward the house.

"I'll follow you," Peebo said, a smirking lilt to his voice.

"I charge a pasturing fee," Anson said.

"I'll bet."

"So, maybe I don't have to pay you cash money for that bucking horse."

"No, you don't have to pay. Because I ain't sellin'."

"Room and board will buy him."

"Maybe he ain't pastured on Box B land."

"As far as you can look with those puny little eyes is Box B land."

"Now, son, don't go and put up no fence between us over a old horse that just wants to chew some more grass before he goes off to that final pasture."

"Peebo, there's a big old fence between us right now. You put it there."

"No, son, I didn't. You're mad because you got throwed. Your dignity got hurt more'n you did."

Anson had wandered, and now he set his steps toward the lampglow from the kitchen window. The sun rose in the east and turned the fog into a gossamer shadow that glimmered with a soft pale light as eerie as will-o'-the-wisp clinging to a morning bog and the cloth of brume parted for the two men as they waded through it like blinded men making their way.

"My dignity ain't hurt at all," Anson said. "I'm just pissed that you went back on your word."

"Seems to me, son, you are pretty low on forgiveness this fine morning."

"Ain't nothing to forgive. A horse that bucks a man off when there's trouble, isn't worth the powder to snap a percussion cap. Seems to me you lack the gifts of a horse breaker to allow an animal like that to carry a man on its miserable back."

They reached the porch and Anson hesitated before climbing the steps. He turned to look at Peebo. "Ain't that right?"

"Horse was broke to ride. He wasn't broke to stand still and get snakebit."

"He got snakebit anyway, didn't he?"

"Seems to me the rider must have been plumb sawing wood when that snake rose up out of the dirt. An experienced horseman would have rid the horse plumb out of danger."

"You got all the logic of a pissant, Peebo. You know that?"

"I can smell breakfast in there. Probably be as cold as a miner's nuts by the time we climb these stairs."

Anson snorted and turned away from Peebo, clumped up the steps and the fog drifted away from the house as the sun rose in the sky and swept the land like a dim torch fixed to the wall of some deep cavernous place.

The two men walked into the kitchen, Anson scowling, Peebo wearing a pleasant grin on his face and sniffing the aroma of food warming on the woodstove. Lucinda turned away from the counter and smiled.

"Sit yourselves," she said in Spanish. "Breakfast is ready."

"Lucinda," Anson said, also in Spanish, "I present you with Peebo Elves. All he wants is coffee and a hard biscuit."

"Oh, no, that cannot be true," Lucinda exclaimed. "A man must eat a good meal to break his fast in the morning."

"Yes'm," Peebo said in English, "I surely do believe that. I'm ready to break my fast in six dozen different ways."

"What does he say?" Lucinda asked Anson.

"He says he has a little bit of hunger."

Lucinda beamed.

Anson and Peebo sat at the table near the center of the large kitchen. Lucinda carried hot tortillas in a covered earthen bowl and set them in the middle of the table, then put on hot plates crowded with scrambled eggs, strips of seasoned beef, red beans and a bowl of *salsa casera,* with a spoon jutting from it.

"Umm," Peebo murmured. Lucinda gave him a cloth napkin, which he put in his lap.

"Don't get used to it," Anson said. "This is the last square meal you'll get for a long time."

"How come you want to just brand stray cattle? Seems like it won't do no good unless they're penned up."

In between scoops of food, chewing and swallowing, the two men talked as Lucinda prepared food for both to take with them.

"Pa says we brand every head of stock we find, no matter where. As the ranch grows, we'll need those cattle for market. We've got several men out branding cattle, calves, yearlings, full-grown, no matter what. It's the brand that's going to make the difference between making a go of it or just drying up and blowing away."

"Seems like it's pretty haphazard, doin' it that way."

"Not as haphazard as it looks. We've divided the ranch into smaller ranches, sections, you might say. We make sweeps through each section at certain times of the year and brand every unbranded head of beef we find. We keep a tally on these, and grade them."

"Grade them?"

"Yeah, later on we might do some culling or want to make a gather to run up to New Orleans, and we look at those records in the tally books."

"Makes sense, I guess."

"It's a jumble now, but someday, it'll all pay off."

Esperanza and Lazaro came into the kitchen, a few moments later.

"Good morning," Esperanza said in Spanish.

"*Buenos días,*" Anson said.

"Mornin' ma'am," from Peebo.

Lazaro hesitated a moment when he heard Anson's voice. He stopped in his tracks and it appeared he would leave the kitchen.

"Sit down, Lazaro," Anson said. "Hungry?"

"I have hunger," Lazaro said.

"I am hungry, you say," Anson said, in a professorial tone. "You've got to start thinking in English, Lazaro."

"Yes, I know."

Esperanza helped the blind boy find his way to a chair. "You sit down, too, Esperanza."

"I come to get the meal for the señora," she said.

"She can come down to breakfast," Anson said.

"Your mother, she does not feel well."

"She'll feel better if she comes down to breakfast."

Esperanza hesitated. She looked at Lucinda.

"I will get her," Lucinda said. In Spanish, she told Esperanza to serve herself and Lazaro. Reluctantly, Esperanza began dishing up food for her and the boy as Lucinda left the kitchen.

"Hello, boy," Peebo said. "My name is Peebo."

Lazaro swung blind eyes in Peebo's direction.

"Peebo?" he said.

"Yeah," Peebo laughed. "Funny name, ain't it."

"It is a funny name. Are you the man with the horses?"

Surprised, Peebo nodded, then realized that Lazaro could not see him. "I brought some horses in yesterday. I had more, but the Apaches stole them."

"I like horses," Lazaro said.

"So do I." Peebo looked meaningfully at Anson. Anson frowned. "Do you ride horses?"

"I would like to ride. Anson, can I have a horse?"

"Too dangerous, Lazaro."

"But I can ride. Can't I, Esperanza?"

Esperanza's facial muscles rippled to take on a sheepish look. "You must not ride unless someone is watching you," she said.

"You tellin' me you got on a horse?" Anson said.

"I did one day. I did not fall off."

"Well, unless you get on a horse that knows where it's going, or where you want to go, I don't see any sense of it. You stay away from them horses."

"Aw, what's the matter, Anson? If the boy wants to ride, let him ride."

"Stay out of it, Peebo."

"Boy needs a horse if he's to be a man," Peebo said.

"A blind boy doesn't need a horse."

Esperanza set the plates of food on the table. She placed one in front of Lazaro, handed him a fork. She sat down, then, and began to eat.

Lazaro bowed down to smell the food, then worked his fork into the beans, sniffed it before he put it into his mouth. Anson looked at him, feeling pity.

"Someday I am going to buy a horse of my own," Lazaro said.

"Good," Anson said, a sarcastic tone in his voice, "you go right ahead and buy whatever you want when you get some money."

"I am going to buy a pretty horse and I will ride him all over."

Peebo watched the boy eat, marveling at the way he managed to find what he wanted on the plate and bring it to his mouth.

"You wouldn't know if it was pretty or not," Anson said cruelly.

"Yes, I would. Horses like me and I can tell if they are pretty or not. I can tell if they are mean, too."

"That's enough jabber about horses, Lazaro," Anson said. "Just eat your breakfast and put such notions out of your head. You're not going to ride any more horses. Hear?"

"I could teach him to ride," Peebo said.

"So could I, Peebo. But, I'm not going to. If he fell and broke his neck, Ma would throw seven kinds of fits."

"I would not fall," Lazaro said.

Anson shoved his chair away from the table, just as his mother entered the room, followed by Lucinda.

"Good morning, everyone," Caroline said, a cheery lyric to her voice.

"Mornin'," Anson grumbled.

Peebo, Esperanza and Lazaro were more kindly in their greeting.

"You can sit here, Ma."

"I'm not hungry. I just came down to see how you and your friend were. Peebo, isn't it?"

"Yes'm." He looked at Anson, then said, quickly, "We were just talkin' about young Lazaro learning how to ride a horse."

"No, we weren't," Anson said, and stood up, glaring at Peebo.

"Why, that would be nice, Peebo," Caroline said. "Would you be willing to help him? He dearly wants to ride, but I've been afraid he might hurt himself."

"Long as he understands horses, he won't have no trouble, ma'am."

"Sit down, Ma," Anson ordered, pointing to his empty chair. "Peebo and I have to saddle up and ride over some range. Peebo, you about finished stuffing your mouth?"

"Anson, don't be so sharp with your friend." Caroline walked over and sat down, smiled at Peebo.

"We've got work to do," Anson said.

"Yes'm," Peebo said. "I could sure teach that boy a heap about horses. Seems to me like he's got a natural bent in that direction."

"Why, that would be nice," Caroline said.

"Peebo ain't goin' to be here long enough to teach Lazaro anything," Anson said.

Peebo finished eating, got up from the table and carried his dishes over to the counter.

"It wouldn't take long," Peebo said, setting his dish and cup down. "Next time we're over this way, I'll take Lazaro for a ride. I'll gentle him a real good horse, Mrs. Baron. You won't have to worry none."

"Call me Caroline, please."

"Yes'm."

"Ma, we're leavin'," Anson said. To Lucinda, he said: "Have you got our grub packed?"

"Yes," Lucinda said. She handed Anson two bundles, wrapped in light towels. He took them without thanking her, his face dark as a thundercloud.

"Bye," Anson muttered, and headed for the back door.

"Good-bye, Caroline. Lazaro," Peebo said.

"Please hurry back and teach me to ride," Lazaro said.

"I will." Peebo followed Anson out of the house.

Anson was waiting for him at the bottom of the steps.

"Seems like a nice boy," Peebo said, grinning wide.

"Peebo, you're messin' in something that ain't none of your chili-pickin' business. That blind boy ain't going to grow up. He's got the pox and it's goin' to eat him alive and gobble up his brain."

"Huh?"

"Never you mind. Just don't get his hopes up, hear?"

"It might help if you was more of a brother to him, son."

Anson turned and started for the barn.

"He ain't my brother," Anson said.

"I thought he was. Looks some like you. A little darker, maybe."

"Well, he ain't. He's just a bastard my ma took in. Like a stray dog."

"Looks to me like that boy puts a whole lot of dotage on you."

"Dotage?"

"He rightly dotes on you, son."

"I don't care if he does or not."

"Not your brother's keeper, eh?"

"Not by a damned site."

"Hell of a way to treat a growin' boy who thinks the sun rises and sets on you, Anson."

"He's blind, Peebo. What if he was on a horse and a rattlesnake bit the horse and he got throwed. He wouldn't even know which way to run."

"Neither did you, son. You was knocked plumb cold. You lived."

"Shut up, Peebo. Just, for once, shut your dumb mouth."

"Sure, son. I'll shut up. I realize it's the truth that hurts."

The two men reached the barn. Before he saddled up,

Anson looked in every stall for the horse that threw him.

"You really did take that horse out of here, didn't you?"

"Told you I did."

Anson walked to the tack room, got his saddle, bridle, rifle and pistol. Peebo did the same and the two men started toward separate stalls.

"Well, if I see that mangy sonofabitch anywhere close to here, I'm going to put a fifty caliber ball in his heart."

"Anson, someday that mean spirit of your'n is sure enough going to get you into a heap of trouble."

"I ain't mean-spirited. I just know what's right."

Peebo looked heavenward, rolled his eyes.

"Lord, I done found me a righteous man," he said. "My worries are over, for sure."

"Peebo," Anson said, "if brains were powder, you wouldn't have enough to blow you to hell."

Peebo grinned and set his rifle and pistol down, walked into the stall with his bridle and saddle.

"I hope you don't step on a rattlesnake today," Peebo called out.

Anson replied with a string of curses that blistered Peebo's ears and caused the horses to neigh in several of the stalls as if they were nervous and afraid of something they could not see or smell.

37

FIDEL RIOS BROUGHT the wagon up to the barn. The wagon was pulled by four strong horses. Fidel wore a six-shot cap and ball pistol, a .32 caliber Colt made in 1851. He had cleaned most of the rust off its metal frame. Luis Selva, holding a lantern, caught the team, held them in place while Fidel set the hand brake and climbed down.

They both called to Paco Cienega, who was inside the barn with the slaves. Paco emerged a moment later, carrying one of the lanterns.

"I am ready to load the blacks," Fidel said. "Where have you been?"

"The Frenchman is talking to the blacks and I have been guarding them."

"With the lantern?" Luis said, not without sarcasm.

"I left my rifle with Reynaud."

"Did you leave your balls with him, as well?" Fidel asked.

"Is he going to shoot the blacks?" Luis asked.

"He might shoot you, if you don't close your mouth," Paco said.

The Mexicans ceased their banter when Matteo walked over from the house. He was smoking a thin cigar and not wearing a hat. The Mexicans could smell the aguardiente on his breath. They nodded to him and mumbled subservient greetings. Matteo nodded back.

"Is everything ready?" the *patrón* asked.

"The Frenchman is inside with the blacks," Paco said. "He is talking to them."

"Good," Matteo said.

Just then, David walked up, appearing out of the shadows. He was carrying his rifle and bedroll, saddlebags. Matteo did not smile.

"I am surprised to see you here, David."

"Why?"

"I did not think your woman would let you go."

"She does not have any say in the matter."

"That is good. A man must be the master in his own home."

"What if I had not come?" David asked.

Matteo shrugged. "I would have told you to work somewhere else."

David said nothing.

"Believe me," Matteo said.

"I believe you."

"Shall we go inside, then? Let us see what Reynaud is saying to the black slaves, eh?"

David followed Matteo inside the barn. Reynaud and a Mexican named Eladio Contreras were lining up the slaves in a single column. Socrates, the tallest, was the last to take his place in line.

Fancy, Buelah's daughter, started to whimper. "Don't cry, child," Buelah said.

"No talking," snapped Reynaud. It was then that David noticed the Frenchman had a quirt in his hand. Reynaud snapped it for emphasis, and some of the Negroes cringed instinctively. Reynaud smiled.

"See?" Reynaud turned to Matteo. "They are already well trained. No need to bind them for this journey. They will behave."

"They do not know this country," Matteo said. "If they try to escape, they will face much danger."

"I have just finished telling them about the Apaches, snakes, wolves, wild cattle, and lions," Reynaud said. "If you are ready, Matteo, we will load them in the wagon and be on our way."

"David will accompany you," Matteo said.

"Very well," Reynaud said, as if it did not matter to him one way or the other.

"How many of the men will you need? They are all well trained and all are expert with the rifle and pistol."

"Just two, I think," Reynaud said, "besides the driver and Wilhoit here."

"Good. Let us go, then. You have a long way to travel."

To the slaves, Reynaud said, "Walk slowly outside, then climb up into the wagon one at a time. You older men help the women and the young ones."

None of the black slaves replied. Socrates started pacing toward the open barn doors. The other slaves followed obediently.

David watched as Reynaud stepped in close, flicking the three tails of the quirt as if to remind the slaves who was in charge.

Fidelius and his wife carried wooden buckets. As the two passed David, he noticed they were empty and smelled as if they had been used before, possibly while the slaves had been in the barn.

"There is much money here, David," Matteo said, as Socrates climbed into the wagon, turned and helped Elmo up. "See to it that Reynaud gets a good price and that all of the money is returned to me."

"I will do my best, Matteo."

"Maybe you will want to get into the slave business one day, eh?"

"No. I don't think so."

"Wait until you see what they are worth, these blacks."

David held his tongue. Matteo was pretty proud of himself, David thought, and it angered him that he could be so insensitive. Perhaps Ursula was right. He should not have accepted Matteo's order for him to ride to the slave market. He was sure he would regret it for the rest of his life. But, he also knew that if he did not go along, the slaves would be sold nonetheless and he was powerless to do anything about it.

"Better mount your horse, David," Matteo said. "Luis has already saddled him."

"I see the horse," David said. It stood beyond the wagon in the darkness under a small leafy box elder. He walked to it as the last slave, the boy named Claude, scrambled into the wagon.

"Sit down and be quiet," Reynaud ordered and the Negroes obeyed him even though he did not crack the triple-lashed quirt.

"Anyone trying to escape will be shot," the Frenchman said. "And those still left will be beaten. Do you understand me?"

All of the slaves nodded, Socrates not as vigorously as the others.

Reynaud walked a few yards away and mounted his waiting horse. He rode up to Matteo and touched a finger to the brim of his hat.

Matteo nodded and Reynaud spoke to the drover, who released the hand brake, rattled the reins. The harnessed horses stepped out and the wagon started to move.

As soon as the wagon was in motion, Socrates spoke to the other slaves, his voice pitched low. He spoke in a dialect of the Bantu language.

"We will escape if you all do what I tell you. Understand?"

The others grunted assent, their voices drowned by the noise of the wagon wheels and the creak of harness.

"I will crush the driver with my arms. You slide off over both sides of the wagon and scatter like the wild quail in all directions. We will wait until we are far from this place. We will do it at a place where it is very dark and there are many trees. This is what we talked about last night. Until then, speak not. Wait."

"What do we do after we escape?" Sarah asked.

"Keep your eyes on the drinking gourd. Make a wide circle and run toward the North Star in the drinking gourd. Be very quiet. Hide and wait until we all come together. Then, we will follow the drinking gourd north to freedom."

"They have rifles. We have no weapons."

"They will shoot," Socrates said, "but when you hear the click and the whooshing sound, drop to the ground very quick, *pese, pese,* and the ball will fly over your head. Each rifle has only one shot. After you hear the ball go by, then get up and run. It will take them time to put powder and ball back in their barrels."

"What if we do not hear the click and the whoosh?" Sarah asked.

"If you listen, you will hear it. Or if you hear a boom, you run left or run right or go down to your knees."

"We might be killed," Pluto said.

"You might choke to death on a bone," Socrates said. "You must think of life and freedom. Not death."

Another started to speak, but Socrates put a single finger to his lips and no other spoke as the wagon rumbled away from the houses and barn into the dark pit of night. The lantern lights finally winked out and the blacks in the wagon let out a collective sigh.

Reynaud rode up to take his position next to Luis, who took the lead. The wagon rumbled on and the night took on the sounds of wood and metal and leather under stress.

Paco flanked one side of the wagon, the left side, and David rode along the other. David could dimly make out the road, rutted with wagon tracks over time. He felt as

if the trees they passed by were all full of Apaches and
they completed the blackness of the night to narrow his
view of where they were going. He looked up at the stars
every so often, and when he looked at the occupants of
the wagon, they, too, seemed to be gazing skyward.

Reynaud did not stay at the head of the small caravan
long. He seemed restless. He rode around to one side of
the wagon, spoke briefly to Paco, and then rode around
to the other side to talk to David, with whom he rode
along for a while.

"You do not like this, Mr. Wilhoit?" Reynaud asked.

"I can think of better things to do."

"Matteo tells me you are recently married. You wish
to be at home with your wife."

"That's one better thing."

"Ah, I wish the same. I am not at home in the wilderness. I am one who likes the fine restaurants, the wine
and food of New Orleans, the clink of glasses raised in
hearty toasts, the smell of the Gulf, the rain on the cob-
blestones, the graceful surrey, not the noisy wagon we
have here. I miss the beautiful women with dark, flirting
eyes, the crayfish and red snapper with their bright aro-
mas. I am, alas, a man of the city, not of this, this bleak
and empty place."

"Is it the money that brings you here, Mr. Reynaud?"

"Oh, it is the money, and the adventure, as well. And,
I have a score to settle with Martin Baron, a matter of
honor."

"A matter of honor?"

Reynaud told him about his sister and Martin and why
he had come to kill him.

"Will you challenge Baron to a duel, then?"

"A duel? With Martin Baron? Why should I do this?
He is not a gentleman. He is not to the manor born. He's
a crude adventurer, a seaman with a disreputable past
come to land, perhaps hiding other peccadilloes he committed in other places. No, I would not challenge Baron
to a duel. He does not even know the Code Duello, I

fear, and, even if he did, he deserves to be shot down like the dog he is."

David struggled with the image of Reynaud stalking Martin Baron and shooting him dead on some street, then walking away. He knew that Matteo was a ruthless man, but he had thought that Matteo had some honor to his character, that he was struggling to build a cattle ranch in a hard land and that he was strapped for money. Reynaud, on the other hand, seemed to be a man who was ready to kill for honor, but didn't seem to understand the word, what it meant.

Reynaud made David feel uncomfortable, more uncomfortable than he was beginning to feel with Matteo Aguilar. Perhaps, he thought, I should judge Matteo by the company he keeps. If Reynaud would shoot a man in cold blood, without benefit of trial, and Reynaud worked for Matteo, then Matteo must be cut from the same bolt of cloth. It suddenly dawned on David that Reynaud had not been hired just to smuggle slaves into Texas, but to eliminate Matteo's competition.

David felt stupid that he had not realized this before. Suddenly, he wished that he'd listened to Ursula and had refused to be a party to the slave trade and join forces with Reynaud, a man he not only distrusted, but was beginning to fear.

Paco suddenly rode up to speak to the wagon driver, Fidel Rios. Reynaud saw this and reined his horse over to take up Paco's space.

"Fidel, stop the wagon," Paco said.

"What passes?" Fidel asked.

"I heard something."

"What?"

"I do not know. A horse, I think."

"You are crazy, Paco. Ride back to your place."

"Stop. I will speak to the Frenchman."

Fidel sighed and tugged on the reins. The team slowed, came to a halt.

Reynaud reacted with quickness. He rode up to the

front of the wagon and reined his horse in a tight circle to confront Paco and Fidel.

"What are you doing?" Reynaud directed his question to Fidel. "I did not tell you to stop."

"Paco, he said he heard some noise."

"What noise? I didn't hear anything."

Fidel shrugged. His gesture was barely visible in the darkness. Reynaud turned his head to look at Paco, who seemed unperturbed, calm.

"I heard a horse let wind," Paco said.

"You heard a horse break wind?"

"Yes, I think that is what I heard," Paco said.

"And, where was this horse that farted?"

Paco waved a hand off to the side of the road. "Somewhere," he said.

"*Merde*," Reynaud spat. "I did not hear a horse farting and I have the very best of ears."

"That is what I heard. Perhaps, too, the *como se dice,* the *pling* of a spur. Off there. In the mesquite."

Reynaud sat his horse without speaking for several moments. He turned his head one way, then the other. Paco looked at him. So did Fidel, and neither man moved while Reynaud was listening. It was very quiet and the horses were still and so were the people in the wagon. David's horse tossed its mane impatiently and began to paw the ground. David jerked the reins with an abruptness and the horse stopped its fidgeting.

"I do not hear a thing," Reynaud said.

"I hear no thing either," Paco said.

"I hear no thing myself," Fidel said.

"Continue," Reynaud said, extending his arm forward to point down the road. "Do not stop again unless I tell you. *Comprenez vous?* Do you understand?"

"Jess," Fidel said.

"Ride back to your flank," Reynaud said to Paco.

Paco turned his horse and rode back alongside the wagon. Fidel clucked to the team of horses and rattled the reins across their back. It sounded like a series of slaps and the horses took up the traces and jolted the wagon forward. Those riding in the wagon swayed back and forth with the momentum as if they were mechanisms.

Reynaud let the wagon pass him by and waited until David was alongside.

"What was that all about?" David asked.

"These Mexicans. They do not want to work. They are afraid of the dark."

"Too bad," David said, but he didn't believe Reynaud. He knew Paco and Fidel. They were good workers and he did not think they were afraid of the darkness. "I guess you told them there was nothing to fear."

"Umm. I left them with the impression that they should fear me."

David did not comment on what Reynaud had said and Reynaud dropped behind him to take up the rear. The black people in the wagon passed one of the buckets among themselves and David heard the sounds of some passing water and, later, one of the slaves emptied the bucket and he smelled the acrid scent of urine on the night air.

He watched Paco, who seemed to be more wary than before. Paco turned his head often as if he was trying to hear something and he checked his rifle more than once.

The wagon moved slowly through the eerie nightscape and David felt sleepy. He found himself nodding off, lulled by the rocking motion of his horse and the steady rhythm and plod of hooves on the wagon track. He managed to wake himself before he fell from his horse and he rubbed his eyes and patted his cheeks to stay awake.

Each time he looked up at the stars, they seemed to have moved only slightly and he realized he could not measure time at night. He looked at the wagon and saw that some of the Negroes were sleeping. But the big man, Socrates, was wide awake and he was watching the stars as if he were reading a map.

38

—

MARTIN SAW ALL that he needed to see after he and the other three men reached the Rocking A. From a distance, and on foot, they observed the loading of the wagon, were able to count and verify the number of Negroes being transported north. Before the wagon left, Martin slipped away with the two nighthawks and Roy to the place where they had hobbled their horses.

"I reckon you got a plan," Tom said to Martin.

"First thing, let's check our ropes, shake them out, make sure they're limber."

"Our ropes?" Tom asked.

"We'll need them," Martin said, and set the example for them when he unlashed his lariat and built a loop, making it ever wider until he threw it. It landed flat as a pancake.

He watched as the others plied their ropes in the gathering dark. Satisfied, he told them to tie their ropes back on their saddles. When he was finished, he climbed onto his horse.

He rode to a place where they could see the wagon depart, count the men going along on the expedition.

Martin recognized Wilhoit and Reynaud. He did not know the Mexicans.

"Satisfied?" Tom asked as Martin reined his horse away from their vantage point.

"We know how many men we have to fight, if it comes to that."

"You aim to lasso them?" Tom asked, his voice laden with sarcasm.

"We'll use the ropes, Tom. Don't worry about it."

"I ain't worried about a goddamned thing, Baron."

"Where to?" Roy asked, mainly just to break the tension between Martin and Tom.

"Follow me," he said, and set a pace for the others at a slow gallop.

"You aim to lasso them Mexes?" Cullie asked, riding up alongside Martin.

"We might just do that, Cullie."

"Be awful hard in the dark and with them shootin' at us."

"Now that we know what we're facing, I think my plan will work. I put it together when we rode up here. I know a place where we ought to have the upper hand. If we do it right, nobody gets shot, nobody gets killed."

"I ain't never roped no greaser before," Cullie said.

"And you won't, tonight. We don't call Mexicans that in this country."

"What?" Cullie asked.

"Never mind," Martin said.

A few minutes later, after thinking about it, Cullie said, "Oh." Martin smiled briefly in the dark.

After riding a good fifteen minutes, Martin led the others back to a place near the road that offered concealment. He reined up in a copse of trees that afforded them a view of the road from a distance.

"Don't make any noise," Martin warned the others.

"How come we're stoppin' here?" Tom asked.

"Let's see how they bunch up," Martin said. "Who's riding where in front of and around that wagonload of Negroes."

"And, then?"

"I know a place up ahead where we stand a good chance of catching them by surprise."

"Yeah?"

"We passed it on the way here. No reason you should have noticed it. But, I was looking for just such a place."

"You knew they'd come this way," Tom said.

"Easiest way north from the Rocking A. If they mean to sell their stolen slaves they have to go north to a market."

"Makes sense."

"It's about all that does," Martin said.

After a while, the small slave caravan rumbled past them. Martin made out a man in the lead, the driver, two flankers and a man riding drag. He could not tell who they were, but he thought he could figure it out.

After the wagon passed, Martin turned his horse and rode well away from the road at a slow pace so that they would not make noise that could be heard from the road above the clatter of the wagon.

"Now what do you know?" Tom asked as Martin picked up the pace, riding a parallel course to the road.

"I figure one of the Mexicans is leading the way. One who knows the road. They've got two flankers and a man riding drag. I reckon they'll change off just to keep from getting bored or stay sharp."

"Meaning?"

"Well, Reynaud would ride drag for a while. The lead Mexican might switch places with one of the flankers. That leaves Wilhoit as a flanker, and he could switch off with Reynaud. I don't figure either of the Mexicans to bring up the rear."

"What about the driver?"

"He might change off, but it doesn't change much if he does."

"So, what do you figure to do? There's four of us and five of them."

"I'm thinking on it," Martin said.

"That sure does give me a lot of confidence."

"I thought it might."

Martin slowed his horse again to rest their mounts. Finally, he stopped. The others reined up with a kind of obedience that granted Martin the leadership he needed. The three men looked at him, waiting for him to speak.

"Roy, I've got a job for you. After I tell you what it is, you tell me if you can do it."

"Why, sure, Martin."

"I want you to ride down alongside that road, keep up with the wagon, but keep yourself out of sight. Think you can do that?"

"I think so."

"You can't let them know we're here."

"I savvy."

"Ride along for a half hour or so, then gradually drift off until you're out of earshot and then come catch up with us. Don't spare the leather. We haven't got far to go before we have to make our move."

"What if I can't find you?"

"Remember the road. We'll keep the same distance we're at now. You won't be able to miss us. Can you figure out thirty minutes of time?"

"I'm pretty good at time," Roy said.

"Watch what they do. When they change positions. See if they look nervous. But, don't get too close."

"I won't."

"Go on, then," Martin said.

Roy turned his horse and rode back toward the road. The land there was crisscrossed with arroyos, shallow gullies, worn out of the land over time by flash floods. It was broken country, thick with trees and grass.

Martin kicked his horse and rode on, followed by Tom and Cullie.

"You trust that youngster?" Tom asked after a few moments.

"He'll do."

"Mighty young to do a man's job."

"He's grown about as much as he's going to. He's about the same age as my boy, and they've crossed some of the same rivers. You just worry about yourself, Tom."

"I'd hate like hell to catch a ball in the back if Roy spoils the cider."

"You've got a right sharp imagination, Tom."

They heard coyotes in the distance, baying at the moonrise, flinging bright lyrical ribbons to the sky that was haunting, beautiful in the stillness of the night. Martin smiled. The coyotes' songs were part of the reason he loved that country, why he felt at home in the brush, why he loved the night, the peace it brought him.

"I've had my leg pissed on before," Tom said.

Martin picked up the pace once more, setting his horse to a gallop. Tom and Cullie had to slap leather to catch up and by the time Martin slowed again, all three horses were blowing. Martin halted, dismounted. "We'll walk 'em down," he said.

The other two men, without grumbling, slipped from their saddles and walked on wobbly heels behind Martin in single file and the coyotes stopped singing and the stars shifted in the diamond-strewn sky. Martin ticked off time in his mind, took long strides as if he knew every inch of ground and how long it would take Roy to catch up with them once he had finished his reconnoitering.

Roy heard the wagon coming long before he saw it, and he backed his horse into the shadows and stationed him behind enough mesquite to make him invisible. He held his breath as the caravan came into view and when he saw the lead rider, he knew it was a Mexican by the red bandanna around his neck and the straw hat he wore. As the wagon passed him by, he saw David Wilhoit and his teeth ground down tight as his jaw stiffened.

On the other side of the wagon was a man he did not know. He figured that must be Reynaud, and then he knew the other Mexican outrider was riding drag. He let the wagon pass by before he turned his horse and rode away from the road at an angle, moving very slowly. It was then that his horse paused for just a slash of a second and broke wind. Roy reined up and cursed silently. The noise had sounded like a thunderclap in his ears. He listened to see if the wagon would stop. Any minute he expected to hear riders crashing through the brush, coming after him.

The wagon did stop and Roy held fast, keeping his horse in check as he listened for any signs that the outriders were going to look for him. It seemed to him that hours passed. He heard the faint rasp of voices, snatches of garbled talk that he could not decipher, and then, at last, the wagon started rolling again.

Roy breathed a sigh of relief and waited several more moments just to make sure they had not sent one of the Mexicans out into the mesquite to look for him. He almost wished that it might be David who would come after him.

He sat there, fingering the trigger on his rifle, pressing his thumb down lightly on the hammer so he'd be ready to cock it back as he drew it from the leather scabbard tucked under his right leg. He touched the butt of his pistol, too, rubbing the cherrywood grip, feeling the brass rivet, the metal strap.

When it was quiet again, Roy set his horse to leave that place, angling away on a path that would take him back to the course Martin and the other two men had taken. He rode through the trees, keeping his bearings in mind and when he neared the track he thought they were on, he leaned over and studied the ground as the horse carried him northward.

Roy carried with him confused thoughts dredged up from deep in his mind by the sight of David Wilhoit, the man who had taken his mother away from him. He won-

dered now if he would have had the courage to shoot
Wilhoit if the man had come after him. He wondered if
he would have been able to kill him and still face his
mother. These were terrible thoughts that he wrestled
with and tried to shut out, but he could not subdue them
in the darkness of night. They were like the thoughts
that came to him when he was about to fall asleep and
would not go away until his eyelids got so heavy they
closed and let the images drift away on waves of sleep.

He spurred his horse into an off-gait and the jolting
helped keep him from falling into a slumberous state that
would have been dangerous. And, he knew he had to
catch up with Martin and the two nighthawks, get ahead
of the wagon.

Finally, he put David and his mother out of his mind
as the horse jarred his body with its jolting gallop.

He almost ran Martin down. One moment the way was
clear and the next, he was in the deeper darkness of trees
and the three men loomed up right in front of him like
sudden apparitions.

"Ho up, Roy," Martin said.

"Hey."

"Any change back there?"

"They're coming at a steady pace," Roy said. "Two
flankers, a point man and one riding drag."

"Good. We're not far from the place I picked for the
ambush."

"How do you figure to get the slaves to the Box B if
you capture them?" Cullie asked. "Walk 'em?"

"We'll borrow Aguilar's wagon," Martin said. "I had
that figured before we even left. He won't miss it."

"Let's see this place you got picked," Tom said.

"Follow me," Martin said, and rode toward the road.
The three men fell into line, their mounts following his
lead with weary, leaden docility as if they were old war-
horses trekking to some nocturnal abattoir where Black
Sabbath witches were in waiting in long midnight robes,

fire-blackened cauldrons bubbling steamy clouds behind them.

Roy felt the eeriness and the muscles of his abdomen tautened as he realized the enormity of what was about to happen. The horses dropped into a dark, featureless coulee, black as the pit of hell, a place choked with brush and he could almost hear the rattlesnakes slither away as the horses clacked their iron hooves on loose stones and sent them clicking like dice against the larger rocks so that they sounded like skeletal bones clacking in some wizard's castle keep.

The four horsemen climbed slowly out of the coulee onto a somnolent plain bristling with mesquite bushes and treacherous with nopal cactus, a long dry wash that led into a series of interstitial gullies worn to desecration over countless centuries, hollowed out by rains and winds and floods until they lay like scars of old wounds upon the land. A few yards farther on, they encountered a deep arroyo, seemingly bottomless in the nightpitch, and Martin turned his horse left, away from it and came upon a gradual rise that led to the road, to a patch of it, bordered by mesquite trees so thick they seemed to be threaded together into a maze's wall that led to God knew where and Roy realized what a perfect place it was for an ambush.

Martin reined up and halted his horse and turned to face his three followers. The others stopped and tried to discern the features on his face, but it was a mask, hidden from them in the darkness of trees and sky and they waited for him to speak and reveal that he was alive and the same man they had followed, not some wraith born out of the night's black illusions.

"This is where we'll jump them," Martin said. "Roy, you'll ride past the arroyo and stay just off the road. We'll let the point rider reach you. Then, I'll take out the driver of the wagon and turn it into the arroyo.

"Tom, you and Cullie take out the near flank rider and

the drag man. I'll stop the wagon and ride back to take the opposite flanker."

"Jesus," Tom said, "you pile up a plate."

"You have to picture it in your mind long before that wagon gets here. Roy, if you can down the point rider quick enough, you can take out the other flanker. He might come riding up on you, anyway."

"See what I mean?" Tom said. "You got a heap more probables than possibles in this little scheme."

"Hell, it's darker'n the inside of a well here," Cullie said.

"Your eyes will get used to it," Martin said.

"Do we shoot or rope?" Tom asked, "or just yell and scare the hell out of 'em?"

"You can do whichever's easiest for you," Martin said. "I'm going to run up on my man after he's shot his rifle and knock him off his horse, then hog-tie him if I have time."

"If not?" Tom asked.

"I'll coldcock him with the butt of my rifle."

"Only thing left to do is have a pie social," Tom said.

"They'll be confused," Martin said. "We'll chase 'em back into those gullies or carry 'em back there and tie 'em up if they're still breathing."

"Cullie," Tom said, "was I you, I'd shoot your man dead and get your pistol ready. And I'm going to duck like hell because I think there'll be lead flying like ducks in October."

"I was thinking that the best thing to do is shoot their horses. Put them on the ground. They'll probably shoot wild and you can ride up on your man and knock him senseless."

"You got an idea there," Tom said, coming around.

"We have the advantage," Martin said. "They're not expecting us. And, with the wagon out of the way, they'll try and run after it. That's the natural thing to do. Go after what you're guarding."

"Only it won't be there," Roy said.

"That's the idea," Martin said.

"I think we can do it, Tom," Cullie said.

"Pick your spots. We haven't got much time," Martin said. "Roy, go on."

Roy rode off. Martin put Tom just above the dip in the road and led Cullie beyond to a place in the trees where he could watch the whole caravan pass by and catch the drag rider from the rear. Then, he rode back and found a place on the opposite side of the road. He had an idea that he might take out the flanker on his side and still go after the wagon driver. If he was quick, it would work.

Soon, they all heard the distant clatter of the wagon. None could see the other, but each man sensed what the others were doing. They unlimbered their rifles, checked their locks, poured fresh powder into the pans and blew gently on the grains, leaving only a film of fine black dust that would explode into fire when the flint struck the iron face of the frizzen.

Some moments later, the point rider rode past. Then, the wagon rumbled up to the precipice of the dip in the road. Two riders flanked the wagon as it bent downward to the lowering road. Close behind, the drag rider rode, oblivious to what lay ahead.

Roy waited until the lead rider was just a few feet past his position and then took a bead on the neck of his horse. He cocked his rifle and led the target slightly. He held his breath, then squeezed the trigger.

There was a hiss and a poof as the spark from the flint struck the pan and the fire shot through the hole. The main powder charge ignited and the rifle cracked like a whip, spouting orange flame. White smoke obliterated horse and rider but Roy heard the ball thunk into flesh.

The horse screamed and then the night exploded with more shots and flames lit the darkness and men yelled as if they had been thrown into the fires of hell.

Roy raced through the smoke straight at where he had

heard the horse fall, his veins tingling, his heart throbbing, his senses running hot with electricity and he wondered if he would ride into a lead ball and never see the stars or his mother again.

39

ANSON AND PEEBO did not speak to each other for fifteen long miles as they rode toward the burned-out jacal that lay within a stone's throw of the Nueces River. Anson's head cleared and he felt no aftereffects of the concussion. The fresh air, the clear blue sky dotted with little cauliflower clouds, the land stretching out forever, all served to change his mood and his outlook. He thought, too, that getting away from the ranch was a big part of the mood that was on him now.

Being around his mother always twanged his nerves, made him edgy, disgruntled. He had not stopped to figure out why to any great degree, but now he thought it might be because he knew she was ill, possibly going crazy, and there was the smell of death about her that brought back memories of Juanito, Bone and what had happened between Mickey and his mother. And, having Lazaro around didn't help any—the boy was a constant reminder of his mother's sin and the terrible consequences they all were forced to bear.

They followed a pair of wagon tracks that had been rutted over the years since Martin Baron had purchased the land from old Aguilar after giving up the sea to raise cattle. Such scars as these lasted a long time, especially with fairly frequent use. The Barons had hauled in supplies from Galveston and Corpus Christi over that route at least twice a year and Anson had used it to find his way to the farthest eastern edge of the Box B for the past couple of years. Each time he rode it, he felt more at home and the tracks were comforting; more or less stable markings on an unmarked land.

They came to a small creek and a watering hole that was still seeing a lot of use. There were cattle and deer tracks in the soft mud around the hole, laced by the tracks of birds, armadillos, coyotes, rabbits, rats, and the boots of men.

Anson reined up and ground-tied his horse in the shade of a husky oak whose branches spread wide as if to provide shelter for wayfarers. Peebo jumped from his horse as if he had just arrived at a picnic spot. Anson spread his body on the ground and drank from the running stream above the water hole.

Then, he took off his hat and dipped it in the water, carried it to his horse. Peebo, watching him, did the same.

"Good thing you got here first," Peebo said.

"Why?"

"I would have watered my horse first, out of habit."

"Our horses would have sucked that hole dry and we wouldn't have gotten a lick out of 'em the rest of the day."

"It's a long country," Peebo said.

"Long and wide."

"And then some."

"If we hadn't run into trouble after you got here with those horses, this is the way we would have taken getting back to the ranch headquarters."

"I figured as much," Peebo said, carrying a hatful of

water to his horse. "Shade feels mighty nice."

"Juanito said God made places such as this."

"I believe him."

"I've been thinking about him all mornin'," Anson said.

"Thinkin'? You must have got your brain back. I thought you must have plumb lost it somewheres yesterday."

"You still got your smart mouth, I see."

"Sometimes it ain't as smart as I'd like it to be."

The two carried another pair of hatfuls of water to their horses. They could feel the light breeze under the tree, cooling them down.

"I probably wouldn't shoot that horse that throwed me if I was to see it right here," Anson said.

"No, I figured you was mad at somethin' else and wanted to take it out on the horse."

"Is that what you figured?"

"I didn't think you'd shoot a helpless horse that hadn't done you no harm."

Anson laughed. The tension had been broken between the two as if it were a cord that had stretched so tight it had snapped under the strain.

He kicked a clod of dirt that had once been mud, rolled up above the creek from some hooved creature by accident. "I probably never would have pulled the trigger."

"Especially if you looked into its big brown eyes," Peebo said.

Anson laughed again. "It would have helped if you had named the damned horse."

"Yeah?"

"Hard to kill something you've been calling Joe or Billy."

"True. A 'course I could have called it Shithead."

"It wouldn't have been too hard to shoot old Shithead," Anson said, laughing underneath his words.

"Or Percy, maybe."

"I don't know if I could kill a Percy."

"Maybe Percival."

"Yeah, I could murder a Percival, no question."

"Well, I'll just have to be a mite careful on what I name my stock with you around, Anson."

"Name them something pretty, maybe. Like Fluffy or Taffy."

"I could do that. When you rode into town you could holler out, 'Whoa up, Fluffy.' "

Anson laughed gruffly, letting out a lot of the tension that still lingered like a stubborn flame that won't go out no matter how many times you blow on it.

"Let's have a smoke," Anson said. "Then, we'll ride another five miles and make camp."

"Or we could ride into the evening," Peebo said. "Make some miles in the cool."

"All right. Let's see how we feel by then." He stepped out from under the oak and looked at the western quadrant of the sky, saw that the sun stood on the low side. "There's another little crick about eight or ten miles farther on. If it isn't dried up."

"My canteen's full."

"So's mine."

They rolled smokes and squatted in the shade. Anson picked up a stick and started drawing in the soft dirt. Peebo watched him, fascinated at his friend's intense concentration. Anson drew several shapes, squares, circles, diamonds, hexagons, triangles, trapezoids, and other curious shapes. He drew curving lines and straight ones all in a row. To one side of this growing pictograph, he drew a large box with sides of straight lines so that it made a square. Inside the square, he drew a large B. He inhaled from his cigarette and blew smoke out of the side of his mouth.

When he was finished, Anson rocked back on his legs, cocked his head and viewed his large sketch with a critical eye. "Know what all this is, Peebo?" he asked.

Peebo blew a stream of smoke out of his mouth and

hunched forward to get a closer look at Anson's strange design. He tipped his hat back from his forehead and scratched a spot on his scalp as if to align his thoughts. "Hen scratches?"

Anson chuckled. "You can do better'n that."

"Looks like some kind of map, maybe. Crude as any kid's scratchin' in the dirt. I give up."

Anson took the stick and waved it like a pointer, or a wand over the entire landscape of his sketch. He finally plunked the point of the stick square on the large B he had drawn.

"This here's the town Ken Richman built. We call it Baronsville. You ain't been there yet."

"No, I haven't. That's for sure."

Anson brought the pointer over to another series of small squares. "This is where we were this morning. Headquarters of the Box B. These little dots over here are where most of our hands live. About a mile, mile and a half from the big house."

"Didn't I see you walking over there last night?"

"Yeah, you might have. I went to see Jorge's family."

"To tell them how he died?"

"Yes. To tell them I was sorry."

"That all?"

"I gave them some money, told them where they could find his body. Look, let's get back to the map. All these other shapes around it are Baron property."

"None of 'em look connected, lessen those lines mean roads."

"They do. Our ranch looks kind of like a patchwork quilt. A piece here and a piece there. With connecting roads. See?"

"Kinda."

"Okay. This little chunk here is where Roy Killian has his itty-bitty spread my pa gave him. Likely, he'll grow it some bigger someday. Buy more land."

Anson made some scrawls to the west of the Killian icon. "He'd have to go this away."

"I can see that."

"Over here," Anson said, raking the stick through the air and pointing at other squares, "is Matteo Aguilar's Rocking A. Box B and Killian come to a point here."

"What's all that jumble to the south?"

"That's the brasada. The brush country. No one claims it. It's wild and thick and full of snakes and wild cattle and God knows what."

"And all this over here? I gather we're just about in the middle of that."

"Yep. More Box B land. Here's the road we're on, see? And up yonder's the Nueces. Down there is the Rio Grande, what used to be called the Río Bravo by the Mexicans because they thought it was a short river."

"How come you drew all this?"

"See these lands around the headquarters?"

"I reckon."

"Well, they're fenced and we have cattle on 'em. This is where we do the crossbreeding and experimenting with different grasses."

"And all this other?"

"What me and the hands have been doing is branding everything on this whole range. I mean to put a Box and a B on every head of cattle I run across and then fence all this in, probably with mesquite at first, and cull 'em down and mix 'em up and see what breeds do best. After we finish branding every damned critter that moves, then we'll gather 'em all up and I'll have me the biggest herd in all of Texas."

Peebo tipped his hat back and ground out his cigarette.

Anson got up, took one last puff and tossed the stick away, crushed the butt of the cigarette into the dirt.

"Seems like you bit off an awful lot, Anson."

"We're just about finished with the branding, near as I can figure. We won't stop, of course, but next thing we'll do is put up the fences, cross fences and then we'll make the gather. We'll have to sell off some stock so I can hire extra hands, but we'll get it all done."

"I think you might," Peebo said.

"First I got to catch that white bull and put my brand on his sorry hide."

"Then, after he kills you, what?"

Anson laugheɑ.

"If he kills me, I'll kill him. But, no, I'm going to make that mean sonofabitch fall in love with me. He's going to love getting his hide burned and he's going to follow me home like a puppy."

"That what you think? Boy, I think that old bull's goin' to stomp your ass right into the ground and piss on what's left of your hide."

"Let's mount up," Anson said, heading for his horse.

Peebo nodded and went to his horse. The two men set out once again, headed east. In the waning hours of the day, the sun played with the shadows and the land took on a richness of texture that made Anson's chest swell with pride.

Peebo, too, was not unaffected by the pastel colors that seemed to shift and blend with the changing light as the sun sank lower in the sky and softened the harsh features of that rugged country. He came up alongside Anson, flashed his disarming grin and began to talk when Anson smiled back.

"Mighty pretty, ain't it?"

Anson knew what Peebo meant. He nodded.

"All this has a way of getting to you."

"It gets inside you," Anson said.

"I could get to love it."

"I already do."

"Makes you want to ride forever and never stop," Peebo said, and fell silent as if enraptured by the spell. Certain places they passed began to haze over and they rode in silence for a time. Finally, it was Anson who spoke, as if he had suddenly found his tongue.

"Peebo, you reckon we can really catch that white bull?"

"I don't know. If our ropes hold, I reckon."

"I really want him bad."

"How come?"

"Well, I got this idea, I mean I've had the idea for quite a spell, and I want to try it out."

"What's that, son?"

"I've been chasing longhorns for years and pa and I have talked about putting more meat on their skinny bones."

"Thought you was crossbreeding some of 'em."

"A few. But, when we fence all this section off, I want to cull out the skinny beeves and put the fat ones together. Try different feeds and grasses."

"Get bigger, fatter calves, you think."

"Yes. It ought to work. Juanito talked a lot about breeding cattle when he was alive. He was an Argentinian and they've been at it for more years than Texas had flags."

"So, you'll try it."

"That bull might be the one I've been looking for, to father a herd of superior longhorns that we could sell with pride anywhere in the world."

"It's a big dream."

"But, I got this feeling a while ago."

"What feeling?" Peebo asked, as the sun fell deeper into the west and the shadows stretched out ahead of them like wraiths unleashed from dark canyons far to the west.

"Do you know the word *doom?*" Anson asked.

"Doom? Something like death, I figure."

"Well, like death, I guess, but the word means something else to me."

"What does it mean to you, Anson?"

"It's like something's going to happen and I don't know what. Something real bad."

"Maybe the word means that, too."

"I feel like something's hanging over my head and I'm not going to find out what it is until it falls on me."

"I've had feelings like that, too. Is it about the white bull?"

"Yeah, I think so. But, it's a lot of other things, too. It's Ma and my pa and that blind boy, Lazaro. A whole lot of things."

"You think too damned much."

"Maybe," Anson said. "But I feel like doom is dogging my tracks."

"Best you put old doom out of your mind, son."

"I don't know if I can."

"It's just the darkness coming on, Anson. It'll go away with the morning light."

Anson sighed. He turned in the saddle and looked at the western horizon. The sky was changing as rapidly as the land and the sun hung just above the edge of the world like a blazing disk hammered out of bronze and gold and the clouds were starting to catch fire, streamers of them stretched across the far reaches of the heavens like tattered banners woven of cotton and flax.

He turned around and sighed again.

"You know what, Anson?"

"What?"

"Back there. When we stopped for a smoke."

"Yeah."

"We missed doin' somethin' and maybe that's what's botherin' you."

"Doing what?"

Peebo laughed. A grin lit up his face even in the shadow that had fallen across it like a vagrant scarf.

"We was sittin' by that stream and we didn't chunk one rock into it."

"I used to do that when I was a boy," Anson said.

"Yeah, me, too. I think you and me are gettin' old."

"Not that old."

"I mean if we had chunked some rocks into that creek, we'd have been boys again."

Anson shook his head, even as he saw that they were coming close to the place where they would spend the night. He could smell the water and the horses were starting to get frisky, tossing their heads and prancing.

"Peebo, you're loco."

"Well, I still think we shoulda chunked some rocks back there. Maybe you wouldn't be riding with doom hanging over your head."

Anson brightened. "Yeah, you may be right, Peebo. We should have chunked some rocks into that creek like we was fuzz-faced boys."

"Damned right."

"We'll do it tonight," Anson said. "Yonder is another creek and that's where we'll spread out our bedrolls."

For emphasis, Anson slacked the reins and touched spurs to his horse's flanks. "Race you there," he called back to Peebo as Anson's horse broke into a wild gallop.

Peebo let out a whoop and chased after Anson. They looked like a couple of boys just let out of school and the shadows raced after them and overtook them and the sun fell off the edge of the earth and left a molten sky flaming as far as the eye could see, as if it were a huge reflection of a blazing prairie fire set there like a painting by some Incan god traversing the heavens in a fiery chariot.

40

ROY RAN ON rubbery legs through the smoke from his rifle, his heart frozen somewhere between his chest and throat, his veins burning hot with adrenaline, his rifle across his chest like a thin shield. He saw the downed horse first, then a grubby Mexican trying to rise from the ground on wobbly feet braced by at least one shattered ankle, the other twisted like a tangled rope.

Remembering what Martin had said, Roy took his rifle by the muzzle, grasping the barrel firmly with both hands. He waded toward the fallen Mexican point rider and swung the rifle like a bat. Luis put up his hands to ward off the blow, but the stock broke both wrists and careened off his head. There was the sound of a loud smack and Luis keeled over as if felled by a twenty-pound maul.

Rifles cracked as Roy fell headlong from the momentum of his rush and hit the ground with a resounding thud that jarred his senses, flashed red explosions in his head. He heard the chilling screams of women, rising high-pitched and shrill. The screams sounded like the raucous gabble of geese fleeing in terror from the red fox suddenly invading the barnyard.

Martin ran his horse down on top of the wagon driver, swerved as he brought his rifle around in a one-handed swing, scything through the air until the butt smashed into Fidel's jaw, cracking the bone and shutting off the Mexican's cry of pain.

The black slaves in the wagon cringed and huddled together as Fidel fell to the side of the seat, his right arm caught on the front board. Martin reached over and grabbed the reins left on the seat like a tangle of snakes. Socrates reached over the board as Martin lifted the reins.

"Can you turn this wagon hard to the right?" Martin asked.

"Sure can," Socrates said, climbing over the board.

"Trust me," Martin said.

Socrates nodded and scrambled into the seat. He grabbed the reins from Martin's hand. "Where do I go?"

"Turn up that draw to your right and keep going until you can't go any further. Wait for me."

"Yes sir," Socrates said.

Martin heard the sharp crack of rifle shots, the sound like a snapping of whips and he turned his horse to see if Tom or Cullie needed any help.

Cullie shot David's horse in the head, just below the eye. It was a brutal shot and the horse twisted its neck as the lead ball smashed through hide and bone and flattened before it ripped out the other side of its head, taking with it the mashed pulp of its flesh and bone, leaving an exit wound the size of a saucer.

David felt himself flying through the air as he lost contact with the saddle. His rifle flew in another direction and he braced his arms for the fall. The horse began to buck and kick with pain and he felt a shod hoof graze his side. He hit the ground like a sack of meal and lights danced in his head before he surrendered to a darkness not born of the night.

Reynaud ducked as a lead ball sizzled over his head. He fired his rifle from the hip, pointing the muzzle straight at Cullie. Cullie took the ball in the chest, grunted as if punched in the solar plexus and doubled over in the saddle. Reynaud slid his empty rifle into its scabbard and drew his pistol, even as he spurred his horse toward Cullie's position. He raced past the dying man and into the brush. Shots and screams filled the air as he disappeared, safe from any harm.

Tom saw Reynaud streak past Cullie and fired his pistol, but knew the shot had gone wild. He rode over to Cullie, who was slumped in his saddle, moaning in pain.

Cullie stared downward onto a saddle drenched in blood.

"Cullie, can you ride?" Tom asked.

The wounded man coughed and sprayed blood on the pommel, clear to the saddle horn. Tom cursed and leaned over to lift Cullie's head. Blood bubbled from Cullie's mouth as Tom looked at his face. He saw the hole in Cullie's chest, small, round, and blurting crimson with every beat of the dying man's heart.

"Christ, Cullie," Tom said, "you caught it for damned sure."

Cullie gargled the blood in his throat. Unable to speak, he flailed his arms, struggling to breathe. Tom held the man against him, listening to the rattle in his throat, the wheezing in his lungs like a blacksmith's bellow. Cullie shuddered and his arms stopped moving. He slumped against Tom, let out a last liquid gasp and did not take any more air into his shattered lungs.

"Tom?" Martin called. "Need any help?"

"Go on, Baron. Do what you got to get done."

"Roy," Martin yelled. "Go after that wagon. Be there in a minute."

Roy swung his horse in a tight turn. He had heard the wagon rumble by, the women screaming and sobbing, and now he raced after it, glad to get away from the smell of burnt black powder and stinking smoke.

Martin rode up along the road, saw David Wilhoit lying unconscious in one of the wagon ruts. Martin did not stop, but turned his horse and trotted to the place where he had sent the black people with the wagon.

"Roy?" Martin called.

"Here," Roy yelled back and Martin saw the outline of the wagon at the end of the coulee, stopped, the women only whimpering now, sounding oddly like the elliptical warblings of mourning doves squatted on dusty perches among a copse of shadowy trees. He heard the black men speaking in a tongue that sounded like the muffled beat of a drum made from a hollowed-out tree.

"Do any of you speak English?" Martin asked, as he rode up to the wagon. The tall black man in front stood up.

"We all do. Some."

"Do you have a name?"

"Sir, the white folks call me Socrates."

"Good name, Socrates."

Roy moved closer to hear the conversation. "I told 'em not to be scared," he said.

"Are you scared?" Martin asked.

"No, sir," Socrates said. "But, we're all powerful curious."

"I don't blame you. I heard you were stolen from your masters. Back in Louisiana, I think."

"Yes, sir."

"Well, you're free now."

"Free, sir?"

"Yes, Socrates. However, I've got a proposition for you and your people, if you'd care to listen."

"I'se all ears, sir."

"If you want work, I think we can find homes for all of you. You would get paid, just like anyone else."

"Paid? With real money?"

"That's right. And, I'll have papers drawn up for each

of you saying you are free. No longer slaves."

"It sounds good, sir. Too good to be true."

Martin laughed. "I know it does, Socrates. My name is Martin Baron and I own considerable property. The man next to me is Roy Killian and he's just getting started in the cattle business. We have a town that would welcome you, I think. There's a lot of building going on there, and you'd get decent wages."

The women made sounds of wonder in their throats and the other men grunted in approval as they listened to Martin's words.

"You talk it over," Martin said. "Roy, you better ride on back there and tend to your father-in-law."

"Father-in-law?"

"David Wilhoit. He's knocked cold."

"Oh, him. Yeah. What should I do? Want me to shoot him?"

"I doubt if that will be necessary. Go on."

"I wasn't serious," Roy said.

"I knew you weren't."

Roy made his way through the dark of the narrow draw and onto the road. Behind him he heard the gabble of Negro voices and he would have given a nickel to know what they were saying.

The road looked different. Not only was the wagon gone, but he saw riderless horses standing still, as if they had been frozen there, their reins trailing. He rode on, saw a man lying by the side of the road, a part of the shadows, unmoving, as still as the stillness itself, and beyond, two more men sitting down, one cradling the other in his arms.

"That you, Roy?" a voice called out.

"Yeah."

"One got away. The Frenchie, I think."

"Tom?"

"Yeah."

"Cullie there?"

"He's done for," Tom said.

Roy rode up to the fallen man, looked down. He could tell it was David, even in the dim light of stars and the sliver of moon that had tacked itself to the dark velvet of the sky, hanging like a shining scimitar above the ghostly land.

"David?"

There was no answer.

Roy swung his right leg over the saddle's cantle and stepped down, pushed his horse aside. The horse stood there, sniffing, its ears twitching, its eyes rolling like marbles at the strangeness of its surroundings.

David did not move as Roy knelt beside him. "You're out cold, all right." Roy lifted David's head and put his ear to his mouth. "Breathing, anyways."

David let out a weak moan.

Roy shook him slightly. "Wake up, Mr. David Wilhoit. You ain't dead, you sonofabitch, but you ought to be." He slapped David's face, both cheeks, hard enough to jar the unconscious man.

"You gonna wake up?" Roy asked.

David's eyelids batted up and down as if the spirit inside were trying to peer out from whatever somber cave wherein it had dwelled. Roy leaned close to him, until he could feel David's breath on his face. "You there, David?"

"Wha?"

"Wake up. It's time to get up and go on home."

"Roy? That you?"

"It better be, or it's the devil himself come to welcome you to hell."

"I—I . . . What happened?"

"You was in the wrong place at the wrong time, Wilhoit. Get your sorry ass up."

Roy stood up. He grabbed David's lapels and pulled the man to his feet. David stood there, swaying, groggy, obviously disoriented. He put out his hands to balance himself as if he had found himself awakened on some high wire stretched taut over some deep chasm unknown by surveyors or chartists.

"Where in hell am I?" David asked.

"You don't know? Hell, you might as well join them slaves in the wagon. They don't know where they are, either."

"Slaves? Oh, yeah. What happened?"

"Somebody knocked you off your horse. They should have shot your sorry ass."

Roy withdrew his hands from David, half hoping he'd fall down. But David touched a hand to his head as if imparting light or knowledge through the bleeding crack in his skull. He touched the slight wound gingerly and winced.

"I remember. Roy, I didn't want to come along. Matteo wouldn't take no for an answer."

"What about my ma? She give you her approval?"

"No. Your mother didn't want me to go."

"So, now you're a goddamned slave trader, are you?"

"I don't deserve that, Roy. You've got it all wrong."

"Hell, you was ridin' with these jaspers, carrying a loaded rifle. I figure you knew what was cooking in that pot."

"I couldn't get out of it. Matteo would probably have killed me if I refused to go."

"Well, I ought to kill you myself."

"Where are the Negroes?"

"Where you can't get at 'em."

"Good. I never cottoned to what Aguilar was doing."

"You sure got a sorry-ass way of showin' it."

"Reynaud?"

"The Frenchie. Never saw him. Run off, I reckon. Damned coward."

"I didn't trust him."

Roy reached down and picked up David's hat, which had fallen off. "Here. Put on your hat, get on your horse and get on back to my mother. She'll be worried if Reynaud shows up at the Rocking A and you're not with him."

"Thanks, Roy. I'm sorry I got mixed up in this."

"I'm sorry you got mixed up with my mother."

"I love her."

Roy turned away, his neck swelling with anger, the blood-engorged veins swelling under the skin like small blue snakes. He mounted his horse and rode away before he said something he knew he'd be sorry for. He turned his horse toward the place where Tom and Cullie were sitting.

"Tom?"

"Roy, Cullie's dead."

"Shot?"

"By that Frenchie, Reynaud."

"Can I help?"

"Yes."

Roy dismounted. Out of the corner of his eye he saw David limp to his horse. A few seconds later, David rode past them. Tom glared after him. "Who's that?" he asked.

"David Wilhoit. I think he got roped into this by Aguilar."

"He's lucky he didn't get a chunk of lead in his gullet."

"He's married to my ma."

"Too bad for her."

"Is Cullie really dead?" Roy asked.

"Yeah. Help me get him on his horse. We'll lash him on and take him back to Baronsville."

"Damn, Tom."

Tom said nothing. He and Roy lifted the dead man, lugged him over to Cullie's horse. They draped his body over the saddle and Tom loosened the thongs on Cullie's lariat. He and Roy laced Cullie with a diamond hitch, running rope through the stirrups. The horse acted up until they were finished, turning, sidling to get out from under the dead weight.

"Where's Baron?"

"He's up that draw with the wagon."

Tom mounted his horse as Roy held the reins of Cullie's horse. Tom rode over and took the reins from Roy. "Let's go," he said.

Roy climbed on his horse and followed Tom to the little draw. He could not take his eyes off the body of Cullie. Not long ago he had been alive and now he was gone. It could have happened to any of them.

Martin had the wagon turned around and was leading it from the draw when Tom rode up, leading Cullie's horse.

"What you got there, Tom?"

"Reynaud killed Cullie."

"That's a damned shame."

"I'll get the sonofabitch one day."

"Reynaud got away?"

"He lit a shuck."

"Lucky."

"Cowardly."

"Yeah, that, too."

Tom noticed that one of the Negroes was driving the wagon. He recognized him from his and Cullie's seeing him on the docks, and later on, riding in that same wagon to the Aguilar ranch.

"Well," Tom said, "you got what you came for, I reckon."

"So it seems."

"They all willin' to go with us?"

"Yes."

"Pretty trustin' ain't they?" Tom looked straight at Socrates when he said it.

"They'll be free men, Tom."

"They cost me a friend."

Martin turned in the saddle to face Socrates. "Just drive the wagon on to the road and turn left. Roy, you see they make it. Tom, ride on up with me so we can talk."

Roy nodded and took Martin's place at the head of the wagon. Tom handed him the reins to Cullie's horse and followed Martin out of the draw and onto the road.

"Tom," Martin said, when they were out of earshot of Roy and the Negroes, "you don't want to go and make those darkies any more miserable than they already are."

"Cullie got killed giving freedom to them niggers."

"Cullie got killed. You can't blame the Negroes for that. They're innocent bystanders."

"Baron, I ain't here to tell you your business, but you're way out on a limb here."

"You think so."

"Them are stolen slaves. Texas, last I heard, was a slave state. You can't just go and turn 'em loose like they was white."

"Mister, I can do any damned thing I want to. The Box B is not a slave state. And, I'm the Box B."

"It sure as hell don't make me no never mind, but I'd sure as hell think twice and then twice't more was I you 'bout payin' out money to slaves born and bred."

"I'm not going to argue with you, Tom. When we get back to Baronsville, you see Ken Richman and draw your pay."

"Might be somebody in Louisiana interested in what happened to them contraband niggers."

Martin stopped his horse, turned to face Tom. Even in the dim light, his face reflected his anger in its chiseled features. Tom reined up and met Martin's stare head on.

"Tom, I'm going to say this only once. If you ever use that word again on this ride, it'll be the last thing out of your mouth."

"Are you threatening me, Baron?"

"I'm warning you. I don't like the term. Those are people back there. Their skins are black and that ain't no fault of their own. As far as I'm concerned, you aren't a damned bit better'n any one of 'em."

"You got a lot to learn, Baron."

"Well, as long as you're riding for me, I'm the teacher."

Tom could almost feel the heat from Martin's glare. He clamped his mouth shut and jerked his reins, turning his horse around. He rode back to the wagon, jerked the reins of Cullie's horse from Roy's hand and rode back up the road.

When he passed Martin, he said, "I quit, Baron."

"Too late, Tom," Martin said. "I fired you five minutes ago. I don't want to see you in Baronsville again. You draw your pay and Cullie's too."

"You ain't heard the last of me, Baron."

Tom rode on before Martin could reply, but Martin knew he'd already said all he had to say to Harris. Men like him were a blight on the land. For once, he questioned Ken's judgment in hiring such a man.

Roy caught up with him.

"Where'd Tom go?"

"He rode on."

"Any trouble?" Roy asked.

"No, no trouble at all."

"He looked pretty mad to me."

"Men like him come and go," Martin said. "They have no roots, no ties to anything. He won't even be missed."

"No, I reckon not. I guess he was mad about Cullie gettin' killed."

Martin didn't answer. He slowed his horse until he was alongside Socrates.

"If you and your friends are hungry, we have grub in our saddlebags," Martin told the driver.

"No sir, we's too excited to eat right now."

"You just let out a holler if your belly starts to rumble."

"Yes, sir," Socrates said, grinning wide. He looked back at his friends in the wagon and nodded his head. They all smiled. "Did you hear that?" he asked. "We can holler for food and that man ain't goin' to cane us. No sir. We be free."

The ex-slaves in the wagon murmured their joy at Socrates' words and, later, they began to chant and croon the old songs they barely remembered. Their singing rose on the night air and floated over the country they passed like flower petals of many hues strewn in their wake that fluttered in the soft winking light of the stars and the bright new moon.

41

ANSON STUCK THE branding irons in his bedroll, tied the bundle in back of the cantle on his saddle. He could still smell the stench of burnt wood although the fire that had consumed the jacal was long since burned out. He and Peebo found the burnt corpse of Jorge, the skull stripped of flesh by buzzards, coyotes, flies and worms, grinning up at the sky with eyeless sockets. He and Peebo buried the remains in a shallow grave, marked it for Jorge's family. They covered the small mound with stones so it would be easy to find again.

"Let's get the hell out of here," Anson said.

"You aim to pick up the tracks of that white bull?"

"Yes. There's been no rain, so we ought to be able to find them."

"Might should have brought more hands with us."

"They'd just be in the way."

"You still goin' to brand any stray cows you see?"

"Yes."

"Hell of a way to earn a living," Peebo said.

"You'll earn every copper."

"And then some."

The two men still had food left after taking two meals on the ride to the burnt line shack, but Anson said they'd have to live off the land from then on. He told Peebo he had flour and coffee and fatback for gravy and soaking bannock.

"You got any sugar?"

"A peck or two. Why?"

"Sweet tooth," Peebo said.

"You never said anything before about having a sweet tooth."

"I just got it." Peebo grinned.

"Just got it?"

"You know how it is when you don't have something. You want it."

"And so you suddenly got a sweet tooth."

"Yeah. But, now it's gone away. Now that I know you've got it."

"Peebo, did anyone ever tell you you were full of shit?"

"Not to my face."

"Well, you are. Don't be askin' what else I got or don't got, hear?"

"Unless some cravin' comes over me."

"It better not," Anson said.

They walked the horses to the creek to drink and filled their canteens. Anson tasted the water first to make sure there was no alkali in it, and there wasn't. As they were about to mount up, they heard noises, something coming through the brush.

"Hear that?" Anson said.

"I'm not deaf, son."

"Listen. It's getting closer."

"Maybe that old bull's coming after us. Better get that branding iron hot and ready."

"Shut up, Peebo."

The two waited, straining their ears. Anson let his

hand drop to the butt of his pistol. Peebo stood by his rifle, ready to jerk it from its scabbard.

"Sounds like a horse," Peebo said.

"Could be. Or a deer. Or a cow."

"Too steady. Horse."

Anson cupped a hand to his ear.

"Scuffing like a horse," Peebo said. "Dragging one front hoof."

"You got good ears."

"Comes from havin' a sweet tooth."

Anson snickered. Peebo grinned. "Horse," he said again.

"Well, it's coming down that old road," Anson said. "Right here where it crosses the creek at the shallows."

"You goin' to draw on it?" Peebo asked.

"Huh?" Anson looked down. He had his pistol half out of the holster. A sheepish look plastered on his face like a sheet of *masa* dough, he slid the Colt .44 back into the leather.

More odd noises mingled with the scuff of that one hoof, a fugue of other hooves, leather under strain, the jingle of spurs, various rustlings and rattlings. Peebo and Anson looked at each other. Anson shrugged, and his brow wrinkled, his mouth bent in a puzzled frown.

"Sounds like a gypsy caravan," Peebo said.

"More like a drummer toting his wares on horseback."

"More'n one horse," Peebo said.

Anson nodded, "Two, three, maybe."

"Four," Peebo said, sorting out the different pads of hooves. Brush crackled and snapped as the noises grew louder and closer.

"We better take some cover," Anson said.

"Yeah, maybe," Peebo said, and pushed his horse toward the nearest oak a dozen yards away. Anson walked in the opposite direction, leading his horse. He took up a position behind the latticework of three mesquite trees.

A few moments later, Peebo and Anson heard splashings in the creek, then the sounds of horse slurping water. A man groaned as he climbed out of the saddle, and there were more sloshings in the creek, farther upstream. Peebo looked over at Anson and held up four fingers. Anson shook his head. He held up three fingers. Peebo nodded.

"Hello," Anson called out. Peebo, behind the oak tree, cringed and waved one hand to silence him.

"Daddy, someone else is out here."

A female voice. Anson's eyes widened.

"Who's there?"

A male voice, thin, querulous.

"Show yourself."

Another male voice, this one deeper than the other, more authoritative.

"Friends," Anson called.

The people of the voices began to converse in low tones. The slurping noises stopped. Anson thought he heard the word *brigands*. His mouth went dry and he licked his lips. The muscles of his stomach tautened like the skin on a drumhead. Then, the conversation stopped and it grew very quiet.

"Show yourself," the man with the deeper voice said.

"You show yourself," Anson said. "This is my ranch you're on."

"Ranch?"

"That's right. You're on Box B land."

More conversation, whispers, sentences rising in tone, as if one or two were doubting.

"Are you Baron?"

"I'm Baron," Anson called back.

"Wait a minute."

Still more talk and Anson's palms began to sweat. Peebo held fast behind the oak. Anson wished the people would ride or walk into view. He was curious about the woman whose voice he had heard.

Finally, a man splashed across the creek, walked between Anson and Peebo. He was carrying a flintlock rifle that was as graceful and as beautiful as any Anson had ever seen, with a curly maple stock, shiny brass fittings. The blade front sight glinted in the sun. The barrel was octagonal and browned. The man wore a loose-fitting cotton shirt, open at the throat, light cotton trousers, boots that had a shine under the dust, a wide-brimmed hat. He carried a possibles pouch and two powder horns, a brace of pistols, both cap and ball Colts, in holsters attached to a wide belt, of Mexican leather. Both belt and holsters were hand tooled with flowery designs.

"Where are you Baron?"

"Over here," Anson said. He wrapped the reins around one of the mesquite branches and stepped out into the open.

"I see you. You look mighty young."

"For what?"

"Are you Martin Baron?"

"I'm his son, Anson."

"My name is Al Oltmen."

"I don't know you."

Peebo cleared his face and Al spun around quickly.

"Don't shoot," Peebo said. "Just wanted you to know there were two of us."

"Just a minute," Al said. He put two fingers to his lips and whistled. "It's okay Doc. You and Lorene come on out."

A man appeared, leading a horse and mule. He was wearing white cotton trousers, a white muslin shirt and a straw hat. His boots were wet from walking through the creek. He was not tall, but wide-chested, stout, and he wore an affable smile. He was unarmed. The mule carried two large wooden panniers that rattled with unknown substances. Behind him, a young girl came forth, leading two horses. She was dark haired, and slender and tall, taller than either Al or the other man. She had brown eyes and a smile curved like a cupid's bow.

"This here's Anson Baron, Doc," Al said, cocking a thumb toward Anson. "He says he's Martin Baron's son. I don't know who that other jasper is."

"My name is Peebo Elves." Peebo left his horse ground-tied behind the oak and walked out into the open. "I ride for the Box B."

"I'm Patrick Purvis," Doc said. "And this is my sister's orphaned daughter, Lorene Sisler. She helps me in my work."

Anson couldn't stop staring at Lorene. He had never seen a more beautiful young woman, nor a taller one. He saw that she had splashed water from the creek on her face and had not completely wiped it all off. Beads of it glistened on her forehead and in front of her dainty, seashell ears.

"Well, gosh," Anson stuttered, "I wish we had some hospitality to show you. Thing is, the line shack we had here was burned down by Apaches."

"We're just passing through," Al said. "On our way to Baronsville."

"Al here's a Texas ranger," Pat said.

"What's that?" Peebo asked.

"Kind of a peacekeeper," Al said.

"Oh, he's more than that, I assure you," Pat said. "There were Texas rangers here in Texas when the Spaniards owned the land; and Rangers when the Mexicans ran the Spaniards out."

"All unofficial, of course," Al said.

"Truth is," Dr. Purvis said, "the Texas Rangers have always looked out for folks, the settlers here in Texas. If they see something wrong, they settle it."

Anson took another look at Al. He didn't look exactly like a soldier, but he was well built, muscular, and he had a cast to his eye that any hunter would recognize, a strong jawline with a shadow from whisker bristles. Anson decided that Al would be a man to ride the river with and wasn't just wearing a six-gun as a fashion accessory.

"How come you're going to Baronsville?" Anson asked.

"I'm to see Ken Richman there," Doc Purvis said.

"Then, he's taking me out to the Box B to see your mother, Caroline."

"My ma?" Anson asked.

"That's right."

"Does my pa know about this?"

"It is my understanding that he probably does not, but he will be informed."

"Does my ma know you're coming?"

"I do not know."

"Seems to me there's a lot of not knowing about this visit."

"I assure you, Mr. Baron, I have the best interests of your mother at heart. Do you know anything about her condition?"

"That's my business." Anson could not help being surly. Talk about his mother had touched a nerve.

"I understand. We need not discuss these matters here. I'll be spending time in Baronsville and I'll see to it that all family members are fully informed of my findings."

"Well, you still have to go through my pa before you go talking to my ma."

"I'm sure that will be arranged by Mr. Richman."

Anson glowered at the doctor, but he held his tongue. Peebo shifted his feet nervously. Lorene gazed at Anson with a look of pity, as if he were some lost derelict found wandering half-mad in the wilderness. Al's face was an impassive mask.

"I'm also coming to talk to Martin Baron," Al said.

"About what?" Anson's tone was only slightly less deprecating.

"There's going to be a war, I think."

"A war? With the Mexicans? The Apaches?"

Al's short laugh was mirthless.

"Not exactly," Al said. "A war between the Northern states and the Southern."

"I heard talk of that," Peebo said.

"What's that got to do with my pa?" Anson asked.

"If there is such a war," Al said, "it will affect all of

us, your ma and pa, you, and Peebo there. The Texas Rangers will play a big part in keeping order."

"Keeping order?" Anson asked.

"Once any man picks up the gun against another, it becomes everyone's business. This would be a civil war, a war between neighbors, friends, relatives."

"How come there has to be war?"

"It's all over the issue of slavery."

"We don't keep slaves," Anson said. "Pa and I don't cotton to one man owning another."

"There are some who believe it's a God-given right to own slaves."

"Let them have their slaves. That's no reason to have a big old war."

Al chuckled again, that dry laugh of his that was bereft of all humor.

"Do you read the newspapers, Anson?" Dr. Purvis asked.

"Seldom. Baronsville has a newspaper."

"I'm afraid the gap between North and South is quite wide and, while it appears, on the surface, to involve slavery, I think the reasons are much more complicated."

"Then, why fight?" Anson asked. "Talk it out."

"I think it all boils down to the independent spirit of the people in the South. Washington is far away from the cotton fields and the issue of slavery. People down here are isolated from the federal government. They want to govern themselves. That is, I think, at the heart of the conflict between North and South that will bring on a civil war."

"Maybe the South has a point," Anson said.

"Yes, we do," Purvis said.

"Then, you're one of those who want the South to secede from the Union?" Peebo asked.

"Not necessarily. I believe in states' rights. I don't believe the federal government should interfere with the decision of a state whether or not it wants to be free or hold slaves."

"Isn't that why we have representatives in Congress?" Peebo asked.

"To be sure," Purvis said. "But, the North has the vote. More representatives."

"Then, something should be done about that," Anson said.

"Here, in this conversation, you have the very arguments brought up in the Congress," Purvis said. "And, there seems to be no easy solution."

Anson lifted both hands in a gesture of surrender. "If the government can't figure it out, then no wonder some folks want to go to war."

"Exactly," Purvis said. "I'm afraid we must be going. We've still a long way to go."

"Yes," Anson said, looking at Lorene. She had not said much, but he had the feeling she knew more than anyone there. For one so young, she looked so wise. Those brown eyes of hers seemed deep with secret knowledge. Her faint smile was enigmatic. He smiled at her, and she batted her eyelashes, smiled back at him.

"I hope to see you again soon," Al said, offering his hand to Anson. Anson shook it and nodded.

"Good-bye," Dr. Purvis said.

Lorene held up a hand, gave a slight wave.

"Be seein' ya," Anson said, directing his statement to her in particular.

"Bye," she murmured.

Anson and Peebo watched the small party ride away. When they disappeared from view, Anson felt a great loss. He stood there for a long time, picturing her beautiful face in his mind. He seemed frozen there.

"We goin' to just stand here all day?" Peebo asked.

Anson turned around.

"No. Let's get going."

"You look smitten, son."

"Smitten?"

"Lovesick. Over that gal."

"Aw, no."

"I've seen moonsick critters before."

"Not me," Anson said.

Peebo brought his horse out into the open. He climbed up into the saddle and looked down at Anson, who still stood there, a look on his face that was lit by an inner rapture.

"Son, if you want to chase after that gal, we can go after that white bull some other time."

Anson shook his head as if bringing himself out of his reverie. "Naw, we're going after that bull. I'll probably never see Lorene again."

Peebo guffawed. "Oh, you'll see her again," he said. "Now that you're on a first name basis."

"What in hell does that mean?"

"It means, son, that you've been bitten by the love bug and you're gonna be mighty sick until you see her again."

Anson sighed and walked over to the mesquite where his horse waited. Peebo was right, he knew. He could not get Lorene out of his mind. Something told him that she was the one he had been looking for all his grown life.

As they rode away, Peebo was smart enough not to say anything to Anson. He knew that Anson was not really there. His body sat atop his horse, all right, but his heart was far away, following Lorene just like a lost puppy.

42

LA MADRUGADA. DAWN. She was the dawn in Mickey Bone's eyes, the breaking light over the dark horizon of night, the song whispered in the heart before sunrise of every new day. When he saw her again, he felt the stones in his heart melt and run like flowing lava in his veins.

"You come at last," she said.

"I have been lost in the white man's world again."

Bone dismounted from his horse, stood there like a beggar at her door. He had been leading another horse and it stood there, tied to his saddle, its head drooping in the heat.

"I know. I have seen you wandering all alone in my dreams."

"Where are all the people?" he asked, looking around the nearly deserted village hidden in the mountains of Mexico. "Where is Red Leg? And Drum?"

"There," Dawn said, and pointed to the high stony peak above the camp, a place of skulls and skeletons, a place where the dead were taken so that they could make the journey along the star path to the other world in the night sky.

"All dead?"

"A sickness came over the village after you left," she said, "and it was like a smoke that one cannot see, that comes in through the nose and takes away the breath. It came in the night and took the old ones and the children. It came like the wind that blows through the cordilleras and then was gone."

"And our son, Juan?"

"He is alive, Miguel. The Great Spirit did not let the wind of death blow on his face."

"And Big Rat? Is he dead, too?"

"No, Big Rat is alive."

"Dream Speaker?"

"He, too, lives."

"I will see him. Dream Speaker."

"Do not talk to Big Rat. He talks against you. He says that you are the cause for all the sickness, the deaths."

"Why?"

"He says you brought bad spirits to the Lipan. He says you brought death to the Lipan people."

"That is not true."

"Counts His Bones said the same thing as he was giving up his breath."

"Counts His Bones is dead, too?"

"Yes. Dream Speaker says that all of the people will die. He says they are the last of the people."

"Why did you come back here?" Bone asked.

"My heart was with the people here."

"You were their slave before I came here."

"I know. My heart told me to come back here. Perhaps I heard the old ones whispering in my dreams, or the young ones cry out in their sleep."

"I want to take you back with me."

"To the white man's land?"

"Yes. There is nothing here. Nothing but death."

"Perhaps I will die, too."

"No. You will not die. I will see Dream Speaker. I will talk to him."

"Ask him where we should go."

"You must not stay here. Our son must not stay in this place."

"Ask Dream Speaker. My heart has gone silent. My ears have gone deaf."

"I would see my son first."

"I will take your horse," she said. "You brought two."

"One is for you and the boy." He handed her the reins. She walked away, leading his horse and the tied one. He followed after, still dazed by all that she had said.

The village was a pathetic sight to Bone's eyes. The few people still alive were gaunt from hunger and the ravages of disease. He could smell death as he walked toward a small wickiup set apart from the others, following in Dawn's wake and she so solemn and quiet, the love for her tore at his heart made his pulse quiver in his temples as his blood pounded in his heart like a small thunder. He felt fear, but could not trace its source. The fear came from no man, but from something nameless, something in the air that seemed to hang over the village like a pall.

People turned their heads away from him as Bone passed their lodges. The stray dogs that had once roamed the camp were absent and he knew they had wound up in the cooking pots, along with the rats and ground squirrels, the grasshoppers and the crickets. There were tiny bones scattered near blackened pots that told him of their fare: birds and field mice, and he knew they had probably eaten lizards and snakes, along with roots and sour grasses that filled the belly but provided no nourishment.

The old woman sat in the darkness of the wickiup, a structure made of sticks and stones and brush that was three sided, its back wall being the rock face of the mountain, blackened long since by the soot from the cook fires. A small boy lay asleep on what appeared to be a collection of soiled rags. Dawn sat down and motioned for Bone to sit across from her.

Bone sat down, looked at the old woman. Something about her seemed familiar to him, but he could not remember a name to go with her face. He looked at his son, sleeping so quietly, so thin and pale his cheekbones stood out beneath the skin.

"You do not remember me, Hueso?" the old woman said.

"I know you."

"Do you remember what I am called?"

"No. It is a name I have not spoken in many moons."

"You know her name, Miguel," Dawn said.

"Yes, I know her name, but it is buried deep in my head. It is like a stone covered with mud."

"I am called Little Bird. The Mexicans call me Pajarita."

Bone's mouth opened, but no sound came out. When he had last seen her, she was a buxom maiden with a round face, pretty teeth, and was always smiling, always hopping about as if she was ready to dance. Now, her teeth were carious, rotted away in her mouth until they resembled little black twigs, and the roundness of her face had melted into straight hard lines, giving her chin a sharpness that was not there before. Her hair was falling out; it was dirty and unkempt, full of burrs and sand.

"Little Bird," he choked. "Yes."

She had grown old before her time. She was not much older than Dawn, but she looked to be her mother or an aged aunt.

"Did you bring food, Miguel?" Little Bird asked. "Your woman brought food, but it is all gone."

"I have some beef that has been dried in the sun, some hard little cakes of flour, what the white men call biscuits, and some dried apples. They are yours," he said. "I did not know how bad it was here or I would have brought food."

"I will fetch what my husband has," Dawn said. She

rose up and left the hovel, pushing aside the woven mat that served as a door. Bone saw that there was nothing made of leather inside the lodge and he knew they had boiled and chewed on what things they had that were made of tanned hides.

"Do you bring death with you this time, too?" Little Bird asked.

"I did not bring death before. Death comes and goes as it wishes."

"That is true. But, death follows some people, do you not believe this to be true?"

Bone thought about it. Somehow, what the woman said made sense in an odd way. Death happened around dangerous people, he knew.

"Death does not follow me."

"I feel there are bad spirits about you."

"You feel bad, so you feel bad spirits."

"Do not tell me what I feel, Hueso."

"I would talk to Dream Speaker," he said.

"He is in his place," she said. She lifted her head and looked up.

"On the mountain."

"Always he is on the mountain. He is a pure man. Death is afraid of him."

He arose and met Dawn as she was coming back in with the staples he had carried in his saddlebags. She bowed her head and let him pass. "You go to Dream Speaker?"

"Yes."

"I will be here."

He left the lodge. He saw that Dawn had unsaddled his horse and hobbled both of them in a place where there was water, some shade from the mountain. She was a good woman, he knew.

Bone climbed the mountain, tracing the old path he had trod many times when he had gone to see Dream Speaker. It was a place close to the sky and below the opposite peak where the dead were taken.

Dream Speaker sat next to the bare flat face of the rock he favored, his legs crossed, his eyes closed. He looked very old, Bone thought. His bare skin was shriveled and wrinkled, the bones of his arms very small and visible under the thin parchment of his skin.

"Did you bring tobacco?" Dream Speaker asked. "I have a pipe."

"Yes," Bone said.

"Sit and we will smoke."

"You knew I would come?"

"Do you hear those crows?"

Bone listened. He heard crows cawing in the next canyon. He could not see them. "I hear them," he said.

"The crows told me Hueso would come this day. They saw you when you were far off. You brought two horses."

"Yes."

"One is for your wife and son."

"That is true."

"Good. Take your family away from this place of death."

"I did not bring death with me."

"No. Some say you did that."

Bone brought forth tobacco from his possibles pouch, handed the leather packet to Dream Speaker. The old Lipan picked up the pipe that was next to him. He cleaned out the dry burnt grass in the bowl with a bony finger and dug out a small amount of tobacco and began packing it into the empty bowl.

When he was finished, he picked up a piece of glass and held it to the sun just above the dry tobacco. The sun beamed through the glass and smoke began to curl upward in small tendrils. Soon, the tobacco caught fire and Dream Speaker set the shard of glass down and blew on the tiny flame. He sucked on the pipe, his cheeks caving in to concave hollows. He drew smoke through the stem and then took the pipe from his mouth. He held the pipe up and offered it to the four directions, slowly blowing out the smoke in his mouth.

"Take the pipe," he said, handing it to Bone. "Offer your smoke to clean the air of the death that has come blowing in here on the wind."

Bone blew smoke into the air, watched it shred and dissipate. He handed the pipe back to Dream Speaker.

"You may keep the tobacco," Bone said.

"I have not had tobacco in a long time."

Bone watched the old man smoke. Dream Speaker closed his eyes and held the smoke in his lungs until there was little left when he exhaled.

Dream Speaker opened his eyes suddenly and watched the expelled smoke as it twisted and curled and floated into shapes and patterns until it became shreds of cobwebs and finally disappeared.

"You have been asked to kill a man you do not want to kill," the old man said.

"That is true."

"You will not kill this man. But, you will fight a battle that is like a war."

"A battle?"

"That is what I see in the smoke."

"Where will this battle be?"

"It will be at a place where you have been before. I see blood and dead men. I see many rifles, many bullets."

"And what of me?"

"You will not die there."

"Where will I die?"

"You will die in the arms of a friend, many years from now."

"Good," Bone said.

Dream Speaker looked at Bone. His eyes were covered with a thin film and Bone realized that the old man was almost blind. Yet he could see things that no one else could see.

"It will not be good. Your life will be filled with sadness, your heart will carry sadness to your wife and son before you have breathed your last breath."

"Then, that is what my life will be," Bone said.

"There will be no more Lipan. You will be among the last."

"There will always be Lipan."

"No, Hueso. There will be men with white faces who kill them all. Life is a great circle. There is no beginning nor end to the circle, but a tribe will fall off for a time and will not come back for many moons, many seasons."

"I do not understand this," Bone said.

"It is of no matter. All of the red men will one day be wiped off the face of the earth. It will be as if they never were."

"What of the white men?"

"They, too, will one day be part of the earth, all in graves, all with the worms at them. Only the earth lives forever and it has seen many tribes come and go."

"All of that is a long way off as we measure time, is this not so?"

"Time is a thing we who breathe measure. The Great Spirit does not measure time. A lifetime, many lifetimes, are but the wink of a firefly in the mind of the Great Spirit. Time is like the sky. It never ends and it has no measurement."

"What am I to do then, Dream Speaker?"

"Take your woman and your son. Follow the path that you see with your eyes. Do not wander from it. Breathe the air and let the sky come into your eyes and your heart. When the end of the path is there you will see it."

"I will go," Bone said.

"When you return to the place from where you rode, you will encounter death again. Not your own, but another's, one that you touched with your hand."

"Who is this?"

"I do not know the name."

"Not my wife."

"No, not Dawn. Another."

"Anson Baron?"

"I do not know."

"Martin Baron?"

"I do not know."

"Matteo Aguilar?"

"I do not know."

Dream Speaker turned away from Bone and smoked the pipe. He spoke no more, and after a time, Bone stood up and walked away. No words were spoken between him and Dream Speaker ever again. He walked down the path into the dying village and looked back up to the place where the old man sat. But, he could not see him and the sun struck his eyes and blinded him for a moment.

Big Rat appeared before him. The warrior held a knife in his hands. He looked very bad. His skin was yellow and hung on his bones.

"I will kill you, Hueso," Big Rat said.

"Go away."

"You will die here," Big Rat said and he took four steps toward Bone before he collapsed and fell to the ground. Bone walked up to him and heard his breath wheezing in his lungs. Then, there was a sinister rattling sound and Big Rat twitched all over and blood ran from his mouth and onto the ground.

"Is this the one who will die?" Bone asked, looking over his shoulder and up to the place where Dream Speaker sat.

"That one is dead," someone said, and Bone looked around and saw Little Bird standing there. "You killed him."

"No. I did not kill Big Rat."

"Go, Hueso. You bring death with you."

Bone looked beyond the woman and saw Dawn and Juan standing by the horses. She was holding the reins. He walked past Little Bird and she hissed at him like a snake.

Perhaps, he thought, I did kill Big Rat. Maybe death follows me like a shadow.

He rode from the camp with Dawn and his son on the barebacked horse and he heard the keening from the women mourning the death of Big Rat and the sound sent a chill up his spine even as the sun was hot and poured down on him and made lakes dance on the land and glisten like tilting mirrors. And the water disappeared as he rode through the desolate land that was empty of all life and he knew in his heart that the whole earth had been like that once and would be again someday.

43

THE WAGON AND its team stood just outside the Rocking A barn. Matteo, Reynaud, and several hands
stared at it as though it was some strange vehicle suddenly landed from the sky. Luis walked around the
wagon, feeling its wooden sides, looking into the bed.
Matteo stood there, watching, his eyes hard as black agates, his lips pressed together in a tight frown.

"*Oye, mira,*" Luis exclaimed. He pointed to the left
front wheel.

"What is it?" Matteo asked.

"There is a chain and a lock. The wagon is chained
to the hitchrail."

Matteo and Reynaud walked around to the other side
of the wagon. They looked at the chain wrapped around
a spoke and around one of the posts of the hitchrail. A
large lock hooked the two ends of the chain together.

"What in the devil?" Matteo said.

"I think Martin Baron is trying to send us a message,"
Reynaud said.

"A message?"

"Look at the chain. The lock. That's the kind they use to shackle slaves."

"*Mierda*," Matteo said.

"Oh, Martin is one sonofabitch, I think."

"You let the bastard get away when he took those slaves from me."

"I had no choice. We were outnumbered. See here, Matteo. We've been over all this before. Baron was smart. He knew where to wait for us. He knew how many we were. He hid beside the road. We were caught by surprise. The same could have happened to you."

"Luis," Matteo said. "How many men did you see when you were attacked?"

"I only saw one. The one who hit me."

"And Paco, how about you?"

"I saw two, I think."

Matteo growled in his throat as if ready to chew Reynaud to bits.

"What went wrong?" Matteo asked.

"It was dark. They caught us by surprise."

"Did you see Martin Baron?"

"I did not."

"Did any of you see him?"

Paco and Luis shook their heads. Reynaud shrugged.

"I think I killed one of the Baron men," Reynaud said.

"You think?"

"I shot him."

"And you rode away, leaving my men to fight alone," Matteo said.

"I do not know how many men Baron had. There could have been a dozen or more."

"What of David?"

"He was caught by surprise," Paco said. "He did not say much to me. I think he knows more than he is saying."

"See?" Reynaud said. "Even your own man admits that we were caught by surprise. As far as that goes, you didn't even see him or whoever it was haul that wagon and team up here."

"Shit," Matteo said.

"What should I do about the lock and chain?" Luis asked.

"Break it. Cut it. Then, I want you to gather all the men and bring them here."

"Yes, *patrón*," Luis said.

At that moment, Matteo saw his wife, Luz, waddling toward them. He turned his head, surprised that she had left the house. Her belly was swollen, using up all the fabric of the light dress she wore so that he could see her knees below the hem.

"I saw them," she said in a calm voice.

"What?"

"I saw Martin Baron and another man bring the wagon back." She stopped next to the wagon.

"When did they come?" Matteo asked.

"Early this morning. They were very quiet."

"Why did you not awaken me?"

"I called your name, Matteo. You could not hear me. You were loud in your snoring."

"You should have shaken me."

"I did shake you. You were in the arms of the aguardiente. I thought you were dead, my husband."

Matteo glowered at her.

"I was not drunk," he said.

"No? Then, it must have been someone else in my bed. The man I tried to awaken was *muy borracho*."

"*Cállate*," Matteo snapped.

"Do not raise your voice against me or I will think you are the same man who staggered into our bedroom last night and yelled at me that you and Paco and Luis had drunk all the brandy in the Rio Grande Valley."

"Woman, shut your mouth."

"I will," she said. "I came to tell you to bring Cora, the midwife."

"What? You are having the baby?"

"The baby is knocking on the door. I broke my water a few minutes ago."

"Why did you not say so, woman? Paco, go and get Cora. Bring her here quick to the house."

Paco stood rooted to the ground for several seconds until Matteo withered him with a look from those steel black eyes of his. Then, he took off running.

"Thank you, my husband," Luz said sweetly.

"Go back to the house and wait," he said.

"Don't you want to know who the other man was who came with the wagon? He and Martin had two horses tied to the back. And after they put the wagon here, they rode away. They seemed not to be in a hurry."

"Who was this other man?" Matteo demanded.

"I do not know," she said. "But he was a big man."

"A big man?"

"Yes, very big. Bigger than you. Bigger than Reynaud."

"I do not know this man," Matteo said. He looked at Reynaud. Reynaud shook his head.

"I think you have seen this man before, Matteo," she said.

"If I saw him, I would remember him. Where did I see him?"

"A week ago, he was in the barn with the other slaves."

"With the slaves?"

"Yes. Do you not remember?"

"What are you saying, woman?"

"The man with Martin was black, my dear husband." Matteo swore.

"Socrates," Reynaud said.

"Was that his name?" Luz asked in that sweetest of her many voices. "I did not know. He was a very big man and he rode his horse well."

Matteo brought his hands up, held them in a strangling stance as if he wanted to choke Luz at that very moment. "*Vete*," he ordered, and waved her toward the house.

Luis crept away, trying his best to go unnoticed. Matteo saw him out of the corner of his eye.

"Bring all the men quick," Matteo said. "Run."

"Is Luis going to bring your soldiers?" Luz asked.

"Yes. Go in the house. I will talk to you later."

"I will go," she said. "Do you want me to prepare your bedroll?"

"I will prepare it."

"So, my husband goes to war, does he? I will be a widow, then."

With that, Luz turned and began to waddle back toward the house. She bore a faint smile on her lips. Matteo stared after her, the veins swollen in his neck, his voice strangled to silence by the grip of his rage.

"War?" Reynaud said.

Matteo whirled on him.

"Yes," Matteo said. "War. You did not kill Martin when you had the chance. So, you are going to get your chance again."

"Isn't this somewhat extreme?"

"Extreme?"

"Drastic."

"Drastic?"

"Declaring war on one man, I mean," Reynaud said.

"Reynaud, you are stupid. You have taken my money, eaten my food, slept in my house, and you have not done the one thing you came for."

"What is that?"

"Kill your enemy, Martin Baron."

"I was going to get around to it, when the time was right."

"Well, the time is right. I am going to get those slaves back and the land Baron stole from my family."

"He did not pay for the land he owns?"

"He did not pay enough," Matteo said.

"How much is enough?"

"His life will be enough, Reynaud."

Matteo walked toward the house, leaving Reynaud standing there.

"What about the wagon?" Reynaud called after Matteo.

"Fuck the wagon," Matteo said.

44

THE LONGHORN KICKED and swung its head from side to side trying to shake off the rope around its neck. Anson kept the rope taut, dragging the cow toward the fire. The cow bawled in protest and stiffened all four legs so that it plowed four furrows in the ground for the last ten yards.

Peebo was waiting by the branding irons stuck in the coals.

"Fun, huh?"

"Yeah, Peebo, more fun than I've had since my last toothache."

"This is a hell of a way to brand cattle. One here, one there, a couple here, three there."

"Every little bit counts," Anson said, swinging out of the saddle. He hung on to the reins, pulled his horse toward him so that the rope stayed tight. "Now, help me throw this maverick down and you can put the iron to him."

"It's a her, ain't it?"

"Don't get smart."

"It's your turn to rope the next one," Anson said.

"Let's get this one burned first."

Anson walked the length of the rope, running his hand along as he went. He circled the longhorn cow and came up from behind. He grabbed the horns close to the boss, dug in his heels and twisted. The cow struggled to get away, dragging Anson around as it turned, shaking its head to break his grip. Anson bent the neck of the cow even further and weighted it down with his body until the animal's legs collapsed beneath it. The longhorn kicked and struggled, but Anson pinned it to the ground until it wore itself out.

"Now," Anson yelled at Peebo.

Peebo jerked both irons free of the hot coals and raced to the fallen cow. He pinned its hind leg with his boot and rammed the iron with the square at its head. Hide and hair hissed as the brand burned into the hide. The hairs smoked and disappeared leaving a raw burned square figure in the hide. Quickly, Peebo jammed the other iron with its small B directly in the center of the square. The cow bawled and tried to kick Peebo away. He kept pressure on its leg so that it could not move much.

"There," Peebo said, and stepped back.

"Now, come around here, Peebo, and grab the end of this one horn."

"Hell no," Peebo said.

"It's going to try and hook me the minute I turn it loose."

"Damned right."

"You sonofabitch."

"Let's don't be bringin' my mother into this, son."

"You bastard."

"My father, neither."

Panting from the exertion, Anson set himself. He gathered his feet under him, pushed hard on the jutting upper horn. Then, he pushed on it for leverage and stood up.

He jumped to the left and ran as the cow swung its head. The long horn just barely missed catching Anson's leg. The cow got to its feet, shook itself and turned its head so that it was looking straight at Anson.

"Hoo, hoo," Anson shouted and grabbed the rope as his horse stepped away to take up the slack.

"That cow wants some of your hide," Peebo said. "Aren't you forgetting something?"

"What?"

"The rope. You need to get it off that cow."

"No. I'm holding that cow hostage."

"Hostage?"

"You saw the tracks. Why we came here."

"Oh, the big white bull."

"He's in there somewhere." Anson cocked his head toward the thick mesquite growth a hundred yards from where the cow stood. "Don't you recognize this cow?"

"Recognize it? I never saw it before."

"Yeah, you did. When we first saw the white bull, he had a bunch of cows with him. This was one of 'em."

"Jesus," Peebo said.

"I'm bettin' that bull will see he's lost one of his gals and come after her. Break out your rope while I get the other one off my saddle."

"You want me to go get another unbranded cow? This is branding the hard way."

"No. I want you to stand by with the rope looped up for when El Blanco comes runnin' up here to get his sweetheart back."

"Like I said, son," Peebo said. "That's doin' it the hard way."

Anson stood there, catching his breath. He hung his head. His shirt was plastered to his chest and back, sodden with sweat. He was covered with dust that clung to the fabric of his clothes so that he looked like a man made out of dirt.

"That makes an even dozen for the day," Peebo said, as he got one of his ropes off his saddle. He began to build a loop. Anson nodded, unable to speak. His lungs burned as if they were on fire as he struggled to drink in fresh oxygen.

"That bull's probably miles from here," Peebo said. "I'll bet he run off when you lassoed that cow there."

"I'll bet he didn't."

"You know," Peebo said, as he walked toward Anson, still shaking out his loop. "I've noticed that we've been driftin' westward the past few days. That mean anything?"

"We've been following that white bull's tracks," Anson said, a disarming tone to his voice.

Peebo stopped walking. He looked around him in all directions. He peered at the sky and marked the course of the sun across the great vault of heaven. He sighed, tipped his hat back on his head and scratched a spot that didn't itch.

"Well, I'll be a ring-tailed sonofabitch," Peebo said.

"What?"

"You are one slick sucker, Anson."

Anson had regained his breath and stood up straight. "Huh?"

"We ain't been follerin' that bull and his harem at all, have we?"

"I don't know what you're talkin' about, Peebo."

"You've been herdin' that bull back toward the ranch. Slow, but sure. I should have caught on a week ago."

"It's time we got back. Likely, we'll need more help."

"It's that gal, ain't it?"

"What gal is that?"

"That Lorene Sisler."

"I don't know what the hell you're talking about, Peebo."

"Sure you do. Well, it don't make no never mind to me. But, why are we standin' here with ropes if you think that bull's goin' to come runnin' up here on us?"

"There's daylight left. I figure this is our best chance to smack a brand on that big old bull."

"Well, I'm waitin', son."

Anson spoke to his horse, slapped him gently on the rump. The horse took a step to keep the rope taut. Anson walked down it to the freshly branded cow and she started bawling when she caught him coming close. Anson kept her moving and bawling as Peebo watched.

"Still waitin'," Peebo said.

"About three or four days ago, I noticed some cows in the brush that looked familiar," Anson said. "They were wilder than the ones we caught and branded. So, I started pushing them westward, closing off their usual places. You could see by their tracks where they liked to be, where they had been."

"I'll say one thing, son. You're a hell of a tracker if you saw all that."

"Something I learned from Juanito."

"Yeah, Juanito. He taught you one hell of a lot."

"If only you knew."

"So, you been drivin' them slow-like thisaway. Now you say this cow's one of that wild bunch."

"Sure enough."

"But you're ready to go home."

"I got that doom feeling, Peebo. Had it for a week. Like something's going to happen and I can't help it none."

"Your ma?"

"Maybe. Yeah, ma, and pa, too. That's the thing about that doom feeling. You can't rightly put your finger on it. But, it's there. I guess *dread* might be a better word."

"*Dread?*"

"Yeah, *dread*. But, it doesn't really put the meaning to what I feel like *doom* does."

"*Doom* is just another kind of word for death, son."

"I know. I'm not ignorant, you know."

"No, you ain't ignorant, son. You're just peculiar."

"Well, I got to get on back home. I can't keep on out here with that doom feeling hanging over me."

Anson made the cow bawl again when he jumped at it and waved his hat.

"I see what you're doin', son," Peebo said.

"You just stay ready, Peebo."

They did not have to wait long. The cow kept bawling its distress signal and soon they heard a crashing sound in the mesquite, then the rumble of hoofbeats. Many hoofbeats.

Anson was watching the bunch of mesquite where he had caught the cow, thinking the bull would come from that direction. But, he was wrong. A stream of longhorns came out of the thicket, not in a solid bunch, but from different directions. The white bull was not in the lead, as he expected, but came charging and bellowing from the rear of another column that seemed to come out of the dust thrown up by the preceding cattle.

He yelled at Peebo, but had to dodge a pair of young bulls with huge horns that braced him. He just barely managed to escape being impaled by them, or bowled over, and by the time he saw the white bull, he was off balance.

He heard Peebo yell something, and then the herd swarmed into the clearing, rampaging through the fire, tossing irons that clattered and rang like church bells. To his horror, the white bull charged toward his horse.

"No," Anson yelled, but it was too late.

The bull cocked its head and aimed a horntip straight at his horse's belly. The horse tried to get out of the way, but was knocked back by other cows and the white bull's horn rammed into its side. The horn went in so smoothly, at first Anson thought he was mistaken. That it was only an illusion. But, his horse staggered and went down and the bull's horn rose in the air, dripping with fresh blood.

The roped cow began to run and shake its head, trying to throw the loose rope. The rope had come loose when his horse went down. Anson heard Peebo's horse scream and then the scream was shut off and the herd picked up momentum, sweeping past him like some mindless tide.

Anson choked on the dust and closed his eyes to keep the grit out. When he opened them a split second later, he saw the cattle running at great speed away from him and the dust closed over them. He heard the rumble of their hooves for several seconds and then a silence that was as monumental as a giant rock.

"Peebo?" Anson called.

No answer.

"Peebo, answer me."

Anson heard a groan. He started to walk to toward the sound. He stopped by his horse and thought that he had never seen so much blood before. The ground pooled with it and still it came. A string of entrails lay like a coiling mass of gleaming wet snakes and his stomach churned at the gruesome sight.

A few yards later on, Anson saw Peebo's horse, more disemboweled than his own, and blood splattered and flung in all directions. A lake of blood began to form around the horse's belly and, beneath the silence, he heard the buzzing of flies.

Peebo lay several feet beyond and Anson's heart dropped in his chest. He feared his friend was dead, for he lay so still.

"Peebo?"

"Ahhh."

Anson knelt next to Peebo, saw that he was breathing. He reached down and touched a hand to Peebo's cheek. Peebo's eyelids quivered for a moment, then slowly opened.

"Anything broken?" Anson asked.

Peebo stared at Anson for several seconds before he answered. "Nothing I can feel right off."

"Can you get up?"

"Son, if I'm still alive, I can get up."

"Want some help?"

"No. Just let me talk to my feet and legs for a minute.

I want to stand up. They want to lie down."

Anson waited. Finally, Peebo grunted and sat up. He looked down at his boots. He waggled his feet from side to side. "Yeah, they still work."

Peebo stood up slowly, groaning as each part of his body moved to a new position. "They gone?" he asked.

"They're gone. We lost the horses. Both dead."

Peebo swore.

"If you feel like it, let's strip the saddles and bridles from the horses and start walking back to the ranch headquarters."

"How far?"

"Not far. Half a day, if we keep at it."

Peebo looked around, saw the dead horses. He winced, shook his head. "Might as well get to it," he said.

They performed the gruesome task of removing saddles, saddlebags and bridles from the dead horses. Anson looked up at the sky and got his bearings. They started walking west, Peebo following a few yards behind Anson.

The two men crossed several trails winding through the scattered mesquite groves and gradually began to encounter more open land, and places where Box B hands had cleared the land of trees. They kept shifting their loads, but they did not stop.

They saw branded cattle grazing on high grass and Anson knew they were getting close to the ranch. "Not far now, Peebo," he said.

"I'm getting my bearings."

The two walked into an expansive grassland and then found the first fence made of mesquite. They crawled through it, pulling the saddles behind them and that's when Anson saw the dun horse grazing by itself near some cattle.

"Say, Peebo, isn't that . . ."

"Yeah, that's where I put him."

"Well, I'll be damned."

"We can ride double."

They walked up on the dun. Peebo laid his saddle and bags down, carried the bridle over to the horse, speaking to it in gentle tones. He slipped the bridle over its face and then examined its leg.

"He's all healed up from the snakebite," Peebo said.

"I see."

"Let me saddle him up and we'll ride to the ranch."

Anson said nothing. When Peebo was finished tightening the single cinch, Anson walked over to the horse and rubbed its nose.

"I'm glad I didn't shoot you, boy." He set down his saddle, bridle and kept the saddlebags slung over his shoulder.

Peebo smirked, then climbed up in the saddle. The horse whickered. "Well, come on, son. Climb up behind me."

Anson grabbed Peebo's hand, stuck his left foot in the empty stirrup. Peebo pulled him up and Anson swung his leg over and sat behind the cantle. He felt the tiredness in his feet and legs drain away.

"I know the way now," Peebo said, and turned the horse toward the ranch.

"Pretty fine old horse," Anson said.

"He'll do."

"I'll come back later and get my saddle."

"Yeah. You might want to ride this old horse back. He's taken a likin' to you."

"Shut up, Peebo," Anson said.

They rode in silence for a time, straight into the falling sun. They passed vaqueros who waved from a distance and the air was sweet with the scent of summer. Anson patted the dun on its rump, felt the power in its rippling muscles.

"You know, something, Peebo."

"What?"

"I never could have made a loop big enough to throw over that white bull. His horns are just too damned big."

"I know. I thought of that when I saw the bastard up close."

"I'll get him one day, but it won't be with a rope."

"You got it figured out yet?"

"No," Anson said, "but I will. I'll put the Box B brand on that wild sonofabitch and we'll put him in with some big cows, see what we get."

"I can see your heart's set on gettin' that bull."

"He's really something," Anson said.

"Biggest bull I ever saw."

The bull was even bigger in Anson's mind as they rode on, flushing quail from the grasses, jumping rabbits and roadrunners. It was still wild country, Anson thought, but he was going to tame it someday and that white bull would be the start of a herd of cattle that would be the envy of every rancher in the Rio Grande Valley.

He was almost disappointed to be going home. He wished he could stay forever out in the brush, chasing down mavericks and putting the Baron brand on their rangy hides. He was glad now that he had not caught the white bull, even though they had lost two horses.

"Let him be wild a while longer," Anson said, just blurting it out without thinking.

"Huh?"

"Oh, nothing," Anson said, as a smile came to his lips.

"I heard you son," Peebo said, to Anson's surprise.

He thought about that last cow he had branded and wondered if the white bull had sired the calf she carried in her belly. Perhaps, he thought, the herd he envisioned had already started to form.

"That's what Juanito told me," Anson said.

"There you go again. Talkin' to yourself, son."

"Juanito said whatever you dream and believe is true, will happen."

"Maybe."

"No maybe about it, Peebo. You just got to believe, that's all."

"Faith?"

"Yeah. Faith."

45

U RSULA HEARD THE front door slam shut. She jumped at the alien sound, dropped the tin plate in her hand back into the washbowl. It sank beneath the soapy bubbles and disappeared.

"David?"

"Urs. Come quick."

She grabbed a cloth and dried her hands as she walked from the kitchen into the front room. David stood there in the center of the room, a pale ashen cast to his face, molded into an eerie visage by the feeble orange light from the single lamp glowing on a table by the door.

"You look like you've seen a ghost," she said.

"I've just been talking to Matteo."

"Well, that would scare me, I know."

"Don't joke. It's serious."

"What's serious?"

"Matteo plans to attack the Baron ranch."

"Attack the Baron ranch?"

"He says he has a trained army. His Mexican hands."

"Maybe you'd better sit down and tell me all about this, David."

"Yes, yes." Clearly agitated, David sat on the divan. Ursula wadded up the damp cloth and sat in a chair facing him.

"Now, what's all this about Matteo and his army?"

"It'll take him a week or two to get all his men together. But he has been training them to fight like soldiers. After Martin brought that wagon back, Aguilar went into a blind rage."

"Serves him right."

David took off his hat and set it next to him on the couch.

"Reynaud is in it with him, I think."

"Reynaud is a snake," she said.

"Anyway, he wants to know if I will fight in his army and I'm terrified."

"Just tell him no."

"It's not that easy. He said if I don't fight with him, then I can move out, that I have no job with him."

Ursula sighed.

She squared her shoulders and drew herself up straight in the chair. "David, if Matteo picks a fight with Martin Baron, that means my son Roy will be in the thick of it."

"My God, I didn't even think of that."

"So, you have no choice."

"I don't?"

"No. We've got to warn Roy. And Martin, too. You can't work for a man like Matteo. He's—he's evil."

"Christ," David said, dropping his head into his hands. "Oh, Christ."

"David. There's no decision to make. We have to leave. Now. Leave everything here. Just ride off."

"My God, what if Matteo sends his men after us? He might shoot us down like dogs."

"Well, there's another reason right there."

"What?"

"If Matteo would do something like that, then you can't possibly ever trust him, let alone work for him. So, we have to go."

"What if he sees us?"

"Shh," she said, leaning over to whisper to him. "We'll wait. We'll pack what we can and leave after Matteo goes to sleep. We'll hitch up your buggy and leave in the dark."

"He'll hear us. Someone will. He's sent for all his hands. He's mad, I think."

"Crazy, you mean."

"Yes. Crazy."

"All right. We'll just take two horses. We don't even need saddles. Just bring two horses here and we'll ride over to Roy's and tell him what's going on."

At two in the morning, David and Ursula rode away from the Rocking A Ranch. No one saw them leave. No one came after them.

Late the next morning, sleepy and weary, they rode up to Roy Killian's house and were greeted by Wanda Fancher and her mother, Hattie.

"Where's Roy?" Ursula asked.

"He's working out back, painting a room we built. I'll go get him."

"You two look like you've rid a piece," Hattie said.

"We have," David said. "I'm David Wilhoit."

"Step down, both of you, and I'll put on a pot of tea."

"Thank you, Hattie," Ursula said, her voice laden with weariness. David helped her dismount. As they were walking to the house, Roy and Wanda came around the side and Urusula wondered if her son had married the woman she had arranged to move in with him.

"Ma, what are you doing here?"

"Roy, you and Wanda better come inside with us. We have a lot to tell you."

A half hour later, Roy had his horse saddled and was saying good-bye to Wanda. "I'll be back tonight," he said.

"You be sure, hon," Wanda said. Her eyes twinkled with suggestion. "Don't you worry about your ma and her husband. That room's ready for them."

"Thanks, sugar," Roy said.

"Should I tell your ma?"

"Tell her what?"

"About us, silly."

"You mean . . ."

"I mean that this would be a good time to get married. While your folks are here."

"Good Lord, Wanda, I can't think about marryin' at a time like this. If we have to fight Matteo Aguilar . . ."

"This might be our only chance, Roy."

Roy climbed up on his horse, adjusted the pistol he wore, rammed the rifle more tightly into its boot. He leaned down and she stood on tiptoes. They kissed.

"We can talk about it when I get back tonight. Don't say nothin' 'till then."

"Anything," she said.

"Anything. Promise."

"All right."

He waved to her and turned his horse toward the Box B. Soon he had the animal at a gallop and Wanda watched him until he was only a dot on the horizon. Then she turned to go back into the house, a playful smile on her lips, a merry twinkle in her eye.

When she walked in on David and Ursula sitting at the table, she smiled wide.

"Mother Ursula," she said, "I've got some good news for you."

46

MARTIN LEANED AGAINST the back porch railing, listening to every word Dr. Purvis said to him. Dr. Purvis had suggested that they go outside so no one else inside the house could hear what he had to say. As the doctor spoke, Martin saw his world crumbling away, turning to dust, blowing away in the hot Texas wind that blew across the land in late April of the year 1861.

"She doesn't have long, I'm afraid. Perhaps days. Weeks. I just don't know. She could go at any time."

"How can you know for sure?"

"The disease she has is advanced. We don't know much about it. But, it has eaten her away inside. It's already reached her brain and that, in my estimation, shows it to be in its last stages."

"She's a young woman."

"I know. I'm sorry."

"Is there anything you can do for her, Doc?"

Purvis shook his head. "I gave her some salve for the lesions on her body. I gather you didn't know how far the disease had advanced."

"No. I knew she had spells. We—we haven't . . ."

"Had relations? I gathered as much. She told me she was ashamed of her body, the sores on it."

"What did you say about her brain?"

"This, ah pox, whatever its name, infects the brain in its last stages. She might go mad before she dies. You might have to take care of her when she, ah, loses control."

"I'll take care of her, Doc."

"Well, that's it, Mr. Baron. Al Oltmen wants to talk to you about another matter, if you're up to it."

"I'll see what he has to say."

"Fine. I'll send him out."

"Thanks, Doc. Do what you can for Caroline."

"I will."

A few minutes later, Allen Oltmen descended the porch stairs. He seemed properly sober about what he had to say and Martin welcomed any conversation that didn't include the subject of death.

"Mr. Baron, I gather the news wasn't good."

"Doc didn't tell you?"

"No, sir. I believe such matters are confidential."

"You say you're a Texas Ranger. I've heard of them over the years. Army?"

"No, sir, the army and Rangers don't get along too well. We're separate."

"What did you want to see me about, Oltmen?"

"Well, sir, Sam Houston mentioned you. He's pretty sick, you know, living down in Galveston. Sam doesn't want war, thinks Texas was wrong to secede."

"Hell, Sam must be getting up in years."

"He's seventy-six, I believe."

"A hell of a man."

"Yes, sir."

"I met him once."

"He remembers you, Mr. Baron. Charlie Goodnight spoke of you to him often."

"Haven't seen Charlie in a while, either."

"No, sir, but that's what I wanted to talk to you about. Charlie and Mr. Sam, they both think you would make a good Ranger, especially if this country goes to civil war over the slave question."

"Oh, I doubt if there'll be any war," Martin said.

"Sir, I think there will be. So does Sam. And, I'd like you to be a Ranger, not let the army grab you."

"Why?"

"Well, in town I talked to Ken Richman and he told me about the slaves you freed from one of the ranchers hereabouts. If the army gets you, you'll be fighting for the slaveholders."

"Oh, I couldn't rightly do that, Mr. Oltmen."

"No, sir. With the Rangers, you'd be helping people. We could use you as a scout. We still have a problem with Apaches and Comanches and, mainly, that's what we Rangers do, look out for folks and keep the redskins off their backs."

"And, if there's war?"

"Well, you'd not have to fight with the army. We aim to stay Texan, but we believe in the Union. Most of us, that is."

"I don't really want to fight anyone from the North."

"No. I don't either. I'm against this war, if it happens, as I believe it will. I have a badge in my pocket, and I'm authorized to swear you in as a Texas Ranger. It would keep the army from getting you and when the war's over you wouldn't have to explain why you didn't fight Yankees."

"I'll think it over," Martin said. "Thanks."

Oltmen hesitated, seemingly unwilling to let the matter drop. He pulled a badge out of his pocket. "This is yours, if you want it. Should I leave it with you?"

"I don't know, Mr. Oltmen."

"Call me Al, will you?"

"If you see Charlie, tell him I said howdy, will you?"

"Yes, sir, I will."

"And, you can call me Martin, Al."

Al grinned. "Why, that's fine, sir. I hope to see you again real soon."

Martin nodded. "I'll go in with you. I want to say good-bye to Dr. Purvis."

The two men went inside.

Before Dr. Purvis and Al left, Oltmen pressed the badge into Martin's hand.

"That's yours," he said. "I couldn't give it to another man. If you don't join us, that's all right, too. The badge is yours to keep."

Martin took the badge without looking at it, put it in his trousers pocket.

After the doctor and Ranger had left, Martin walked upstairs. Through an open door he saw Esperanza in her room with Lazaro and Talia, one of the ex-slave girls who now worked for him, along with Socrates, Fidelius and his wife, Petunia, and Elmo. The other Negroes worked in town and were doing fine, he knew. Roy Killian had hired on the young men, Pluto and Lucius.

He walked to Caroline's room, knocked politely.

"Who is it?"

"It's me."

"Come in."

Martin opened the door and walked inside the bedroom he had once slept in with his wife. He closed the door softly. The room smelled of unguents and oils.

"Did you speak to Dr. Purvis?" she asked.

"Yes. I'm sorry, Caroline."

"Umm, yes. It's bad news for me. Good news for everybody else."

"Please, hon."

"Hon. You haven't called me that in a while."

"I know. I've been a bastard."

She sat next to the window on a chair he had bought for her. She was still wearing her nightgown. He could not tell by the way she looked that she was dying. "The sun is setting. It will be dark soon."

"Yes."

"No," she sighed. "I shut you out. I kept you away. I didn't want you to see the marks of my sin on my body."

"You don't have to talk about that," he said.

"All right. What did Roy Killian want? I saw him ride up last night, then ride away again. You didn't say why he came all the way over here."

"It's nothing."

"Marty, I saw his face. That man carried a lot of worry with him."

"He said Matteo Aguilar was putting together an army of his Mexicans."

"Are they going to start the civil war everybody's talking about?"

"I don't know. No. He's mad because I took his slaves."

"So, he's going to fight you. Me. Us."

"I doubt if it will come to that. Probably all bluff."

"You know Matteo better than that. He's a snake. And, he doesn't bluff. If he says he's going to do something, he does it. That family."

"I'll take care of it," Martin said.

"I know you will." She arose from her chair and came close to Martin. She looked into his eyes. For a moment, she seemed free of disease, almost beautiful. He felt a wrenching in his heart as she studied his face. "You might want to go into town and bring that cannon back out here. It worked against the Apaches. It ought to work against Matteo."

"But . . ."

"I know," she said, waving his unsaid words away, "I'm over that. Besides, what difference could it make now? I'm dying, Martin, and you won't have to live with my madness anymore. I won't have to live with it, either."

"Caroline . . ."

She turned away from him abruptly.

"Martin?"

"Yes," he said.

"Will you do me one last favor? I promise not to . . ."

"Sure. What favor?"

"Sleep in my room tonight. Sleep with me. One last time."

"You don't have to ask, Caroline."

"Yes, yes I do. I don't want you to do anything. You can't. But, I would just like to have you in my bed before I die."

He heard her choke back the tears and he felt his own eyes brim up, start to sting.

"Now, go, will you?" she said. "Come back tonight."

"Let's have supper together," he said.

She turned, wiped her eyes. "Yes, I'd like that," she said.

"Damn, Caroline. . . ."

"Just go for now, will you? I want to dress up for you."

He left the room and heard her loud sobbing after he closed the door. He choked back his own tears and walked down the stairs. As he passed Esperanza's room, he noticed the door was closed. He could hear whispering inside and wondered if they knew about Caroline's condition.

Martin walked out on the front porch, sat in one of the chairs. He needed to be alone, to think. The wicker seat was turning cold as the sun stood behind the house. The eastern horizon was still and gray, as empty as his heart.

Then, he saw the horse with two riders emerging out of the long shadows of afternoon. There was still sunlight on the high ground so he could see that it was Peebo and Anson riding in. He stood up, walked to the railing.

He knew he had been cold to Caroline, never forgiving her for letting Bone violate her. He knew that it probably wasn't her fault, but she could have fought him off. That's what he thought, and yet he still had doubts about what had really happened.

It was long past time to forgive and forget, he knew. Caroline was dying and he must forgive her sin. He was sure that God already had, because she had suffered the past few years for that sin and deserved no further punishment.

"Anson, Peebo," Martin said as the two rode up. "A good way to wear out a good horse."

"We had some trouble," Anson said.

"Step down, son. I need to talk to you. Peebo, you come to supper after a while, will you? Lucinda should have it ready soon as the sun goes down."

"Thanks, Martin," Peebo said.

Anson slid off the horse's back and walked to the porch as Peebo rode toward the barn.

"Something wrong?" he asked.

"Better sit down for this, son."

Anson climbed the steps, threw down his saddlebags, which were nearly empty. He sat in one of the chairs. Martin turned and leaned against the railing, pressing his butt up against it for support.

"You ran into Dr. Purvis," Martin said.

"I did. Was he here?"

"Left a while ago."

"Ma?"

"She's dying, Anson. Maybe you ought to go upstairs and . . ."

"Christ, Pa."

"She's dressing for supper."

"How long does she have?"

"Hard to tell. A day, a week, a month. Doc didn't know."

"I'm sorry."

"I know. Me too."

"I don't know what to say to her," Anson said.

"I can't help you there, son. She's your mother. You'll think of something."

Anson sighed and stood up.

"I'll go on up and see her. She coming to supper?"

"Yeah. I'm going to stay with her tonight."

"That's good, Pa. Damn." Anson opened the door and left his father alone on the porch. He listened to Anson's footsteps until they faded away.

Then, he walked down the steps and around to the side of the house to watch the sun set. The tears started to well up in his eyes and he let them spill over and course down his cheeks.

The sun sank below the western horizon and the clouds pinked to a soft pastel that deepened to a reddish hue. There was a golden rim on the underside of the largest cloud and the rays stood in the sky like a fan made of airy streamers.

"God, please take care of her," Martin said, and the tears gushed from his eyes and he shook from the great sobs that burst from his throat like the strangled screams of souls damned to eternal hellfire.

47

MARTIN WAS STILL awake. Caroline had fallen asleep several minutes before. It was full dark outside and the moon was waxing full as it rose in the velvet sky. He wondered if she would see another day. She looked so tired, so frail.

She turned over in her sleep like something sleek and sweet, like a graceful seal rolling lazily in the ocean. And he looked at her in the dark of the room, saw the moon shed light on her face and arms as it streamed through the windowpane, magnified, streaked through her dark hair with pewter fingers.

At that moment, he thought she was beautiful because the dim moonlight softened her, took away her age, ironed out the wrinkles in her face and sculpted her to a youthful, graceful woman in repose.

This was the time to look at her. This was the perfect moment to forget the bitter quarrels, the words laden with anger that coursed between them like arrows barbed and cutting, like sharp stones shot from a leather sling.

Here, in the calm silence where good thoughts were born, where the bad past could be forgotten, where memory and history could be altered to reflect a kindness he had not shown her in the past few years.

Finally, he thought, he could love her again. He could love her without any screen between them, any animosity. He could think of her as the child she once was, as the innocent, before the world and its ways corrupted her. Now, he thought, it was a sweet, clean love and she was as beautiful in repose as a woman in an old painting. She was forever, now, somehow timeless, wonderful to behold.

He wondered if she knew how much he loved her. He had tried to tell her after supper, when they were alone. But, there really was no way to tell her how much he loved her. Not now. Not after so much time had passed without any expression of love between them.

It was too complicated now, so confusing. He could feel the love, as he felt it now, but to express such feelings was beyond his ability with words. Maybe this was the best way. Look at her asleep and let the love he felt wash over him, wash over her. Like healing waters, like balm.

He looked at her and it seemed he could feel her love him, too. He wanted her to love him. Like this, quietly, and without boundaries, without restrictions, amendments, qualifications. Maybe, he thought, such love could only exist at night, when the world was invisible, when only the two of them were alive. But that was only a small part of love, not even half. You had to love during the hard times, too. The bad times. And, she had done that, he thought. But, he had not. He had been wrong. You had to love in the harsh light of day as well as in the soft spell of evening.

He wanted to awaken her, but he knew that if he did, it would all go away. Most of it, anyway. No, let her sleep. Let her be like this and tomorrow he would tell her how he had looked at her, and brushed a hand across her face, stroked her hair, nestled against her, secure in the darkness.

Tomorrow. It might never come. He might close his eyes and never awaken. No, Caroline might not awaken. He felt terribly mortal just then. She seemed so close, yet so far away. She was lost to him, lost in the ocean of sleep, unaware of his presence or his thoughts.

"I love you," he said softly into her ear. She did not stir and he wondered if the words could go through sleep, could penetrate the subconscious and work through the dream, become part of memory. "I love you," he said again, more loudly and she stirred, turned away from him.

Maybe she knows, he said to himself. Maybe she knows that I feel this way about her all the time. But, I buried it in hatred, buried it all so that she never knew that all the time I did not touch her, I loved her, wanted her.

He put an arm across her waist, closed his eyes.

He vowed to tell her about all this. Tomorrow, he would tell her that he had looked at her while she was sleeping and that he had felt a great love for her that had built up over the years. He would wait until she was wide awake and had had her coffee. That's when he would tell her how he had felt looking at her as he had.

He did not sleep for a long time because he kept trying to put all of it in words and none of the words said what he had felt. The words kept getting tangled and mixed up and he finally gave up.

"Good night, sweetheart," he said and those were the right words, finally.

"Good night," she replied, turning over, taking him into her arms. "I love you."

And there it was, the loving nocturne he could not put into words because it was too complicated. He opened his eyes and kissed her, but she was already back to sleep. Fast asleep, a smile on her face barely showing in the soft light of the rising moon.

During the night, Caroline stopped breathing and, for some reason he could never explain, her stillness awakened him. He took her lifeless body in his arms and held her tightly until his arms ached. And, then he laid her by his side and smoothed her hair and brushed his lips against hers.

"Good-bye, my love," he whispered.

It seemed to him, then, that he heard her voice, from some faraway place, heard it in his ear and in his heart. And, hearing it, he felt at peace with himself even as he felt empty inside, hollow, as if a part of him had been torn out and flung into the vastness of the night sky where, in his grief, he thought Caroline might be, might even take with her that part of himself that had been part of her from the first moment he saw her and fell in love with her.

The love that he thought he had lost was now eternal and he knew he would carry his love for Caroline forever in his heart.